THE CHILDREN OF DARKNESS

WITHDRAWN

D1568930

DAVID LITWACK

FIRST EDITION SOFTCOVER
ISBN: 1622534344
ISBN-13: 9781622534340

Editor: John Anthony Allen
Senior Editor: Lane Diamond
Cover & interior layout & design by Mallory Rock

Printed in the U.S.A.
www.EvolvedPub.com
Evolved Publishing LLC
Cartersville, Georgia

Other Books by David Litwack

Along the Watchtower

The Daughter of the Sea and the Sky

www.DavidLitwack.com

For Mary Anne, who always knew I would write again.

PART ONE
LITTLE POND

"Whoever undertakes to set himself up as a judge of Truth and Knowledge is shipwrecked by the laughter of the gods."

— Albert Einstein

Chapter 1

A Dreamer of Dreams

Orah Weber kept watch on the twilight-shaded woods, longing for Nathaniel to appear but wishing he'd stay away. Behind her, the people of Little Pond warmed themselves around a modest bonfire. Every evening for the three weeks leading to festival, the mound of logs would grow until the finish of the games. Then the grand fire would be lit and the feast served. Although this night was only the first, the fire blazed brightly enough to light up the square.

She gazed at the bell tower above the commons. Perhaps Nathaniel was right, and on this night, he was in no danger. The bell had not yet tolled; the vicar had not yet arrived. Spicy-sweet wassail still bubbled in its cauldron, and the music played on.

A trio struck up a lively reel, and she turned to listen, tapping a toe and patting her thigh to the rhythm. At the fire's edge, a girl bobbed up and down to the beat in a purple hat with three snowflakes embroidered on the brim. Nearby, young couples looked on while elders sat on the porch of the commons with firelight flickering across their faces.

She had spent that afternoon with Nathaniel, sitting on a log by the pond. The leaves in the surrounding forest had completed their autumn change, and stunning hues of red, yellow and orange reflected off the still water. She'd stared at the colors, struggling to find a way to convince him. After her fifth try, she stood and planted her hands on her hips.

1

"I forbid you to come," she said.

"Since when are we in the habit of forbidding each other."

"Since you've come of age and grown too bull-headed to take care of yourself."

She'd been close with Nathaniel for as long as she could remember. Even as a small boy, he'd wondered what the world must be like beyond their tiny village, but now he was an adult and she on the threshold. She'd always been the mature one, bothered by his childish notions. Time to forego his fantasies and become more responsible.

Yet he resisted, stubborn as always. "What would you have me do, Orah? Cower in my father's cottage."

"Not cower but be less conspicuous when the vicar arrives."

"Only one in three are taken."

She bent low and pressed her palm to his cheek to force him to face her. "It's not worth the risk. Have you forgotten the look of those who've been taught, the far off gaze, the dreams seemingly ripped away?"

He grasped her wrist and eased her hand aside. "What good are dreams if they stay unfulfilled?"

They'd had this conversation many times before, every day for the past month since he'd come of age. He'd brood on this one thought—life was passing him by.

"But we're so young," she'd say, "our future so filled with possibilities."

He'd scoff at her, never satisfied with the way things were. "What possibilities are there in Little Pond?"

Little Pond was the smallest village along the edge of the mountains, much smaller than Great Pond, which had two shops and an inn. The pond that gave her home its name was a lovely spot, filled with lake trout and frogs with huge eyes, but Great Pond was triple its size with an island in its middle. It bettered Little Pond in every way.

Nothing much ever happened in Little Pond, and so nothing much happened in their lives. Yes, they were both good at many things, but he always wanted more. At seventeen years, he was already one of the strongest in the village, though he'd never been tested in a fight. He could run fast, among the fastest in footraces at festival, though he'd never finished first. Like her, he possessed a fine mind, the two of them the smartest students in school, though he always scored second to her.

And so, despite her encouragement, he brooded. Was he destined to be good at everything but fall short of greatness? What if the opportunity for greatness came only once in a lifetime, a single perilous choice to change the world? Would he charge forward, believing in his own courage and strength, or run away? That, he claimed, was the test of greatness. Yet he feared their preset life in Little Pond offered no chance to find out.

She was different. Her family had been weavers in Little Pond for as long as anyone remembered. Unlike the surrounding farmers, her days followed a predictable pattern. Five days a week, she worked the loom. Two days, she traveled to Great Pond to trade for yarn. The flax never failed, and her neighbors always needed cloth.

Still, she wondered. Should she be more like Nathaniel? Should she long for something beyond the village of her birth?

As a seven-year-old, she'd watched her father die. She could still see his sunken eyes, so filled with hope as he whispered his final words.

> *Now, little Orah, don't cry. You have a wonderful life ahead*
> *of you. Study hard in school and don't let the vicars set your*
> *mind. Think your own thoughts, big thoughts based on grand*
> *ideas, and find someone to love.*

She yearned to think big thoughts as he'd urged, to do important things with her life, but not so much that she'd take risks like Nathaniel.

Now, as she stared at the bonfire on this night before the winter blessing, a new worry consumed her. Though one in three were taken, none ever recounted what happened during the coming-of-age ritual. Every child in the village grew up fearing the teaching, all except Nathaniel. She suspected a part of him hoped for it.

"At least I'd get to see Temple City," he'd say, "the light's eternal fortress against the darkness. At least something different would happen."

Orah startled from her reverie, as Thomas separated from the crowd, pointed to the tree line and cried out. "Well look who's come to do us honor in the village square."

Next to Nathaniel, Thomas was her best friend, the three inseparable since they'd learned to talk. While Nathaniel was prone to notions, Thomas found trouble wherever he went, too often relying on her to rescue him. He'd taken to needling Nathaniel at that age when boys' voices change. In a period of a few months, Nathaniel had shot up to over six feet, a full head taller than Thomas. For a time, he was gangly and unsure what to do with his arms when he walked, prompting Thomas to tease him to no end. One day, when Thomas had gone too far, Nathaniel challenged his shorter friend to a fight behind the schoolhouse.

She stepped in between, urging them to stop their boyish nonsense and remember they were friends. Nathaniel picked her up and moved her aside.

Before the fight could start, Thomas winked at her, dropped to one knee at Nathaniel's feet, and begged. "Please, holiness, don't hurt Thomas. Thomas is your friend."

She'd laughed despite herself, and to this day recalled the incident as a fond memory of childhood. No fight occurred between friends that day and none since.

Now, as she watched Nathaniel saunter in from the woods, she was pleased he'd come despite her protestations. Her face grew warm from something more than the heat cast from the fire, but she held back, letting Thomas make first contact.

He tugged at Nathaniel. "Come on. I've been waiting for you to get our first wassail."

"I thought I'd find you with the players."

Thomas's face sagged. It'd been all he'd talked about the past few weeks—the chance to play his flute at festival now that he was of age. Apparently the players didn't dare let him take part. Music was frowned on by the Temple of Light. By rule, a group was restricted to no more than a drum and two winds. Other instruments, such as strings, were banned as remnants of the darkness.

"I tried," Thomas said. "They told me to wait my turn. I'll have to settle for wassail."

He gestured to the cauldron bubbling in front of the commons. The familiar smell filled the air—fermented apples with cinnamon and honey. Everyone claimed wassail was the best use of the harvest, but only those of age were allowed to indulge.

Nathaniel shook free. "I haven't said hello to Orah yet."

"She can have some too.... Oh, I forgot. She's not of age."

4

Orah forced a scowl. "A couple more months and I won't have to take that from you anymore, thank the light."

She smoothed her gray skirt so it flowed to her ankles, and tugged her gray vest until it properly displayed her slender form. All would change to black when she came of age. Once satisfied with her appearance, she stepped halfway to Nathaniel and let him fill the space between them, only then allowing her fingertips to brush his arm.

"I was hoping you'd make a smarter choice," she said.

"And miss being with you and Thomas?"

"Better than taking the risk."

Thomas shoved her aside. "Let's get a cup now before the kettle runs dry."

Orah's back stiffened. Though only two fingers taller than Thomas, she could loom over him when she wanted.

"Leave him be, Thomas. He shouldn't stay just because you want wassail."

"I've always come for the celebration," Nathaniel said. "I didn't want to miss it now... just because I've come of age."

Orah's eyes shifted to him and lingered. She wanted him to stay, but her practical side took over. "If you're an adult, you need to act it."

"You both worry too much," Thomas said loud enough to attract the attention of Elder Robert and Elder John, who were playing checkers at the far end of the porch. Thomas clasped his hands to his chest and pleaded. "Come on, Nathaniel. I missed the music. Don't make me miss the wassail."

Before Nathaniel could respond, Orah blocked his way. "You should consider before starting on wassail. It's frowned on by the vicars."

"So?" Thomas said. "They don't like music either, but we still play."

"The vicars teach us to avoid frivolous foods like honey. They're trying to help us lead a better life. They don't like the name either."

"Oh, I'd forgotten. The name comes from one of the—" His eyes bulged and his voice rose. "—old, forbidden languages."

The two elders glanced toward them with that look of scorn the old reserve for the young.

Orah waved to quiet him, but he sailed on. "Next they'll ban friends meeting in threes. Come on, Nathaniel, or are you so afraid of the vicar?"

Orah grabbed both by the elbow and dragged them to the edge of the shadows cast by the fire. There, she placed a hand on each of their shoulders, drew them into a circle and lowered her voice. "It's unwise to openly mock the vicars, especially now."

Nathaniel raised his chin and glared at her. "I'm not afraid."

"Me neither," Thomas said. "I'd welcome the chance to go with the vicar to Temple City, to see the tall spires and the officials standing in line to greet me. I'll bet they've never met my like before."

"Well I'm quite sure of that," Orah said, "but not for the reasons going around in your big head."

"Why so glum? Wouldn't you like to visit Temple City? I'm sure Nathaniel would."

Her response sliced through the night air. "Nathaniel is not going to Temple City."

Nathaniel brushed the sleeve of her tunic in that way he had when she became agitated. The firelight reflected off his features, highlighting the stubborn eyes that refused to accept the world as it was.

"Tomorrow's the blessing," he said, "nothing more. Here's my deal. I'll lay low and watch my words while the vicar's here. After he's gone we can gather at the NOT tree to celebrate our own festival."

The "NOT tree" was their name for a shelter deep in the woods, built by Nathaniel's father as a place to play their games when they were little. They'd named it the NOT tree, using their initials— Nathaniel, Orah and Thomas. With so many years gone by, she doubted his father remembered it, but the NOT tree remained their special place.

She flicked a strand of hair from her cheek and brushed it back. "A fine deal. We'll meet there tomorrow after dusk."

Thomas reached into his tunic and pulled out the wooden flute he'd carved years before, and which he always carried with him. "And with the vicar gone, I'll be able to serenade my friends."

When all three nodded in agreement, Orah lifted her face to the sky with arms extended, palms outward as she'd been taught.

"Praise the light, giver of life. Let us end tomorrow safely, together at the NOT tree."

6

Just as she finished praying, the bell atop the commons began to toll, ringing sixteen times, each clang echoing in the night air. All music stopped, and parents took children by the hand. Cups of wassail were set down, and faces turned toward the entrance of the square.

Thomas slipped the flute back into his pocket.

The vicar strode through the east gate of the village with all the pomp of temple clergy, bearing a pack on his back and the weight of divine authority on his shoulders. He stopped near the fire and confronted the villagers.

"Greetings," he intoned, enunciating every letter. "Don't let me interrupt your festivities. The blessing is for tomorrow, not tonight. Please, dear friends, continue your celebration."

No one stirred.

The vicar approached a table, lifted one of the abandoned cups to his nose, and closed his eyes. As he inhaled, he shook his head.

"Honey in your drink. We'll speak more of this tomorrow, but for now, my friends, enjoy your evening. Blessed be the light."

The surrounding crowd muttered, "Blessed be the light."

Orah touched hands with Nathaniel and backed away.

Though no one appeared to move, within seconds the villagers had faded from the square

.

***

Orah lingered behind the trunk of an oak tree, invisible in its shadow. She needed to learn more, to understand the threat to her friends.

Nathaniel had always been a dreamer.

When they were children, she'd organize games in the woods, elaborate adventures pitting the light against the darkness.

Nathaniel would try to add to the game, conjuring up stories based on bedtime tales told by his father, beyond what temple rules allowed. He'd pretend the darkness had been lifted by a knight, slashing about with a sword and riding an armored horse, though weapons and the riding of animals had long ago been banned. He'd insist the knight had built Temple City, then scaled the mountains outside Little Pond and discovered a great ocean on the other side.

As he grew older, she'd warned him to keep such notions to himself. Nathaniel and his notions. She prayed he wouldn't pay the price tomorrow.

She sniffed the air, trying to read the breeze, before glancing back to the clearing where the unattended fire had begun to die.

The vicar stood alone in the middle of the square. With a sigh, he set down his pack, carried all the way from Temple City. Inside would be two of the Temple's most essential mysteries: the season's medicine and the sun icon, greatest miracle of the light.

After stretching his shoulders, the vicar squared them to the bonfire, picked up an abandoned cup of wassail, and poured its contents onto the embers, which hissed and spit out a sweet-smelling steam. His lips curled upward into his hollow cheeks, until his teeth showed and his face displayed a rarely-used, but perfectly genuine smile.

Chapter 2
A Teaching

Following his meeting with the elders, the vicar had two hours to roam the village prior to the noontime blessing. He assumed the posture he'd been taught — back arched, head up, eyes focused on the path ahead. His beard was freshly groomed, a pencil-thin mark that traced the contour of his jaw. His hair had been razor cut to an exact line that intersected the middle of each ear. On his head was the not-quite-square hat of a junior vicar, narrower in front than in back, all black, with no red stripes as yet. Even so, the villagers would treat him as a proper envoy of the Temple. He'd followed the rules and so would they. Little Pond would yield one of its young for a teaching.

He measured his stride — three foot lengths per step. As each heel struck, it made a mark that mimicked the hat, forming a sequence of almost-squares in the dirt road. The squares detoured only to avoid the occasional puddle left from an early morning drizzle.

Whenever he came upon villagers, he tried to engage in conversation.

"The autumn's been warm, thank the light. Did that make for a productive harvest?"

This brought the trite responses he'd come to expect and was able to ignore.

Next, he would ease into more personal topics. "Is everyone in good health? Was the medicine sufficient for your needs?"

Then, intermingled, the contentious questions: "How goes the struggle against the darkness? Have you noticed a change in behavior, anyone showing signs of being tainted, someone who might need my attention?"

Most of the villagers, like villagers everywhere, chose their words with care, answering at length but saying little.

"Oh yes, Anne bore Matthew a son. Elder Robert's daughter married a young man from Great Pond. The light's strong in the people of the Ponds. We're true to the faith."

They'd been conditioned all their lives to parrot back the litanies of the Temple, and viewed this conversation as another ritual. By midmorning, he was growing impatient and began pressing harder.

"Do the young congregate in unruly ways? Have some become rebellious?" Then more bluntly, "Do any speak ill of the Temple? We must be vigilant, my friends, or the darkness will return."

Back in Temple City, a red stripe awaited his hat. Others had achieved monsignor by his age, but he sought more than status. A promotion would allow him to pass off the Ponds to a younger vicar.

How he loathed this village, a nasty little outpost at the edge of the world, bounded to the west by a barrier of white granite mountains ending high up in a sawtooth. Locals claimed ancients had scaled these peaks and found beyond them a sea so great its far side could not be seen. But no one in the age of light would have dared such a quest. Since it was forbidden to speak of the time before the light, at least in civilized places, the rumored trek had never happened. Yet here at the edge of the world, they still told tales.

Not much changed in Little Pond, and he was bound to keep it so. There were no big problems, only minor distractions. If someone strayed, he exercised his duty as visiting vicar to correct the transgression before it grew. Even a small change might undermine the light. The line must be drawn, he'd been taught, before the darkness had a chance to return. Be vigilant always.

It was usually the young who deviated. The young, so adventuresome and curious, had not yet learned the full horror of the darkness. Schooling was less strict here, teachings less common than in larger towns, so once each season he traveled to Little Pond and listened in the prescribed way, searching for a candidate for a teaching. For the past three seasons, however, they'd resisted the will of the Temple, tarnishing his record.

Ahead, the steeple of the commons loomed, the completion of the loop near. Small villages often lacked enough young ones to teach, but if he failed this time, a full year would have passed. Less than an hour remained until the blessing—barely time to communicate to his superiors.

As he paused to consider his options, a white-throated sparrow landed in a puddle to begin its morning bath. With a blur of wings, it splashed about, lifting its neck and singing with a whistle too passionate for its size. Its song was five notes, two long and three short, with the last ending in a trill. The bird seemed unaware of his approach.

He knelt down, picked up a stone the shape of an acorn, and straightened, never taking his eye off the bird. Then he took aim and threw, just a flick of the wrist so as not to startle it.

The rock missed by a feather and the bird flew off.

He'd redouble his efforts. This time, he'd find one for a teaching, an example so the light would shine forever.

On the porch of the commons, he found the two elders, John and Robert, who had resumed their game from the night before.

He strode toward them. "Greetings, my friends."

The two barely looked up, but stopped their play.

"Elder Robert and Elder John, I believe?"

They nodded.

The vicar reached into the pocket of his robe and pulled out a waterproof pouch. He removed a piece of paper from inside, making no effort to hide the printing that the superstitious villagers took to be nothing less than temple magic.

"Little Pond has had no teaching in almost a year," he said. "As elders, you know the importance of discipline. I need your help in finding a candidate."

The elders looked past him as if wishing he would disappear.

The vicar stayed quiet, letting the silence become a physical presence.

The two men fidgeted in their chairs. Finally, Elder Robert spoke. "We're a small village. Enough have been taught that we can keep the faith."

"Children come of age all the time. Surely some need... correction."

Robert's voice grew resolute. "We take care of our own and are loyal to the Temple. We give no reason to believe otherwise."

The vicar noted the white mourning sash draped across Elder John's chest. Perhaps he'd be more pliable.

"I note you've had a passing to the light, Elder John."

John looked away, as if the ache inside was none of the vicar's concern. "I lost my wife of forty-four years."

"I'm sorry. May she dwell in the light everlasting."

John nodded in gratitude, but the vicar gave no reprieve.

He pulled the paper closer and read deliberately. "Temple records show two comings of age within the past half year and, as you know, the records are never wrong."

John's voice cracked. "I don't recall."

"Why surely you attended the ceremonies."

"I'm getting old. I can't remember."

"Perhaps, if you saw the names...." He turned the paper toward them so they could read the bold writing done by no man's hand. "The records tell of Thomas Bradford and Nathaniel Rush."

"Two fine young men," John said after a moment. "From strong families faithful to the light. The Bradfords work hard on a farm at the south of town. They're good folks and kind to their neighbors. Nathaniel's mother died in bearing him. He was raised by his father, William, one of the elders. You met him this morning. You have no cause to bother either."

The vicar rocked on his toes. "It's not for you to say... what's a bother to the Temple of Light."

John slid toward the edge of his seat and matched the vicar's stare. "William was sent for a teaching when he was young, a week after coming of age. It was the longest this village has ever known. Is that not enough for the Temple?"

The vicar pressed his face closer to John's. "I will get my teaching today, if not one of these young men, then another." He glanced at the paper. "The records show you have grandchildren. A little old, perhaps, but maybe I should choose one of them."

John's fingers tightened on the arms of his chair and he began to rise.

Before he could get to his feet, Elder Robert intervened. "I've heard one making light of the Temple. A teaching might help him lead a more responsible life."

John turned to him and licked his dry lips, but said nothing.

The vicar narrowed his eyes into slits. His mouth twitched at the corners. "Elder Robert and Elder John, you are true children of light. Once you give me a name, I'll need speak of your families no more."

The elders' every muscle sagged as they avoided each other's gaze.

***

The somber villagers assembled in the square, old and young, men, women and children. Orah settled on a bench at the rear between Nathaniel and Thomas, while the elders moved to the front.

As she waited for the ceremony to start, she took stock of her friends.

Nathaniel sat straight-backed, eyes unflinching, focused on the altar like a good child of the light. Thomas only grinned. Both bore the obligations of all males who'd come of age: the temple-prescribed black tunic beneath the ceremonial robe, the hair trimmed to the temple-ordained length, and the thin beard marking their jaw line. But that's where the similarities ended.

Though Thomas was a few months older, he looked younger. Where Nathaniel's whiskers could use filler, only charcoal could make Thomas's sand-colored fuzz look like a beard. He had boyish features that seemed like they might linger well into middle age, and he acted younger too. When they'd been in school, Thomas loved to chide her for studying too much, but she spent much of her time keeping him out of trouble and covering up for him when he misbehaved.

The vicar stepped to the front, and a hush settled over the villagers. Everyone turned to face the stone altar. Little Pond was too small to have a building dedicated to the blessing, so its inhabitants had built the altar at the request of the Temple generations before.

13

With no resident vicar, they often used it for other purposes, such as holding festival pies. Such use would have enraged the vicar had he known, but the people of Little Pond took advantage of what they had.

Now the altar gleamed, covered by a satin cloth, pure white but for the emblem of the Temple, a yellow orb whose rays beamed down on an adoring family: father, mother, and child. A gold icon three hands high stood at its center—an image of the sun.

While her neighbors wasted little time dwelling on the light or worrying about the darkness—they had enough to do to get by in their daily lives—all were respectful of the ceremony. They reserved their true awe, however, for the sun icon. Through it, they heard the grand vicar speaking to them four times a year from far-off Temple City. Each time, he'd astound them with his knowledge—babies who were born, couples wed, young people who'd come of age. It was a true miracle.

The vicar approached the altar to the right of the sun icon, and faced the congregation with arms raised and bony fingers pointing toward the heavens.

"Dear friends," he intoned. "The Temple brings you greetings. Another season is upon us. Blessed be the light."

The congregation responded in a monotone. "Blessed be the light."

"The grand vicar is the human embodiment of the light in this world. He sees into your hearts and knows if darkness dwells therein." The vicar pivoted toward the icon and stared at its center. "Holiness, is this village worthy of receiving the blessing?"

Like the others, Orah held her breath—not because the answer was in doubt, but because the voice emanating from the sun icon always inspired her. A crackling rose from its metallic center, and children would later claim it glowed.

"People of Little Pond." The voice resounded through the square. "This past season, we have felt your love as you walked in the light, and so, you have been blessed with a fruitful autumn. We welcome three new children."

The disembodied voice went on, listing the names of newborns along with their parents. As each was mentioned, eyes turned. Heads nodded approval as if the births were not complete until acknowledged by the Temple. Afterwards, the chief clergyman recognized one marriage, a cousin of Orah's to Elder Robert's daughter, and the death of Elder John's wife. The people took it positively — their communal father dispensing approval and sympathy.

The grand vicar finished with the usual blessing. "May those newly arrived be welcomed, those departed be remembered, and all be embraced by the light."

With this cue, the vicar asked with a tremor in his voice, "Holiness, are they deserving of the gift of life?"

"The people of Little Pond are deserving."

The vicar turned to the audience. "Let the elders approach."

The five elders, including Nathaniel's father, stepped forward, with the two oldest, John and Robert, bearing a sack that contained donations collected in the past week.

"What is it you bring?" the vicar said.

"We give what we can to support the Temple," Robert responded.

The vicar took the sack of medicine from his pack and handed it to the elders in a simultaneous exchange. The medicine was a gift from the Temple, enough to last until the next blessing. Like every child in Little Pond, Orah remembered the magic in that sack, white tablets for headaches, pink powder for stomach ailments, and miraculous blue capsules that healed infections during cold winter nights. Its contents would be stored in the village pharmacy and dispensed freely according to need.

"Bless you, people of Little Pond. Through your generosity, the light shall thrive." The vicar stuffed the tithe in his pack and turned toward the icon. "Holiness, will you lead us in the precepts of faith?"

The crowd rose to their feet. When the grand vicar began the precepts, everyone recited with him.

"Blessed be the light. Blessed be the sun, the source of all light. Blessed be the moon, the stars, and our own world which revolve around its light. The light is the giver of life, the darkness of chaos and death. Those who seek the darkness shall be doomed to darkness never-ending, but those who embrace

15

the light shall dwell in the light everlasting. While we believe and are true to the light, the darkness shall never return."

Once the voice from the sun icon had quieted, a sense of satisfaction settled over the villagers. Orah waited for the vicar to dismiss them with the usual intonation: "Go with the light."

When he hesitated, she grew restless. Her heart pulsed louder with each beat.

After too long a delay, the voice from the sun icon spoke again. "The light is stronger than the darkness, but we must be vigilant. For hundreds of years, the Temple has armed a few to be soldiers of faith. Little Pond is honored this season to have one of its own chosen for a teaching. Come forward, Thomas Bradford of Little Pond."

The crowd went silent.

Orah turned to her friends. Nathaniel bore a look she'd seen before, whenever he spoke about the death of his mother. Thomas's face had gone ashen.

"Come forward, Thomas of Little Pond, and be taught the horror of the darkness, so you may keep the light shining in Little Pond."

Thomas stood and drifted forward on wobbly knees. Orah lunged to touch him, but he'd moved beyond her reach.

The vicar spread his arms. "Welcome, Thomas. You shall accompany me to Temple City and return to your people wiser. Now, my friends, go with the light."

A subdued village repeated the benediction.

Orah squeezed Nathaniel's arm. "What will happen to him? Will he be all right? When will he be back?"

The vein in Nathaniel's forehead throbbed. "Who knows? No one ever talks about teachings, but it's a three-day trek to Temple City and three days back, so he'll be gone at least a week." When she remained disconsolate, he added, "He should be home for festival."

As the villagers dispersed, Orah rose on tiptoes to peer over their heads. She caught sight of Thomas, hands held high in triumph, the mask of his face painted with a grin as if he'd just won a race, but she knew him better. Even at that distance, she could see the glow in his eyes had gone dim.

Chapter 3
The Darkness

Thomas squinted, trying to see the opposite wall. It had to be near, because his boots pressed against it, but try as he would, he couldn't penetrate the darkness. Not a flicker of light to help, only the darkest dark he'd ever known. No moon, no stars, no hint of dawn—a dark to haunt one's dreams.

He could guess the size of the teaching cell by touch. The floor covered at most one pace square, enough to sit up straight with legs bent. The wooden hatch that formed the ceiling hung well short of his height, so he had to hunch over when he stood. He could sustain the position for only a few minutes before dropping back down.

He'd given up trying to find a comfortable position. The Temple hadn't designed the cell for comfort. They intended the teaching to be harsh. No way around it, so now he stared into the darkness with his knees drawn to his chin.

The voices of the vicars echoed in his mind. "Let us record the first teaching of Thomas Bradford of Little Pond, blessed be the light. Do you understand why you are here, Thomas?"

"Yes sir." Temple City still dazzled him then, with its lofty towers and arched halls that boasted row upon row of larger-than-life statues. He'd felt privileged to be there.

"Why is that?"

"To learn to defend the light against the darkness." He'd been a fool.

The senior vicar had leaned forward and glared. "Do you know what the darkness is?"

"Yes sir. The darkness is the time before the light, a time of chaos and death." The standard answer learned in school.

The vicar's response struck like a slap in the face. "You know nothing of the darkness, because you've never been taught. The darkness would terrify a child, but you're of age now, Thomas, a full child of light. We chose you for this teaching, so you'll guide your life hereafter to ensure the darkness never returns."

They asked him to say the precepts, an easy test, and with a grin he recited what he'd memorized as a child. "Blessed be the light. Blessed be the sun, the source of all light. Blessed be the moon, the stars, and our own world, which revolve around its light. The light is the giver of life...."

When he finished, they said he'd recited the words with "insufficient sincerity," and sent him to ponder the meaning of the darkness.

He'd crouched in this cramped cell ever since. Time passed, but he had no sense of it.

At first, he felt no fear. The Temple preached no harm to others. Weapons, war and violence were of the darkness and forbidden. Gradually he realized that the teaching caused him no harm, that the pain came from within. The constant dark gave no measure of space and masked the passage of time, leaving him awash in a sea of nothingness so large he couldn't see the shore. He longed for the light of a firefly, for news of the day. These thoughts gnawed at him like a physical pain.

Deacons brought food and water at intervals, but never enough. His stomach growled, and his throat stayed raw and dry.

His legs began to throb. To escape the cramping, he imagined himself separated from his body, floating in the air overhead, but he kept glancing down at the wretch below. He could envision himself clearly, all except the eyes.

Exhaustion reigned above all. At first, he hurt too much to sleep. After a while, he'd drift in and out, his head nodding until his chin dropped to his chest and woke him.

Sometimes, he'd startle as the ceiling cover grated open. Light would pour into the cell, flooding him with exhilaration. Such moments meant more than food or water. He'd stand, stretch his limbs and look into the plump faces of the vicars surrounding him, seniors all with their decorated hats. They, in turn, would look down on him with sympathy before reciting a litany of the horrors of the darkness.

In the darkness, they claimed, people spoke different languages and worshipped different gods. Their leaders used these differences to separate the people—each from the other—and then rail against their enemies to turn focus away from their own shortcomings.

At first, they fought with simple weapons, similar to the pocketknife the vicars had taken from him. Then their wise men studied in schools and toiled for years to create bigger weapons to destroy their enemies in greater numbers. *A tale to scare children,* Thomas would think, *and I am not a child.*

Then they would close the cover, and the darkness would return.

He'd awaken after a time, his mind confounded by sleep, and watch the air above him shimmer. Visions appeared, showing ranks of people rushing toward each other with strange weapons. They chanted the name of their god as they attacked, each side in a different language.

It had to be a dream.

The vicars returned and asked why he carried the flute. They warned that music, taken to excess, might facilitate the return of the darkness. For in the darkness, the young gathered at night to dance to forbidden music, a way of worshipping death.

Later, his cell lit up with visions once more. Boys and girls, tenfold all those of the Ponds, crowded in the dark with strange lights flashing above them. Their shirts bore images of skulls, and some had etched symbols of death into their skin. A piercing sound pained his ears, a kind of music played not with the sweet flute and drum of festival but with impossibly loud instruments. The people swayed to the beat, oblivious to each other's presence.

Another dream? He began to wonder.

The vicars told how scholars had created a liquid that melted flesh off bone, and the leaders of the darkness allowed them to drop it from the sky so they'd be deaf to the cries of their enemies. In their arrogance, they even created a false sun. They dropped this too, so its heat scorched those on the ground, leaving nothing but the outline of their bodies in ash.

This time, when the vision startled Thomas awake, he pressed his eyes shut to block out the light, but the flash of the false sun glowed through his eyelids.

Perhaps the horror had been real.

Again and again, the vicars told of the darkness. Again and again, what they'd described showed in the dreams.

The vicars came so many times he lost count. Each interview started with the same question: "Do you know the darkness?"

"Yes sir," he always replied.

They'd ask him to recite the precepts. With each response, he spoke with more sincerity, until one day he sobbed and struggled to get out the words.

Then suddenly, the interviews stopped. No more questions, no more visions. He waited in silence.

His cracked lips measured the passage of time. With no taste, no smell, no sight, no sound, he exercised the last of his senses by groping at the walls. They had the feel of stone, rough-hewn by unskilled workers, but worn smooth by thousands of desperate fingertips. Like so many before him, he'd been abandoned. If light was the giver of life, his would soon end.

Then, as the wings of death fluttered in the darkness overhead, a new vision appeared, no longer a nightmare from the past. He saw Little Pond in the spring, its sparkling waters, its hills strewn with apple trees newly bloomed, its granite mountains looming in the distance—and the utter loneliness of his circumstance struck him. He imagined Orah and Nathaniel strolling along the path to the NOT tree together, hand in hand, without him. No longer their burden, he'd drifted from their memories. He reached out, trying to touch his old life once more.

The vision vanished and the ceiling board creaked open. He looked up at the panel of vicars and staggered to his feet.

This time, they asked a different question: "Thomas, are you happy with your life in Little Pond?"

"Yes sir."

"Do you care for your family and friends?"

"Oh, yes sir."

"And would you like to go home?"

His throat seized up. He nodded.

The clerics leaned in and consulted with each other, and then the senior vicar turned to him. "So you still may, Thomas. You've learned of the darkness. We believe you may become a faithful child of light."

Thomas waited.

"The Temple offers three teachings. The first demands understanding, allegiance and proof. You must convince us you understand the darkness. Once you've done so, you'll prove your loyalty by swearing allegiance to the Temple. But know this, if you go back on your oath, you shall endure the second teaching, a hundred times worse than the first, and you'll dwell in the darkness to the depths of your being. If you stray after that, the Temple of Light will deem you an apostate, and the people of your village will do as is written in the book of light:

> *If there comes among you a prophet, or a dreamer of dreams, and gives you a sign or a wonder, saying, 'Let us return to the darkness,' you shall not hearken to the words. If your brother, or your son or daughter, or your wife, or your friend, who may be as your own soul, entice you saying, 'Let us abandon the light and serve the darkness,' you shall not consent to him, but you shall surely kill him. Your hand shall be first upon him, and afterwards the hand of all the people. And you shall stone him with stones, that he die, because he has sought to thrust you away from the light.*

"That is the third and final teaching, Thomas. Think before you answer. The Temple loves its children but will do what it must to prevent a return to the darkness. Do you understand?"

Thomas tried to concentrate. *A prophet? A dreamer of dreams?* He was no dreamer. He just wanted to go home.

He nodded.

"Thomas of Little Pond," the speaker's voice resounded through the circular room. "Do you know the darkness?"

"Yes sir."

"Can you recite the precepts of faith?"

He did, his voice growing stronger with every word.

"One final test and you'll be free to go. Enlighten us as to where the seeds of darkness have started to grow in Little Pond. Tell us the names of those who have questioned the light."

Thomas's mind again switched out of his body. He regarded his face, dust-covered with streaks of tears.

"But why, holiness?"

One vicar said, "It's not for you to question—"

The senior vicar cut short his colleague's words with a wave. "You've endured much, Thomas, but what you've learned is merely a symbol, far less horrible than the real darkness. That's why the Temple exists—to prevent a return. You say you're happy with your life, but this happiness does not come cheaply. Prove your faith by giving the names of others who need our help. Show your loyalty, and we'll allow you to go home."

What were they asking? *For me to betray my friends.*

"I cannot," he said.

"Then, Thomas, you do not yet know the darkness."

He sat down without being asked.

They slammed the ceiling cover shut, and the darkness returned.

Chapter 4
Emptiness

Orah worked the loom, trying to focus on the task at hand: shift and weave, shift and weave. She marveled how her fingers passed the shuttle back and forth while her feet rocked the treadle, weaving the weft through the warp without engaging her mind.

Though most of her neighbors were farmers, her family had been weavers for generations. Like everyone else, they kept a vegetable garden, cultivated flowers to adorn their cottage, and raised a few animals for milk and eggs, but they spent the bulk of their time at the loom.

Local farmers delivered wool or flax to Great Pond, where a community of spinners turned the fibers into spools of yarn. They sent these to families like Orah's, masters of the weaving craft. The weavers kept some of the resulting cloth for their own needs and distributed the rest to the farmers and spinners, receiving food and yarn in return. Everyone had enough to eat and wear, a balance so sensible Orah could imagine no other way.

Her mother had taught her the craft at eight years old, and Orah had been taking her turn at the loom ever since. Weaving had become as natural to her as walking.

Yet now she wished it took more concentration, that it didn't leave her free to think of other things.

She needed no calendar to tell that festival was near. She tracked the date by the shadow on the sundial in her family's garden, a beautiful piece with a face of white granite, inlaid black numbers and a bronze shadow maker. Her grandfather had carved the dial as a present for her tenth birthday, after her grandmother died that spring. He'd used the sundial to take his mind off his sorrow and force himself to look forward to the granddaughter he doted on.

It had taken half a year to finish. First, he trekked two hours to the base of the mountains, then climbed to where the vegetation thinned and the granite began. He needed several trips to locate rock pure enough for the face, weeks to carve out the piece, and nearly as long to drag it back. He went whenever he found the time. Overall, he took the entire summer to gather the materials and bring them home.

Every night that fall, he worked on the sundial by candlelight. Orah would stay awake as her grandfather chipped and rubbed at the hard rock until her mother insisted he go to sleep. Finally, in November, he went to Great Pond and had the blacksmith craft a bronze shadow maker. When all was ready, he brought Orah to a flat spot in the garden and sited the shadow maker to point true north.

In the weeks leading up to festival, and for a number of days thereafter until her birthday, Orah watched as sunset grew earlier and later, and the shadow longer and shorter. Her grandfather supervised while she recorded her findings in a log. For the past six autumns, she'd continued the tradition, writing down the date and position of the shadow, learning to forecast the seasons.

This year, she struggled to keep the log. Her grandfather had died in late winter, shortly after her sixteenth birthday, unable to hold on for her coming of age. As she penned each entry, she thought of him and continued for his sake.

Then the vicar took Thomas. Despite her best efforts, she could find out little about his plight, and no one dared predict the date of his return. The day Thomas left, she had drawn a double line in the log, contemplating a different kind of entry—not the trivial movement of the shadow on the sundial, but the progress of her life. Yet each day, she wrote nothing more than a brief note to Thomas: *Be brave* or *Stay safe*. Now the number of entries emphasized how long he'd been gone.

The three friends had never been separated this long. When she and Nathaniel came together, they felt Thomas's absence, but staying apart was worse. So each evening after dark, despite the encroaching cold, they met at the NOT tree.

On this morning, she could hardly wait. She worked faster, but the thoughts kept coming. Thomas seemed to cry out to her from a cramped and lonely place, but she had no way to help. She concentrated on the loom until her hands flew—shift and weave, shift and weave—but her mind gave no rest.

***

Time passed no more easily for Nathaniel. He pressed his father for information about teachings, and with each day Thomas was gone, he found himself slipping closer to impertinence.

That morning, his father had asked him to help stack firewood. Nathaniel waited on the porch, surveying the mounds of wood the two of them had split through long hours at the chopping block. They looked like mountains.

His father stepped outside, rubbed his hands together and blew into them. "Are you ready, Nathaniel?"

He stood tall for a man of the Ponds, but shorter than his son by a hand. Hard work on the farm had thickened his muscles in a way that would not come to Nathaniel for years. His hair had grayed only at the edges, and his chin remained prominent. Deep-set eyes showed both the pain and joy of life. Nathaniel knew the pain came from the loss of his mother, and he himself was the joy—the son she'd left behind.

Nathaniel nodded, then held out his arms while his father piled three logs onto them. "I can take more, at least four or five."

"We don't need to carry all at once." His father grabbed a couple of the larger logs and led him to the lean-to.

They laid down an evenly spaced row on parallel beams and placed the next row crosswise to allow the wood to dry. After several trips, sweat began to bead on Nathaniel's forehead.

When they'd completed the third cord and a fourth had grown to Nathaniel's waist, his father held up a hand. "Let's stop for a drink." He set a water bucket onto a bench—nothing more than a plank

25

nailed across two tree stumps in front of their cottage — filled a ladle and offered it to his son.

Nathaniel refused the offer and glared at his father instead. "Why won't you tell me what they're doing to Thomas?"

His father withdrew the ladle and took a swallow before returning it to its hook. "We've discussed this, Nathaniel."

"When will he come home? It's already ten days."

"They'll teach him until he's taught, another week or more."

"That's almost festival."

"It's not for us to rush the Temple of Light."

He turned away, attempting to resume their chore, but Nathaniel blocked his way. "Will he be all right?"

"Yes. The Temple does not harm its children. You know that."

"You said it might change me if I were taken."

"Change is different than harm. Yes, he'll probably be changed."

"In what way?"

His father's shoulders slumped, and he let out a long stream of air. "After teachings, people become more serious and sadder too. Thomas will learn the stark reality of our past. He may go through a... period of mourning. He'll need time to recover and might be distant with you and Orah. But as far as permanent change, I can't say."

Nathaniel studied the toe of his boot, which did its best to dig a hole in the ground. He'd come of age, no longer a child, and deserved the truth. "Why are teachings so mysterious? They're not described in any of the books, and every time I ask, you avoid answering."

His father rested a hand on Nathaniel's shoulder. "I've explained all I can."

Nathaniel felt an unfamiliar tremor. Fear. He'd never seen his father afraid before. He tried to lock eyes with him, but his father released his grip and went back to the woodpile.

"Now hold out your arms."

Nathaniel opened his mouth to argue, but before he spoke, his father loaded him up with logs until he grunted under the weight.

"Take these to the shed. One more effort like the last and we'll be done by sunset."

Nathaniel dumped his load on the ground with a thud. "You're hiding something from me. Why?"

His father flushed and grabbed the logs himself. At the entrance to the woodshed, he spun around. "You forget yourself, Nathaniel. I'm your father and you'll show me respect."

In his young life, the two had never exchanged such words. Nathaniel knew he'd overstepped but couldn't bring himself to admit it. Without answering, he whirled about and ran off.

***

Susannah Weber glanced up from the kindling to find Nathaniel approaching on the path to her cottage. Usually, he bounded along, all arms and legs with only a hint of how to make them work together, but now his limbs hung limp, making his whole body sag. *The vicars and their teachings, honestly.* The boy looked awful, and her daughter seemed no better. The girl worked the loom as if her father had passed to the light that morning. Still, poor Thomas would be worse off.

She did her best to soften her expression and be welcoming. "Why, Nathaniel, what are you doing here so early? The farmer's life must be easier than I presume."

Weaving demanded less physical effort than farming but took more time, especially in the winter. She and her daughter spent long hours producing cloth to trade for their needs.

"Good morning, ma'am. Is Orah here?"

"Of course, but she's taking her turn at the loom. I'd prefer you don't disturb her until she's done."

"I'd really like to see her."

She resumed her work, half-heartedly tossing kindling into a basket on the porch. "We all want things. We don't get them the instant they pop into our heads."

"Yes, ma'am, but it's been so hard since Thomas was taken."

She thought of herself as kindly. When someone asked for help, she never paused to consider her own inconvenience. Once she understood the young man's mood, she set down her load and gave him her full attention. "Yes, I've seen it in Orah as well. Her turn will be done in an hour. Can I give her a message?"

"If you please. Tell her to meet me as soon as possible. She'll know where."

Susannah laughed. *The three friends and their secrets.* She knew vaguely of some meeting place in the woods behind the Rush cottage. "Would you mean the NOT tree?"

Nathaniel nodded shyly.

She imagined how his deceased mother would have responded, and cut short her laughter, pursing her lips as if to say "poor boy." Like everyone else in Little Pond, she liked Nathaniel and hated seeing him unhappy.

"I'll tell her, I promise, as soon as I've finished with this firewood. I'm sure she'll want to meet you when her work is done."

Nathaniel thanked her politely.

As he walked away, she shook her head and—after glancing around to check that no one could hear—mumbled to herself. "Why in the name of the light don't the vicars leave these young people alone? Honestly."

***

Nathaniel wandered about the village, reluctant to go home, but after a while, he worried he'd draw attention and retreated to the seclusion of the NOT tree. He checked his tracks before entering the hidden path. No trace of his passing showed on the hard ground and, unusual for so late in the season, no snow had fallen.

When he arrived at the clearing, his heart sank. His mind held an image of a magical place, but now, with no greenery to brighten the view or night to cloak the scene in mystery, it seemed bleak and cheerless. As a child, he'd played their summer games here—make-believe adventures with his friends--but for him, they were much more. He'd go home and reflect on them as he lay awake at night. In the dimness of his bedchamber, the darkness they'd fought would transform into grotesque creatures, winged and scaled and breathing fire, or fanged serpents with slit tongues. Yet always, the hero of his imagination remained the same: tall, a plumed helmet upon his head, a gleaming sword with a bejeweled hilt grasped in his right hand. And on his chest, an obsidian medallion, all blackness, the oval talisman he'd used to capture and imprison the darkness. For nothing could destroy the darkness that dwelled in each person's heart. Only great courage could constrain it.

A deep sigh. The scene before him triggered none of those fantasies. Beneath the noonday sun, the hut seemed small and bare, a skeleton of his childhood.

Usually by this time of the year, they'd have performed their winter ritual, cutting down boughs of balsam fir and covering the frame. Usually snow would have covered the land and... usually the three friends would be together. Nathaniel's throat started to close, and the world weighed on him as if the adulthood that had hovered over him since his coming-of-age had come crashing down.

He heard a crackle of dry leaves and turned to catch Orah jogging along the path. Her breath burst out in gasps, and the color had risen in her cheeks.

"I came as quickly as possible," she said. "I didn't finish my turn, but I'll make up for it tonight." She grimaced at the bare shelter and stepped forward to touch the wood. The circle of slats held fast in the frozen ground, and their tops remained tightly bound. Nathaniel's father had done well by them.

When she looked back, her face was drawn. "Do you remember how the three of us would play our games?"

Nathaniel forced a smile. "You'd always set the rules."

"I did not."

"You most certainly did." He mimicked her voice. "'Thomas, go off to the right, and Nathaniel to the left. I'll stay here and count to ten, saying one Little Pond, two Little Pond, which should give you plenty of time.'"

"Well maybe, but you and Thomas would argue with me."

"That's why we came up with the Pact of the Ponds." He placed his right hand over his heart and thrust his left in front, then gestured for her to do the same.

Her hand ventured into the space between them, but pulled back. "It won't work. We need three to form a circle."

"Then let's pretend Thomas is here."

She glared at him but finally gave in, covering her heart and grasping his wrist.

"Pact of the Ponds," he said weakly. "No more arguments and the game will begin."

"This is no game." She yanked her hand away and stared beyond the tree line, as if searching for Thomas in far-off Temple City. "Something terrible is happening to Thomas. I can sense his loneliness and fear, even at a distance. Do you believe that?"

Nathaniel nodded. More than once in their years together she'd seemed able to read his thoughts. "It's possible... for friends since birth."

"Can't we find a way to help? Your father's an elder. What does he say?"

Nathaniel gritted his teeth as the shame from that morning rushed back. He told her what had happened, and she had the same questions.

"How will he change?" she said.

"He might be sadder."

"A sadder Thomas? What a horrible thought. Why didn't you press for more?"

"I tried. I don't know why he wouldn't tell, but I said things I never should have said. Since Thomas was taken, we're all in a foul mood." He glanced at the hut skeleton. "Why don't we cover the shelter now, you and I? It'll cheer us up and give Thomas a pleasant surprise when he returns."

A crease formed between Orah's brows and her eyes narrowed. "Our special ceremony without Thomas? How can you think such a thing? He's gone less than two weeks and you'd forget him?"

First he'd snapped at his father, and now Orah had snapped at him. The world had gone awry. This morning, he'd been angry with his father for one of the few times in his life. He'd *never* been angry with Orah before. "This is the Temple's fault, with all their rules and ceremonies."

"You mustn't say such things."

"Why not? No one's listening."

"Because the Temple protects us from the darkness." She recited from the book of light, a verse the elders used to admonish children. *"Beware the stray thought. Like water dripping on rock, it can erode the strongest mind and open a path for the darkness."*

"We don't even know what the darkness is."

"The darkness is the time before the light, a time of chaos and death."

He stepped toward her. "That's what we learned to recite in school, but what is it really? You're the smartest person I know. Can you tell me what the darkness is?"

He studied her as she pondered his question. Her looks came from the Weber side of the family, with olive skin and delicate but unremarkable features, more than offset by flaring dark eyes. The sole gift from her mother was a striking red tint to her hair. Together, they combined into a fierce beauty, especially when outraged like now.

At last, her outrage vanished and she came closer, enough so he felt her breath. "Yes, Nathaniel, I can tell you. The darkness is when a son hurts the father he loves, when friends are separated, and when those who care the most about each other raise their voices in anger." Her expression hardened, and her delicate features disappeared. "By that meaning, I swear the darkness will never return."

The strong words narrowed his vision, so he saw her now as through a tunnel. When the moment passed, he noticed something cold on his cheeks.

A light snow had begun to fall.

Chapter 5
Festival

As festival approached, Orah came to agree with Nathaniel. Covering the NOT tree would affirm their friendship with Thomas rather than deny it. Despite her distress at his absence, she had no way to help. So the day before festival, she and Nathaniel gathered to wrap the structure in green to welcome Thomas home.

Before they entered the forest, Nathaniel fetched an axe from the woodshed while she rummaged about for twine. They met as dark settled upon the clearing outside the village.

Stars winked into being and a moon rose, less than half-full but bright enough to light their task. She picked a branch lush with needles and prodded Nathaniel to chop it free. As it fell, she grabbed the end, and together they dragged it to the shelter. After she located the perfect spot, they bound the branch to the slats with twine before returning to the woods. In less than an hour, they had remade the bare structure into an enclosed dwelling that seemed, under the stars, to have stood there forever.

Orah ducked inside and waited amused as Nathaniel crawled in on all fours. Beneath the cover of branches, her breathing quieted as if she'd entered a holy place. The smell of freshly-cut balsam filled the air like incense, a comforting memory of childhood.

Custom prescribed a blessing when they'd finished their work. This year was Orah's turn. "May the light bless our shelter." She stopped at the tired old phrase, uttered without thought. This year's blessing had to be real. "Not the light the Temple claims to own, but the true light that burns in our hearts." She grasped Nathaniel's hands and spoke for the both of them. "Dear friend Thomas, we're sorry to have covered this shelter without you, but know we have not forgotten you. We're here in the darkness with you. Not the darkness of the Temple, but a warm and loving darkness that will soon embrace the three of us again."

Nathaniel gasped at her statement—too close to heresy.

She squeezed his hands to regain focus. "Thomas, we are with you. Say it with me Nathaniel, so it will be stronger."

Both inhaled deeply and spoke. "Thomas, we are with you." Then she added, "Return to us safely and soon."

In what moonlight filtered through the branches, the puffs from Nathaniel's breath filled the space between them.

***

For as long as Orah could remember, she'd looked forward to festival, but Nathaniel's coming of age and Thomas's absence made this year feel different. She'd tossed in bed last night, a cloud of uncertainty hanging over her, but when she awoke this morning, the usual excitement filled the air.

The celebration began at noon with footraces. The youngest competed first, followed by the older children, and finally those of age, from seventeen to twenty-five. Boys and girls raced separately, so she and Nathaniel could cheer each other on.

She'd always been fast, but now, as the oldest in her group, she managed to win all three of her races—the sprint around the commons, the longer run through the village, and a scramble between obstacles. The scramble required more agility than speed, and favored the younger girls, but this year she competed with a special intensity.

Age worked against Nathaniel. As a new adult, he competed with men whose muscles had thickened and minds had grown accustomed to the length of their limbs. Deriving no inspiration

33

from her victories, he ran poorly in the first two events. Then, in the scramble, he fell at the finish, lunging in an attempt to make the final three and skinning his knee.

When all the races had finished, the elders awarded prizes to the winners—by tradition an elaborate wreath made from the flax that grew around Little Pond.

Flax filled a vital need for the people of the Ponds, harvested for both its fiber and seeds, but in the spring when its blossoms bloomed, families would go out among the stalks and search for the most beautiful flowers—the whites and lavenders, and the blues valued most of all. Orah recalled long June evenings with her father before he died, sitting and weaving stalks into rings. Then the flowers would be hung on the walls to dry, looking like the wings of a butterfly. A simple prize, but even the oldest decorated their cottages with festival wreaths won long ago.

The elders often delegated the awarding of prizes to someone close to the winner—a parent or, for the older ones, a betrothed. When the time came for Orah to receive her due, Elder William Rush called on his son. Nathaniel gaped at him, but his father smiled, offered the victor wreaths and gestured toward Orah.

Everyone knew Thomas had been away a long time—longer than the usual teaching—and most had watched the three friends grow up together. The crowd murmured its approval as Nathaniel placed the wreaths on Orah's head so gently he disturbed not a hair.

But both Orah and Nathaniel had forgotten the last part of the tradition: male presenters were expected to kiss a female winner, once on each check. Their neighbors, however, had a better memory and urged them on. Nathaniel took on a look that said he preferred to be elsewhere, but in response to the crowd, he rested a hand on Orah's arm and leaned in to brush each of her cheeks with his lips.

She laughed and rolled her eyes, but a sudden glow warmed her skin, and a flush of crimson added to the color of the flowers.

***

By the time twilight came, Orah waited eagerly for the feast. All the races had been run. Happy winners pranced about, sporting wreaths on their heads. Food and drink covered every surface, from the railings of the commons to the Temple altar. All that remained was the lighting of the bonfire and the festival tree.

A spruce stood in the village square with candles attached to every branch. *Would the vicar disapprove of this tradition as well?* He never joined them for festival and no villager ever discussed the celebration with him, so the unseen and unspoken was allowed.

The lighting of the tree started at the top. This year, the elders chose Nathaniel to help. He planted himself at the base while strong arms hoisted a nimble ten-year-old onto his shoulders—a role once filled by Thomas at a similar age. The boy paused to balance and then straightened. Nathaniel's father passed a pole up to him with a flame attached to its tip. He kindled the topmost candle and worked his way down. Once the top third of the tree blazed with light, the boy vaulted to the ground and many hands lit the rest.

Orah watched open-mouthed as one by one, the burning candles chased away twilight. Then Elder Robert grabbed the burning pole and, amidst an air of expectation, tossed it into the bonfire stack. Within seconds the dry wood crackled, and the flames shot higher than the festival tree.

A cheer went up. While a few of the revelers stayed to watch the fire spread, most headed for the food, but as they turned, they froze in place. A hush rolled across the crowd, and Orah stretched for a better view.

There stood Thomas at the edge of the firelight, lingering like a part of the shadows.

What did they do to him? His pale skin stretched over cheeks so hollow that his face showed no sentiment save exhaustion.

The adults hesitated to approach, and their children caught their fear. Even Nathaniel wavered, too stunned to move.

But Orah rushed forward. "Thomas, you've returned to brighten our festival. What a gift." She reached out to touch him, but he recoiled.

"A drink." His voice rasped as if he hadn't used it in days. "May I have a drink?"

Someone offered a cup. His hands shook so much that the liquid spilled on his soiled tunic. After two gulps, he glanced at the festival tree and began to well up.

Nathaniel finally pushed through the crowd to join Orah. "Have you been to Temple City? Did you see it?"

Thomas growled like an offended stranger. "I saw nothing but darkness."

Two elders placed restraining hands on Orah and Nathaniel.

"He'll need time," Elder Robert said. "Give him a few days."

Orah pulled away and pressed closer. "What is it, Thomas? Did they hurt you?"

Thomas's head snapped around. He lifted his chin and straightened as if about to deliver a sermon. "The Temple of Light does not harm its children. Only in the darkness was violence done. The vicars have shown me the truth. Horrible things happened in the darkness. I'll dedicate my life to ensure it never returns."

The elders muttered how the teaching had made him wise beyond his years, but now he needed to rest. Gentle, older hands led him away.

"He's home at last," Nathaniel said as their neighbors strove to regain their festive mood, "but he's no longer our Thomas. Only time will tell whether what's been taken from him returns or is forever gone."

Forever gone. Orah shivered. *Nathaniel's wish has come to pass.*

Something had finally happened in Little Pond.

Chapter 6
Winter

Winter settled on the Ponds and into the bones of its people. No blizzards blew in from the mountains, but a light snow fell every few days, leaving the pathways coated in white. Twilight seemed to come right after noon, and the dark and cold stalked everyone.

For the farmers, winter meant idle time. By the first snowfall, they'd completed the chores saved until after the harvest—cottage repairs or fence mending—and the few animals they kept took a small effort each day. The indoor season provided a chance to create little luxuries, to tool leather or carve wood, and to catch up on reading.

Only the Temple provided the printed word, and the vicar frowned on the owning of books. On the rare occasions when he brought a new one, he placed it on the shelves in the commons to be shared by all. But during winter months, the shelves lay empty. Neighbors passed books to each other without ever returning them to the commons.

Orah had read them all, each a variation on the same theme-- praise the light and damn the darkness. She reread them anyway, hoping to gain a fresh perspective.

When not reading, she consumed most of her daylight hours weaving or contemplating her needle as it dipped in and out of the resulting cloth, sewing garments to trade. Once a week when weather allowed, she trekked the two hours to Great Pond with a few bolts of fabric to barter, and returned with a pack laden with spindles of yarn.

Though the people of the Ponds stayed inside more and saw their neighbors less, she managed to meet Nathaniel every day. As for Thomas, he never ventured from home.

She let him be, heeding the caution of the elders: *He'll return to himself by spring, though he won't be quite the same.*

This gave her little comfort.

Occasionally she'd invite him to join her and Nathaniel, leaving notes with a place and time. She offered to help or listen. She promised not to judge.

He never came.

***

William Rush watched his son with concern. Nathaniel had become withdrawn since Thomas's return, and the gloom of midwinter seemed to affect him more deeply this year.

The idea first came up during a visit to Susannah Weber. He'd brought over a bushel of grain to trade for a new coat for Nathaniel, whose growth had left his sleeves two fingers short of his wrists. William found he could talk to the affable woman more easily than to his sullen offspring and quickly discovered that Orah shared the same malady.

Susannah Weber looked different from her daughter, with freckled skin and a short head of red hair, but she was just as direct. "Well William, the time has come to intervene."

"What do you suggest?"

"Leave the grain. Orah and I will bring the coat to Nathaniel tomorrow at dinnertime."

He nodded, slowly at first, and then more rapidly. "I can make a meal."

"And I'll bake bread."

Maybe together, they might lift the two young people out of their low spirits.

***

Nathaniel jumped at the knock on the door. He'd been balancing on his toes all evening, waiting for Orah to arrive. While he always looked forward to her visits, he especially relished them now as they broke up the long winter days.

She handed him the new coat and helped him try it on. It fit perfectly. The smell of freshly baked bread filled the air, and at first everyone relaxed, but once they sat down for the meal, the conversation wilted. The parents tried to carry the discussion, but the mood around the table dampened every attempt. Eventually, the room quieted until no sound remained save the clinking of forks on plates.

After they finished eating, Nathaniel's father suggested they settle by the fireplace while he prepared tea. Nathaniel tossed two logs on the fire. The wood sputtered and cast off sparks as if resisting the flames, and then erupted into a peak of yellows and reds. Soon, with their chairs close by, all felt a warm glow on their faces.

After a respectful pause, Orah's mother dove in. "So how is young Thomas?"

"We don't know," Nathaniel said. "He won't let us near."

"He's not the first to be taken. Recovering from a teaching takes time. He may need help."

"But the elders told us to leave him alone."

"I heard what they said, but some wounds don't heal on their own."

Nathaniel threw his hands in the air. "Everyone tells us what to do and what not to do, but no one will tell us what happened. How can we help without knowing?"

Orah's mother grabbed the poker and prodded the perfectly good fire. After a painful silence, she stood and hovered over Nathaniel's father.

"They're right, William. It's time we tell them why we heed the words of the vicars... and why we hate them as well."

Hate the vicars? Nathaniel knit his brows. Not the usual parental sermon. He steeled himself, waiting for them to impart some harsh truth.

"We're loath to talk about it, William, but for their sake, we must."

After a puzzling hesitation, Nathaniel's father nodded.

Orah's mother shifted over to Nathaniel and took three long breaths as if buying time to compose her words. "The Temple took your father for a teaching just after coming of age. It lasted long, weeks longer than Thomas's. When he came home, he was all closed up inside. The Temple had stripped the joy from him, but as the elders say, he recovered in time. He's grown into a fine man and a good father, despite the teaching and the loss of your mother."

Nathaniel grimaced and sucked air in through his teeth. *My father taken, and longer than Thomas?*

Before he could respond, Orah's mother moved on to her daughter. "They took *your* father as well. We'd grown up together, much like you and Nathaniel." Her eyes glistened, and she needed a breath to continue. "My sweet young man... when he returned from Temple City, something in him had changed. We married, you were born, but he was never the same. The teaching haunted him in his dreams. He'd wake up in the middle of the night in a cold sweat, and I had no way to comfort him. After he died so young, the vicar tried to console me, but I refused to listen. Though I'd never shout it from the bell tower, I blamed — I still blame — the Temple and their teaching. Your father had a gentle soul, and the vicars broke his heart."

Her chin sagged to her chest, and she collapsed in her chair. Orah squeezed her mother's arm.

As Nathaniel struggled to moderate his breathing, his father buried his face in his hands. *What could have happened so many years ago to affect him so?*

"Why didn't you tell me?" Nathaniel said, careful to keep the edge from his voice.

His father's hands began to move, scrubbing his brow as if trying to remove a stain. When they dropped to his lap, his eyes were red. "I was ashamed, Nathaniel. You don't know what a teaching's like. They show you deep into the darkness so you appreciate why the Temple stands. You see horrors beyond imagination."

He went on to tell of the small cell, the lack of light, the thirst and hunger, the exhaustion and what he could only describe as visions of the darkness.

40

Orah asked what Nathaniel feared to ask. "Why ashamed?"

Nathaniel's father licked his lips as if recalling the thirst. At last, he stood and gazed down at the two of them.

"The end of the teaching is up to you. After a while, you beg to return to your normal life. Shortly thereafter, you offer a limb just to go home, but the vicars want more."

Nathaniel sputtered, hardly able to spit out the words. "If it made no sense, why didn't you tell them what they wanted?"

A sorrow seeped into his father's bones, making his shoulders droop. "You've admired courage and honor since you were no taller than my knee. That's what the vicars demand from you before the teaching ends. To go home, you must surrender your courage and honor."

"I don't understand," Nathaniel said.

His father spoke so softly he had to strain to hear, but a single word rang out: "Betrayal."

"Betrayal? Who could you have betrayed?"

Orah's mother jumped up. "Enough, William. You've told more than I intended."

He shook her off, and his back stiffened. "To end the teaching, you must betray a friend. Why does Thomas avoid you? More than likely, he betrayed you."

Orah's mother blocked him from their view and stepped closer. Her voice rose with each word. "You must never blame him. He had no choice."

Nathaniel's eyes widened as the fire buzzed and flared. "What happens next?"

"Most who are betrayed are never taken. The vicars find enough candidates on their own. Time passes, we grow older. The betrayal becomes nothing more than an entry in the Temple records. That's why I finally told. They led me to believe that...." He turned away, unable to finish.

Orah let out a slight, almost imperceptible gasp, and then clutched the edge of her chair and rose. Her lips contorted around a single unbearable question. "Who did *you* betray?"

Nathaniel failed to comprehend. What had she heard that he had not?

Her mother grabbed her by the arm, but she twisted away.

"Who," Orah said, shouting now, "did you betray?"

Her mother waved wildly. "Enough William. Say no more."

He brushed her aside and came to within an arm's length of Orah. Their eyes met, and his expression melted into shame.

Orah let out a shriek and fled from the cottage.

Silence filled the emptiness left by her flight. Then the topmost log of the fire settled, crushing the embers below. The pyramid of flame dropped as well, and the room dimmed.

***

A few days later, Nathaniel attended Orah's coming-of-age. Though not as big a celebration as festival, the occasion still bore the weight of a major life event.

While awaiting the guest of honor, he kept twisting around, hoping to spot Thomas. He peered past the crowd of well-wishers, friends and relatives hugging and murmuring good cheer as they awaited the ceremony. No sign of Thomas.

He wanted to tell his friend he knew what had happened and welcome him home. He and Orah had discussed what they'd learned, trying to understand. *Impossible.* He would never understand the teaching, but one thing he knew with certainty—he blamed neither his father nor Thomas. He blamed the Temple of Light.

Finally, Orah emerged and took her seat on a platform erected in the village square. Her mother had the honor of cutting her hair to the prescribed length, just covering her neck. Afterwards, three female relatives accompanied her inside the commons. Moments later she reemerged, the gray clothing of youth shed. She now wore the black vest and long dark skirt of age—a full child of light.

Next, Elder Robert stated the precepts of the Temple, one at a time, waiting as she repeated each, even though she'd known them since first school. Finally, Robert led the assembly in the blessing of life, recited upon attaining major milestones.

"Blessed is the light that has given us life, allowed us to thrive, and brought us here to this day."

Nathaniel studied Orah, trying to read her mood. When the ceremony ended with the communal "blessed be the light," he caught her mouthing the words. What struck him most, however, was how

42

she'd grown. Coming of age had added a fierce intensity to her normal seriousness. The Temple had changed his two friends. Had it changed him as well?

At the end, Elder Robert marked Orah's name on a card that the next courier would take to Temple City.

Now came the time to celebrate. Most people proceeded to the feast, but Nathaniel lingered to congratulate Orah. He grasped her by the waist and swung her around, and as she flew, she caught a glimpse of something over his shoulder.

"Thomas," she whispered.

Nathaniel set her down gently and turned. Thomas lurked in the last row like a distant relative from another village. The two of them approached their friend as if coming upon a bird they wished to view more closely but not frighten away.

Orah tried on several expressions before she settled on gratitude. "Oh Thomas, I'm so thankful you've come. You've given me the best present I could have."

Thomas took a small step toward them. Nathaniel froze in place, afraid that any motion might scare him away. He glimpsed a hint of his friend behind the mask the teaching had imprinted on him, but Thomas came no closer.

Remembering his father's distress, Nathaniel chose his words carefully. "We'll always be your friends, no matter what you've done. We're here when you need us. We'll listen when you want to tell."

At the front of the commons, the feast awaited. Relatives shouted out to Orah to receive her first toast. Thomas balanced on the balls of his feet. When the villagers called a second time, he spun around and fled. The mask of his face had never changed.

***

As dusk settled on the village, Orah tired of entertaining, so Nathaniel drew her away to the refuge of the NOT tree. He brushed the snow off a flat rock outside the shelter, and the two huddled together for warmth.

"What does this coming of age mean?" Orah said. "I feel no different. You've been of age longer. Can you tell me what it means?"

Nathaniel shrugged. He had no answer and knew she had more to say.

"I'll tell you what I think, Nathaniel of Little Pond. It means two things. First, we can no longer harbor illusions. We must let them fade into the thin air from whence they came. Second, we'll need to make choices, and that will be the hardest."

A crunch of snow on the path, and Thomas emerged from the woods. Nathaniel waited, wondering at all the times he'd longed for change and how, now, he ached for things to return to the way they were.

"I guessed you'd be here," Thomas said, his voice strained but close to his own. "I always know what the two of you are thinking. That hasn't changed."

One side of his mouth did its best to curl upward, passing for his familiar grin. Then all three moved toward each other, silent as the snow-covered woods, and met in a steadfast embrace.

Chapter 7
Orah's Log

My coming of age seems like a good reason to start my new log, no longer to chronicle the changing of the seasons but to record the progress of my life.

Last night, following the ceremony and our reunion with Thomas, I dreamed of my father in a teaching cell, but I was the one being taught. The vicars insisted they'd release me only if I betrayed him.

"How can I betray him?" I cried. "He's passed to the light."

The Little Pond vicar with black beads for eyes glared down at me. "You must renounce his deathbed wish."

My father's final words came back to me: Don't let the vicars set your mind. Think your own thoughts, big thoughts based on grand ideas.

I shook my head and sat back down. The cover thudded shut, thrusting me into darkness. Tears began to flow for the first time since my father died. What else could I do? To renounce his wishes would be like watching him die again. Yet unless I betrayed him, I'd stay in the teaching forever.

The air above me shimmered as Nathaniel's father had described. I braced for visions of the darkness, but my father appeared instead, younger than I remembered and with the delicate features he'd bequeathed to me. "Why are you crying, little Orah?"

"The vicars demand I betray you."

"Not me. No one can betray those who are gone. They're asking you to betray yourself."

My lower lip trembled and my words emerged with a quiver. "What should I do?"

My father offered that familiar smile and spoke as if reading me a bedtime story. "Your mind and heart are your own. No one can control them, even with temple magic. Find your purpose and be true to yourself. Nothing else matters."

The image flickered, the dream faded, and I awoke.

I lay in my bed, staring up at the ceiling until the dawn crept past the edges of my window shade.

Now, as I write this, my first log entry, I wonder: What is my purpose?

I've come of age and am more confused than ever. I'm certain of only one thing – I boil with rage at the vicars.

But to what end?

Chapter 8

Confession

Nathaniel battled against a howling headwind that stole his breath and stifled all speech. A storm had blown in from the north and swirled through the Ponds for the past two days, leaving in its wake drifts to the eaves of his cottage. That morning, after the sky cleared, Orah had insisted they get Thomas outdoors. So now Nathaniel trudged along, breaking a path for his friends through the newly fallen snow.

He paused to catch his bearings—another hundred paces to Elder John's cottage. Once the steam from his lips slowed, he drove his knee forward and set out again.

They'd managed to get Thomas outside every day except for the height of the storm. Whereas before the teaching he'd complained about the slightest discomfort, now he seemed to thrive on the cold. That morning, he'd rewarded them for their efforts.

"The darkness lurks in the past," he said, "or in the cells of Temple City, but not in Little Pond with my friends."

As they made their daily treks, neighbors noticed the three out and about and gladly invited them in. One by one they came forward, first with sympathy, and then with stories of teachings.

"My Uncle Edward—he's long gone—had a teaching. Wouldn't let on what happened until his fortieth birthday. He was a good man, but after he told his story, he was a better man."

"My brother Richard—you remember him, gone off to work in Great Pond—had a teaching. Came back, said nothing for two months. Then went to the village square and spat at the altar. After that, he was fine."

Elder John never spoke about teachings, but for some reason he insisted they visit every few days. As soon as the storm had cleared, Nathaniel decided the next visit was overdue.

When they reached the recent widower's cottage, he stood in the doorway waiting to usher them in. They stamped the snow off their boots on the weather-beaten slats of the porch and bustled into the warmth of the living room, where a fire blazed in the stone hearth. Elder John hung a kettle over the flames and hovered while the water came to a boil. Once they had settled in their chairs and wrapped their hands around steaming mugs, he gave them a lesson on the Temple.

"Despite the Temple's imperfections, it offers us the best chance for a good life. We read in the book of light about the horrors of the darkness, but the memory of bad times fades. The vicars claim even a small step backward might lead us to violence, chaos and war." He checked that each of them heeded his words. "I don't know myself, but I trust the vicar's wisdom."

Orah's eyes flared. "Can't they find a better way to show us the darkness without hurting anyone?"

John sighed. "You don't understand. They don't mean to impart knowledge, they mean to impart fear. They take one in three, sometimes more, at a young age. By making them afraid through the teaching, they make us all afraid, even as we respect what the Temple stands for. For all these centuries, these methods have kept the darkness away."

Nathaniel tried to follow the elder's words. He'd grown up fearing the darkness and had always been faithful to the Temple... except in his innermost thoughts, shared only with his closest friends. What cause would the vicars have to take him? So what if Thomas had given his name? They selected only one in three. The rest became nothing more than entries in Temple records.

But Orah's warning rang out in his mind.

No more illusions.

***

March arrived. The drifts settled to knee-high under their own weight and then melted to the ankles. In the common pathways, many boots beat down the snow, and the villagers spread ash over it to make walking easier.

The warmer weather made Nathaniel worry more. Within weeks, the roadways would clear, and the vicar would come for the spring blessing.

As the snow thawed, so did Thomas. Gradually, more details of his teaching emerged.

Orah worked with him like a mother easing a splinter from a baby's finger, using insight gained from Nathaniel's father. "In this dark hole," she'd ask, "were you cold and wet as well?"

He'd answer sometimes, but never mentioned the betrayal.

One day, as the three wandered through the village, making irregular tracks in the snow, Thomas lifted his face to the early March sun, letting it give back warmth. He seemed more content than at any time since the teaching.

For the moment, Nathaniel's worries eased, and he shared his friend's good mood. He stepped in front, causing the three to pause and form a circle. "I have something to tell you, Thomas. Whatever they forced you to do wasn't your fault. From what my father said, even the strongest character would give in to the teaching. The vicars had no right to demand my name, but know that as of this day, I forgive you."

Thomas's good mood vanished, and the sallow look from festival returned. He stared past them, as if seeing a far-off place. "They dangled the hope of leaving, but always out of reach. I had to tell.... It was the only way to go home."

In those few words, he'd said more about the teaching than ever before.

Orah urged him on. "They killed my father, Thomas. Don't let them destroy you. So what if you gave them Nathaniel's name. You had no choice."

"Not just his name. They wanted more."

49

Nathaniel's head snapped around. "More? What else could they want?"

Thomas began to sob. "They wanted to know your dreams."

Nathaniel's heart thudded in his chest as a foul mix of outrage and fear tore at him. He pictured Thomas in the teaching—exhausted, frightened, and broken—and he intended to comfort his friend, but the question would not be contained. "You told them about my dreams?"

Without another word, Thomas turned and stumbled off.

Orah wavered for a second before confronting Nathaniel. "Blame the Temple, not him. We have no choice but to forgive, and as for whatever trials may come, we'll face them together."

Nathaniel gaped as she caught up to Thomas, clutching him in her arms and letting his tears make moist stains on her tunic.

Chapter 9
First Test

The equinox, barely dawn, the morning of the spring blessing. Nathaniel tossed in bed. What if the voice from the sun icon should call his name? Would he submit like his father, and if not, would he ever see Little Pond again?

He gave up on sleep and swung his feet to the floor. While he waited in the dim light for the chirping of birds to signal sunrise, he pondered the value of honor and the cost of losing it.

Ten years earlier, he'd spent a similarly somber night following the funeral for Orah's father.

***

He startled awake from a nightmare and cried out for the mother he never knew.

His father rushed into his room, settled on the bed, and wrapped an arm around his shoulders until he calmed enough to describe the dream.

"Mother appeared to me there in the doorway. She whispered my name, but for some reason, she stayed hidden in the shadows. I wanted to tell her Orah's father was coming to join her, so I stood and came closer. She reached out as if to give me a hug, but before we touched, a moonbeam flashed through the window, and I saw she had no face."

"It's a dream, Nathaniel, nothing more."

"At least Orah knew her father. I know nothing about my mother."

His father sighed. "I miss her so much, sometimes I forget to share her with you."

"Tell me what she was like."

"She was tall, with deep brown eyes that pierced your soul. I believe she had a special sense and could tell what those close to her were thinking."

"Like Orah can with me?"

"Yes, your mother would have liked the comparison. She loved you more than anything. When you were still in the womb, she'd tell you stories about all the wonderful things you'd do. She believed one day you'd make the world a better place. If the darkness ever returned, you'd be the one to drive it away."

***

On this morn of the spring blessing, what would his mother think of him as he shivered in his underclothes and helplessly awaited his fate? Were her dreams merely the aspirations of a young woman expecting her first child, or a premonition? If he was so destined, what choice should he make now?

After a time, he gave up on sleep, dressed and went outside to pace. In the watery light of pre-dawn, he easily found his way. His stomach growled, and he stepped inside the storage shed to hack off a slice of ham. As he sat hunched on a bench eating, he caught sight of his travel pack hanging on the wall, and an idea began to form. What if he filled the pack with food and a jug of water? His sheepskin jacket hung nearby, and a brightening sky foretold a good day to be outdoors.

He'd never win a battle with the vicars. Even if he could resist their strange powers, the dread they inflicted on the villagers would make it impossible to defy them, and once in their grasp, he'd either lose his honor or never return.

He had one other choice: vanish for the day. The Temple required everyone to attend the blessing, but a few always found excuses— business elsewhere, sickness, or a visit to a distant relative. If he missed the ceremony, the vicar might forget to call his name and do without a teaching for the spring. He could hide until the vicar departed.

Nathaniel's heart sank as soon as the idea formed. His first test since coming of age, and he planned to run away. What other option remained?

Yet in the fantastic dreams of his childhood, his knight would never have made such a choice.

***

As the hint of sunrise flared on the horizon, he donned his jacket and hurried off to the NOT tree.

Once inside, he sat cross-legged and stared blankly at the balsam walls. Time passed slowly. After an hour, he began to worry. He was too near the village, and if temple magic found him, this place might implicate his friends. So before Little Pond rose for the day, he headed deeper into the woods.

Five minutes later, he stumbled upon a familiar trail. At some point, all schoolchildren of the Ponds made the two-hour trek to the mountains in the west. They'd hike to the foothills and climb through bushes and scree to the base of the white granite, where their teacher would tell them to touch the rock and feel the edge of their world. *Here you may come, but no farther.* Most never forgot that moment, but few came back. Despite the old stories, everyone believed the mountains insurmountable.

As a more adventurous sort, Nathaniel's father used to bring his young son and his friends there for summer outings.

Before he knew it, Nathaniel had set out on the path. The excursion would give him something to do, take him far from the village and let him think more clearly. When he returned, he'd claim to have forgotten the vicar's visit and gone off to the mountains to celebrate his first spring since coming of age. The elders would chastise him but might believe the young, absentminded romantic.

Still, he hoped for something more. This path — if the legends were true — led over the granite peaks to the ocean... and beyond. Perhaps, in his uncertainty, it might also lead to answers.

As he hiked, his mind wandered to younger days on the trail with his friends. His father would make up games to reinforce their schooling and keep them from getting bored. He'd start with a quiz about the land, giving them five seconds to answer.

"How many ponds in this region?"

"Five."

"Their names?"

"Little Pond, Great Pond, Middle Pond."

"The easy ones, Thomas. Nathaniel, you must remember the rest."

"Beaver Pond and East Pond."

"How far to Temple City?"

"Three days."

Then, when the children began to fidget, he'd switch to numbers.

"How much is seven and nine?"

"Sixteen," Orah would call out.

"I had the answer," Thomas would protest, "but Orah always shouts it out first."

"I understand. This next one is just for the boys. This is the year 1132 of the age of light. I was born in 1101. How old am I?"

Nathaniel would glare at Orah, daring her to speak out of turn, and then answer, "Thirty-one."

"A hard one now, again for the boys. Nathaniel's grandfather was born in 1073. How old is he?"

Thomas would look to Nathaniel, who stammered until the time had passed.

"Five seconds is up. Orah?"

Her hand had already shot into the air. "Fifty-nine, sir. I knew it right away."

Nathaniel and Thomas would make faces at her until his father reprimanded them. "You'll learn as well if you work hard. It may take a bit more time." Then, he'd look up as if surprised. "Ah, we've arrived."

***

Nathaniel had kept a steady pace for two hours, and finally the mountains loomed. No wonder teachers brought students here—an experience to impress. The ground fog had burned off, revealing a brilliant sky, and the morning sun shone strong from the east, bouncing its rays off the white cliffs and making them glow.

Now, with an unobstructed view of the edge of the world, he needed to rest. He plopped down on the spongy moss, settled his back against a boulder, and took a swallow from his water jug. Then he tipped his head back and stared at the massive rocks, a scene from a storybook.

This far from the village, he dared defy the vicars and imagine his knight, fresh from defeating the darkness, coming to take on his next quest. Perhaps the knight had scaled the mountains and built a boat to cross the sea, and to this day his descendants lived on the far side of the world, with no vicars, no Temple and no teachings.

Exhausted from a restless night, with the sun warm on his face and visions of knights in his head, he drifted off to sleep.

***

An hour later, he awoke with a crick in his neck from the hard rock and needed a moment to recall why he'd come. As his mind cleared, he decided he'd made the right choice. He'd avoided the vicar and saved himself for the great deeds that surely lay in his future, while also rediscovering this spot from his youth. He resolved to bring his friends back as soon as possible.

He stared at the craggy hilltop, seeing the mountains anew, and noted a dark patch a third of the way up the rock face. *Why does it fail to reflect the light? Dense bushes? Moss on rocks?*

The more he stared, the more he envisioned no rock at all, but a pass through the mountains and a trail leading up to it. A foolish notion, Orah would say, but he needed to know.

He began to work his way up, fighting at first through knee-high undergrowth, some thick with thorns. Once through the vegetation, he found a series of switchbacks climbing up the rocky slope. He moved with no plan, trudging steadily upward until sweat streamed down the small of his back and his breath came in short bursts. Exhaustion overcame anticipation, and he paused to rest. For all the distance he'd covered, his goal seemed farther away than when he'd started. To cross the mountain, he'd need provisions and perhaps some rope, but as his breathing returned to normal, he realized the pass was no illusion.

As he eyed the steepening path, he pictured his knight, battered from his battle with the darkness, scaling this mountain. He would have shed his helmet and armor, too heavy for the climb, and burdened with nothing but his sword and the talisman round his neck, slashed his way through the thicket and carved out a passageway. On the far side, he'd have built a boat and sailed away, taking the magically constrained darkness as far as possible from the children of light.

On a whim, Nathaniel glanced back to gauge how far he'd come. From his perch on the high ledge, he spotted the village of Little Pond. The place that had been home for all his life looked tiny from here, but he recognized details: his father's farm, and the bell tower of the village commons.

At once, his circumstance became clear.

The sun approached its midday peak. Soon, the blessing would commence. His absence would embarrass his father, and in the glare of the noontime sun, he recognized his coming here as an act of cowardice. Whatever might have happened, he should never have run out of fear.

Forgetting his discovery, he turned downhill and raced back toward the village.

***

Breathless and sweating despite the chill, Nathaniel rushed into the square. A few villagers lingered, but most had returned to their homes. He blew out a stream of air.

The altar lay bare. The vicar had gone.

Relief turned to worry when he picked up a murmur among those who remained. He asked for the cause of their concern, but they only shook their heads, so he searched for someone more familiar.

Susannah Weber! Her face had gone pale as chalk, and her cheeks were moist with tears.

"What happened?" he said.

"Oh Nathaniel, first my sweet young man and now my daughter."

When he stared blankly at her, she cried out. "Orah has been taken."

Chapter 10

Temple City

Nathaniel stretched his legs until the muscles sang. He'd been ready to rush off to Temple City at once, but his father had forbidden him to go. As a loving son, he was loath to openly disobey, so he'd waited until the wee hours of the morning before leaving. By dashing off before sunrise, he'd cut the vicar's lead in half. Now he hoped to close the remaining gap with his long stride. Whenever his legs tired, he pictured Orah in the teaching cell and pressed on.

He paused to rest near one of the temple trees that loomed over the landscape, with its stubby branches and garish green needles. His teachers had proclaimed these towers a miracle of the light, possessed of magic and to be avoided, but his father had taught him a more practical use. Set at intervals of exactly ten thousand paces, they provided a good way to measure distance — two hours apart at a normal stride, but he'd passed the last few in less. If only he could keep up this pace.

He arched his back to expand his lungs and drew in a deep breath, then started off again.

Thomas had tried to stop him, insisting no one could prevail against the vicars. "They're too strong and instill too much fear."

Nathaniel had dismissed him with a wave. He felt no fear. Nothing could shame him more than this — after waiting his whole life, he'd failed his first test of courage. He'd run away, and the vicar had chosen Orah in his stead. Now he must pay the price.

Like the knight of his dreams, he'd charge into Temple City, but this time, he had no doubt what to do. He'd go to the vicars and offer himself up in her place.

***

"Let us record the first teaching of Orah Weber of Little Pond. Blessed be the light. Orah, do you understand why you're here?"

Orah gazed up at the three men and forced herself to match their stares. "No, my lord, I do not. I've done nothing wrong."

"We concern ourselves less with the doing of wrong than the tendency to make choices that allow for the darkness to return. You *do* know what the darkness is?"

"Yes sir. The darkness is the time before the light, a time of chaos and death."

The vicar in the center wore a hat with six red stripes and a beard two hands long—an arch vicar. She'd learned the rankings in school, but had never seen a vicar so powerful.

He glared at her unblinking, thick brows hooding his eyes. "The darkness was much more. This teaching will help you learn the truth about the darkness, so you shall never forget the need to obey the Temple of Light."

Orah tried to stay focused, but her gaze kept wandering up to the arches, which were lost in the shadows cast by flickering candles dotting the surrounding walls, and back down to the panel of vicars.

The clergymen sat at a curved desk mounted high on a platform, which forced the person standing before them to crane their neck. A tapestry hung behind them, covering the wall halfway up the dome. Its colors had faded, but its meaning remained clear. On one side, the sun beamed across rows of vicars with arms uplifted in prayer. On the other, a black thunderhead threatened the advancing host. The battle of darkness and light.

Beneath her feet lay the hatch hiding the teaching cell.

She shook off such thoughts and answered with a firm voice. "I look forward to your help. I'm an excellent student and eager to learn."

"And so you shall, Orah. Isn't that a name from one of the forbidden languages?"

"It may be, sir. I'm told it comes from the word for light." She conjured up an image of her father, and raised her chin. "It's a proud name passed down in my family for generations."

"But forbidden, nevertheless. Rules exist so the darkness may never return, yet you play loosely with those rules. That means you do not fully appreciate the horrors of the darkness. Orah of Little Pond, whose name means light, we shall ensure that you learn—" He leaned forward for emphasis. " —to the depths of your being."

She withered under his glare and swung her hands behind her back, hoping to hide how much they'd started to shake.

***

Nathaniel could no longer contain his sense of awe. The Ponds had only one-story buildings, all made of wood, but even from a distance Temple City soared. Elaborate stone structures rising six stories or more challenged the low-lying clouds. In place of the modest sloped roofs of his home, sculpted spires rose above all, as if aspiring to the light.

His impression changed once inside. While the official buildings dominated the horizon, the dwellings within had been crammed together off trash-strewn streets—half-built hovels no one in Little Pond would deem fit to live in—and he found no hint of the hospitality of the Ponds. People cast suspicious glances as he passed. Children fled into their homes or ran into the soiled aprons of their mothers. All seemed fearful of strangers, and trudged about in tattered tunics with the bent-over gait of someone recently beaten.

Though quick to reach the gates of the city, he'd lost time finding his way inside, wandering in circles and passing the same buildings again and again.

On each circuit, he'd run into bands of men marching four abreast—temple officials, he assumed, but not vicars. They wore no hats, and their black tunics matched his except for an insignia on their chests—the sun icon shining down on the adoring family of three. In the center of the sun lay a gem in the shape of a star. It held no color of its own but reflected the colors from its surroundings.

The men strutted about with disdain for all they passed. He took a hint from the locals and shied away from them.

After the third loop, he became desperate. Time flowed like lifeblood leaking from his veins.

He finally approached a woman whose kindly appearance reminded him of Orah's mother. "Pardon me, can you tell me how to find a vicar?"

Her brows crumpled together, forcing a crease above the bridge of her nose, and the kindness in her eyes disappeared. "By the light, man, why? No one speaks to the clergy unless spoken to first."

"Please help me. My friend's been taken for a teaching, and I have to find her."

The woman's pupils grew large. Her mouth opened as if to respond, but no words came out. Instead, she showed him her back and scurried off.

After the third such rejection, he changed his approach. When a boy trudged by with his head down and a sack of flour under his arm, Nathaniel stopped him. "Who are these men, marching with the mark of the Temple?"

"Why, sir, they're deacons, defenders of the light."

"Do you think they'd take me to a vicar?"

"They might, or they might beat you for sport. I'd keep my distance if I were you." The boy took a few steps away, then called back as he broke into a trot. "Don't go near them till I'm gone, and don't let them know we spoke."

Nathaniel's head throbbed, and the air around him grew thin. The sounds of the city became muffled, as though he were underwater. *What good is courage without a plan?* He finally gave in and approached the deacons directly.

After a series of rude questions, the vicar's henchmen aligned in a square-shaped formation with him at the center, and marched him through the arched gateway of the main Temple building, with stern statues of deceased clergy eyeing him as he passed. The corridor ended at a massive chamber with hundreds of officials bustling about.

A low-level lackey ushered him before one of the dozens of desks that lined the walls, where an ill-tempered clerk scribbled Nathaniel's request down and repeated it in a nasal whine. "You say your friend has come for a teaching, and you're offering to take her place. Is that correct?"

"Yes sir."

The clerk paused and punctuated his writing before looking up. "Hmmm. Most unusual." He folded the request, marked it with a wax seal in the shape of the sun, and handed it to one of the couriers dashing about everywhere.

After so much time lost, the chance to keep Orah from the teaching had passed, but Nathaniel still hoped to save her from the worst. He stepped forward to accompany the messenger, hoping to speed up the process, but the clerk signaled for him to wait.

With the flurry of business in the hall, he worried he'd wait for hours, but the courier returned in minutes and gestured for him to follow.

They ended up in a round room with vaulted ceilings much as his father had described. Three clergy sat at a raised desk along the back wall, all well-fed and with beards greater than any he'd ever seen—senior vicars with more red stripes on their hats than he could count.

The one in the center with the most stripes began. "You are Nathaniel Rush of Little Pond?"

"Yes sir."

"And you are here to... request a teaching in place of Orah Weber?"

"Yes sir."

The senior vicar shook his head. "Extraordinary."

The vicar on the left leaned forward. "No one ever requests a teaching."

"Nevertheless, I've come to offer myself in Orah's place. I'm of age, from the same village, and would serve your purpose as well. My father's an elder and my neighbors regard me with favor. My teaching will make Little Pond stronger in the light."

The vicar on the left grumbled and murmurs of disagreement spread between the three.

Nathaniel edged closer to eavesdrop, but they noticed his approach and fell silent.

"Nathaniel of Little Pond," the senior cleric intoned, trying to restore order to the proceeding. "We'll need time to confer alone. Our servants will bring you to a holding area in the meantime."

61

He rang a bell with a miniature sun icon for a handle. Four deacons marched in, formed the well-practiced square around Nathaniel, and prepared to escort him out.

He rose to his full height, arched his back, and refused to go.

The men of the Ponds stood a good hand taller than the people of Temple City, and Nathaniel stood a hand taller than them, so he towered over the deacons.

They wavered, looking to the clerics for guidance.

The vicar on the right waved them off with a flip of is hand. "What now?"

"My request is urgent. I want my friend relieved of her teaching at once, or my offer will not stand."

The vicar in the center stared at him, stroking his beard, and an impish expression stole across his face. "Your friend has only arrived this morning. We've just finished with her, and will deliver our pronouncement soon. Now with your permission...." He waggled his thick brows and pointed using only his eyes. "Follow these gentlemen to your... guest quarters."

He gestured for the leader of the deacons to approach, leaned in and whispered a few words. The deacons reformed and guided Nathaniel away.

As he walked out, he glanced back over his shoulder.

While the two younger vicars stared in bewilderment, their superior gazed after him, deep in thought.

***

The deacons led Nathaniel down a narrow stairway to an underground hall. On one side, the wall bore no markings other than the etched decay of years. As his boots echoed on the stone floor, his imagination turned these scars in the stone into images—demons with exposed skulls or shrieking birds of prey. He turned away. On the other side stood a more ominous sight, a row of stout doors, each with a tiny window concealed by a metal slat controlled from the outside—and each anchored by an iron bolt.

Nathaniel understood the true purpose of this place—not a guest house but a prison. They'd keep him locked up here until they handed down the judgment. He prayed he hadn't condemned both Orah and himself to a teaching.

One of the deacons opened the door and escorted Nathaniel inside. The room was not the cramped cell he feared, with a wide floor and headroom to spare. A serviceable cot lay to one side and a table and chair to the other. Though windowless—the walls were below ground—a tarnished brass receptacle on the table held a lit candle. At least he'd have light.

He settled on the cot and stared at the walls as the deacon shuffled out and locked the door behind him. Years of decay had worn down the stones, leaving a layer of dust on the floor and a stale taste on his tongue. Yet he refused to be discouraged, still determined to save Orah. He hoped the vicars would accept his offer.

As for his notions of Temple City, he'd been deluded. This place had not a whiff of ancient greatness. Men of honor would never build such a prison.

"So this is the great Temple City," he said with a sneer.

"Not quite."

Nathaniel froze. Had someone actually answered, or had he already gone mad? A grating came from the opposite wall, like the gnawing of a rat on stone. He grabbed the chair for defense, but what happened next took him by surprise.

A flicker of light filtered through a hole in the wall, followed by a muffled voice.

"You see, they built many Temple Cities. This is only one. Not the biggest either."

Nathaniel set the chair down and edged toward the wall. "What did you say?"

"Not the biggest. I've seen only three, but one was bigger, at least as far as I can recall. They brought me here so long ago."

Nathaniel came closer. "Who *are* you?"

The voice on the far side of the wall gained strength. "You see, the Temple designed their world on a grid—east to west, north to south—a Temple City every six days, each location responsible for children of light within a three-day-walk. Do you know for what purpose?"

Nathaniel had no idea how to respond.

"Control, of course. To control you and me and everyone else." The voice became deep and mocking. "So the darkness shall never return. Why else do you think we're here in these cells? To protect the world from the darkness? No. To control our thoughts."

Nathaniel had never heard such blasphemy spoken so bluntly — and here in Temple City.

The man's rant sailed on. "The self-righteous vicars and their henchmen who strut about. Deacons they call them, defenders of the light, but they're only rough men, uneducated, who do as they're told because the Temple provides them power they could never obtain on their own."

"But who are you?" Nathaniel said, trying to be more assertive.

The man cackled. "I'm the guest in the next room. Their favorite guest because they never let me leave. 'If there comes a prophet,'" he boomed, mimicking the vicars, "'you should stone him, even if he be your own child.' But if I'm a prophet, why haven't they stoned me? Do you know why? They're afraid to let me stand before my people, terrified of what I might say."

"How did this hole between the cells get here?"

"I bored through the stone myself, yes I have, scratching with a bit of this and that. Through a wall as thick as a grown man's head." He tried to laugh, but only an unhealthy cough emerged.

A madman, surely, but Nathaniel couldn't let such a claim go unchallenged. "That's impossible."

"Impossible? A persistent man can do anything. It took twenty years, but I wore down the stone before they wore me down."

Twenty years. Nathaniel sucked in a breath but stayed silent.

"Let me have a look at you," the man in the next cell said. "I see so few people."

Nathaniel peered through the hole but saw nothing.

"No, no, not so close. It's only a small hole. Go back to the far wall. Your turn will come."

Nathaniel did as asked.

"A young one, eh? Fine-looking and tall. Let me give you advice, young man: don't stay as long as I have. Tell them whatever they want and go on your way." He attempted a long sigh which quickly degraded into a wheeze. Once he caught his breath, his voice rose. "Lie if you must. Why did they bring you here anyway?"

Nathaniel opened his mouth to answer but stopped. This wasn't Little Pond. The whole city brimmed with intrigue, and he was fast learning mistrust. "Let me see you first. It's my turn."

He heard scuffling steps from the far side and put his eye to the hole.

In the neighboring cell stood an old man with skin so loose the outline of his skeleton showed. He panted and his mouth hung open, exposing a tongue covered with sores.

Nathaniel looked away.

"Not pretty, no." The man's voice became clearer by the moment. "This is what happens to a body given hardly enough food and water to survive. The Temple doesn't harm its children, oh no, but they don't know what I am, so they keep me here. Would *you* like to know what I am, young man?" He paused, seemingly more for effect than expecting a reply. "I'm what they fear most: the truth. So here will I stay forever."

Despite his revulsion, Nathaniel returned to the hole and looked again. What did he behold? An image of madness? Or courage beyond anything he'd ever imagined?

***

The clergy reconvened in a windowless room that was brightly lit despite the absence of candles. A pale glow flickered off the arch vicar's face as he gazed into the glass panel, giving his actions a mystical cast—the light bestowing wisdom on its high priest.

He tugged at his beard, nodding repeatedly, and spoke without looking away. "Perfect."

"What is?" the junior vicar said.

"The boy's background, his family, his profile... all as I suspected." He faced the younger man. "I had him placed in the cell next to the old prisoner."

The younger vicar stared back, his lips spreading agreeably, but his eyes narrowed. "But holiness, the plan failed the last time."

It had failed, but the concept was sound. The last time, the arch vicar had spent weeks begging the council for approval, overlooking how they indulged him like a child. Let the old prisoner die, they had said. The secret's nothing but a legend. Finally, to humor him, they conceded. When his plan ultimately failed, they shrugged it off and said: *No matter. The secret will die with him. It's nothing but a legend anyway. A myth.*

65

Alone among his peers, the arch vicar had immersed himself in the archives, where he'd found snippets of proof. He believed the place existed.

Should he try again? This time, he'd have to act on his own. An unauthorized attempt, discovered too soon, might damage his standing with the council—support he'd need when the grand vicar passed to the light. Maybe they were right. Let the secret die with the old prisoner.

Yet still, that ancient place haunted his dreams.

His chest tightened at the thought of it, and his breathing became short. Why did that daunting remnant of the darkness pull at him so? In the archives, hints of what lay there had tempted him, almost more than he could bear. What did he hope to find that would justify risking a lifetime of service? If found, would he have the faith to resist its temptations, to destroy it once and for all?

And why, at the thought of its destruction, did he already mourn its loss?

Now, the light had granted a second chance. The boy from Little Pond had fallen into his grasp, a boy perfect for the task.

The arch vicar waved his hand and the mystical glow vanished. "The last time was different. Our man was not true of heart."

"The old man's cynical, Holiness, suspicious. He'll never—"

"I tell you this is different. The old man's health is failing, so he's more likely to trust someone, and the boy is naïve, but brave—a vessel waiting to be filled."

"How will you convince such a brash young man, Holiness?"

"I'll ask him to commit to the Temple, to lead the people of the Ponds in the light."

"But, Holiness, how can you be sure he'll believe us?"

The arch vicar consulted a slip of paper. "According to his friend... Thomas, our boy Nathaniel fancies himself destined for greatness. We simply offer an opportunity worthy of him." He turned and headed to the door, but stopped and reversed himself. "And if that doesn't work, he'll believe us anyway."

"Why, Holiness?"

The arch vicar's pupils darkened to black embers, but a wicked twinkle showed in them. "Because he cares about the girl."

***

Nathaniel stood again on the mark at the center of the room and looked up at the three vicars. Only a few hours had passed.

"Nathaniel of Little Pond," the speaker proclaimed. "We have decided to grant your wish and send the girl home."

Nathaniel raised his chin and beamed at the arches spanning the peak of the dome. He'd done it—Orah would be set free. In his elation, he almost missed what the vicar said next. He quieted his thoughts and tried to concentrate.

"We have one condition. You seem a fine man, eager to learn of our ways. Rather than a teaching, we believe you might better serve the light by becoming an envoy of the Temple."

An envoy of the Temple? He can't mean.... "I don't understand, Holiness."

"Let me be more specific. We're offering to train you in the seminary to become a vicar."

The arch vicar's words dragged Nathaniel down, seeming to cast him into the cell beneath his feet. "But I'm just a boy from a small village."

"Not a boy, a man of age who has asked for a teaching. We offer you more—the chance to serve your people, in addition to helping your friend. What do you say?"

"Holiness, I...."

"We know this is a difficult decision. Serving the Temple is a great honor but also a lifelong commitment. Once you've chosen this path, you cannot go back."

"There must be another way."

"There is no other way. If you agree, we'll give you a week to go home and settle your affairs before returning to Temple City. Otherwise, the teaching of your friend will resume. You have two days to decide. In the meantime, you'll remain our guest." He leaned forward for emphasis. "Two days."

The vicars rose to leave, but Nathaniel stopped them with a shout. "Wait! I'll consider your offer, but only if my friend can join me while I decide."

The younger vicars snapped their heads around in astonishment, but the arch vicar ignored them. "Very well, Nathaniel of Little Pond. While her teaching awaits, she may share meals with you. Her presence may help you choose the right path."

Nathaniel stammered. What more could he say?

The audience had ended. The arch vicar dismissed him with a flip of his hand, and the deacons led him back to his cell.

Chapter 11
The Keeper

A scratching at the peephole intruded on Nathaniel's thoughts.

"I'm sorry you came back," the old man said. "I hoped you'd tell them what they wanted and go home."

He had intended the words kindly, but Nathaniel waved him off. After a time, the old man put the slate back into place and hobbled away.

Nathaniel slumped on the cot and buried his fist in his cheek. He'd dashed from Little Pond to this cursed place, hoping to help Orah, but what had he accomplished? An impossible choice lay before him: commit to the Temple, or send her back to the teaching. Either would haunt him for the rest of his days.

He'd had no food since arriving at Temple City, and though eating was least on his mind, his stomach growled. Thankfully, at that moment, a young deacon unlocked the door and brought in a tray, a simple meal—brown bread, apples and goat cheese—but much to Nathaniel's relief, enough for two. Moments later, a guard ushered Orah into the room.

Dust coated her from head to toe, but her spirit seemed intact. "Nathaniel of Little Pond, and here I expected to share lunch with the grand vicar."

He gestured at the tray. "I arranged a little snack for us."

Each took measure of the other.

How must I look in her eyes? Less battered he presumed, but far from the confident hero—just a boy from a remote village who'd reached beyond his means. Seeing her made his choice all the more burdensome. He couldn't help but imagine her in the same state as Thomas at festival. No words seemed appropriate, and every attempt to speak caught in his throat.

Orah's eyes widened, and she reached out for him, but her hand hovered in mid-air without touching him. "Why are you here? Did they take us both for a teaching?"

She'd see through any evasion, but he tried anyway. "I came to rescue you. I offered to replace you, but they turned me down. The light knows what will happen next."

Orah sat on the cot with the tray between them and let her gaze wander from the cell door to the food and finally back to him. She drew in a breath and let it out slowly. "I should be angry with you for risking yourself like some fool hero." Her features eased into a smile, and she brushed his cheek with her fingertips. "But thank you."

His head still down, he rolled his eyes up to glance at her, and grimaced. "Believe me, I'm no hero."

Shame kept him from saying more, but a flash of pain in her eyes told him she'd heard enough and knew he was hiding something. Whether out of pity or hunger, she refrained from pressing for now.

She grabbed a loaf and broke it in half. "We should eat. Who knows when we'll get the next chance?"

He accepted the bread from her, grateful for the reprieve. They ate in silence, showing little appetite but managing to clear the tray.

Once finished, she fixed him with a piercing stare. "What aren't you telling me? If they turned you down, why was I released?"

Before he could answer, the familiar scraping of the peephole cover sounded from across the room.

Orah startled. "What was that?"

"My new friend, the prisoner in the next cell. He's been there so long he misses companionship."

Then, another, more ominous noise came from the walkway outside, the thump of deacons' boots on the stone floor.

"Quickly, Nathaniel, before they come. What are you hiding?"

70

He dreaded the moment but had to tell. The choice seemed dragged from his lips — her teaching or his commitment to the Temple. She listened open-mouthed, but for once had nothing to say.

"I made my offer," he said, "and they made theirs. They granted me two days to decide, and in the meantime, they suspended your teaching and let us share meals. I thought seeing you would help me decide, but now my misery's complete. I'm no hero, but I won't let you go to the same fate that befell Thomas and my father and yours. How could I live with that?"

She stood, rising to her toes so she appeared taller. "You will not do this for me. I forbid it. I'm not frail and will survive the teaching better than any of them." Her face reddened to match her hair, and her breath came in short bursts. "As far as living with your choice, if you become one of them, you won't live long enough to be ordained. I'll kill you first, the Temple and their darkness be damned."

He pressed two fingers to her lips, but he never could calm her when her blood was up.

She twisted away and lowered her voice to a hiss. "The darkness — a tale they made up to control us. Why don't they leave us alone?"

"Hush, Orah. Think of where you are. Don't make things worse for the both of us."

The grate of metal on metal quieted them as the bolt slid open. Two stout deacons motioned Orah to follow.

She glared over her shoulder as she crossed the threshold. "Think hard, Nathaniel. I pray you come to your senses before our next meal."

The deacons led her off, one at each arm. The door slammed shut behind them, followed by a deafening silence.

***

The silence didn't last long.

The old prisoner barely gave him time to collapse on the cot. "A strong woman, yes?"

Nathaniel kept still, staring at the opposite wall, but for now companionship seemed preferable to quiet. "Yes, a strong woman."

"The teaching won't destroy that one. No."

71

Nathaniel turned and spoke to the hole, his voice rising. "I won't let them take her."

He imagined the old man chewing over his words before saying them aloud. "But to become a vicar? You know what they are."

"I don't know anything, and neither do you."

"You'd be surprised."

"How could you know? You've been locked away in that cell for twenty years."

"What better way to know what they are?" The old man let the thought sink in, backing off and then returning to the peephole. His voice became less scattered. "She was right, you know. They lie about the darkness. The darkness was not as they teach."

Nathaniel's eyes narrowed. He sat up straight and listened for more. When no more came, he slid to the edge of his cot and whispered, "How can you be so sure?"

Snippets of muttering filtered from the other cell. The man seemed to be having an argument with himself. "It's time to tell, Samuel. He may be the keepers' last hope."

Nathaniel crept closer and peered through the opening.

The old man stood more erect with the look of someone who'd made a decision.

Nathaniel placed his mouth to the hole. "Who is Samuel?"

"I am Samuel," the old man said. "Yes, there's still a person here after all these years, a man with a name. And she called you Nathaniel?"

"Yes, I'm Nathaniel."

"Pleased to meet you."

Nathaniel checked back through the hole to catch Samuel bending at the waist with hands straight to his sides, a formal bow that seemed to cause him some pain—the bow of a once proud man.

"How can I be sure about the darkness?" Samuel said, his voice gaining strength with each word. "Because the vicars failed to erase the past. Everywhere you look, bits of it remain. Haven't you seen its vestiges in your village, things the Temple hasn't ordained?"

Nathaniel thought of wassail and festival, of Orah's name from a forbidden language. He nodded, then realizing the man couldn't see, said, "Yes."

"What they call the darkness is nothing more than our past, but they show us only the worst."

Nathaniel had to ask. "Were you sent for a teaching?"

Samuel let out a laugh. "A teaching's a trifle compared to what I've been through. I'm aware of what they show in teachings—and yes, all the evil they claim is true. I also know what they hide, the good they've erased. Like a foolish parent trying to save us from our own wickedness, they've given us a world of limits and not a world of possibilities. Do you understand what I'm saying?"

Nathaniel began to feel lightheaded, and tiny black dots fluttered before his eyes like gnats. "Nothing is as it seems. I have a lot to think about."

"Yes, and so do I."

The old prisoner moved away and settled on the wicker chair next to the table. His shoulders heaved, and his breath came in short bursts as he stared at his hands.

Nathaniel staggered toward his cot, but stopped and went back to the peephole. "One last thing, Samuel. What's a keeper?"

Samuel glanced up. "A story for another time, my boy. For another time."

***

Time passed swiftly. At breakfast the next day, Orah begged Nathaniel to reject the vicar's offer, but he refused to send her back to the teaching. Her parting stung more each time the deacons led her away.

Samuel eavesdropped through the peephole during their morning meal but said nothing. After the cell door closed following the second lunch, he spoke at last. "I told you my story was for another time, Nathaniel. Well, now's that time."

"What did you say?"

"Come close so I can whisper. I'll tell you about the keepers."

The term had piqued Nathaniel's curiosity since their earlier conversation, but what could he believe from his fellow prisoner? What fantasies had the poor man concocted over twenty years?

He shuffled toward the wall as if approaching a precipice in the dark. "I'm here."

73

"Our forebears lived in time of wonder, filled with magic and strife. When the Temple came to power, the vicars preferred order to wonder. The darkness, they screamed from their pulpits, a time of chaos and death. They determined to erase the glories of the past so we'd forget them forever, but the wizards of that age resisted. To save their treasures for the future, they concealed them from the vicars in a place called the keep."

Nathaniel pressed his ear to the wall and listened, as he had as a child when his father told tales at bedtime.

The old man continued. "The time would come, the wizards believed, when a generation would arise that embraced their wonders once more, but the vicars ruled with a ruthless hand, intent on eradicating the past. The keep would need to stay hidden until the coming of the new age, so they created a puzzle, a rhyme that led to the keep, and divided the verses into pieces for safekeeping, one piece to one person, with directions to find the next in the chain. Those chosen to preserve the clues they called keepers."

Nathaniel's heart pounded. "How many keepers are there?"

"Each keeper knows of the next and no more—all except the last one. If one link is broken, the secret will be lost forever, the reason why every keeper takes an oath to pass on his clue before he dies."

Nathaniel's dilemma flitted from his mind, replaced by the vision of an armored knight with a plumed helmet and a flashing sword. To the darkness with teachings and the coming of age. The idea of the keep had awakened something in him he thought he'd lost forever.

"But who'll solve the puzzle?" he said.

"A vanguard of this new generation would arise first, driven to seek the truth at all costs, even at the risk of their lives. These few would take the lead. The founders of the keep called them seekers, and their task would be to solve the puzzle and rediscover the keep."

"What's in the keep?"

"The chain started so long ago, even the keepers aren't sure. The keep may not even exist."

"Ancient magic?"

"More. Something the Temple fears. Something that might change the world."

Nathaniel's hands shook. *I'd be a seeker if I could.*

The other cell went quiet.

Nathaniel checked through the peephole to find the man slumped on the cot, his chest hardly moving. He should leave him be, but....

"Samuel?"

"What now?"

"Are you a keeper?"

"It's just a story, Nathaniel, and now I need to rest."

***

The final dinner before Nathaniel's decision came and went. As the door slammed shut and the bolt snapped into place, Nathaniel wondered if he'd ever see Orah again. Horrific images flashed before his eyes: Orah in the darkness cell; himself with the not-quite-square-hat of a vicar reciting the blessing; or worse — snatching the child of some neighbor for a teaching.

First thing in the morning, the deacons would escort him to the round chamber, and he'd gaze up into the unyielding faces of the clergy. They'd demand his decision.

The word decision stuck in his mind, so he almost missed its echo from the peephole.

"I've made my decision," the old man said. "We each face a difficult choice, and so we must help each other."

"Help each other? I have no way to help you, and what can you do for me?"

"I can offer a third way, and you can keep the chain alive."

Nathaniel gasped. "You *are* a keeper."

"I am the first keeper. For twenty long years, I've kept faith, but if I die without passing on the secret, the chain will be broken."

Nathaniel tried to count three breaths before speaking, as Orah would urge him to do, but the words burst out as if on their own. "What do you want me to do?"

"I'll pass my clue on to you. You tell the vicars you'll join them. They'll give you time to go home and settle your affairs before returning. Then... don't return."

"I'm to become a keeper?"

The old man's chortle resounded strangely off the stone walls, but he caught himself and spoke more distinctly than ever. "You misunderstand, my boy. The time for rediscovery has come. You will become a seeker."

The cell walls seemed to contract. "But Temple City's the farthest I've ever roamed from home. What do I know of the greater world?"

"Don't doubt yourself, Nathaniel. You had the courage to come alone to Temple City and offer yourself to save a friend. Such passion will serve you well as you seek the keep. Accept my offer. You may be the drop of water that wears down the rock of the Temple."

Suddenly, Orah's voice echoed in his mind. *No illusions.* His eyes narrowed. "Why would you trust me?"

"I have no choice. When I die, the first clue of the keepers will die with me, and the chain will be broken. You're our only hope."

The moment had come, Nathaniel realized. More than the decision to run to the mountains or to follow Orah to Temple City, he now faced the *real* test. He took a deep breath, puffed out his chest, and relaxed. "I'm ready."

The old man dragged his cot aside and knelt on the floor. He then picked at the far wall with his fingernails, and a pebble came loose, revealing a hidden compartment. He groped inside and pulled out a rolled-up parchment, ordered Nathaniel to step away, and squeezed the scroll through the peephole.

Nathaniel grasped it as if it were spun glass. "What is it?"

"All you need to begin the search: the city, the symbol, the pass phrase and the rhyme."

Nathaniel unrolled a parchment unlike any skin or paper he'd ever seen, pure white but with a hard sheen, so the surface looked wet but felt dry. He wanted to believe in the keep, but when he unfurled the scroll, his doubts returned.

"It's blank."

"The words will appear when held over a flame. Don't worry. The scroll won't burn. The words will show for a few seconds and then vanish when they cool."

Nathaniel rushed to the candle, but the old man barked for him to stop. "Not here. Not anywhere near Temple City. They must never learn what's on the scroll. Look when you're far away."

"How will I understand what it means?"

"That's the seeker's task, but I can start you on your way. Each scroll contains the name of a town and a symbol. Use these to find the next keeper. After that come the phrase you must speak and the required response of the keeper. In this way, you'll know to trust each other."

A cough racked the first keeper. Only when it subsided did he continue. "Finally, you'll find a part of the rhyme that shows the way to the keep. Each scroll will contain one four line verse. Don't try to make sense of it until you've discovered the final scroll. The rhyme must be whole to be understood."

Nathaniel stared, trying to make the words appear with the heat from his eyes.

"One last warning: don't dawdle. The keep's waited too long and may already be dying." More coughing, and when he resumed, his voice sounded rasping and raw. "I've told you all that's been passed down through the ages. My twenty years of suffering is nearing an end. My life's work is done."

The old man limped to his bed and collapsed.

Nathaniel mouthed a silent prayer, not to the Temple, but to the light. "Be blessed in the light, first keeper." He rolled up the scroll, concealed it in his sock, and lay down.

But he found no rest that night. Here in this cell, as the candle flickered and his hope dimmed, he'd found what he'd been searching for his whole life.

Something to change the world.

Chapter 12
Nightmares

Thomas leaned against the split rail fence and glared at the hard ground.

His father had sent him to prepare the southwest field for planting, though the earth had not fully thawed. Better than brooding, he'd said.

The teaching had left him weak in body, and this chore he'd grown up with seemed harder this year—his shoulders burned, and he needed a moment to rest—but his spirit ached as well. After months of nights haunted by dreams, he'd begun to find some peace... until his friends had been taken.

He poked at the ground with the spade, rolling a clump of stubborn sod, but his mind ventured into the dark place where his friends must be. Memories of his teaching brought nightmares, but the thought of Orah in the vicar's cramped cell frightened him more. He'd tried to dissuade Nathaniel from going, but his friend's growing bond with Orah defied reason. Now, he had nothing to do but wait.

Their fates were his fault, the result of his cowardice. His friends would fight harder than he did and resist longer. Light knows how long their teachings might last, or, when they returned, how much would remain of their spirit. Like Nathaniel's father, he'd bear this guilt for the rest of his life.

He propped the spade up against the fence and switched to a pitchfork, lifting it high overhead until his shoulders shuddered. He took aim and pounded the prongs into the clump again and again. When he could no longer lift his arms, he stared at the pitchfork, now buried in the frozen earth.

My friends. How he wished he could help them, if only he could be as brave.

Chapter 13
The Scroll

Nathaniel shifted the pack on his shoulders. Temple servants had filled it with provisions and slathered it with oil until the leather gleamed in the sun. The newly restored pack rested soft and supple against his frame, but he kept fidgeting with the straps to give his hands something to do.

Orah marched three paces in front, her jaw pointing to the road ahead.

Each time he tried to catch her, she sped up until he had to jog to keep up. Finally, he conceded and let her walk alone.

That morning, the deacons had brought her to the city's western gate, the one leading to Little Pond. When she'd spotted Nathaniel approaching, pack on his back, she'd turned to her captors and insisted they return her to her cell. The bewildered guards assumed she misunderstood and, speaking slowly, explained she'd been released.

By the time Nathaniel reached the group, she'd started shouting at them, demanding an audience with the vicars. The deacons told her to go home. Once a judgment had been handed down, the Temple was to be obeyed.

Nathaniel had grabbed her by the elbow to draw her away, but she turned on him instead. Taking advantage of the distraction, the deacons slipped off, leaving the two odd young people and their outlandish village ways on their own.

Once alone, Nathaniel had tried to persuade her to give up the fight and come with him. "For now, thank the light, we're free."

He'd waited for her to argue, to scold, to get angry, but she did none of these. Instead, she pressed her lips into a thin and bloodless line, squared her shoulders toward the west, and glared as if challenging the horizon. After several awkward moments, she'd stomped off toward Little Pond.

They'd now been on the road for more than an hour, and she had yet to say a word. He longed to catch up and face her so he could reveal the reason for his deceit, but the towers of Temple City still rose behind him in the distance. He bit his lip and vowed to say nothing more until the accursed place faded from view.

He'd wait until twilight, at that evening's campsite, and hope that when she learned the truth, she'd forgive him.

***

He picked the perfect clearing as the sun settled to the treetops. A thick layer of pine needles carpeted the ground, good for a soft night's sleep. A small stream bubbled nearby, and a rocky outcropping sheltered them from the road so no passing traveler would see their fire.

Before twilight fell, he went deeper into the forest to gather firewood. Though Orah still fumed, she remained responsible enough to help with the chore.

He knelt beside her as she gathered an armful of dead branches. "Still angry?"

When she refused to answer, he reached across and touched her for the first time that day. She grasped the kindling like gold, her forearms tight and unyielding, but he pressed gently until her load clattered to the mossy earth.

"You're so stubborn," he said. "Your anger has made you blind."

She spun around and faced him. "What don't I see, Nathaniel? The vicars have set the both of us free, neither locked away in a teaching cell. Would you have me believe they've suddenly discovered mercy and let us go without you bartering your soul?"

He was consumed by anticipation and dread—anticipation of sharing the story of the keep, and dread she might receive it poorly. How would she react?

"With all your learning, Orah, have you ever heard of the keepers?"

Her eyes widened with surprise. Then a hopeful uncertainty crossed her features, and she shook her head.

In the midst of the trees, as they knelt facing each other, he poured out the tale: the founding of the Temple, their invention of the darkness, the eradication of the good along with the evil, the elders who saved their treasures in a place called the keep, and the generations of keepers who preserved its secret for the coming of the seekers.

Her expression changed as he spoke, from anger to disbelief, disbelief to openness, and finally to wonder. By the time he finished, her eyes had become mirrors reflecting the fading light, as if the dreams of their youth had come to pass. "How do you know this, Nathaniel of Little Pond?"

He told her of Samuel, kept prisoner for twenty years, the first of the keepers.

She waited, considering all he said.

She wants to believe, Nathaniel thought, *but has one last doubt.*

"How do you know the story's true? What if all those years in prison addled his brain?"

Without a word, Nathaniel reached into his stocking and pulled out the scroll.

Her eyes went from mirrors to moons. "What is it?"

"The first clue in the chain."

She reached out, but he yanked the scroll away. "Be careful. It's survived for hundreds of years."

Orah laughed—a wonder to see again. "I'll care for it as if it were you as a baby."

Once she grasped the scroll, she let her fingers glide along its surface. "I've never seen such a parchment. It ripples like paper but feels like glass. Is it temple magic?"

"Maybe magic from before the Temple."

She unrolled the scroll and raised it to her eyes in the dim light, but her wonder turned into a scowl. "There's nothing on it. Is this one of your tricks to distract me from never speaking to you again?"

He drew in a deep breath and prayed the old prisoner hadn't misled him. "The first keeper claimed the founders used their magic to hide the clue on the parchment. To view it, we need to hold it over a flame. The scroll won't burn, but the heat will reveal its contents."

Orah stared at the blank scroll, running her fingertips over its surface as if touching the words would make them appear. Then she popped up and rushed off.

"Where are you going?" Nathaniel called after her.

"To make a fire."

He laughed. "Well you might want to bring some wood with you."

She fought back a blush and returned the scroll to Nathaniel.

After collecting their kindling, the two hurried back to the clearing.

***

By the time they lit the fire, twilight had settled over the land. Nathaniel found four green branches to make a frame, each as long as his arm. While he whittled off their twigs, Orah fetched twine from his pack.

"What happened to your pack?" she said. "The leather looks like new."

"They cleaned it for my journey."

"Why would they bother?"

"The benefits bestowed on a future vicar."

An edge came into her voice. "But you're never going to be a vicar."

"They don't know that, do they? Come on, now, I'm ready."

He pressed two sticks together, and Orah bound them with twine, and then they did the same with the second pair. He held both parallel while Orah slipped the scroll in between. Finally, they squatted by the fire.

Until this moment, he'd thought of the keep as only a story, no different than the bedtime tales told by his father. If the clue failed to appear, they were lost. With nowhere to go, the vicars would punish them harshly for their deception.

Nathaniel glanced at Orah and hesitated.

She brushed his arm and nodded.

Gripping the ends of the frame, he eased the parchment over the fire.

He waited. The parchment did not burn, did not even blacken, but black markings wriggled on its surface, forming themselves into a picture and words. He watched spellbound until the wood began to smolder, then laid the frame on the ground within the glow of the firelight.

At once, the wonder of his childhood returned. He whispered as in a place of worship. "The city, the symbol, the pass phrase and the rhyme."

Orah raised her brows. "What does that mean?"

"Just as old Samuel said. Look." He pointed to the first word. "Adamsville, the city where we'll find the next keeper."

Orah brightened. "Adamsville. A town to the east. The shopkeeper in Great Pond married a woman from there."

"Do you know how to get there?"

"Not yet, but I can figure it out. What's next?"

"The symbol, which tells us how to find the keeper within the city."

Below the name of the city was a drawing of three identical objects, two side by side and a third behind and slightly above, each round at the bottom and tapering to a dome near the top.

"They look like mountains," Nathaniel said, "but I've never seen any so perfectly formed, and what would mountains be doing in the midst of a city?" He began to panic. What if he proved too dim-witted to solve the first clue?

"I know what they are," Orah said in her I-know-the-answer voice.

He whirled on her. "Tell me."

"Not now. I'll tell you when the time is right."

"Don't make me wait, Orah."

Sparks glimmered in her eyes, reflecting the firelight. "Who had me waiting all day, worrying he'd bartered his soul to become a vicar?"

Nathaniel lowered his head. "I'm sorry. I did what I thought best for both of us."

She lifted his chin with a finger. "Much as I hate to admit it, you may have been right. What comes next?"

84

"The pass phrase." He tapped the next lines. *The first born says to tell you he is doing well, blessed be the true light. May the true light shine brightly upon him and disperse the darkness.* "We greet the next keeper with the first phrase, and he responds with the second, a way to trust each other."

Orah turned back to the parchment and chanted the final words aloud.

> *To the North, behind the rock face*
> *To the East, towering o'er the lake*
> *To the North, through forest of stone*
> *To the East, the entrance shall be*

She glanced up, pleading for an explanation.

He gaped at her open-mouthed and shrugged. "The rhyme that leads to the keep."

"What nonsense. It's not even a proper rhyme."

As they concentrated, hoping to wring more meaning out of the words, the letters faded and the parchment once again turned blank.

Nathaniel kept staring, willing the words to return. Then he remembered the advice of the first keeper: "Each scroll contains one verse of the rhyme. Don't try to make sense of the rhyme until you've received the final scroll. The rhyme must be whole to be understood."

When he glanced up, twilight had flown and night was ascendant. The time for storytelling had ended, and the two of them readied for sleep.

As he lay on the pine needle carpet, in the darkness and under the stars, the seeker's burden came tumbling down upon him. After so many generations, he alone had been entrusted with the mystery of the keep—a dream come true.

Why then, in the darkness and under the stars, did he feel so small?

Chapter 14
Pact of the Ponds

The third day of their flight from Temple City dawned with the blessing of groggy forgetfulness. Nathaniel awoke to a low-lying fog that soon burned off with the sun. He insisted he and Orah start immediately on the final leg of their trek, taking little pause for breakfast.

His heart lightened as they entered familiar terrain. He'd traveled farther from Little Pond than ever before, and relished his return.

He lifted his face to the sun and proclaimed his feelings aloud. "How good to come home. How wonderful to see our families again."

How reckless to rush off the week before, and how lucky all had ended so well.

Yet when he looked back at Orah, she'd turned grim. "We must learn to never think that way again."

He stopped and faced her. "Why won't you let me celebrate our good fortune?"

"What good fortune would that be?"

"We've challenged the vicars and returned unharmed."

He resumed walking with a hint of a swagger, but Orah cut him off. "Unharmed, but not unburdened."

He sighed, heaving his shoulders up and down more dramatically than necessary. "Don't I deserve to enjoy my homecoming before taking off to light knows where?"

"You promised the vicars you'd return in a week. The farther away you can get in that time, the better. Once they discover you misled them, they'll come looking, and if they find you, you might pray for a teaching as the lesser punishment."

She was right, but he tried to cling to the good feeling. "A few days won't—"

"Generations of keepers died to preserve the secret, and you'd sleep late for a few days?"

"What would you have me do?"

"Leave at first light."

"First light tomorrow? I can't be ready by then."

"Of course you can... with my help. Adamsville is just the first stop, with no hint of which town will come next or how many towns will follow. You'll need water skins for dry stretches, food for at least ten days, warm clothing, a sharp knife and a hatchet. I'll contribute the few coins my grandfather left me. We can start collecting supplies as soon as we get home. Thomas will help too. We'll gather them in small bunches to avoid notice and store them in the NOT tree."

He considered her plan. Though he hated to leave so quickly, they could be ready by morning. Yet provisions remained only a part of the challenge. "What about my father?"

"We'll make up a story."

"You mean lie?"

"A necessary story. No one in Little Pond has ever gone to the vicars and volunteered for a teaching. We'll tell them you so impressed the clerics they decided to send you on a mission. You're not sure how long you'll be gone, and you're forbidden to discuss it further."

"They'll believe this?"

"We've been to Temple City, but neither of us bear the look of a teaching, and too little time has passed and.... They'll have to believe us. How else could we have returned so soon?"

Nathaniel nodded. He'd never lied to his father, but the story would work. His father would let him go on a mission for the light, and not worry, at least for the first week.

He stood there open-mouthed as Orah spun around and resumed her march.

"Come along," she called back. "We can make Little Pond by noon if we hurry."

***

Nathaniel had crossed less than half the footpath to his cottage when his father rushed out to embrace him. After they separated, he held his son at arm's length and delved deeply into his eyes. "It's you, Nathaniel, and unchanged."

"There's been no teaching, not for myself and not for Orah."

Astonishment spread across his father's face. "How is that possible? When I read your note, I assumed the vicars would consume you both."

Nathaniel swallowed hard and chose his words carefully. "I had no plan when I arrived in Temple City. It's the biggest place I've ever seen. The people were all afraid, and deacons marched everywhere."

"Such a reckless thing to do. I'd have stopped you if I could."

"That's why I didn't give you the chance."

His father took a step back and eyed Nathaniel with the look of one who's discovered his old friend had changed while they were apart. "How did you free Orah?"

"I went and offered myself in her place. Well, the vicars had never seen such a thing. My actions impressed them so much they thought I might serve the Temple in better ways than being taught. They decided to send me on a mission for the light."

His father winced as if struck. Though a loyal child of light, he mistrusted the vicars.

Nathaniel pressed on. "I'm to go far away, seeking something of enormous significance to the Temple." That part at least rang true. "Who knows how long I'll be gone, and I can't say more than that. They forbid me to reveal details."

The light drained from his father's eyes. "Then I'm to lose you again, and maybe forever."

"Of course not. I'll come back, and when I do I'll have changed, but only in ways that will make you proud."

His father waited, digesting his son's words before his expression softened. "I'm already proud of you, Nathaniel, and that will never change."

***

Nathaniel arrived with a satchel of supplies: bags of dried apples, flatbread and smoked meat, two water skins, and a hatchet—enough to fill nearly half his pack. He itched to start the journey, but the talk with his father weighed on him. What if his father was right? What if he'd never return? He waited for Orah to ease his misgivings.

She arrived in a whirlwind, bearing a bag bigger than his. "I brought most of what we need. Thomas agreed to fetch the rest: some twine, a pocketknife and two blankets. A bit more food and we'll be ready."

Nathaniel sized up the bag on the ground. A sheaf of paper caught his eye. "What's this?"

Orah flashed a smile. "Paper for my log. I'll need it to record our journey."

His head snapped around as the implication struck him. "Orah of Little Pond! There's no way you're coming with me. Not a chance. I forbid it."

"Since when do we forbid each other anything?"

"You forbade me to become a vicar."

"That was different. You were about to make an awful choice to protect me."

"I'm trying to protect you now."

"I can't let you go without helping. I'm in your debt for rescuing me."

Nathaniel looked away, embarrassed, but he recalled his father's concern. How could he place her at such risk? "Seeking the keep is not child's play. Think what they'll do if they catch us?"

"And if I stay, what will happen when you fail to return? They'll come back and take me for a teaching, or worse. I've had a taste of their darkness and don't yearn for more. Besides, you can't seek the keep without me."

"Why not?"

"Because only I can find the next keeper. I've figured out the way to Adamsville and know what the symbol means. I can get us there and you cannot. So it's settled."

Then to show her strength, she hoisted the two satchels, one in each hand, and tossed them into the shelter.

***

At scarcely first light the next morning, Nathaniel fidgeted while Orah organized her pack, her breath emerging as rapid puffs of white. Why had she insisted on coming? Why had she abandoned her orderly world? To search for the elusive keep or to be with him? For years, she'd humored him, listening to his dreams, never believing they'd come to pass. Now dreams had become reality. They were about to leave Little Pond, maybe forever.

He was glad she'd come.

She'd exchanged her black skirt for pants tucked into lambskin boots. Both wore the woolen jackets common to the Ponds, which they'd need until midmorning for warmth. Soon lighter clothing would suffice, but they had to prepare for the worst. How long would they be gone? If they needed these jackets again when winter returned, they'd be gone a long time indeed.

They divided the load between them, with the heaviest items—the hatchet, water skins and dried meat—going into Nathaniel's pack, all except the paper for her log.

With their provisions squared away, nothing remained but to wait for Thomas, who'd insisted on seeing them off. The two took turns touching the NOT tree for luck, realizing they were about to do more than depart Little Pond. They were about to leave their youth behind.

Nathaniel startled to a crashing in the woods.

Thomas stumbled into the clearing, grinning foolishly and breathing out steam. He lugged a pack as big as theirs, though it appeared larger on his smaller frame. He apologized between breaths. "Sorry, haven't got used to this thing. A strap caught on a branch."

Orah and Nathaniel spoke as one. "What are you doing, Thomas?"

He forced a look of surprise. "You didn't think I'd let you go without me."

Orah collected herself first. "You have no idea what this is about."

"I know you're going on an adventure and bringing lots of food. I'd guess it's something the vicars won't like, which means it's perfect for me."

She crossed her arms and dug in her heels. "This isn't a game, Thomas. You can't come."

"How do you plan to stop me?"

"For the last time, go home."

She turned to Nathaniel for support, but he considered the gloom that had settled over Thomas at festival — and the spark that flared in him now.

Orah seemed to read his thoughts. "Don't you dare, Nathaniel."

"*You're* coming. How's that different?"

She arched her back and lifted her chin. "I was with you in Temple City."

"He went there too and suffered more than either of us."

"No matter. You can't come, Thomas, and if you follow, I'll make your life miserable."

Thomas grinned. "I've been made miserable by the vicars. You don't hold a candle to them."

She snorted, hoisted her pack, and signaled for Nathaniel to do the same, but as she turned to go, Thomas blocked her way.

His grin had disappeared. "You can't deny me."

"Why not?"

His lower lip trembled. "I thought I'd never see you again, because you'd never give in as I did. I'm ashamed, and helping you is my only way to make amends. Besides, when the two of you go missing, they'll come take me for the second teaching. You *will not* leave me behind."

Nathaniel gave Orah time, knowing her, knowing how she'd decide.

At last her arms went limp, and she nodded.

With a sly smile, Nathaniel slapped Thomas on the back. "Pact of the Ponds." Orah opened her mouth, but before she could argue, he reminded her of the rule. "No debate after the pact's declared."

Thomas squeezed between them to form a circle, covered his heart with his right hand, and thrust his left into the center.

Nathaniel did the same, gripping Thomas's wrist, and waited for Orah.

She finally gave in, sealing the pact, but insisted on the last word. "So be it. Against my better judgment. We're now three seekers, and may the light protect us all."

PART TWO
THE SEEKERS

"The beginning of wisdom is found in doubting; by doubting we come to the question, and by seeking we may come upon the truth."

— Pierre Abelard

Chapter 15
Flight

Orah led Nathaniel at a furious pace, leaving Thomas lagging behind. She kept to trails they'd explored as children, winding paths most adults had forgotten. When she finally stopped at a clearing, she glared back at the path for a full minute before Thomas appeared.

He staggered in and collapsed on a log, apologizing between breaths. "I'll do better, Orah, I promise. How much farther to go?"

Why did he have to come?

She had no choice but to help Nathaniel—how could she leave him alone to bear such a burden? Now she had to watch out for Thomas as well.

"We let you join us," she said. "Isn't that enough?"

Nathaniel set his pack down between them. "His question deserves an answer. Time to tell us where we're going."

A deep sigh. They always expected her to have answers, but she only pretended to be a leader, an act perfected when they were little. In what seemed like an instant, through the villainy of the vicars and a quirk of fate, she'd been drawn into this reckless venture so counter to her nature. She was a weaver, and weavers took no risks. The flax never failed, and her neighbors always needed cloth. Nathaniel was the brave one, charging into Temple City. On her own, she'd never have taken such a chance.

With the sole of her boot, she brushed away leaves and smoothed the dirt into a circle, then found a stick to draw with. Her friends huddled behind.

"Here's Little Pond." She made a mark on the ground. "Three days east is what we've been calling Temple City, the place so recently a kind host to us all. From what the old prisoner told Nathaniel, the Temple has set up a grid, north to south and east to west, with other Temple Cities, each responsible for everyone within a three day walk. From that we can conclude they're located here, here and here."

She scratched the letters "TC" to the east, north and south of the first Temple City, and paused to be sure they followed.

"The shopkeeper in Great Pond told me his wife travels to Adamsville twice a year to visit family. A five-day walk, he said, as the crow flies, but six to loop around the Ponds. We know the five ponds follow a crescent to the southeast." She sketched in the ponds, starting at Little Pond and continuing southeastward. "I asked the shopkeeper if Adamsville is so far from Temple City that they never see a vicar. He said no, a vicar visits more frequently, because he comes from a different place just a day away. So Adamsville must be to the southeast and about a day northwest of the lower Temple City. That places it here."

She carved an "x" and checked to see if they were impressed. "One last thing. The main roads follow the grid." She drew connecting lines between the Temple Cities. "I think we should avoid them."

Thomas contemplated his tired feet and wiggled his toes. "Are you sure we have to? That'll make the trip harder."

Sure? She wasn't sure of anything. Since the day the grand vicar had called her name, her life had spun out of control. Now she raced through the woods toward light knows where. Thomas and Nathaniel always expected her to have answers, but never before had the answers mattered so much.

"I'm not sure of anything, Thomas. I only said I think we should."

She glanced from one to the other. This far from Little Pond, she was starting to realize how rash this undertaking might be. They'd have to make a number of decisions with no clear answers, and with only an inkling of the power of the vicars. Against such power, the three of them might be more fools than seekers.

Please think kindly of me, Nathaniel, and on this journey, forgive me the mistakes I'll surely make.

"Orah's right," Nathaniel said as if he'd read her mind. "We'll avoid the main roads. We can follow a route to the southeast, using the sun for direction, and cut through the woods when necessary."

Orah nodded in gratitude, then erased the drawing with her boot so as to leave no trace behind.

***

For the first couple of days, Orah found well-marked trails, but by the start of the third she was forced into the woods. She tried following gullies formed by rainfall, but they often led them astray, and so, afraid of wandering too far off course, she had them scrambling over downed trees and through thick brush. By nightfall, they had wasted much of the day traveling in the wrong direction.

They camped at the closest they could find to a clearing. The next morning, she awoke stiff from the uneven ground and sore with scratches from the prior day's trek. Moreover, when she shared her ailments with the others, she discovered they'd slept fitfully as well. The gravity of their undertaking had begun to sink in, and an overcast sky offered no consolation.

They broke camp and trudged on. She did her best to keep to a straight line so they'd eventually emerge from the woods. Sure enough, after a few more hours of thick brush, the vegetation thinned and they caught a break in the trees. It had to be a road.

As it came into view, she froze at the sound of gruff men cursing and laughing ahead. She signaled for her friends to drop to the ground, and peered through the underbrush.

Deacons.

She stayed low, clawing at dried leaves as if grasping for the soil beneath. The smell of decay filled her nostrils as she hugged the earth and tried to slow her heartbeat.

My first mistake – underestimating the Temple of Light.

Once the clamor had passed, she raised her head. "They're searching for us."

"Not likely," Nathaniel said. "They couldn't possibly have expected me back so soon."

"We were fools, Nathaniel. They never trusted you and sent deacons to spy. Had we lingered a day longer, they'd have caught us in flight."

Thomas crouched on the ground, clutching his legs and rocking back and forth.

Nathaniel rose to one knee and surveyed the road, then turned to Orah. "You were smart to stay off the main roads. From now on, we avoid all roads in daylight. From now on we think differently about everything."

Orah stood and brushed herself off. "We need to keep moving. Once we've made it three days past the nearest Temple City, I think we'll be safe. The next city won't know about us yet. Even the vicars can't send word that far, that fast."

Thomas released his knees to let the blood flow back into his arms. "Are you sure this time, Orah?"

"No, Thomas. I said I *think* we'll be safe." She looked at him with resignation. "We've left 'sure' behind."

***

They arrived at the outskirts of Adamsville on the seventh day, covered with the dust of the road. Orah felt more vagabond than seeker, with the way every passerby stared at her, but as the clay path turned to the gravel of the merchant district, her mood improved. People there seemed more accustomed to strangers, and scurried about lost in their own affairs.

This town was less grand than Temple City but many times the size of Great Pond. Where the latter had one road with a few stores and an inn, several streets crisscrossed Adamsville, all teeming with commerce. Most of the buildings stood two stories high—unheard of in the Ponds—with a storefront below and a residence above, and unlike the wooden dwellings of Little Pond, those of Adamsville had been constructed of brick. Everything seemed tall and exceedingly solid.

Orah startled to a new sound—boots crunching on the stony surface. From around a corner, she spotted four deacons parading abreast. Their spotless black uniforms gleamed, and the stars on their chests flashed in the sunlight. They paused at a post between buildings, and the tallest held a scroll taut to the wood while a second nailed it down.

Once the deacons reformed and marched on, the three travelers reemerged.

Thomas turned to flee, but Orah grabbed his arm and whispered, "Better to know your enemy."

She strode to the message on the post, and her lips moved silently as she read. The top of the paper bore the heading "Temple Bulletin" in bold lettering. The first part listed minor infractions committed by the locals—hair trimmed too long, improper dress and unsanctioned foods—but it was the second section that raised bumps on her skin.

When finished, she signaled the others to follow as she ducked between buildings.

Her worry spread to Thomas. "What did it say?"

"It lists those they're searching for... with names and descriptions."

"Are we on it?"

"No, only vagrants and people traveling without permits. I told you they can't send word that fast. Adamsville is controlled by a different Temple City."

"I wish you were more certain of that."

Orah whirled on him. "It's not my fault you're here."

Nathaniel wrapped a long arm around each of them and lowered his voice. "But we *are* here, and we shouldn't linger in the open. Time to tell us. Where can we find the next keeper?"

At least she knew this answer. "Isn't it obvious?"

"Not to me. I see no mountains here."

"They're not mountains, Nathaniel. They're spindles. The symbol of the three spindles is the sign of a yarn store. Our second keeper, if he exists, is a spinner."

Nathaniel stared out, seeming to reassess the symbol in his mind, and then stepped from the shadows. "In that case, let's find this spinner and get off the road."

Chapter 16
The Spinner

Around the next corner, Orah spotted a brass symbol that matched the image on the scroll, hanging over the doorway of a two-story brick building. The shop's open door beckoned, yet she hesitated to enter, plagued by a sudden wave of doubt. What if the chain had been broken? What if the keep itself had ceased to exist? What if both were the delusions of the old prisoner's deranged mind?

She searched for answers in the building. White curtains and a flower box marked the upper floor as lodging. The store on the ground level had a window large enough to display an impressive pyramid of yarn. Behind the glass, the shopkeeper stacked spindles on shelves above the counter.

"What if he's not the owner?" Nathaniel said. "We should be certain before we blurt out the pass phrase."

She shifted sideways to avoid the glare and peered inside. "Too proud to be a laborer, too old to be an apprentice. He looks like the shop owner, but I can't be sure."

"You've dealt with spinners before. Why don't you go in and pretend to bargain?"

She considered a moment and nodded. After patting the dust from her clothing and checking her hair in the reflection of the window, she marched in with Nathaniel and Thomas trailing behind.

Up close, the shopkeeper seemed older than he'd appeared through the window, and he moved with difficulty, using an unusual walking stick with a mallard's head carved into its handle. His left leg hardly bent at the knee as he shuffled about with his back to them.

Orah rapped on the counter.

The man turned, took them in with a glance and raised a skeptical brow.

"Excuse me, sir," she said, trying to sound confident despite his reaction. "I'm a weaver from the Ponds and have come to find the best yarn available. I'm interested in seeing your wares."

The brow remained raised, but his eyes narrowed. "Young lady, are you looking or are you prepared to trade?"

"I'm prepared to trade, but not yet. First, I want to compare your work with the others."

He smiled in a way that seemed neither patronizing nor unkind. "Then you won't be back for some time, my dear, since my nearest competitor is a two-day walk from here. I'll be happy to do business with you when you return. Now, I don't mean to be impolite, but I have things to do." With that, he resumed his work.

Orah gathered her will, but a tremor crept into her voice, betraying her uncertainty. "The first born... says to tell you he is doing well, blessed be the true light."

As she held her breath, praying for the correct response, the man climbed a ladder behind the counter and placed two spindles on a high shelf. The clatter of them falling into place echoed throughout the shop. After a few seconds, she spun around and fled the store with Thomas and Nathaniel at her heels.

"What do we do next?" Thomas whispered. "What if he's not the one?"

"I don't know," she said. "He's all I can think of."

Nathaniel gathered them into a circle. "What if he's hard of hearing? We should try again."

Orah turned to respond, and caught the shopkeeper eyeing them from the behind the curtain. She lifted her chin, rose to her full height, and strode back in.

"Sir...." She tried to speak louder this time, but the words came out forced, as if mimicking an elder at festival. "The first born says to tell you he is doing well, blessed be the true light."

The old man's hands began to shake. He grabbed her and drew her farther inside, with the others close behind. After checking that no one was watching, he pulled the shade down over the display window.

Finally, he spoke. "May the true light shine brightly upon him and disperse the darkness."

Orah stood dumbstruck. They'd done it. They'd found the second keeper.

"Why didn't you answer the first time?" she said

He stared past them as if remembering times gone by. "I've waited so long I thought I'd never hear the words." Then he smiled. "And if you'll pardon me, the three of you don't look the part." He glanced up at the ceiling as if afraid he'd offended them, and proclaimed to no one in particular, "The seekers have come. Blessed be the seekers."

He closed his eyes as if sleeping, and when he reopened them, they glistened. "Such a miracle that you found me after so many generations. At times I believed my father's tale a myth. But I haven't yet fulfilled my mission. Come with me."

He led them to a supply room in the back of the store and had Nathaniel slide a wooden cabinet aside. Dust underneath showed the piece had not been moved in years. Starting at the base of the wall, he counted with his walking stick sixteen bricks up. From there, he tapped three to the right and stopped at the fourth. He tried to remove the brick but his knobby fingers were too weak to dislodge it.

Nathaniel stepped forward and tugged until the brick came loose.

From the hole, the shopkeeper removed a scroll exactly like the first. He grasped it in both hands and presented it to Orah. "The city, the symbol, the pass phrase and the rhyme. Blessed be the seekers."

The hair on the back of her neck tingled as she accepted the scroll.

The shopkeeper bent his head, almost a bow. "My life's purpose as a keeper has been to wait for you and, now that you've come, to lead you to the next in the chain. The rest is up to you, but I can give directions. The next leg of your journey will require a trek of several days, and I see you're already road-weary. Please honor me by accepting my invitation to dinner. Then stay the night and rest. In the morning, I'll replenish your provisions and start you on your way."

All three nodded in appreciation. As Orah rubbed the glossy surface of the scroll with the pad of her thumb, the realization struck with much more force than one of Nathaniel's notions--the keepers were real.

The keep must exist.

***

Since leaving Little Pond the week before, Orah and the others had survived on cornmeal crackers and dried mutton, usually eaten in a rush while squatting on the ground. Now, as she washed off the dust of the road, the second keeper prepared a fine meal. The first inkling came from the smell wafting up the stairs of seared lamb aromatic with forbidden spices--perhaps a hint of mint or thyme — and yams glazed with honey.

When she arrived downstairs, the table had been set with the spinner's finest crockery, and a mouth-watering dinner awaited. Her mother had never cooked such a meal.

In no time, she'd cleared her plate and asked for more.

Afterwards, the friends sipped apple cinnamon tea and learned about the keeper. He'd been born and raised in this house and had learned spinning as a boy. At his coming of age, his father asked him to swear loyalty to the family business. The spinner's ancestors had run the Adamsville shop with a fanatic commitment, longer than anyone could remember, but only as his father lay dying did he reveal the reason: the place held a clue in the keeper's chain.

He'd married here, and his wife had borne him a son who arrived sickly into the world and survived less than two years. They'd yearned for another to fill the void, but had drawn the white stone at their nuptials. They had pleaded with the vicar, but the clergy enforced the rules rigorously: a family of the white stone may bear only one offspring. Had their child been stillborn, they'd have been allowed another. When rules are made for the

DAVID LITWACK

many, they're cruel for the few. His wife had passed to the light several years before, and he'd since lived alone.

After dinner, he led them upstairs to a small but comfortable room with a single window in back and eaves in the corners. It had been his bedroom as a child, he explained, and his son's nursery for the time he had lived.

"My wife left it unchanged for years," the keeper said, "a kind of memorial for our boy. After her death, I removed all painful reminders of my family and turned it into a guest room."

The seekers had not slept in beds for a week. With their stomachs filled and the doubts of the day diminished, they could barely stay awake.

Seeing this, the second keeper bid them good night and departed.

Despite her exhaustion, Orah itched to peek at the scroll. She stretched the shiny parchment over a candle flame, and though only Thomas had never seen the change, all three held their breaths until the words appeared.

This time, the city read "Bradford."

Thomas lit up at mention of his forebear's former home.

Orah took this to be a good omen and moved on to the symbol, a poorly drawn square, with one end longer than the other. She glanced at Nathaniel for guidance. He only shrugged.

But Thomas gasped, and the blood drained from his face. "I know what it is. I see it every night in my dreams—a vicar's hat."

"It can't be." She gaped at the not-quite-square, and then squinted, trying to force the picture to change. When the perception lingered, she buried her concern to steady her friend. "We'll go to Bradford and find a better explanation."

Thomas released his breath. "I hope so."

"At least the pass phrase is clear." She read the words below the symbol, wanting to move on before the letters vanished. "'We travel toward the dawn to seek the light of truth,' followed by, 'May the light of truth keep you safe and show you the way.'"

The rhyme, however, taunted her, as mysterious as before.

> Twixt water and dark walls of pine
> A cave made by men who must die
> The Temple of Truth you shall see
> Golden doors that are closed for all time

"What does that mean?" Thomas said. "How do we get in if they're closed for all time?"

"It's worse than the other." Nathaniel scowled. "What's a cave between water and dark walls?"

Orah hid her disappointment, needing to keep their spirits up. "Remember what the first keeper said. The rhyme makes sense only if complete. We're the seekers. Look at how many obstacles we've already overcome. When the time is right, we'll know what to do."

Yet she knew at this moment the title of seeker meant little. Before they reached their goal, each would be called upon to do more than they'd dreamed possible, and only then would they earn the name.

The words faded and the day rested heavily upon her. Their journey stretched beyond the horizon, with no end in sight.

***

After the others had gone to bed, Orah rummaged through her pack and withdrew her log. At long last, she found a moment to chronicle the events since that day the vicar had dragged her off to Temple City. She wrote for an hour and then paused, the pen poised over the paper.

The story lacked something—a meaning, a hope, a fear.

Here she sat on this bed in the home of a stranger, a seven-day trek from Little Pond. She'd abandoned her mother and all she'd ever known, beat through the brush, slept in the woods and fled from the deacons... but to what purpose?

She began to write.

> The meaning: To right a wrong. The Temple and its teachings exist for a single purpose – to keep the people from questioning the vicars. What are they hiding?
>
> The hope: To lift the constraints on my people. As the first keeper told Nathaniel, to give them a life of possibilities rather than a life of limits.
>
> The fear....

She raised the pen. What did she fear most? To rot away in the prisons of Temple City? To die a death by stoning? To lose Nathaniel?

The last gave her pause, and she shook her head. What good were any of these if she lost herself? She recalled her father's deathbed words, and with sudden clarity, denying them became her greatest fear.

> *The fear: To let the vicars or anyone else set my mind. To aspire to be less than I might be. To be unworthy of another's love.*

Satisfied with the entry, she restored the pen and paper to their waterproof container and stuffed it away in her pack.

***

Orah stirred first. A sliver of sunlight found a gap in the curtain and landed on her right eye. She opened it, closed it, and then startled awake—the light of midmorning, not dawn.

She staggered to her feet to rouse the others, but paused when she caught an odd tapping on the stairs—the click of a walking stick on stone, but approaching too fast.

The old spinner burst into the room, his face ashen. In his right hand he waved a crumpled piece of paper.

"Deacons. Searching from house to house. They'll be here in minutes."

Thomas jumped up and began filling his pack, while Nathaniel rubbed sleep from his eyes.

"They can't be looking for us," Orah said. The keeper handed her the paper, and she read it aloud. "Urgent bulletin. Three friends of the darkness believed to have arrived in Adamsville overnight: a tall, dark-haired man; a shorter one; and a slender girl with auburn hair. If sighted, report."

Thomas snarled at Orah as he rolled a blanket and jammed it into his pack. "I thought you said word couldn't travel that fast."

She glared back at him, but he kept his head down, continuing to fill his rucksack.

Nathaniel started packing as well and urged her to do the same.

"We have time," the spinner said. "The deacons are clumsy fools, so quick to harsh treatment they've foretold their coming. I have bags ready for each of you, with food for ten days. I'll fetch them while you finish. Fold your bedding and clean up. Leave no sign you stayed here. I'll return in an instant. Please hurry."

106

They finished with the linens just as he returned with the bags. The three accepted the food, secured their packs, and rushed toward the stairs, but a knocking at the door froze them in place.

The shopkeeper placed a finger to his lips, came close, and whispered, "I've planned for this. It wasn't hard to guess how the Temple would feel about the seekers." He turned and pointed. "That window leads to a small alley out of view from the front of the house. The building has no back door, so they won't suspect anyone trying to leave that way."

Orah glanced out. "I can see why. It's too steep a drop."

The keeper's response restored her confidence. "Bricks are wonderful things. They hide secrets, and when removed provide hand and footholds."

He slid the window open.

Thomas leaned out and turned back with a grin. "He's made holes every couple of feet like a ladder. Climbing down will be easy."

The pounding on the door grew louder.

Orah pointed to Thomas. "Go."

Thomas put his nimbleness to use, vaulting over the windowsill and scrambling down.

Once he gave them an all-clear, she gestured to Nathaniel. "You're next. I'll toss you the three packs. They'd be too heavy for me, and you can catch me if I fall.

Before he could argue, she cast him a look of such urgency he obeyed. After he'd climbed down, she dropped the packs to him.

As she turned to make her goodbyes, the second keeper drew her close. "Travel east for six days, past the roads that lead south to the Temple Cities. Then turn north at the next opportunity. Two days more and you'll arrive at Bradford."

She repeated the words, hoping to remember, and scrambled over the sill.

He called after her, "Go quickly. The keep won't wait forever. May the true light speed you on."

Once over the side, she found the holes an easy fit for her feet, but in her haste, she lost her grip near the bottom and would have landed awkwardly if not for Nathaniel.

They dashed around the corner, out of sight of the window, and she again took charge. "He said to go east. Let's get as far from here as possible."

Nathaniel stopped her. "The bulletin claimed we were three. If we go separately, we'll be harder to identify."

"I won't split up," she said.

"It'll be safer. That's all that matters. I'll go north, you go east and Thomas south. We'll meet on the road, ten minutes east of the town. Whoever arrives first should hide in the woods and signal when the others appear."

She began to argue, but stopped when she heard the keeper's voice unnaturally loud, berating the deacons for manhandling an old man. She gave in and took off in her designated direction with a prayer they'd meet as planned.

***

Orah slowed her jog and began scanning the woods. The terror of being caught had diminished, but all would be wasted if one of them was caught.

Then two sharp whistles, a birdcall to anyone else. She turned to catch Thomas emerging from the trees.

Her remaining fear became a single word. "Nathaniel?"

Thomas made a sweeping gesture with his arm, and Nathaniel's tall form emerged through the branches. Bits of leaf clung to his hair and beard as he beamed at her. "We did it."

"Yes," she said, "but let's never separate again."

He nodded soberly and brushed her cheek with his fingertips.

To feel his touch, to know he was safe.... How painful the minutes apart had been. Was this her punishment for following his dream? But for now, their escape stirred her blood and drove off any emotion save exhilaration.

Their journey would grow harder with another eight days to Bradford, assuming they found their way, but something more gnawed at her, something... subtly wrong. Yes, Nathaniel had broken his vow to the arch vicar, but why should three villagers from the edge of the world merit such attention?

She stared at the road ahead. Eight more days to Bradford. Eight more days of looking over her shoulder and checking for deacons. Eight more days of pondering her fate.

108

Chapter 17
Bradford

After more than two weeks, Orah had wearied of the seekers' journey. Their goal remained a long way off, assuming the keep existed and could be found. For each moment of elation or instant of peril, she slogged through hours of tedium.

At least the April weather had been kind. Mild nights seldom required a blanket, and cool days allowed for a brisk pace—that is until they headed north, away from the second Temple City. When the sweltering heat arrived, she imagined the vicars had sent temple magic to break their will. She trudged along, each footstep landing with a thud upon the earth.

Thomas complained that his feet hurt and that as the smallest, his pack weighed heavily on him.

Their pace slowed, and two days after turning northward, she'd glimpsed no sign of Bradford.

Nathaniel did his best to raise their spirits. "Think how much we've accomplished. We dodged the deacons and secured a second piece of a puzzle for the ages. Are we sure to find the keep? Not yet, but the possibility should stir our passions."

She knew he was right, but still....

Unable to act or plan, she fretted constantly. How many keepers remained? What if, after all these generations, the chain had been

109

broken? Even if the chain remained intact, how would she solve such a baffling rhyme?

She viewed solving the rhyme as key to their morale. That night, after dinner, she pressed Nathaniel to bring out the scrolls, and she memorized every word.

The next day, as they hiked in the heat, she chanted as she went:

> *To the North, behind the rock face*
> *To the East, towering o'er the lake*
> *To the North, through forest of stone*
> *To the East, the entrance shall be*
>
> ~~~
>
> *Twixt water and dark walls of pine*
> *A cave made by men who must die*
> *The Temple of Truth you shall see*
> *Golden doors that are closed for all time*

Occasionally, she'd gain insight into a phrase and bring it up with the others. As they debated its meaning, their pace would quicken.

"We go north," she'd announce. "Then, when we come upon a rock cliff, we turn east."

Thomas wrinkled his nose. "How can there be a forest of stone?"

"Maybe they mean petrified trees."

"If the keep is the Temple of Truth, why would they build it in a cave?"

"To hide it, of course."

Thomas persisted. "Where?"

"Behind the golden doors."

"Which are locked forever."

Round and round they went. By midafternoon, black clouds billowed and surged in the west, rising angrily as if at odds with the heavens. They were a wonder to behold from a distance, but as the storm drew nearer it seemed to target the seekers. The closer the clouds came, the faster they moved, until they blotted all blue from the sky. An immense wind came up, too warm for April—a wet, hot wind that turned the newly sprouted leaves inside out and ripped the weaker ones away, stirring the litter far down the dirt path and raising whirls of dust. Soon, thunder boomed and lightning flashed, followed by heavy droplets of rain driven sideways by the wind, as if some power had heard them mocking the rhyme.

The three fled for cover into the trees.

The squall raced past as quickly as it had arrived, leaving the air cool and fresh. April had returned, and as the storm moved on to the east, a rainbow arced across the sky. Her friends gazed at it in wonder, trying to see to its end, but—practical as always—Orah emerged onto the now muddy road and checked the way forward.

What she saw made her smile, a weary hope fulfilled. "Look there."

Nathaniel rushed to her side. "What is it?"

"A signpost. We've come to Bradford."

***

After their narrow escape in Adamsville, Orah refused to enter Bradford without scouting the town first. But which of them should go? Thomas didn't offer, and she didn't ask.

Nathaniel volunteered, but she insisted his height would make him too conspicuous, and people would more likely trust a young woman alone. He finally gave in.

She wrapped a headscarf round her hair to conceal the color, and left her pack behind. After smoothing her clothing and shaking off the dust of the road, she sauntered off to Bradford like an everyday visitor.

Bradford, like Adamsville, had homes at the outskirts and a merchant district within, but this city featured a square in its middle bordering a well-kept park. At the park's center stood a cheery gazebo built from latticework and roofed with copper, surrounded by a small flower garden. Snowdrops hung in bloom, joined by buds of crocus barely visible above the newly thawed soil. The square seemed a place more for recreation than ritual.

Two-story brick buildings lined the adjoining cobblestone streets, some with ornamental facades. From the heart of the town rose the largest structure, crowned by a steeple and topped by an image of the sun.

Beside its entrance, a post for notices foreshadowed the Temple's presence, but neither paper nor nail marked its surface. No other signs of the Temple showed, and no deacons marched about. More striking, no one crossed the square to avoid her. Each passerby nodded a greeting or tipped their hat, and some asked if she needed directions.

She'd promised her friends to bring back as much information as possible, and so she traversed every street, checked every window, and pretended to shop in every store. She could report with confidence that Bradford was a friendly town, without a whiff of danger, but as yet, she'd found no sign hanging over a door or picture on a wall resembling the symbol on the scroll.

Nathaniel had warned her to avoid taking risks, but she refused to return without a plan. The day grew late, and the number of people thinned as more returned home for dinner. Time to change her approach.

She accosted an elderly man as he crossed the square. "Excuse me, sir, may I bother you for help?"

He stopped at once. "Why of course, child. It's no bother."

Thomas's interpretation of the symbol burned in her mind. She had to eliminate the possibility. "I'm newly arrived here and have been traveling for days. While away, I missed the blessing of the light. Can you tell me when the vicar comes next?"

He puffed out his chest and beamed. "My dear, you're in Bradford. We have our own vicar, a man who's one of us, born and raised here. We're most fortunate because he's the best to be had."

Orah considered the offer made to Nathaniel. Could a vicar be a keeper as well? "Where may I find him?"

"Why you're standing in front of his house." He gestured to the building with the steeple.

Of course – the rectory of the vicar. Orah wavered. Should she press on? "How may I get an audience with him?"

The man chuckled. "An audience? No need. He's available day or night. He ministers to our sick and comforts the afflicted. That's why we love him so. Wait a bit and see for yourself. His class should be ending about now."

Orah's heart skipped a beat. She felt ill prepared for an encounter. "Thank you, sir. The day's getting late, and I won't bother him now. I'll come back in the morning."

The man wished her good evening and ambled off, taking a shortcut across the lawn.

She slipped around a corner to watch. Moments later, the double doors to the rectory swung wide, and the sound of laughter filled the square.

This vicar, Bradford's native son, emerged with six children in tow. He knelt and thanked them for coming. When the little ones began to race off, he froze them with a command. They stopped, gazing up at him cheerfully.

He reached inside his robe, pulled out a handful of sweets, and placed a candy in each child's palm. After receiving their treats, they skipped off.

Orah clung to the wall for support. Of all of the possibilities, this seemed the best. Tomorrow, they'd have to take the chance.

***

That night, after the others had gone to bed, Orah stayed awake to write in her log.

After two weeks of stumbling through this journey – relying not on our wits, but on good luck – our fate has come to this. All rests on my judgment.

I used to believe the world made sense, that counting numbers and assessing facts yielded the proper decision. Not anymore. All I once relied on now rests on shifting sand.

I've studied the town of Bradford, its streets and stores and people, learning all I can in so short a time. Yet every fact leads me to the person I most fear: the vicar.

This evening, I passed what I learned onto my friends.

Nathaniel listened, demanding I repeat the story three times, challenging every assumption. At length, he agreed to my plan.

Thomas took the decision badly. I told him he hadn't witnessed the kindness of this vicar, but it gave him little comfort.

No facts prove my case; no numbers give the answer. I can only guess. Never before has so much balanced on a whim, but where else shall we go? The path forward remains a fog, and deacons await behind.

113

As I finish this entry, and try to get some sleep, only one fact remains: If I'm wrong, all will suffer, but the fault will be mine.

***

Orah awoke to what sounded like a wounded bird caught in a trap—Thomas moaning in his sleep. She got up and knelt beside him, touched his shoulder and shook him gently. When he failed to rouse, she stroked his cheek and whispered in a singsong voice, "Thomas, wake up."

His eyelids fluttered and opened, and he stared at her, dazed. "I dreamed I was back in the teaching cell alone."

"It's all right, Thomas, it's only a dream."

He pulled away, and his voice filled with dread. "It's no dream. Tomorrow, you'll take me to the vicar."

"I've seen him, Thomas. He's not like the others. The people of Bradford love him."

"What if it's a lie? So much of the Temple has been lies."

"We have to try."

"What if tomorrow will turn out like my nightmare?"

"It won't be like your nightmare, Thomas."

"Why not?"

"Because if I'm wrong, you won't be alone."

Chapter 18
The Holy Man

Nathaniel gazed up at the clouds as if searching for guidance. When none could be found, he hoisted his pack and joined his friends on the road to Bradford.

Minutes later, he stood before the rectory in the main square. They had no choice but to seek the next keeper, and Orah had insisted their only clue lay here. Still he hesitated, with something more than mistrust gnawing at him. He'd never met a vicar outside of formal ritual. A veil of mystery shrouded these men, these guardians of temple magic. Though he'd lost faith in them, he was loath to speak to one.

The decision was made for him.

The double doors carved with the symbol of the sun swung open, and the vicar of Bradford emerged, a small man in his middle years. Curls of hair slipped lower than temple rules allowed, framing a face marked with experience. If its lines could be read like words, they'd describe someone kind and slow to anger, a person who had lived a satisfying life.

He bounded down the stairs with arms extended. "Welcome, travelers, I've been expecting you."

No need to respond. Their expressions answered for them.

115

"Oh, don't be surprised. I've been reading about you for days, though I only guessed you'd come here. The tallest must be Nathaniel, the young lady Orah, and the third Thomas. I'm pleased to meet you."

Nathaniel froze. Too late to flee, though nothing about the man seemed threatening. To be safe, he placed himself between the vicar and his friends. "How do you know our names?"

The vicar offered a half smile as if enjoying a private joke. "I *am* an official of the Temple and receive all their bulletins. They usually tell of miscreants and felons, but the latest described three young people from light-fearing families, wandering far from home without permit and heading my way." He switched to mock officialdom. "'If sighted, report at once, but make no attempt to contact.' Extraordinary. Why would such as these travel so far and defy their Temple? It made me wonder, and then it made me hope."

Nathaniel glanced over his shoulder. Orah had fallen back a step, while Thomas shifted sideways preparing to run away. Yet he sensed no flight would be necessary.

"Your people say you're generous and kind. You won't betray us to the Temple, will you?"

The vicar blanched. "Oh my, I'm sorry. How insensitive of me. I forget you're strangers to Bradford. Our town lies far from the nearest Temple City and has always been served by a local vicar. I minister as I see fit and not always by the rules. Now I'm your host, and you're my guests. Please join me inside."

None of them stirred.

"I promise you'll be safe. You can ask my people. I've never once eaten their young." He chuckled at his joke and opened the door to the rectory.

After an awkward pause, Nathaniel ventured inside, with Orah and Thomas lagging behind.

The vicar led them through a large assembly hall with rows of pews and an altar in front, into some sort of classroom with a polished oak table in its center. A door in the back led to his private quarters, and in one corner a narrow stairway spiraled down to the lower level. Besides the conference table and chairs, the meeting room was modestly furnished, containing no high benches or ominous murals. The only mark of the Temple lay at the far wall—a cabinet with brass doors engraved with the sun.

He took his place at one end of the table, on the lone high-backed chair, and bid them sit on either side. "Now that you're settled, feel free to say what you choose."

All three began to speak at once, but Thomas asked his question first. "If no vicars come here, how do you administer... teachings?"

"I do them myself, like the vicars before me." Then noticing Thomas eyeing the spiral staircase, he added, "Just a store room, nothing more. I teach differently than they do in Temple City. No harsh treatments here. I sit with the children around this table and teach more light than darkness."

Nathaniel went next. Though the vicar's manner made him feel at ease, he wasn't about to let instinct dominate reason. "I'm curious why you hoped we'd come to Bradford, and specifically to you."

The vicar folded his hands and studied them, but a tremor in his fingers exposed an unsettling uncertainty. "A foolish notion, one I harbor whenever strangers draw near. Each time, I find myself deluded, but I have faith that one day the right visitor will reward my hope." He straightened and met Nathaniel's stare. "If today be that day, I'm not the one to speak first. Answer me a question and only then, if my query is well answered, will I respond."

"A question?"

"Why did *you* come here?"

The room seemed to shrink and grow dim. The vicar leaned forward, his knuckles whitening as he clasped his hands more tightly, and a keeper's intensity replaced his cordial demeanor. "You're safe here, but if you seek a worthy goal, you must speak first."

Nathaniel's vision narrowed so he saw only the man's eyes. He searched in them for a reason to believe. After a moment, he'd seen enough.

A deep breath in and out. "We travel toward the dawn to seek the light of truth."

The vicar of Bradford raised his clasped hands to his chest, threw his head back and glanced at the unseen heavens. His retort brought a glow to the room.

"May the light of truth keep you safe and show you the way. Praise the light. At long last, the seekers have come."

117

***

Nathaniel struggled to make sense of the situation. This ordained envoy of the Temple was the third keeper, guardian of a secret that might destroy that same Temple. As the day progressed, he discovered something more: this humble man led an exemplary life, far better than he himself had aspired to.

The vicar invited them to share lunch, assuring them they'd draw no attention. He often welcomed travelers who passed through town, because hospitality was a virtue of the light. He warned them, however, to expect a modest meal. The people of Bradford willingly provided whatever he desired, but he'd be wrong to exploit his position. Despite the imposing rectory, he led a simple life, accepting their largesse only to meet his most basic needs.

He brought out a basket of bread and cheese with a bowl of strawberry jam, apologizing as he served. "This isn't Bradford's best season. Had you come a month from now, I'd offer you the most wonderful blueberries around."

After they'd eaten their fill, the three swamped their host with questions. He held up a hand and promised each their turn, offering to answer Orah's first.

"As a vicar," she said, "you must know the secrets of the Temple. Will you share them with us?"

He pursed his lips as he listened and then nodded. "I'm at the lowest rank. Only those higher up have access to the greatest mysteries, so I may know less than you presume. Your question, however, shows a misunderstanding of our positions. I may be a vicar, but I'm a keeper first. My life's work is to aid the seekers. Of course, I'll tell you all I know."

Orah balanced on the edge of her seat. "How did word of us travel so far and so fast?"

"To answer that, I must start with things not written in the book of light. What preceded the Temple was not darkness, but an age of innovation and genius. The people of the world enjoyed boundless freedom of thought and harnessed nature in unimaginable ways. The Temple's founders abandoned that knowledge due to the harm it caused, but kept the more useful inventions to themselves, especially those that can control the populace, such as the medicines they distribute to the children of light, thinking machines to track information, and the answer to your question--a remarkable system of communication."

Nathaniel had heard similar claims from the other keepers, but here, right in front of him, a vicar disputed the Temple's primary precept. He could not let the presumption pass. "The book of light tells us, 'Thus ended the darkness and the age of enlightenment began.' We're taught that as the basis for the existence of the Temple."

The vicar winced. "I'm sorry, my son. I'm aware of what you were taught, but you're a seeker now and must learn the truth. A more honest assertion would be, 'Thus ended the age of enlightenment and the darkness descended.'"

Thomas's eyes popped wide, and Nathaniel let out a whistle — their world turned upside down.

But Orah honed in on the details. "How does the system work? What lets them talk over such distances?"

"A difficult question, Orah. Do you know of the temple trees?"

"Yes, of course."

"Apparently, words are made to fly through the air. Each temple tree receives the words and passes them on to the next. The Temple issues all clergy machines to catch these words, either as sound, such as the grand vicar's blessing from the sun icon, or on paper, like the bulletin warning me of your approach."

Thomas gasped. "Temple magic!"

"Magic, perhaps, but not of the Temple. They stole these wonders from the past."

Orah folded her hands between her knees and leaned in. "What makes the words fly, and how does the machine recapture them? There must be an explanation."

The vicar shrugged. "Perhaps, but I don't know it. I've tried searching the ancient texts from prior keepers and taking apart the devices, but nothing reveals how they work. I'm not even sure the gray friars know."

"The gray friars?"

"Ah, of course. How would you ever encounter them? No temple devices to maintain in Little Pond. The gray friars, so-called wizards of temple magic, serve the clergy largely in secret. We study the book of light, while they ponder the knowledge of the past to better service the Sun icon, printing machines and other devices, but I don't believe they understand what makes them work."

Orah's eyes widened, and she spoke in a whisper. "Can they listen to our words?"

"I... don't think so. To converse requires a device on either end activated by speaker and listener. Maybe in the distant past but...." He hesitated, then shook his head. "No, I'm quite sure, because if the hierarchy possessed such a capability, they most certainly would have used it."

Orah's voice returned to normal. "What else can they do?"

The vicar paused to organize his thoughts. "Have you seen the deacon's star?"

"Yes."

"It exists not merely as decoration but to solve a problem. The deacons are unruly men. The star lets the vicars track their whereabouts, showing their location relative to the nearest temple tree. While not precise, it keeps the deacons in line." He wrinkled his brow as if straining to remember, but finally shrugged. "I wish I knew more. According to keeper legend, so much was once possible, but most has been lost."

"How did the Temple come to rule," Nathaniel said, "if the prior age was so powerful?"

"A good question. I can only surmise. Perhaps the quest for knowledge brought change faster than it could be assimilated. For every benefit, an offsetting harm occurred, as our penchant for evil found ways for abuse. Eventually, the bad outweighed the good. Those who preferred order to progress revolted against unfettered thought, and the wonders were banned.

"Fortunately, the greatest of that era preserved their treasures in the keep, and set up a trail so others might someday rediscover them. We keepers are small steps on that trail, but we've kept faith across the generations, until at last you've come—the seekers."

Thomas brightened at the mention of the keep. "Do you know what's there?"

"I wish I did. All I'm certain of is that the place embodies the wisdom of the past." The vicar's eyes took on a far off glow, the look of a dreamer. "How I envy you. Who knows what wonders await? I only pray it's intact."

Orah nearly rose from her seat. "Intact? Why wouldn't it be intact?"

"Nothing goes on forever, Orah. The founders hoped the seekers would arise in a few generations, not centuries. The keep may have exceeded its intended life."

"If the keep was at risk, why wouldn't the keepers have acted sooner?"

"The keep's purpose is to restore the world to its former greatness. Creating a new world is like the making of a fine meal, requiring both ingredients and fire. The keep holds only the ingredients. The fire comes from us. If we found the keep too soon, we might lack sufficient fire. The world would remain unchanged, and we would lose the chance forever. The emergence of the seekers is supposed to show the world is ready."

A tremor rattled down Nathaniel's spine. *Have I emerged, or did the old prisoner choose me as an act of desperation?*

He put his concerns into words. "Why *did* it take so long? How do we know *we're* the true seekers?"

"Why so long? Because the Temple is skilled at extinguishing the fire in our hearts. That's the very purpose of a teaching."

Thomas rose suddenly and drifted to the window.

The vicar crumpled his brow and eyed him as he went.

"He's had a teaching," Orah whispered.

The vicar put a hand to his breast and drew in a quick breath. "Oh my, I've been insensitive again."

"It's not your fault." Nathaniel rose. "Come back, Thomas. We don't have time for—"

The vicar waved Nathaniel off and went to Thomas instead. The clergyman reached out, a father about to comfort his son, but his hand wavered in mid-air.

He's stuck, Nathaniel realized, *torn between vicar and keeper. His temple caused the harm. Does he have the right to heal the pain?*

Finally, keeper vanquished vicar, and he touched Thomas's arm. "Forgive me. I misspoke. A teaching can never snuff out your fire, but can only drive it deeper."

Thomas turned, his face a hopeful question. "Then can it burn again?"

"That, Thomas, is up to you."

121

The vicar led him back to his chair and riveted Nathaniel with a gaze. "Are you the true seekers? We'll only know after you find the keep and use its contents to change the world."

Nathaniel's dreams, once airy like gossamer, now took substance, threatening to crash to the floor of their own weight. *Why me?*

The vicar glanced out the window, noting the angle of the sun. "You should leave soon if you hope to travel today, but before you do, I have one last obligation."

He opened the cabinet on the wall, exposing the sun icon, and slid the shelf aside. From a hidden compartment beneath it he withdrew the now familiar scroll.

Orah raised an eyebrow. "You hid the keepers scroll beneath the sun icon?"

He gave a half smile. "My little joke."

Nathaniel rose to accept the scroll, but the vicar strode past him to Thomas.

"Why give it to me?" Thomas said.

"Because *you* are a seeker."

Thomas hesitated, and then accepted the scroll.

The vicar beamed. "Next you go to Riverbend, a trip as far as all the distance you've traveled till now, but I can help you get there. Have you ever seen a map?"

"Do you mean a treasure map," Orah said, "like we made when we were little?"

"Similar, but on a broader scale."

He fetched a paper from the cabinet and unfolded it on the table. "This map describes our whole world—another secret the Temple conceals."

Thomas pointed at a spot on the map. "That says Bradford. Is that where we are?"

"Yes, Thomas, and at the far left is Little Pond."

Orah traced their journey from Little Pond to Adamsville and Bradford, and then released a sigh. "I wish we'd had this when we started."

"To find the next keeper, you must go...." The vicar slid his finger along the parchment, not stopping until the word Riverbend.

Orah gestured at an unusually windy road. "What's that?"

"A river. From the breadth on the map, I'd say a wide one."

"And this?" She pointed farther north to scribbles along the edge.

The vicar shrugged. "Maybe wilderness or the edge of the world."

Nathaniel's shoulders slumped. *So far to go, so much unknown.* He squinted as an orange ray of light streamed through the window from the low afternoon sun.

Time to leave, but one last question gnawed at him. "We're grateful for your help, so it pains me to ask, but how do you resolve the lie between vicar and keeper?"

No sooner had the words come out than he worried he'd offended his host.

The vicar grimaced and blinked twice, but then the grimace turned into a smile. "My son, every age comes with its good and evil. The Temple brought much good, overcoming the chaos of the prior age, but over time it's become corrupted itself. Someday a new order will replace it. That's not my task. My role as keeper has been to watch and wait. In the meantime, I do what I can for my people, but make no mistake—when the world changes, I'll support the new way. You three may be the impetus for that change."

The day had flown by. The light through the window diminished.

Light diminished in Nathaniel as well. When his first test came, he'd fled to the mountains. When Samuel offered the scroll, he'd thought only of childish dreams. He'd let his impatience with Thomas get the better of him, where the vicar had treated his friend with kindness. This gentle man, who'd kept the secret all these years, still managed to minister selflessly to his people. Both he and the vicar were dreamers, but only one was worthy of the keep.

He went to his pack and took out the first two scrolls, and as the others watched, presented them to the vicar of Bradford.

The vicar looked bewildered at first, but then shook his head. "No, Nathaniel, you must bear this burden, not I. The people of Bradford need me." He forced a warm smile. "And if a vicar tried to seek the keep, he wouldn't get very far."

"You're more deserving than I am."

"More deserving?" The vicar's eyes flared. "That depends not on how hot your fire burns today, but how you stoke the flames when the time comes. Until then, no one knows who's deserving."

Thomas went to Nathaniel and handed him the third scroll, and Orah pressed his fingers until they curled around the three. It was settled.

"I'll gather supplies if you like," the vicar said, "but I hate to send you out so late. I'd be pleased to host you for the night so you can leave refreshed in the morning."

Orah glanced longingly at the roof overhead and began to answer, but Nathaniel cut her short.

"Thank you, but you've shown us the magnitude of our task. More than our comfort's at stake. We should start right away."

The vicar of Bradford, third keeper of a great secret, regarded the three of them with a wistful look in his eyes. "My heart wishes you'd stay, but my head tells me you're wise to go. Those messages from the Temple carried the utmost urgency, and I fear for your safety. Wait here while I fetch you supplies." Then he vanished down the spiral stairs.

As the light faded from the rectory, Nathaniel dwelled in his thoughts. The journey had begun as a dream and continued as an adventure. In Adamsville he'd learned to appreciate the risks, but only here in Bradford did he finally understand the stakes.

The seekers were the bridge to a new world.

Chapter 19
The End of the Chain

That night, as soon as the campfire flickered into life, Orah pulled out the third scroll. Thanks to the vicar of Bradford, she already knew the city—Riverbend. The symbol depicted a shoe, suggesting a cobbler, but the pass phrase sounded more baffling than the others. The seekers were to say, "We have traveled far, but our journey has just begun. The true light drives us on." And the next keeper would respond, "May you find the end you seek, and may the truth you discover hasten a new beginning."

The wording troubled Thomas. "A beginning? If Riverbend's the beginning, my feet'll fall off before we find the keep."

"Oh hush. It's just an expression. Let's move on to the rhyme before the words fade."

She prayed to glean more meaning from the latest verse, but the lines on the third scroll proved no clearer than the others.

> For a full eight days you shall race
> Two doors to the mouth of the snake
> Once great, it now stands alone
> Sixteen stars shall set the doors free

She stared in silence as the letters dissolved into flecks of black and vanished into the white background of the scroll.

Thomas intruded on her thoughts. "What if the founders had gone mad?"

"They were the most brilliant of a brilliant age," she said. "The puzzle's meant to be hard. The burden is on the seekers to solve the rhyme."

Thomas persisted in that annoying way he had of focusing on silly details. "Brilliant, sure, but they couldn't have been happy. Their world was crumbling around them. I'd be angry, at least, if not mad."

She closed her eyes and shook her head. "No, Thomas, they were not mad."

"How else do you explain these verses?"

She lost patience with his pestering and struck out with a scowl. "Maybe you're not smart enough to understand the rhyme."

"And you are? Then tell me what it means?"

Rather than continue the debate, she withdrew to the edge of the shadows and dropped cross-legged on the ground with her back to her friends. The heat of the fire failed to reach where she sat, so she clasped her arms around herself, rocked back and forth, and did her best to hide a shiver.

After a time, she heard the others readying for bed. She strode to where the scroll still lay in its holder, and in a single motion grasped the wooden handles and swung the frame over the embers. The words reappeared, and her lips moved soundlessly as she committed them to memory.

When she finished, she glanced up to find Nathaniel eyeing her.

"Are you all right?"

"Tomorrow," she said, "I'll add these words to our marching song, but tonight I'll dream of them. The answer will come to me, Nathaniel of Little Pond. I swear it."

***

No dreams came to Orah that night, and she hardly slept. Instead, the rhyme rattled round in her half-awake brain but continued to make no sense. As the moon set and the breeze stilled in the trees, she wondered if their quest also made no sense—spinners and vicars preserving secrets across centuries, leading them on a race to a place that may not even exist. She wished she'd never left the comfort of Little Pond.

Then she recalled Thomas's blank stare, her father's gaunt face, and the tears on her mother's cheeks when she told how the teaching had killed him. She pictured the pompous panel of vicars, preaching their truth to her—a truth based on lies.

With a sigh, she roused herself and tossed a few branches onto the dwindling fire. The flames crackled and spit sparks into the air, floating like shooting stars until they burned themselves out.

Once the fire burned bright enough, she grabbed paper and pen from her pack and began to write.

> *Here's what I know:*
>
> *We found three keepers in the chain. We hold three verses of the rhyme.*
>
> *The keep remains a mystery. No one's sure if it exists, or knows what's hidden inside.*
>
> *In addition to the scrolls, I carry a map. At least five of the towns listed are real—I've visited every one. Does this far-off Riverbend exist as well? To find out, I must spend the next two weeks of my life sleeping on hard ground.*
>
> *What then? How many more towns? How many more keepers? What if the chain broke long ago? Will our quest never end?*
>
> *Or will the deacons hunt us down first, long before we have a chance to change the world? Will our sacrifices be in vain?*

***

Orah referred to the map several times a day, matching landmarks to symbols on the paper—her only proof of progress. By charting their location, she never worried about wandering off course. *Such a simple idea. So helpful.* If the keep housed more ideas like this, perhaps its discovery would justify their trials.

Now, as this leg of their journey neared its end, each landmark seemed to bring Riverbend closer. *The sooner, the better.*

Ants had found their way into a packet of food and, as a result, their provisions ran low. A weary Thomas whined constantly about the size of his rations, and her own stomach had begun to growl by mid-afternoon.

At last, a cemetery of the kind that sat on the outskirts of so many towns signaled their arrival. A waist-high wall surrounded it, with a stone arch providing the only entrance. Orah pulled her friends inside.

The gravestones bore witness to Riverbend's past. Some stood knee-high, while others rose as obelisks with a sculpture of the sun on top. Some inscriptions remained legible, while others had been worn smooth by weather and time. In the back, the oldest stones had crumbled, the latest generation having no cause to maintain them. Nearest the gate lay a fresh plot, the ground moist and mounded, as yet unmarked by a headstone.

She directed Nathaniel and Thomas to sit with their backs to the wall, out of sight from the road, while she crouched before them. "We've seen little of the Temple since Bradford, so you might be tempted to take chances, but with words flying through the air, we need to be wary."

"Come on, Orah," Thomas said, gesturing to the cluster of homey cottages in the distance. "This place seems more like Great Pond than Temple City."

She sniffed the breeze as if to gain a sense of the town, but only the dank odor of freshly turned earth came to her. She shook her head. "Too risky."

"It *does* feel more like the Ponds," Nathaniel said. "No deacons, and we haven't met a soul in days."

"Oh, Nathaniel, don't you start being irresponsible too. We mustn't—"

Thomas jumped up. "I'm going in. I've slept on hard ground for two weeks, and we've nearly run out of food. The shadows are deepening. If we wait much longer, we'll end up hungry and sleeping in a graveyard."

Orah looked at Nathaniel, pleading silently for support, but he stood as well and accompanied Thomas out the gate. She glared after them, but then surveyed her surroundings. Not wishing to be left alone in a cemetery, she followed.

***

Orah had to concede that Riverbend *did* feel familiar, with friendly people and pathways easy to navigate. After a two-minute walk, the dirt road they'd traveled upon passed through the heart of the town, becoming its main street. On one side stood a modest inn and on the other, three single-story shops.

A cask hung above the nearest doorway, the mark of a cooper. The next had a bowl and mug, which, along with the smoke from its kiln, indicated a potter. Much to Orah's relief, the third displayed a shoe that precisely matched the symbol on the scroll. Perhaps for once, they'd find an uneventful episode in their journey to the keep.

Inside, shoes and boots lay scattered across the shelves, and the smell of leather filled the air. In one corner stood a workbench, covered with scraps of hide and an assortment of tools. A girl sat there, tapping away with hammer and awl at a half-soled boot. She glanced up when they entered.

Her youthful face showed she had not yet come of age, and curls hung down to the middle of her back. A white mourning sash lay across her gray vest, and the rims of her eyes appeared raw and red.

An apprentice, for sure. Orah lowered her voice out of respect for the grieving girl. "Excuse me. Is the master shoemaker here?"

The girl set down her tools and rose to greet them, almost making a curtsy. "If you mean my father, no. He's gone."

"When will he be back?" Nathaniel said.

Her voice quivered. "He's gone and will never return. He died two weeks ago and I'm alone."

Orah shuddered as she recalled her own father's passing, and offered the customary response. "May he go to the light everlasting."

The girl's eyes shifted down and to the corners before rising to meet Orah's gaze. "Thank you, ma'am, but if you please, I'm not sure he'd want your blessing. That wasn't his way. I'm Lizbeth. I suppose I'm the master shoemaker now."

Orah shifted uneasily. *Did the keeper pass the scroll on to his daughter, or did he take the secret to his grave? What if we've come all this way to find the chain newly broken?*

Lizbeth misread Orah's discomfort. "Don't be concerned if you need new shoes. I apprenticed to my father since I was little, and he left me with the best of his tools and skills. You won't find better workmanship in the North River valley. Let me show you my wares."

Before she could reach for the shelves, Thomas blurted out what Orah held back. "We didn't come here for your shoes."

Orah tried to cushion his words. "I'm a weaver and, like you, I learned my craft from a loving master. I'm sure your father left much of his skill with you. Excuse us, Lizbeth, we didn't mean to bother you in your grief."

She started to leave, but before she could reach the door, Nathaniel grabbed her arm and whispered, "We need to try." He spun around to the girl. "Please, we had other business with your father."

The girl's eyes widened. "You knew my father? Then you must stay and be my guests. I'd love to speak with anyone who could set his memory firmer in my mind."

"I'm sorry," Orah said. "We never met your father, but we believe he had a passion other than shoes."

"My father lived for his craft. He had no other business."

Nathaniel's shoulders sagged, but Orah pressed on. "None? Look deep into your heart, Lizbeth. We've traveled far to seek him, and you're our only hope."

The girl staggered back a step. After a moment, her tiny hands curled into fists, and she rose up on the balls of her feet, no longer appearing a child. "He taught me all things are possible. Whatever you had to say to him, you may say to me. We are as one."

Orah checked with Nathaniel. When he nodded, she stepped forward and spoke in the same voice she'd used with the spinner. "We have traveled far, but our journey has just begun. The true light drives us on."

The girl's tears began to flow. "He'd waited all his life and now, might I fulfill his wish so soon? I haven't earned it."

Orah grasped her by the arms. "Do you have an answer?"

Lizbeth steadied herself, lifted her chin and announced, "May you find the end you seek, and may the truth you discover hasten a new beginning."

The chain was intact. Relief filled the shop and all embraced.

After some time, the young keeper pulled away and wiped her eyes. "My father hoped you'd come soon, in his lifetime, or all would be lost. When he fell ill, he berated himself for being weak, for failing the seekers and leaving me with such a burden before my time. He feared if the vicars took me for a teaching, I might reveal the secrets, and so he told me little."

Orah grabbed at the thought. "You knew the pass phrase. Did he tell you anything more?"

She nodded. "He cobbled a special boot, just one, not a pair. He said to give it to you if you came."

She slid a chair to the wall, stood on it, and stretched on tiptoes to retrieve a solitary boot from the topmost shelf.

Nathaniel grabbed it before she stepped down. He fumbled inside but found nothing. The girl smiled faintly at his search until he growled in frustration.

"I thought as a seeker, you'd find the scroll with ease." Lizbeth took the boot from Nathaniel and slid the heel back, revealing a hidden compartment. After carefully withdrawing the scroll, she placed it on Nathaniel's outstretched hand.

He rushed to open it.

"Oh, there's nothing to see. My father said you had a way to show the words but were not to tell me."

"Thank you, Lizbeth," Orah said. "We'll take the scroll from here."

Nathaniel held up a hand. "You can help us in one other way. Do you know this region well?"

"Oh, yes, sir. Every spring, I'd go off with my father to take orders for shoes and deliver those purchased. I've traveled all over since I was little."

"Then you can direct us to the next city."

"Please, sir, I don't understand what you mean."

"Leave her be," Orah said. "She doesn't know what's on the scroll."

Lizbeth spun around. "But I do, ma'am. He told me its contents — a four-line verse — but I've never seen the words."

"There must be a city too."

The girl pursed her lips and shook her head. "No, ma'am, that's not what he told me. 'A four-line verse,' he said, 'one piece of the rhyme.' He called it the rhyme that was not, because it did not rhyme. There's nothing else on the scroll, not another mark or word."

Orah opened her mouth to argue when the realization struck. Her face grew warm, and the small hairs on the back of her neck tingled.

She switched her tone to gratitude. "Thank you, Lizbeth. You've given us all we need. Your father would be proud."

Not a mark, not a word. Nothing but the verse.

Lizbeth was the final keeper.

Chapter 20
The Rhyme That Was Not

Though twilight approached, Nathaniel had no urge to rush off from Riverbend. Their two-week trek had worn him down, and he desperately needed a good night's sleep. More importantly, he had no inkling of where to go.

The shoemaker's family had a longstanding relationship with the innkeeper across the way and traveling peddlers who bought shoes for resale stayed as guests at the inn. In exchange, the innkeeper received footwear for his growing children. Lizbeth secured a pleasant room for the three friends, and promised to deliver fresh provisions the next morning.

Nathaniel listened politely as the innkeeper told the story of every amenity in the room—pictures painted by his wife, bed quilts sewn by his grandmother—but as soon as the door closed, he pulled out the scroll.

According to Lizbeth, he held in his hand the final piece of the puzzle, but was acquiring the scrolls enough? The founders of the keep believed the seekers would arise one day, part of a new generation disaffected with the Temple and eager to learn the truth. Yet no such change had occurred. Yes, people feared the vicars, but not enough to fire a revolt. The Temple had ruled for longer than anyone could remember, and no one challenged the established order because no one could imagine a different way. Even he, for all his notions, had never considered opposing the Temple until he met the first keeper.

He quelled his doubts: no sense in worrying his friends.

Before exposing the words on the newest scroll, he tried to temper their expectations. "Fellow seekers, we now have all the scrolls, clues that haven't been joined for centuries, but we shouldn't expect to solve the puzzle in an instant, especially at the end of a long day. No matter what the flame reveals, let's be gentle with ourselves."

He waited for Orah to nod before placing the scroll over the candle. The rhyme appeared as before, but nothing else.

> *One more past four falls in a line*
> *Inside, you must enter and fly*
> *Climb its stairway, fourteen and three*
> *When touched by the lines of the rhyme*

He sighed. The final scroll indeed, but the newest verse was as murky as the rest.

"I know I'm not the one to figure this out," Thomas said, "and I'm exhausted. I'm going to sleep."

Nathaniel agreed. He rolled up the scroll and opened his pack to store it with the others, but Orah snatched it away.

"Leave it," he said. "Solving the puzzle will keep till morning."

"Thank you for your concern, but I want to add this verse to my memory before I sleep, so for the first time, I can see the full rhyme in my dreams."

Too tired to argue, Nathaniel and Thomas readied for bed.

***

After she had snuffed out all the candles save one, Orah studied the verse until the words fixed in her mind. Then she stored the scroll with the others, doused the flame and went to bed.

But not to sleep. She lay awake, listening to the breathing of her friends. The first keeper had warned them not to decipher the partial verses, but now that they'd completed the rhyme, she felt no closer to solving it.

Yet one thought nagged at her, the master shoemaker's remark to his daughter: *My father called it the rhyme that was not, because it did not rhyme.*

134

Orah repeated these words until her eyelids drooped and she fell asleep.

***

Nathaniel awoke to the scrape of wood on the floor. His muddled brain perceived a wraith with a candle gliding across the room, but as his head cleared, he recognized Orah bustling about in the middle of the night.

He jumped to his feet. "What...?"

She'd slid a bench to the center of the room, taken three candles from their bedsides and a fourth from a sconce on the wall, and set them on the bench in a row. As she lit the first candle and proceeded to light the others, their reflection made her eyes glow.

"Get the frame," she said.

For weeks, Nathaniel had carried the frame attached to his pack. He hurried to retrieve it now.

Thomas awakened as well and fetched the scrolls.

Orah wedged them in, starting from top to bottom, and then directed the others to align the four over the candles. The room dimmed as the scrolls obscured the candlelight and they waited for the words to appear.

"Hold still," she said. "I'll need a minute."

Nathaniel examined the verses. They seemed as incomprehensible as before.

> To the North, behind the rock face
> To the East, towering o'er the lake
> To the North, through forest of stone
> To the East, the entrance shall be
> ~~~
> Twixt water and dark walls of pine
> A cave made by men who must die
> The Temple of Truth you shall see
> Golden doors that are closed for all time
> ~~~
> For a full eight days you shall race
> Two doors to the mouth of the snake
> Once great, it now stands alone

135

Sixteen stars shall set the doors free
~~~

One more past four falls in a line
Inside, you must enter and fly
Climb its stairway, fourteen and three
When touched by the lines of the rhyme

Orah's eyes stayed riveted on the scrolls. Her expression evolved from studious to intense, through an instant of worry, and ultimately to triumph. All the while, she muttered what sounded like an incantation. "Not rhyming yet, but I'll beat you and forge you until you rhyme."

Nathaniel watched, worrying her mind had snapped from the strain.

After another minute, she eased into a smile. "I have it. Face rhymes with race, lake with snake. To make a proper rhyme, take the first line of each quartet and place them together, and then do the same with the second, third and fourth."

"What are you talking about?" Thomas said.

"Recite the words using only the first lines. Then do the same with the second and so forth. Like this." She chanted like a vicar during the blessing.

To the North, behind the rock face
Twixt water and dark walls of pine
For a full eight days you shall race
One more past four falls in a line
~~~

To the East, towering o'er the lake
A cave made by men who must die
Two doors to the mouth of the snake
Inside, you must enter and fly
~~~

To the North, through forest of stone
The Temple of Truth you shall see
Once great, it now stands alone
Climb its stairway, fourteen and three
~~~

To the East, the entrance shall be
Golden doors that are closed for all time
Sixteen stars shall set the doors free

When touched by the lines of the rhyme
Nathaniel blinked, but before he could react, Orah confirmed his suspicion. "I don't yet understand every word, but at least the verses rhyme, and now we know their purpose."

Thomas cast about curiously.

Nathaniel explained. "The directions to the keep."

***

In an underground chamber in Temple City, the arch vicar's eyes probed the faces of his younger colleagues. None bore his gaze for long. *To the darkness with the politics of the Temple.*

The voice from the box at the center of the table droned on. "After further investigation, we find you blameworthy for taking undue risk without council approval. Do you wish to say anything in your defense?"

The arch vicar pulled the transmitter close, wary of admitting guilt in front of his underlings. "The situation demanded action. As senior vicar on the scene, I had the authority."

He shot a glance at the others. One of them had betrayed him to the council in an attempt to besmirch his record. He detected nothing but a shift in the eyes of the new monsignor, who had formerly ministered to the Ponds. Perhaps he'd only imagined it. They'd all mastered the mask of calm in the seminary.

The box on the table buzzed. "Nevertheless, our ruling stands. From now on, we trust you'll keep us informed as this matter progresses."

This matter. You treat it like a piece of bookkeeping. Don't you know the stakes? He understood the temptation of unfettered thought, as he himself had been tempted. When promoted to bishop and granted access to the archives, he'd been drawn to the underground rooms, where he spent long nights studying the past. Only after years did he realize the truth—one could not separate the thirst for knowledge from the lust for power. His kind needed to be kept simple. Better ignorance than chaos, better innocence than violent death—that was the lesson of the darkness.

The voice in the box cared only for "this matter," and pandered to its superior. "Holiness, do you have anything to add?"

The grand vicar spoke next. "We trust you appreciate our concerns. This issue has broad implications for the future of the Temple."

The arch vicar scoffed. The awe the old man evoked in others surprised him. He'd never been impressed.

"Your record until now has been exemplary," the grand vicar continued. "Please ensure no repeat of this offense. Blessed be the light."

The spectacle had ended, and the assembled began to rise. The arch vicar checked their faces for a hint of gloating, but the politics of the seminary prevailed.

So clerical affairs have devolved to this—better to avoid mistakes than take risk. Cowards and fools. None but he would have acted with such boldness, and none but he would reap the rewards when at last he found the greatest threat to the Temple.

The young people from Little Pond were leading him to the keep. When they found it, he'd be the one to destroy it, making the Temple and humanity safe for all time.

Chapter 21
The Rock Face

Orah awoke to a knocking at the door. She staggered across the room and fumbled to release the latch.

The shoemaker's daughter barged in, bearing three bulky bags of provisions. "This is all I could gather in so short a time —" She stopped, spun on her heels and glanced about the room.

What must she be thinking? Midmorning and the seekers still sleeping like shiftless drifters.

The bench that had rested against the wall now stood in the center of the floor, with four spent candles stuck to its surface and their melted wax forming a sequence of mystical patterns. Considering the scene, the girl's reaction seemed muted.

Orah steadied Lizbeth with both hands and gave her a kiss on the cheek. "Good morning. We overslept. With so much to consider, we stayed up late."

"If you please, ma'am, my place is to serve."

Orah nearly urged the girl to call her by name — no one had ever addressed her so formally — but she recalled her own brief stay in the teaching cell and shuddered. The less Lizbeth knew, the better.

As Orah's senses cleared, she became aware of a clamor outside and went to the window to check. A crowd of people milled about on the street below.

139

"What's going on?"

"Don't you remember?" Lizbeth said. "Today's the first of May, the Festival of Light."

Orah shot Thomas a glance, hoping to keep him from showing the seekers' ignorance of the local custom. She leapt in before he could disillusion the girl. "Of course we remember, but we've been on the road so long we've lost track of the date."

Thomas swung his feet to the floor and stretched in a yawn. "And where we come from, festival's celebrated a bit differently."

Lizbeth smiled. "Here in Riverbend, people travel from all over. We play games in the afternoon, followed by a feast. You're welcome to come. With so many visitors, no one will spot you for strangers, and you'll find plenty of food."

"Thank you," Orah said, "but you've done a great deal for us already. We can't ask for more. In any event, our mission's pressing and won't wait. We should take our provisions and be on our way."

"Leaving so soon?" Lizbeth arranged the bags on Orah's bed and counted them a second time. "I hoped you'd stay for the parade."

"I'd love to stay for the parade," Thomas said, "and the food as well."

Orah glared him into silence, and then peeked past the curtain at the crowd. She considered the first lines of the rhyme.

> *To the North, behind the rock face*
> *Twixt water and dark walls of pine*
> *For a full eight days you shall race*

A possible interpretation: head north past an outcropping of rock, to a road along the river with a well-treed cliff on the opposite side.

She hoped to learn more from Lizbeth about the surrounding area, but pictured the girl in a darkness cell. Her questions required a circumspect approach. "Where do these people come from?"

"From all over, ma'am. From villages and farms to the east and west and south."

"None from the north?"

"No, ma'am. The North River blocks the way. It's impassable at any time of year, but especially now when the water's high."

"No bridge?"

"No bridge and no road. No one ever crosses the river."

Thinking Lizbeth had misunderstood the question, Orah tried a different approach. "How do people travel to towns in the north?"

Lizbeth's brows rose and her eyes widened. Orah guessed at her thoughts. Her father had foretold of the wise seekers. How could they know so little about the world?

"There are no towns to the north. On the far side of the river you'll find only wilderness. From Riverbend, we have only the road going west to east."

Orah tapped her teeth with the tip of her thumb. *No passage north? The rhyme seemed clear on this point.* Then a new thought occurred to her. "Why do you call it the North River if it runs west to east?"

"Oh, if you please, ma'am, because it does run north. A ten minute walk east of here, the river takes a sharp turn and goes off into the wilderness — the bend that gives our town its name."

Orah suppressed a grin and nodded to the others, but she was reluctant to probe further.

Nathaniel jumped in. "Where the river turns, does a road run alongside?"

"No, sir, nothing but the road that goes east." Lizbeth heaved a sigh. "No one wants to go north. It's nothing but a barren wasteland."

Best to change the subject before the questioning becomes too explicit. Orah focused on the rock face, a term that might imply a hidden trail behind a cliff. "This is such lovely country, Lizbeth — so green with rolling hills. Is the surrounding area like this, or does it change?"

"Thank you, ma'am. The terrain's the same as far as I've traveled."

"No cliffs or rocky ledges? Where we're from, the mountains turn to slabs of stone above the tree line."

"We have hills but no mountains, and few exposed rocks. That's all the landscape I've ever seen." Her eyes drooped at the corners, and her smile turned into a frown. "You ask a lot of curious questions. Why so much concern about rocky ledges and roads that go into the wilderness?"

Realizing she'd pressed as far as possible, Orah signaled for the others to let the girl go. The three lined up to thank her, wish her well, and say their goodbyes.

After Lizbeth departed, Orah stared out the window at the gathering crowd and beyond them, to the trees at the edge of the town.

141

They'd found the final keeper and had in their possession all the pieces to the puzzle. She'd unraveled the verses and mastered the rhyme. Now, the keepmasters directed them to head north into a wilderness with no road and no people.

No choice but to take the next step.

They'd proceed to the bend in the river and search for a rock face, a dark wall, or any hint of a trail heading north.

***

At Nathaniel's urging, Orah gave in to Thomas's nagging and let him watch the parade. They were about to head off into a wilderness filled with towers, caves and snakes that fly, with no notion of how long they'd be gone. So she hefted her pack, prayed for luck, and followed the others down to the inn's common room and out the front door.

The sun shone high overhead as throngs lined the main street. Riverbend's elders had arranged excited children in rows on the opposite side. Each held a stick in one hand, the thickness of a broom handle and half as long.

Music drifted on the air, and soon Orah spotted a large drum decorated with red and green ribbons. It boomed with a sound deeper than the Little Pond drum, and people clapped to its beat. Other instruments appeared as the parade approached. Sunlight reflected off one fashioned from brass. A player pressed his lips to its end and blew, puffing his cheeks out with each breath to make a braying sound, harsher than Thomas's flute and much louder. A second player grasped what looked like a saucepan with bells affixed to its edges, and shook it in time with the drum.

Behind the musicians came men in white masks with skull-like sockets for eyes. Each held a pole with a creature on top, made of pressed rag pulp and painted black. These resembled no animal in the Ponds, and their warts and horns and fangs made Orah shudder. The adults hooted and the children waved their sticks.

The leader of the troubadours held up a hand. The parade halted and the crowd hushed.

"Children of light." He sounded like a vicar. "The creatures of the darkness come to defile your Temple. What say you?"

A wave of jeering spread across the crowd.

"Will you destroy the creatures of the darkness?"

They responded with loud cheers.

"Bring them forward."

The men in masks held up their poles. Adults counted out five children, tied brightly-colored scarfs about their eyes, and positioned them, each one in front of a creature. When given the word, the children swung their sticks until they found their mark. The creatures shattered as they were struck, and sweets tumbled to the ground from their insides. Following a few additional thumps for good measure, the children removed their blindfolds and fell on all fours to gather their reward. Then the next five took their place.

Orah wavered, unsure whether to take pleasure in this game or shudder at its meaning.

Thomas leaned close and spoke in his most melodramatic voice, but softly to avoid being overheard. "Then the seekers, agents of the darkness, go forth to undermine the light."

Orah elbowed him in the ribs so hard the air puffed out from his lungs.

Yet he wasn't far from the truth. Their mission placed them at odds not only with the Temple, but with their whole world.

***

Nathaniel stood behind his friends, taking in the parade. *Nothing more than children's games.* He checked past the players to the opposite side, trying to gauge the mood of the crowd. He detected no yelps of fear or sneers of hatred. Like his neighbors in Little Pond, the people of Riverbend used their festival to celebrate.

As he scanned the crowd, he noticed several men keeping apart, clearly strangers. Although dressed like everyone else, they stood with backs too straight and bearings too formal, and their expressions showed no pleasure at the festivities.

Deacons — out of uniform, but deacons nevertheless.

The tallest among them turned, and their eyes met. Nathaniel tensed, but the man's posture never changed. He stared for no more than a second and glanced away.

Nathaniel tapped Orah on the shoulder. "We need to leave. Now!"

He eased them from the crowd until they rounded a corner, and then took off at a sprint.

***

Orah slowed to a stop at the bend in the river. No enemies marched on the road ahead, and she saw no pursuit from behind.

"Deacons so near?" she said as she caught her breath. "Then why haven't they followed? Either you're mistaken or they failed to recognize us."

Nathaniel lowered his pack to the ground, and his face turned grim. "I don't know, but we need to find this path north... in a hurry."

Orah surveyed the countryside. The sole feature worth noting stood a hundred paces ahead, well past the turn—a nondescript boulder, twice as tall as Nathaniel and wider than his arm-span, but far from the mysterious cliff that hid the trail to the keep.

Thomas saw it as well. "That's the only rock we've seen for days other than pebbles. How will we find a rock face in this terrain?"

They split up to search, but even with her most vivid imagination, Orah found no hint of a trail. On the one side, the riverbank fell so steeply as to deny footing, threatening to cast a wayward traveler into the current. On the other, the prickly scrub grew so thick a child would struggle to slip through. Her every attempt ended with an assortment of cuts and scratches.

At last, they regrouped where the river turned, resting on the roadside and nursing their wounds.

Thomas flung a handful of dirt at the trees. "No path there. An eight-day trip through those woods would take a lifetime."

"We'll find it," Orah said. "We just need more time."

"More time? With deacons on our trail?"

She refused to be goaded and turned away.

Thomas tempered his tone. "I'm sorry, Orah, I didn't mean to sound like it's your fault."

Nathaniel rested a hand on her shoulder and glared at Thomas. "You might help by suggesting a solution rather than always pointing out our problems."

"You two are the smart ones. Where are *your* ideas?"

144

Orah's neck ached and her head began to throb. She closed her eyes and took a cleansing breath. "A month of travel and deacons nearby will fray our nerves. Let's remember why we came. The founders hid the keep to protect it from the vicars. As the true seekers, we're tasked to find it, no matter how hard. We mustn't get discouraged or give up."

Thomas drew small circles in the soft earth. "I'm not saying to give up, but so much time has passed. The scrolls may never age, but the rest of the world does. Trees grow. Soil gets washed away and weeds fill in. The road from the rhyme may long ago have vanished."

Orah wandered off, unable to bear another word. She ambled along to the east, searching the woods for inspiration. A sniff of the air brought only the scent of the pines, and the gentle breeze carried only the rush of the river and the caw of a distant crow. After a hundred paces, she threw her hands into the air and gave up. Any path would have to be nearer the river.

As she turned back, something about the large boulder struck her. She squinted and let out a cry. "The rock."

Nathaniel and Thomas leapt to their feet and ran toward her. She held out a trembling finger as they came near.

"What about the rock?" Thomas said.

"Not from that side. From over here."

They crept closer, eyeing the rock but not turning until they'd reached her.

"Now let your minds roam free."

Nathaniel's fists unclenched when he saw no danger there, but Thomas recognized it first. "It looks like the head of a man."

From where she stood, the rock had taken on the appearance of an old man in profile, with an overarching brow and a great beard, staring out with wisdom for the ages.

Orah renewed her faith in the founders of the keep and prayed to never doubt them again. From now on, she'd avoid relying on the obvious. They'd found no trace of a cliff or a stony ledge, but here before them stood the rock face of the rhyme.

Chapter 22
Water and Dark Walls

The terrain behind the boulder bristled with thick brush, but Orah could picture its past. On either side, a line of ancient trees rose higher than the scrub in the center, setting the boundary for what once must have been a major road. This terrain, directly behind the rock face, convinced her they'd found the way north, though its passage remained challenging.

She fought through bushes as high as her waist, many with thorns that grabbed her pack and snagged her clothes. After a few dozen yards, she twisted her ankle, staggered, and nearly fell.

Nathaniel caught her. "What happened?"

"Not sure. Something hard on the ground, hidden in the brush."

A few steps later, Thomas stumbled as well. Nathaniel groped through the undergrowth and picked up a chunk of strange rock. Its flat black surface contrasted with an underside pitted with gravel, seemingly stuck together with glue.

He held the rock up for Orah. "What do you make of this?"

"I've never seen anything like it. Are there others?"

Nathaniel kicked around and found a half-dozen more. The fragments seemed to fit together like pieces of a puzzle.

As he passed them around, he wondered aloud. "They seem man-made, but for what purpose?"

Orah let her fingertips glide along the smooth surface. "Possibly a layer to harden the road."

"Why would anybody bother?" Thomas said. "That's a lot of work to avoid muddy boots."

Orah scanned ahead, trying to imagine a thousand-year-old roadway covered with black rock. "At least they provide some good. Along with the high tree line, these rocks will guide our way. Let's just watch our step."

After half an hour, road and river converged. Walking eased where seasonal flooding had thinned the vegetation and washed away any sign of black rock. Ahead Orah spotted where the trail left the river and started to climb.

What if the river becomes inaccessible?

They each carried two water skins—enough for three days if the weather stayed mild. The rhyme claimed they'd reach the falls in eight days. If they had no access to water before then, they'd face a dry march.

They stopped to refill their skins at the last clearing before the trail rose. Orah welcomed the respite. She'd battled both the terrain and her own doubts since leaving Riverbend, but now they'd left the deacons behind, and the best tracker would struggle to follow. Their path seemed more certain, and she tried to relax.

What a beautiful spot. The sun dappled the river with sparkles, and a rushing sound filled the air.

"The current's much stronger than the Ponds," Thomas said. "If I tried to swim here, I'd be swept away."

Orah gazed north as if trying to see to the river's source. "The water comes from snow melting in the highlands, and is strongest in spring."

"Where does it go?"

"Maybe as far as Little Pond, or all the way to Nathaniel's mythical ocean."

She rested on the bank and admired the river battling to reach its goal. The torrent struggled around rocks that jutted out everywhere, and frothed about the roots of trees that inexplicably grew in the stream.

Thomas hacked off a twig with his pocketknife and tossed it into the water. As the current carried it away, it inspired another idea. He cut a second branch and made a dramatic slash in its bark. "A mark for our first day. Seven more and we'll be at the falls, and soon thereafter, the keep." He smiled and tucked the improvised calendar into his pack.

But Thomas's good feeling eluded Orah. She stared at the water and brooded.

Nathaniel tapped her with the toe of his boot. "What now?"

"Something's not right. Things fit together too well."

"What do you mean?"

"Why haven't we been caught?"

"Because you're both so clever," Thomas said, "and the deacons are fools."

Orah shook her head. "Or they're smarter than we think. When they passed us on the road outside Little Pond, they made more noise than usual for people on the hunt. In Adamsville, the old keeper heard them blocks away, and they stood at the door and shouted when they could have easily shoved past. The notice sent to the vicar of Bradford said if he saw us, he should notify the Temple but not detain us. Now, at Riverbend, the deacons spotted us but let us go."

"You think all that's deliberate?" Nathaniel said. "Why?"

"I'd guess they want to follow, to scare us a bit but not stop us."

"We've worked so hard to avoid being tracked," Thomas said. "All those days in the thicket, those nights in the woods, and the deacons appeared mostly within sight of towns. How could they follow from so far back?"

"I'm not sure, Thomas, but... Nathaniel only broke his promise to become a vicar, a sin too small to set the entire Temple after us." She flicked a stone into the stream. "I'm afraid they know about the keep."

A cloud of gloom settled over them.

Orah studied the river as if seeking an answer in its flow. "A way to follow without being seen. Something I'd never have believed possible before Bradford."

The waters streamed past like the days of her life, some as smooth as springtime before Thomas's teaching, and others raging like the morning they fled Temple City. She recalled her fury when Nathaniel appeared with the gleaming pack on his back.

The pack. She jumped up and turned to Nathaniel. "Can I look in your pack?"

"If you like, but what do you expect to find?"

"It's our only possession that was in the hands of the deacons."

Nathaniel fetched his pack and emptied its contents on the ground. Both Orah and Thomas took turns poking around inside, checking each compartment to no avail.

"Nothing," Thomas said. "Your imagination's gone wild. Deacons make us all nervous. I'll help repack." He picked up a bundle of dried meat.

Orah grabbed the pack before he could store it. "There must be something."

She grasped the leather lining and yanked it bottom up. As her fingers caressed the seams, she cried out. "Thomas, give me your pocketknife."

Nathaniel stared at the spot where her fingers lingered. "I don't see anything."

"That's because you relied on me to make coats for you. Look here."

She dragged the pack into the sunlight. A patch of fresh leather clearly showed, distinct from its more worn surroundings and held in place by fine, nearly invisible stitching.

Thomas handed her his knife. She picked off the threads without marking the leather, peeled away the lining and pulled out a stone cast in the shape of a star.

She held it up to the light. "A deacon's star. Now we know how they followed."

"But there are no temple trees in the wilderness," Thomas said, doing his best to cling to the fleeting sense of safety.

"No, but we passed one near the bend in the river, close to where we entered the wilderness." She turned to Nathaniel. "What should we do?"

"Bury the cursed thing," Thomas said, "so no one will find it."

"We can't. The signal would keep on and lead them to this spot. We mustn't let them discover the trail."

Thomas took two flat rocks. He laid one on the ground and held the other poised above. "Put it here. I'll crush it to end the signal."

"A worse plan. They've already tracked us nearby. Destroying the star would tell them we found it and speed up the chase."

"Then how will we escape?"

Orah considered a moment before handing him back his knife. "My dear Thomas, can you and your pocketknife whittle me a very small boat?"

Thomas understood at once and soon had assembled a dozen interlocked twigs into a raft small enough to fit in the palm of his hand. Orah bound them together with twine and placed the device in its center, then wove additional netting to stretch across the top.

"There, the device will float downstream, even if flipped in the current. Since the river runs along the road, we'll give our deacons something to follow."

"Brilliant," Thomas said with a nervous laugh. "Now we've lost them for good."

Nathaniel stepped forward and took the boat, which looked tiny in his big hands. "I'm afraid not. Sending the star down river gives us only a reprieve. Eventually, the raft will get caught on the rocks or be grounded. Our little trick might confuse them for a while, but once it stops, they'll figure out the ruse and return to Riverbend with a vengeance."

Thomas's gaze flitted about as if the deacons were already near. "Then can we never be safe?"

Orah wrapped an arm around him. "We'll be safe in the keep, Thomas. The keepmasters were the wisest ever and will know how to protect us."

With a flip of his wrist, Nathaniel tossed the boat into the stream.

Orah watched as the current whisked their latest threat away— another danger avoided, another obstacle overcome.

She stared until the little package vanished round the bend, then glanced up and noted the sun racing across the sky. "We'd best start moving. The farther we get from here, the better."

Nathaniel refilled his pack and headed toward the trail, but a sudden need to bless such an important moment made her call him back.

"We can spare ten seconds." She urged them to gather round, glanced up to the sky and raised her arms. "Praise the sun, giver of life. Grant us success in our search. Guide us together safely to the keep."

Thomas gaped at her. "Isn't the keep the opposite of the light?"

"No, Thomas, the keep is the opposite of the Temple. That makes all the difference."

They donned their packs and moved out.

From the first step the trail rose, and the land to their left dropped off. Soon they had climbed to a ledge above the water, wide enough for all three to walk abreast. To their right, the hillside banked steeply, covered by tamarack pines soaring to the sky. Their naked trunks rose fifty feet or more before branches emerged, providing a thick canopy. Where the odd gap appeared between them, hardy spruce filled in, adding a blue tinge.

Orah gazed to the north. With the river rushing on one side and the forest rising on the other, she recognized at last the vision of the rhyme. For a full eight days they must race on this well-marked path, 'twixt water and dark walls of pine.

Chapter 23
The Falls

The trail soon leveled and travel eased. With the mild weather and a wind wafting from behind, Orah led at a brisk pace, the trio stopping only for meals and an occasional drink. Their progress convinced her they'd beat the time foretold in the rhyme.

By the second day, curiosity rather than weariness slowed them down. Here, far from the world she knew, lay remnants of an older civilization—things foreign to her, which she tried her best to understand.

Along a well-protected section of trail, a line of tall poles rose at hundred pace intervals, each with the girth of a tree trunk but unnaturally straight. A shiny gray coating suggested they were man-formed, if not man-made, and all appeared planted in place for no reason.

Nathaniel rapped on one with his knuckles, and it made a hollow sound. "I wonder what these were supposed to be."

"Look," Thomas said, pointing to their tops. "Some have lengths of black rope hanging from them."

He found a sample on the ground nearby, and wrapped one end around each hand and pulled. The cord proved lightweight and supple but extraordinarily strong. He took out his pocketknife and tried to cut through. The black skin peeled away, revealing a hard inner core with the same texture as the scrolls.

From the top of the next pole, a hundred-foot stretch dangled intact. Thomas grabbed the nearest loop and yanked, but the other end stayed stubbornly attached.

"Come help, Nathaniel."

"Just leave it."

"You can never tell when a sturdy rope might come in handy. You're the strongest. Give a tug."

Nathaniel braced himself and pulled. The rope hardly budged.

Thomas approached the pole and wrapped his arms around it, testing his grip. "I'll climb up to release it."

"You'll do nothing of the sort," Orah said. "It's too dangerous."

"If we're caught, they'll lock me in a teaching cell until I go mad, and you're worried about a fall? Nathaniel, give me a lift."

Nathaniel cupped both hands and boosted Thomas ten feet up the pole. His nimble friend clambered up, clutching hand and footholds in the weathered surface, and reached the fastening in seconds. With two twists, the rope was free.

Nathaniel coiled their find and offered to carry it, but Thomas insisted on bearing the prize himself.

The next day, looking down the embankment, Orah noticed the remains of a covered bridge. The roof had collapsed, revealing a surface made of the mysterious black rock. Two reinforced tracks lay on top, too far apart for the wheels of a cart—another riddle from the mysterious past.

After three days, the trail began to climb, tracking the river toward its mountain source. The slope rose so gradually she detected it not in her legs but as a chill in the air. Farther down, the tips of pine boughs displayed the bright green of new spring growth, but here the needles remained dark. Patches of old snow increasingly dotted the hillside, sheltered in gullies and beneath the shadows of trees.

On the morning of the fourth day, the trail rose more quickly. For now, the river appeared accessible, but possibly for the last time. Orah jiggled her water skin. Only a couple of mouthfuls sloshed inside.

She turned to Thomas. "Can you climb down to the river?"

He eyed the embankment. "I can climb down, but maybe not back up, especially hauling skins full of water."

"What if we used your rope?"

He grinned. "I knew you'd find a reason for bringing me along."

Orah had him tie the rope around his waist, and she and Nathaniel eased his descent. They then used it to lower the empty skins and pull up the full ones. At last, it served to secure Thomas. They braced themselves to support their friend, but he scrambled up like a goat, scarcely breathing hard. Orah never sensed tension on the line.

***

Despite his misgivings, Thomas had to admit the venture was going well. They'd found all four keepers, and though he still fretted about the rhyme, he trusted Orah would solve the puzzle in the end. She always did. The deacon's star would be far away by now, hopefully carried all the way to Nathaniel's ocean. Best of all, he'd found small ways to help his friends.

If only he could shake off the vision of three vicars, sitting at their high bench and spying on his every move.

Near sunset of the fifth day, the rains came and the temperature dropped—a last gasp of winter. A wind from the west lifted droplets from the river and turned them to pellets of ice. The sleet stung his face as he huddled behind Nathaniel and did his best not to complain, but the footing became treacherous.

He cried out over the winds, "We have to stop. We can't go on."

"We can't stop in the open," Orah said. "Too risky."

He cupped his hands around his eyes and glanced beyond Nathaniel. "There's an outcropping ahead. We can crouch beneath it, put blankets up and tie them down with the rope."

Orah wavered but then agreed.

The three hurried to the overhang and removed their packs. Thomas uncoiled the rope while the others pulled out blankets. Within minutes, they'd built a makeshift shelter and huddled inside.

Darkness settled in, and Thomas felt more than exposed on the ledge. The blankets flapped in the wind like walls closing in, and the air grew heavy, as if a millstone weighed on his chest.

He forced himself to breathe, and pulled out the calendar stick to give his hands something to do. Careful not to cut anyone in the close quarters, he made a slash.

"One, two, three, four, five. Only three days left to the falls."

Orah moaned. "Three more days this close to you and I'll go crazy."

Nathaniel countered. "That's assuming we survive the night."

As if in response, a gust of wind ripped loose their covering. They scrambled to grab the blankets and tie them down more securely. The blast of cold air combined with the exertion made breathing strained.

Thomas lay still, catching his breath and listening to the creaking of the pines. Finally, he wondered aloud. "It's as if the forces of darkness are conspiring to stop us."

"I don't believe in the forces of darkness anymore," Orah said. "That's not what frightens me."

"Then what *are* you afraid of?"

"That we'll come all this way and fail. That the secret of the keepers will be lost. That we'll never find the keep."

The thought hung in the air, competing with the wind to chill them. Thomas studied their profiles in the dark. Even Orah had doubts. Even Nathaniel had fears.

When he spoke at last, the certainty in his voice surprised him. "Do you know what I believe? I believe in my friends. I believe we're the true seekers and we'll find the keep... or at least Orah will find it for us."

Orah said nothing, but leaned in and gave him a kiss on the cheek.

After a few minutes, the storm blew past. The wind calmed and the drumming on the blankets quieted.

Orah eased into a smile. "We may survive the night after all."

Survive the night. Maybe Orah is right. What if the keepmasters possess magic stronger than the vicars? The keepmasters will keep us safe.

Thomas peeked outside the blanket and made a small bow to his friends. "I never doubted it, but what happens when we find the keep? What do the keepmasters expect of us? When a seeker finds what he seeks, what does he become?"

All fell silent, lost in their own thoughts.

The next morning, the trees bore an icy glaze that made their boughs sparkle, and the rising sun melted the sleet on the trail. Orah had them collect water from the dripping branches, enough to last until the seventh day. They'd go thirsty after that.

He licked his lips, recalling the thirst of his teaching. He hoped they'd reach the falls soon and find them—unlike the rock face—to be real.

***

From high above the river, Orah spotted the lake that must have been its source, a vast body several times the size of Great Pond. Shortly, the breeze bore a hopeful sound from ahead, growing louder as they approached—the whoosh of rushing water. She picked up her pace, determined to forego their normal rest.

No one spoke as they focused on the sounds of their own hurried breathing, and on the unceasing roar of the falls.

Around the next bend, her optimism faded. Tree limbs and debris lay scattered across the trail where the hillside had ripped away, likely during the recent storm. Of bigger concern, a boulder too broad and sheer to pass around had blocked most of the trail, leaving a scant foot's width of path between it and the drop-off.

The slope down appeared treacherous, and the cliff to their right too steep to climb. Behind them, they'd find no water for days, and their skins hung empty from their packs.

Nathaniel prodded the rock. The boulder had lodged itself firmly in the path, far too heavy to move.

He glanced at Orah, but she had no guidance to offer. Turning back meant the unthinkable, abandoning the search for the keep. They had only one choice—the way forward.

Nathaniel insisted she go first as the slightest and least likely to disrupt the ground. She secured the rope around her waist, while he grasped the other end and braced.

She patted his hand. "Don't drop me, Nathaniel."

"I'll do my best. We don't want to lose our best seeker." Once set, he nodded.

Orah passed around the boulder, clutching its every knob, sliding her small feet painstakingly from side to side. After she cleared the rock, she threw the rope to Thomas, who did the same. Then both grabbed the end and waited for Nathaniel.

He tossed the remaining rope across to their side.

156

"What are you doing?" she cried.

"If I fall, I'd only pull the two of you down with me. Better I cross alone."

He stood out of view, blocked by the boulder, so she shouted across to him, "If you fall, Nathaniel, you better die, because if not, I'm coming down to kill you."

As he started around, she closed her eyes and prayed to the light, knowing his feet were too big for the space and his heels would hang over the edge. A yelp from the far side made her jump. Pebbles skidded off the path and echoed as they tumbled to the valley below. She peeked around and caught Nathaniel balancing on one foot as he groped for cracks in the stone. The misstep had created a hole the size of her fist.

"Stay with me, Nathaniel. Don't look down."

He finally shifted around the hole. Then one step, two more, and he was across.

She grabbed him as soon as he reached solid ground. "Don't ever do that again."

"I don't plan to if I can—" An expression of wonder crossed his face as he glanced past her.

"What now?" She could handle no more surprises.

He began laughing. "Look behind you."

Less than a minute ahead, the first of the falls plummeted from the slope above all the way down to the lake below.

Another obstacle? No, thank the light. The cascade shot out over the cliff face while the trail passed dry underneath.

A few paces farther and she saw them all. This time at least, the rhyme was literal. Before her lay four falls in a line.

Despite her disapproval, Thomas stuck his face out under the nearest torrent and emerged with his cheeks red.

"The water's freezing," he said, "but delicious."

***

Orah suggested they camp between the falls. As the day ended, the wind stilled and the clouds evaporated. Soon, stars flickered into being one at a time, until they sparkled in clusters throughout the heavens. Behind the seekers, the thickly-treed slope had turned black, obscuring the ridgeline from the darkened sky. The mountains to the west had grayed, but a lingering glow radiated from their peaks. Shortly after, a full moon rose, fat and orange on the horizon, climbing until its beams shed a path of gilded glass across the lake below.

Thomas pulled out his flute, but before playing, he checked with Orah. "Are we far enough from the vicars now?"

She laughed. "I don't think they could hear you even with their communication devices."

"Then with your permission, may I serenade my friends?"

She glanced at Nathaniel and both nodded.

Thomas began slowly, but with each passing note he poured more of his being into the instrument. He played a tune of sadness and hope. The song flowed into the air and hung over the valley, matching the light of the stars.

That night, they slept to the sound of rushing water. One more day and they'd be done with the first verse, but Orah worried more about the second. Would it be literal like the falls or symbolic like the rock face?

She gazed out over the river valley and silently mouthed the words:

> To the East, towering o'er the lake
> A cave made by men who must die
> Two doors to the mouth of the snake
> Inside, you must enter and fly

Chapter 24

The Iron Snake

Orah started the next morning with a hearty breakfast. They had food enough for only two days, but one extra serving would make little difference, and they'd earned a decent meal. She doled out a double portion of meat and flatbread to her friends, but ate less herself, offering the remainder to Thomas. When they finished, they filled their water skins from the falls and set off.

The day progressed without care except for the second verse, which she analyzed constantly. "The first part's obvious. We're looking for a man-made cave high up on the hillside to our right."

"So you told us," Thomas said. "Five times."

"I'm trying to fathom the rest, the part about the snake and flying."

"Don't worry so much," Nathaniel said. "For six weeks, we've faced each step as it comes. Wait till we find the cave."

"I know, but I like to be prepared, especially when giant snakes are involved."

Then she'd recite the verse again.

The trek to the falls had taken the predicted eight days. According to the rhyme, they should find the cave after one more day, so by late afternoon, she hardly flinched at the sight of a man-made tower looming ahead.

"*To the East, towering o'er the lake,*" she announced. "Below is the lake and here is our tower."

The stone tower rose some sixty feet and, like so much of the old civilization, was crumbling with age. She scanned to its top and saw at once what lay there—a platform forming the entrance to a cave. She shifted her gaze, cupping a hand over her eyes to filter the glare, and studied the far side of the river valley.

After a moment, she drew in a sharp breath and pointed. "Look there."

The others followed her gesture. To the west, hundreds of paces away, lay a mirror image of the tower and cave.

Thomas scrunched his nose and rubbed the stubble of his scraggly beard. "What do you suppose that means?"

She smiled her I-know-the-answer smile. "It means the old masters had few limits. The vicar of Bradford described an age of innovation and genius. We're looking at one of their miracles."

"What're you talking about?"

"They must have built a road to cross the valley, suspended between the two towers. The tunnel cut through the mountain on the far side and reentered here."

Thomas gaped at one cave and then the other. "Impossible. A thousand men couldn't build such a thing."

She patted his arm. "Before we're done, Thomas, we may have to redefine impossible."

Once the friends got over their wonder, she turned her attention to the next challenge: how to scale the tower. She discovered iron rungs embedded in the back side of the stone, the lowest within Nathaniel's grasp, but when he tried to pull himself up, the rusted metal broke apart in his hand.

The two of them studied the problem, debating solutions, while Thomas circled the base.

At last he spoke up. "I can climb it."

Orah stopped mid-sentence. "What did you say?"

"I said I can climb it. The bricks on the outside may have crumbled, but they left holes to a solid core. The rungs have rusted, but the fasteners remain." He scanned the length of the tower, and he nodded to himself. "I know every hole and fastener I'd use. Once at the top, I can secure one end of the rope and drop the rest down to help you two up."

Nathaniel eyed the tower and then Thomas, letting the idea sink in.

Orah checked the angle of the sun. "All right, we'll try it your way... but not now. Too dangerous so late in the day."

"But—"

"I won't start now, Thomas. We're already tired, and if we have a problem, we'll be solving it in the dark. Better first thing in the morning, especially with a giant snake at the top."

***

Early the next morning, Orah regarded the tower and pondered. Elders long gone and with extraordinary powers had laid out this path, but what if the seekers had taken too long to emerge?

The tower offered a good example. Had the seekers come sooner, they could have used the ladder to climb up, but now success depended on the agility of a nimble seventeen-year-old.

Thomas coiled the rope around his left shoulder, leaving his right arm free, and headed to the base.

She followed uneasily.

He grinned. "Move aside. You won't be able to catch me if I fall, and you'll only get hurt."

Her eyes widened. "Maybe we should find a safer way."

Thomas winked. "Stop worrying. This'll be easy."

He jumped on Nathaniel's shoulders and stood exactly as he'd done with a different tall boy years before at festival. After steadying, he scampered up, using the grooves in the stone and the fasteners of the ladder. In less than a minute, he reached the top.

He waved to his friends, attached one end of the rope to a tree, and lowered the rest.

That morning, Nathaniel had tied a series of knots in the rope. He now used these to ease his ascent. Though not as nimble as Thomas, he was stronger, and with the aid of the handgrips soon joined his friend.

After he'd hauled up the packs, he signaled for Orah to follow.

She gave a skeptical tug and started off, but with Nathaniel anchoring the rope, the climb turned out to be easier than expected.

Still she breathed more easily when he locked hands with her and boosted her up to the platform.

The feeling of relief passed quickly once she assessed the entrance to the cave. It had straight walls that rose as tall as a Little Pond cottage before curving into a perfect arch—clearly made by men—but inside, no light entered. No matter how much she squinted, she could pierce the darkness no more than a few paces.

They'd need torches. She prompted the others to gather dry brush, and then bound them to green branches with twine. After a longing gaze at the bright expanse of the river valley, she lit a torch and plunged inside.

Walking became difficult. The rocky surface within the cave crunched underfoot, interrupted by solid planks raised high enough to trip her. After a while, she realized the roadbed was made of timbers buried in gravel at regular intervals. To speed her pace, she needed to skip from plank to plank, a normal gait for Nathaniel, but one that required her to stretch unnaturally. Even so, she soon mastered the rhythm and was loping along.

After a time, she was struck by the sense of sameness. The walls, the ceiling and the distance between timbers remained the same, no matter how far she went. The rhyme had been specific about the length of the journey so far, but made only a vague reference to the cave. She'd assumed its passage would be brief. What if she had misunderstood? They had water for two days, food for one, and the cave offered nothing but dust and gravel. When their kindling ran out, they'd be cast into darkness as deep as a teaching cell. If she believed the primary precept of the Temple, that the sun was the giver of life, this place could become their tomb.

She needn't have worried.

Since they entered the cave, their torches had cast flickering shadows on the walls and the ceiling above. Now, suddenly, firelight scattered in all directions. She stood not in a cave but a large chamber. Torchlight reflected off metal signs overhead, most rusted, but some with numbers still distinct enough to read. On either side, she detected vague shapes, shadows in the darkness.

Nathaniel suggested they fan out, but she refused, reminding him of the giant snake. She turned to her left, only to bump into a chest-high wall. The right was the same. She advanced twenty paces and tried again. No change. The walls were not walls at all, but the sides of a trench between platforms.

Nathaniel picked one side and hoisted Thomas up. After he'd explored a bit and declared the footing solid, the others joined him.

Once on top, Orah paused to listen. She heard no sound but the echo of their rushed breathing.

She moved on, maintaining a straight line until blocked by a wall. The flickering light from her torch revealed bits of tile covering its surface, most intact but for a few fragments that had broken away.

"Thomas, come closer," she said. "There's writing here. Hold my torch up with yours so I can see better."

As she rubbed off the grime with the flat of her hand, a blackening appeared against a white background. "It's the start of a word."

Thomas brought the torches closer, and the biggest letter P she'd ever seen came into focus.

She took the skin from her pack and began dribbling water over the next letter.

Thomas grabbed her hand. "What are you doing? We have little enough as is."

She jerked away and kept pouring. "It's a message from the keepmasters."

Her skin ran empty just as the words became clear. *Please mind the gap between the platform and the train.*

"What does that mean?" Thomas said.

"I don't know, but it might be important like the rhyme."

"Or it may be ordinary, a simple everyday message."

Orah's eyes narrowed. "The keepmasters did nothing ordinary."

"I hope you're right, but I doubt it. Unless they were gods, they were ordinary most of the time, like the rest of us."

She had no time for bickering—the torches were burning low— so she swept her flame across the chamber and was rewarded with a flicker in response. "Over here."

The others rushed to her side and stood with torches in a row. The firelight reflected off a huge shape ahead. She shuffled forward, hand outstretched, until she touched the object's metallic skin. Its rounded sides stood as tall as a man, and extended some distance in either direction.

"I think we found our giant snake," she said.

Thomas edged closer but stopped an arm's length away. "Is it alive?"

"No. It's a creation of the keepmasters."

Nathaniel ran his fingertips along the dusty side, then rapped on its surface with his knuckles. "For what purpose?"

"Remember the road across the valley?" Orah said. "This looks like a wagon that carried lots of passengers."

"Then why would the keepmasters call it a snake?"

"Maybe they feared we'd forget its name, so they used a timeless shape instead."

Thomas finally mustered enough courage to brush the metal with his fingertips. "How can you be certain this is the snake of the rhyme?"

"*Two doors to the mouth of the snake / Inside, you must enter and fly.* Think, Thomas. The rock face wasn't a cliff, but a boulder in the shape of a man's head. Why couldn't the snake be a long round wagon? And even though 'fly' means to soar like a bird, we use the word in other ways. What did the elders say after you won a race at festival?"

Thomas grinned. "'That boy can fly.' All right, maybe the snake's a wagon. So let's find its mouth."

They wandered along trying to find its entrance. Doors on the side would never be considered a mouth, and all had rusted shut.

She worried the kindling would run out and they'd be left in the dark. "We don't have much time. Where would a mouth be?"

"In the front, of course," Nathaniel said, "but which direction is that?"

"Not where we've come, I hope, or these wagons will really have to fly when they find no bridge across the valley. Let's check the far end."

No longer afraid of some monster, she agreed to split up so they could more quickly check each wagon. Once alone, she felt the small hairs on the nape of her neck tingle as her world shrank to the pool of light from her torch. Luckily, the shouts of her friends soon echoed across the chamber.

"Nothing on this one."

"None here either."

Then Nathaniel called out, his words resounding above all. "I found something, different from the others. Its front is more... like the head of a snake."

Orah and Thomas ran as fast as they dared in the dim light, until they joined him at the far end. All three gawked at their find. This wagon *was* different, newer and undamaged by time, and the luster of its translucent skin amplified the light like the surface of the scrolls. Most importantly, a hatch lay at its tapered head.

Had they found the carriage that would bring them to the keep?

Thomas broke the spell. "We don't know how to get in, and if we did, we wouldn't know how to make it go."

"Believe," Orah said. "Believe in the keepmasters."

She brushed her fingertips against the surface, and it responded with a hum. She jumped back, but the wagon did not fly. Instead, it stirred slowly as if waking from a long sleep. The interior began to glow and in a few seconds became bright as day. The humming grew louder, and the hatch lifted, rising gracefully until it exposed a doorway wide enough for four people to enter abreast.

Thomas fell back a step and eyed the hatch, then peered inside without coming any closer. "It's magic."

"Yes," Orah said, "but not temple magic. We're witnessing the genius of the prior age. When something's the work of the keepmasters, anything's possible, and now, they're inviting us in." She dropped her torch and entered. "Well, what are you waiting for?"

Thomas hesitated, but seemed unwilling to let Orah be braver. He squared his shoulders and stepped inside.

Nathaniel snuffed out his torch and followed.

The interior held rows of padded chairs of the kind that would have been appropriate around a Little Pond fireplace, but there the similarity ended. Had they come with two hundred seekers, all would have fit.

They sat in the nearest seats, facing the front. After days of travel and hours of wandering in darkness, they took the chance to savor the light and rest. For several minutes nothing else stirred. Then, just as smoothly as the hatch had opened, it swung shut. The hum grew louder, approaching a roar.

Thomas leaned in and whispered. "What happens next?"
"I'm not sure," Orah said, "but if I were you, I'd hold on."
As if on cue, the great wagon of the keepmasters began to fly.

***

The wagon did not fly, but it moved faster than anything
Orah had believed possible, driving forward with a roar
that echoed through the cave. The light cast from within
showed the walls of the tunnel passing in a flash.

She tried to measure their progress but gave up. They might cross the world in hours in the heart of this beast.

Then, as suddenly as it had started to fly, the wagon began to slow. The echo spread into a larger chamber, perhaps bigger than the first, and they eased to a stop.

Moments later the hatch lifted and they stumbled out. When the doors closed behind them and the lights faded, Orah stared into darkness once more.

She wavered and nearly fell, her mind flying past shadows while her feet stayed rooted to the ground, but even after adjusting to the loss of speed, she remained unsettled. *Where are we, and what should we do next?*

Then, as her sight adjusted to the darkness, she noticed a brightening at the front of the chamber.

At the far end, a sliver of light filtered down from above. The platform ended at the base of a metal staircase, and though the oddly grooved steps had warped and corroded, they appeared passable.

She set foot on the first tread, glanced up, and a smile spread across her face.

The topmost stair glowed with the reflected light of the sun.

Chapter 25

The Golden Doors

Orah emerged onto the ruins of a street broad enough to hold all the streets of Temple City, but the black rock that covered its surface had buckled, and tangles of weeds sprouted through the fissures.

What once must have been a bustling park ran along its center, lined with trees planted at intervals. A few still survived, but most had succumbed to age and fallen, their rotting stumps visible only as moss-covered mounds. Scattered among them, bits of fences bordered the remnants of gardens, now ragged and overgrown, with the occasional wildflower all that remained of their former splendor.

Ahead, buildings stretched as far as she could see. These rose to staggering heights, some topped with needle-like towers that stabbed at the sky, but most had crumbled as if the heavens had struck back, leaving their bases littered with stones. Vacant windows stared out like hollow eyes, silent and sad, not monuments but memorials.

Thomas tipped his head back and gaped. "Did the darkness do this?" His voice sounded hollow, like the empty shells of the ruined city.

"If we're to believe the keepers," Orah said, "the keepmasters built this and the Temple destroyed it."

Nathaniel fidgeted with the straps of his pack and stared off into the distance, apparently too impatient for contemplation. "We must be close. I only hope we don't find the keep in the same state. Where does the rhyme lead next?"

Orah shook herself from her reverie. "This has to be the forest of stone. The rhyme says to head north to the Temple of Truth."

They stood at the intersection of great roads. With so many tall buildings, she had trouble getting direction from the sun, but guessed north would be down the broadest of boulevards—fitting for the approach to the keep. "This way. The Temple of Truth shouldn't be far. Even with keepmasters' magic, this many buildings can't go on for long."

They passed buildings beyond counting, each with an entrance more impressive than any she'd ever seen. Some had walls of black granite, while others displayed faded murals and the fractured remains of statues, their broken limbs littering the floor.

So much lost. How could a place so grand have fallen into such decay?

In the distance, the boulevard ended at a structure far different from the rest, dwarfed by the surrounding buildings in height, but ceding nothing in grandeur. Its façade gleamed with white marble, and a broad staircase rose up to a portico fronted by massive columns, each too wide for Nathaniel's arms to embrace.

Anticipation quickened Orah's pace as they approached. She jogged along with the others, reciting the third verse between gulps of air.

> *To the North, through forest of stone*
> *The Temple of Truth you shall see*
> *Once great, it now stands alone*
> *Climb its stairway, fourteen and three*

Running as fast as she dared on the uneven surface, she finally arrived at the first of the steps.

Thomas stared up reverently. "Is this the Temple of Truth?"

Orah counted fourteen stairs of granite, each as pure as the sundial in her garden. These climbed to a landing, from which three more continued to the top.

They'd arrived.

Nathaniel made a bow to Orah. "You go first. You've earned the honor."

She started up the stairs, climbing slowly out of respect for the new-found Temple, placing one foot in front of the other and holding her shoulders square. She paused at the landing and gazed back over the ruined city. When she glanced down, her eyes widened, and she beckoned for her friends to join her.

A golden plaque inlaid on granite adorned the landing, but its words, so caked with dust, were hard to read.

"Thomas, give me your water skin."

She reached out, but he pulled back. "I'm not wasting any more."

With an exasperated sigh, she dropped to her knees and began wiping away the grime. Thomas tried to raise her up, but she twisted away. "Leave me alone. I believe... even if *you* don't."

"It may not be important."

"Hush, Thomas. This is the Temple of Truth."

She returned to the plaque, rubbing with the sleeve of her tunic. Where the dust was too thick, she added spit to the task. At last, the first part became clear.

The greatest truth must be....

She scrubbed harder, but the next several words were gone, the metal melded with the stone. Her shoulders strained as she pressed on, intent on restoring the rest. When she'd finished, she could make out the final phrase.

...that in every child is the potential for greatness.

She slumped over exhausted, while her friends waited, giving her time.

Finally, Nathaniel eased her up. "There's more to discover."

At the top of the stairs and behind the columns, a corridor extended in either direction. Several stories high, its arched ceiling must have once been decorated with artwork, but now only splotches of color remained.

Nathaniel glanced to his left and right. "Which way?"

"'To the East, the entrance shall be.' We've been heading North. East is to the right."

She felt more than ready to find the keep and discover its hidden treasures, but the enormity of the situation slowed her pace. Each footstep echoed behind her as she strode down the corridor. At its end, the ceiling opened into a dome painted with white stars on a blue background.

In the back wall of the chamber stood two massive golden doors with no visible hinge, fitted so tightly together that the seam between them barely showed. She gaped as if trying to see through them, but only her reflection stared back, a bedraggled twin trapped in the keep and begging to be released. The gleaming surface betrayed no lock, no keyhole, no handle, and the doors seemed bolted shut with such conviction they might have been closed for all time.

They'd come to the last lines of the rhyme, the final phase of their journey. Orah approached the doors, eager to touch them, knowing the keep lay behind. She rapped with her knuckles—they hardly made a sound.

"Do you know how to open them?" Nathaniel said.

"I hope so. We have only two lines left."

> *Sixteen stars shall set the doors free*
> *When touched by the lines of the rhyme*

Thomas gaped at her and then up at the dome. "There are the stars, but how do we get to them? Even I can't climb that high."

Orah laughed. "I don't think those are the stars, Thomas. The ones we're looking for are much closer."

She gestured to the shadows at the left of the doorway. A box made of a substance similar to the coating of the scrolls sat embedded in the wall. On its surface were four rows of four buttons, marked from one to sixteen, each in the shape of a star.

"I knew the last lines referred to a puzzle, a sequence of numbers that would unlock the doors. It took me a while to figure it out. The one thing I didn't know was where to find the stars, and now, here they are."

"Well," Thomas said. "What are we waiting for?"

"Nothing at all. With your help, I'm ready." She asked him to kneel on the floor. "When I studied the verses, I noticed many included numbers, but none higher than sixteen. The numbers to unlock the doors are in the rhyme. I'll recite the verses, and each time I say a number, write it in the dust. Take care not to miss any."

She began chanting.

> *To the North, behind the rock face*
> *Twixt water and dark walls of pine*
> *For a full eight days you shall race*

Thomas listened spellbound, unable to take his eyes off her, and she needed to prod him. "I said eight, Thomas. Write it down."

He stirred from his stupor and focused on the floor. "Now I understand."

One more past four falls in a line

He wrote one and four unprompted, then two for the doors. As she neared the end of the rhyme, he raised his head. "Is it fourteen and three? Not seventeen?"

"Yes. That was one of the clues. I wondered why they didn't say seventeen and realized that would have exceeded the number of stars."

After Thomas recorded the final number—sixteen—she directed Nathaniel to the box on the wall. "I'll read the numbers from Thomas's list, and you touch the matching star."

Nathaniel positioned himself next to the box, while she stood over the markings on the floor.

"Eight."

He pressed the eighth button. Much to her delight, the star lit up.

She moved on. "One. Four. Two. Fourteen. Three."

Her voice grew stronger with each successive number, until she shouted out the last. "Sixteen!"

Nathaniel settled his finger over the sixteenth button, and glanced over his shoulder at her.

She nodded.

He pressed and stepped back from the doors, giving them leeway.

They all waited.

Nothing happened—no movement, no sound, no change in lighting. Nothing. After a few moments, the stars went dim.

***

Orah sat cross-legged on the floor, sullen and silent. When Nathaniel had tried to cheer her up, she'd sent him off with Thomas to explore. Better to brood alone. A half hour later, they returned to report they'd found nothing. The Temple of Truth was as lifeless as the rest of the keepmasters' city.

Unable to face them, she focused on the floor. "You were right all along, Thomas. I'm not smart enough. The secret of the keep is beyond me."

171

Thomas plopped down next to her, brushing her shoulder as he sat. "Not smart enough? You've been brilliant. We'd never have come this far without you. Not that Nathaniel and I haven't contributed, but you were the best."

She rocked to one side and bumped him playfully, before becoming thoughtful again. "What if you were right about another thing? What if the seekers took too long to arise? What if we did everything as we should, but the doors no longer work?"

Nathaniel had been pacing the room, poking at every crack and corner, but now he spun on his heel and faced her. "Then we're not to blame. Other generations had the chance, and we've accomplished more than all of them. We have nothing to be ashamed of."

He dropped down on her other side and placed an arm around her as she drew circles in the dust.

She finally looked up. "You're the best of friends, and I'm so grateful you came with me, but we're supposed to be the seekers, the most curious and persistent of our generation. Are we now content to accept failure because of the order of things?"

"*The order of things.*" Nathaniel jumped up and strode to the doors as if he'd suddenly discovered the key. "We haven't failed yet. You mentioned the word order — the order of the rhyme. Maybe they mean not the numbers *in* the rhyme, but the *lines* themselves."

Thomas looked perplexed, but Orah encouraged Nathaniel to continue.

"There are sixteen stars and sixteen lines to the rhyme. What were the exact last words? '*When touched by the lines of the rhyme.*'" His eyes took on a glow, as if reflecting the light from the stars. "I'll show you what I mean."

He found a fresh section of floor and wrote down one through sixteen. "Now, Orah, recite the rhyme, one line at a time."

She took a breath and glanced to the unseen heavens. "*To the North, behind the rock face.*"

"No number in that line, so we remove it." His boot rubbed out the number one.

She stirred and rose to her feet, hovering over his drawings and rattling off the remaining verses.

> *Twixt water and dark walls of pine*
> *For a full eight days you shall race*

172

One more past four falls in a line

He erased the two, but three and four stayed. When Orah had finished, a new sequence remained: *three, four, seven, twelve, fifteen.*

She nodded. "It's worth a try. I'll read the list and you press the buttons."

"No. You do it this time."

Her face grew warm. "It's not my place. It was your idea."

He came closer and placed a hand on her cheek, adding his warmth to hers. "Thomas was right. We needed all of us to make it this far. Besides, I'm only guessing. Maybe you'll change our luck."

She took his face in her hands, pulled his head down and kissed him. Then she went to the box at the side of the golden doors. "I'm ready."

Nathaniel read the list, and she touched the stars.

When he called out the final number, her finger hovered. She briefly closed her eyes, a quick prayer to the light. "It'll work this time, Nathaniel of Little Pond. I can feel it."

She pressed the final button.

Slowly, the structure came alive. The floor began to vibrate. The grinding of gears, unused for centuries, echoed off the starred dome. In moments, the doors began to swing inward.

The power of the Temple had been thwarted, the challenges of the masters met.

They'd found the keep at last.

PART THREE
THE KEEP

"In searching for the truth be ready for the unexpected."

— Heraklietos of Ephesos

Chapter 26

The Magic Window

The golden doors led to a much less impressive corridor. No vaulted arches or marble columns, no statues or artwork—only windowless walls and a low, flat ceiling—a place built more for utility than splendor. Orah advanced with care, wary of hidden defenses. The power of the Temple had surprised her, and she had no intention of underestimating the keep.

A dozen paces in, she startled to a recurrence of the gears grinding and spun around to catch the doors swinging shut. Thomas raced back and tried to stop them from closing, though each outweighed him tenfold. Nathaniel yanked him free before they crushed him.

"What are you doing?" she said.

Thomas clawed at the metal. "We'll be trapped in the dark."

Daylight from outside faded as the doors came together with a thud, but darkness never came. A glow rose all around them, brightest where they stood but with no identifiable source.

On the wall next to the doors, Orah spotted a twin of the box with the sixteen stars. "Don't worry, Thomas, this isn't Temple City, and the keep is no prison. The keepmasters have helped us get here and now we're their guests. Come, both of you, and join with me."

She reached out, took their hands, and bowed her head. "Blessed is the light that has given us life, allowed us to thrive, and brought us here to this day."

Thomas winced. "Should you be quoting the book of light in here?"

"I'm praying to the true light, not to the Temple. The keepmasters will understand."

With their endeavor properly blessed, she led them down the darkened corridor. As they approached the boundary of light, new illumination appeared. The glow, it seemed, would follow them wherever they went.

The corridor ended with two doors, more modest than the golden ones that guarded the keep. Before the three seekers reached them, they slid open on their own, revealing a circular chamber filled with hundreds of seats, all facing forward like a Little Pond classroom, but much larger.

As Orah struggled to guess the room's purpose, everything went dark, save a sequence of red lights in the floor that outlined an aisle to the front.

"Well," she said. "What are we waiting for? They're showing us the way."

The three followed the lit path and fanned out to explore, Nathaniel to the left, Orah to the right, and Thomas straight ahead.

As she groped for the wall, a crackling sounded behind her like paper being crushed.

A light flashed, and Thomas yelped. "A window... just appeared. That wall turned bright as day."

Nathaniel rushed to his side. "A window? Where?"

"Don't you doubt me, Nathaniel! I know what I saw."

"I don't doubt anything in this place," Orah said. "Show us where."

He spun about, trying to regain his bearings, and pointed to a spot on the darkened wall.

Orah inhaled and blew out two breaths as if about to start a race at festival. Her legs seemed made of water, but she forced them to move forward.

The air crackled again and a window appeared with people on its far side. They looked unthreatening, but she backed away before they could see her.

The window disappeared.

She froze in place and listened, but heard only the sound of her breathing and the low hum she'd noted since arriving in the keep.

"Do you believe me now?" Thomas said.

Orah nodded and turned to Nathaniel with a will-you-come-with-me look in her eyes. Before them lay what they'd sought all these weeks, a chance to speak with the masters. She grasped his hand, and together they approached the front of the chamber.

The window reappeared.

"They sense we're here," she whispered, "and have opened this window to welcome us."

"Or eat us for dinner," Thomas said.

The people became clearer. At a plain metal table sat two men and a woman, all elders. The woman wore her grey hair long, and dressed like a man in trousers. The first man had a full beard, not the jaw-line cut prescribed by the Temple but a bushy beard like an arch vicar, red in color with speckles of grey. The second was clean-shaven but had hair longer than the woman's, tied in back in a tail.

The man with the beard stood, stared straight at Orah and calmly approached.

She planted her feet so they wouldn't run away. "I am Orah of Little Pond." Her voice rose and trembled like a scared little girl pretending to be brave. "We came here following the clues of the keepers, to seek the—"

Oddly, the man ignored her, gazing past her as if deaf and blind.

Nathaniel stepped closer and waved a hand in front of the man's eyes.

Not a blink.

The man came to a halt and stood at the ready, like a teacher waiting for students to settle before class. Nathaniel made circles with both hands this time.

No response.

He checked with Orah, then inched closer to the window. His finger extended a hair's breadth at a time, until he touched the man's nose.

The image dissolved into liquid, like a reflection in the ripples of a pond. Nathaniel jerked his hand away, and the face resumed its form. The keepmaster never lost his composure.

Orah blew out a stream of air as she and Nathaniel retreated to Thomas. What she now realized to be a picture — a moving picture — went dark once more.

"A message from the past," she said.

Nathaniel agreed, though his eyes flitted everywhere. "Only an image of the old keepmasters."

"Sure," Thomas said. "How could they be alive today?"

Orah discovered the window would also brighten if they sat in the chairs. The intent was clear — visitors were to enter the room, take their seats and listen.

The three settled in the front row and waited for the message to restart.

After a few seconds, the man retraced his steps and addressed them with these words: "Greetings, seekers."

Orah sat transfixed as he welcomed them to the keep with all the manners customary in the Ponds, but she was beyond manners. She slid to the edge of her chair and waited for more. *Why have they brought us here?*

With niceties finished, the keepmaster began. "We are the founders of the keep, built before the darkness descended on the world. You who have come here have justified our hope, that even after centuries of stagnation some would long for more. You are the courageous few, able to overcome not only the Temple of Light, but the obstacles we placed in your path. You have earned the treasures preserved here."

Nathaniel sat up taller and Thomas puffed out his chest, but Orah recalled the empty seats on the flying snake, saw the empty seats now, and a fear crept into her heart.

The master continued. "So why the keep? In our time, the Temple had already existed for a hundred years, but the vicars had not yet solidified their dominion over the world. They allowed dissimilar points of view not because they accepted the beliefs of others, but because they lacked the power to suppress them... until the foolishness of our leaders drove the disillusioned into their arms. The vicars began to control everything — the teaching of the young, the exchange of information, travel. We came to accept that no one could reverse their growing power."

The man in the window pressed closer, his face turned grim.

"Our age of enlightenment was ending. We grieved for the loss of knowledge, the demise of the spirit of innovation, and a number of us resolved to preserve these for the future. We fled to the ruins of the greatest city of our age, through what had become wilderness. There, inside a world-renowned center of learning, the keep was born.

"History has recorded periods of stagnation before, but the human spirit is resilient and has always revived. So we constructed the keep to last a thousand years, if need be, and planted within it the seeds for those who would surely emerge.

"The best of our age—scholars, artists, thinkers—dedicated their lives to recording their knowledge so that, when the time came, the new generation could learn from the past. We began in the year ninety-two of what the Temple cynically called the age of light. As we record this message, the year is one hundred and forty-two. We have finished our task. The rest is up to you."

Orah whispered to Nathaniel. "Fifty years to finish the keep."

"And nearly a thousand since they recorded these words." Even in the faint glow cast by the floor lights, she could see the anger smoldering in his eyes. "It's a disgrace we've taken so long to find the keep, and a miracle it still functions."

The bearded man returned to his seat, and the woman took his place. She began in a muted voice that gained enthusiasm as she spoke.

"We constructed the keep for long-term use and stored in it all the knowledge of our age. You'll find a lot to learn here. We've made provision for you to stay as long as you wish, with ample food and water. The food has been dried and sealed without air to last for an extended period. It may appear strange to you, but when water is added, it will taste acceptable and provide all your nutritional needs. We embedded panels on the roof that soak up the energy of the sun. There'll be light wherever you go and a comfortable temperature throughout the year, cool in summer and warm in winter.

"You'll meet many helpers in the keep, recordings we made to help you learn. You can access them through the same kind of screen on which you're viewing us now. Each shows a different field of knowledge— history, art, science, and much more.

"The screens will light up as you approach, as this one did. If you ask questions, they'll respond. If you're done with a topic, say 'stop.' If you're confused, say 'help,' and an explanation will follow."

She paused to take a sip from a porcelain cup on the table. When she turned back, she had a quiet dignity about her.

"All the exploits of our age, the triumphs and failures, are here. Humankind was imperfect in our day, as I'm sure it will be in yours. In some ages we've been at our best and in others our worst, but overall the race moves on. The Temple of Light stopped that progress. You are the spark that will bring it back to life. Accept our knowledge as a bequest from the past. Take what you believe to be good, discard what you think to be bad, but above all, move forward from where we left off. We encourage you to stay, learn, and then teach others."

The woman resumed her seat, and the final keepmaster, the one with his hair in a tail, took her place. He rocked on the balls of his feet, and his voice rose and fell as he spoke.

"We congratulate you on the success of your revolution. Your presence means the Temple has at last been defeated, or its power so diminished that the keepers felt safe to reveal the rhyme. We can help by arming you with knowledge.

"You are the leaders of a great movement. Bring your followers here. We built the keep to educate hundreds. The keep is yours. Its knowledge will dispel the darkness and light the way so the world may be reborn."

The window darkened, and the glow from the hidden lights returned. When Orah glanced back at her friends, their faces had gone pale.

She spoke for them all. "At least now we know what the seekers were supposed to be."

"Yes," Thomas said, "and it wasn't us."

***

None of them spoke for several minutes, each lost in their own thoughts. Orah clasped her hands between her knees and contemplated the floor while Nathaniel slumped in his chair, his long legs stretched out before him.

Only Thomas stood, circling the chamber as if hoping to find a window with a different message.

After his second loop, Orah could bear his pacing no more. "Come sit, Thomas. We need all our brains to think this through."

182

Thomas stopped, but stayed standing. "What's to think about? The message was clear. We don't deserve the keepmasters' congratulations. We're not what they hoped for. They expected the elders of a new generation, not three young seekers filled with delusions."

"But seekers nevertheless."

Thomas spun around, his face flushed. "Don't you understand? The keepers were supposed to wait for a rebellion to begin, but we took too long. They got desperate and stumbled upon us in their final breath. Our success was luck, not the stuff of legend. We're not the seekers they expected. We're... an accident."

Nathaniel rose, using his height to intimidate Thomas. "You're right. Our forebears failed, but now there's only us, and our fate depends on what we make of it. So what if we came here by accident? The bigger concern is what to do next."

The question hung in the air. Orah pressed her lips into a thin line, for once devoid of answers.

"Well, I know what we should do," Thomas said, and then paused, waiting for their full attention. "I heard one thing that impressed me. The keepmasters may be useless to protect us, but they've left plenty of food. I'm going to find something to eat."

Orah eased into a smile. "I knew we had a reason to bring you along."

She joined Thomas and beckoned to Nathaniel. "Better than sitting here feeling glum."

Nathaniel hesitated as if searching for a more noble answer, some battle to fight, but no enemies lurked in the vicinity, and no great cause flared like a beacon on the horizon. So he followed his friends to explore the keep.

Chapter 27
A Question for Heroes

The keep consisted of a honeycomb of circular chambers, most with corridors extending from them like spokes. A small window graced the wall by the entrance to each corridor, and lit up with words describing its treasure whenever anyone came near.

Orah paused before one that displayed the word *Botany*.

"Bo-tay-nee," she said aloud. "What does that mean?"

Nathaniel stood behind and rested a hand on her shoulder. "The keepmasters claimed we could ask the... screen... for help. Give it a try."

She hesitated, recalling her discomfort in the welcome chamber, then said the word "help" with little conviction.

A woman appeared, much younger than the others and eager to serve. "What is your question?"

"What is Bot-a-ny?" Orah tried to be precise with her pronunciation.

"Botany is the study of plants."

Orah beamed, pleased with her success.

Then, as the helper waited, Thomas stuck his head in front with a more pressing question. "Can you tell us where to find food?"

The helper responded at once. "Proceed to the flashing screen."

Orah glanced about and picked out the only blinking screen. On it were the words *Dining Hall*.

***

Tables lined the dining hall, each with a gray speckled surface and space to seat eight. Screens covered the surrounding walls, a dozen or more like the others in the keep, except for curious red and blue pipes sticking out beneath them. Each screen displayed images of food — meats, fruits, vegetables and grains — vivid enough to make Orah salivate.

She approached one and said, "Help."

No helper appeared this time, but a pleasant-sounding voice asked the question she'd been hoping for. "What would you like to eat?"

She thought a moment. "Lamb — with sweet yams and honey."

The image on the screen vanished and a list appeared. The voice instructed her to touch a selection. She scanned the menu, disappointed at the absence of yams, but delighted to find lamb. She pressed her fingertip to the word, feeling a bit foolish, and waited.

A small door opened in the wall and a shiny package slid out. She held it with both hands and shook, but nothing happened. After a brief inspection, she grasped its corner and tore off the top, but when she checked inside, her brows knitted and the corners of her mouth drooped.

Thomas glanced over her shoulder and his features drooped as well. "The food's spoiled. We'll starve."

Orah waved him off. She sniffed at the lumpy brown dust. "Smells like lamb." She licked a fingertip, dipped it in and touched it to her tongue. "Tastes like lamb."

She glanced up at the screen. "What do we do with this food?"

A helper appeared, this time a portly man who seemed appropriate for the dining hall. "Please repeat your question."

She repeated the same words but louder this time and more slowly, as she might speak to a child.

The helper froze as if he was struggling to understand. He finally replied. "Food is for eating."

She rolled her eyes and groaned. "I know that."

"Do you have another question?" the helper said in the exact same tone.

Orah sighed. Talking to the helpers seemed trickier than talking to a child. They must have guessed what questions would be asked and recorded their answers, but the burden was on the seekers to find the right question.

After some thought, she came up with a new approach. "How do I prepare this food?"

"All food in the keep is dehydrated. You just add water."

"And where may I find water?"

"Hold the package beneath one of the spigots, red for hot and blue for cold."

The curious protrusions scattered along the wall were apparently spigots, although none had a pump handle to work them. She held the parcel beneath a red pipe. Hot water poured out in exactly the right amount, sending the aroma of freshly cooked lamb wafting through the room.

The three spread out, each to a different screen, and ordered a variety of foods, more than they'd be able to eat in a week. When they needed hot, the water poured out steaming like tea heated in a fireplace. When they wished for cold, it emerged as frigid as the waters of Little Pond in winter.

Though the food looked unappetizing—not much more than colored paste—the offerings tasted right and some even strange and wonderful. Keep fare might be no match for home cooking, but it seemed wholesome, filling and, most importantly, plentiful.

As Orah inhaled the last of a buttered potato, she pictured the keepmasters eating meals where she sat. "Imagine, this is how they ate for more than fifty years, spending their lives here, hiding from the vicars and recording their knowledge."

Thomas poked at one of the packets—some kind of fish. "Yes, imagine. Fifty years with nothing solid to chew."

"I don't think food mattered," she said. "They were doing a labor of love, a selfless service for people they'd never meet."

"For people who never cared about them," Thomas corrected, "who over the centuries forgot they existed." He took a sip of purple liquid. "I wonder how long we'll be here, eating this food and hiding from the vicars, before the world has forgotten us as well."

***

Orah sat at the table, unable to budge. Debris from their meal lay strewn across its surface. She would have found their gluttony amusing had their prospects been less grim.

Time to confront the issue. "Well, Thomas, we're fed. What other ideas are rattling around in that head of yours?"

Thomas leaned back and contemplated the ceiling, then sat up straight and shrugged. "How about just staying here? We'll be safe, warm, and never go hungry."

Orah studied her reflection in the tabletop and stroked its surface as if trying to brush away the speckles. "We can't stay here forever."

"Why not?"

"Because we can't spend the rest of our lives hiding. We need some purpose."

"I don't. I just want to avoid the vicars, with their deacons and words that fly through the air and light knows what other dark magic."

"The keep may not be as safe as you think," Nathaniel said. "After a thousand years, it's aging and may not support us much longer, and while the deacons may struggle to find us without the rhyme, they're still searching. But more than that, what kind of life would we have here?"

"Where else can we go?"

Orah turned sideways and gazed at the now darkened screens that lined the walls. The longing she'd suppressed on their journey welled up within her. "What if we went home to Little Pond?"

Nathaniel clenched his teeth and sucked air in between them. "That's the first place the vicars would look. Even our neighbors might turn on us. Who knows what crimes they've accused us of?"

Thomas's mood turned hopeful. "Don't give up so fast. The vicars want to find the keep. We can use its location to barter for mercy and ask for our old lives back."

Orah flushed. "Betray the keepmasters after what we've learned? I want to go home but not at such a cost."

"To the darkness with the keepmasters. If they can't protect us, we need to look out for ourselves."

"They sacrificed their lives to preserve what's here. How can you think such a thought?"

Thomas scowled and hunched his shoulders, and his mind seemed to go somewhere she shuddered to imagine.

When he spoke again, his brashness had vanished. "Tell me something, Orah. How long did you stay in the teaching cell?"

"What has that to do with anything?"

"It has everything to do with it. Tell me."

"Three or four hours."

Thomas stared at her unblinking. "I measured my time not in hours, but eternities. I'd rather die than be taught again."

His response rolled round in her mind. She wanted to win the argument—not just for the sake of winning, but because the keep was so vitally important—but she couldn't hurt Thomas further, hated the thought of hurting him. She bit down on her little finger and prayed the keep was worth the sacrifice.

"I'm sorry, Thomas. I can't betray the keepmasters."

She'd tried not to cause him pain, but his expression said otherwise.

"Do you know," he asked, "what tomorrow is?"

"I'm not sure. The summer blessing?"

Thomas's lower lip quivered. "Tomorrow I turn eighteen. What do you think I want most for my birthday?"

The question hung in the air. She didn't answer because no answer was expected.

"I want my life back. I'm not like the two of you. I want to marry, father a child, or two if the Temple allows, work my family's farm and play music for my neighbors at festival. That's enough for me. Can you give me that life back?"

"I would if I could," Orah said, "but that opportunity died the day you were taken for a teaching. I don't trust the vicars. We might forsake the future and still be punished." She turned to Nathaniel and held out her hands, imploring. "Tell him, Nathaniel. We can't betray all this."

Then she saw it. While she and Thomas were debating, Nathaniel's face had taken on a distant expression, the look of a dreamer. He prepared to speak, and she felt a stirring of hope.

"What should we do now?" he said. "A question for heroes. We should neither barter with the vicars nor hide here forever, but do as the masters intended. We may have found the keep by chance, but we're their only hope. Time to change the world. We didn't come out of a rebellion, so we should start one."

Orah's hope drained away. He'd gone mad. "What you ask isn't possible."

"Not possible?" Nathaniel's jaw tightened and twitched. "The keepmasters didn't worry about possible. They believed in an idea and gave their lives for it. Since leaving Little Pond, I've learned courage is different than I thought. To be courageous means you do what's right even in the face of impossible odds. Most of what we've been taught is based on lies. What's right is to tell the world the truth."

Thomas curled up in his chair and stared at the floor, but Orah's spirit wilted, afraid something between her and Nathaniel was about to be lost.

"We're not children anymore, Nathaniel, and this isn't one of our games at the NOT tree. Your rebellion is an illusion, a choice too much to ask."

His cheeks flushed, and he retreated to the far side of the room to contemplate the white wall.

Orah bit down on her lower lip as if to punish it for letting out the words. She stared at Nathaniel's back, at the hollow between his shoulders, trying to see through to his heart. She'd always been able to read his moods, but so much had changed since their coming of age.

What is he thinking?

She closed her eyes and concentrated. She sensed Thomas hovering nearby and could hear his breath coming in quick bursts, but otherwise silence.

Speak to me, Nathaniel.

The scuff of footsteps approached, and she opened her eyes.

Nathaniel had come back to her, stopping less than a pace away. His chest swelled as he took in a breath, and, when he exhaled, its warmth brushed her cheeks. "Whatever happens, the three of us need to agree. The vicars won't distinguish between us. Whatever punishment befalls one will befall all."

Orah's words emerged in a whisper. "How do we reach that agreement?"

"The hot weather's almost here. The trip back across the ridge would be hard with no shade or water. Let's spend the summer in the keep." He lifted his chin so his jaw jutted out—a gesture he'd inherited from his father. "My father always said there's no wisdom without knowledge. By summer's end, we might gain enough knowledge to make the right choice."

Orah gazed at him, her Nathaniel, her friend since birth. If only they could go back to Little Pond and resume their lives as if none of this had happened.

A deep sigh, and the practical side of her took over. "If nothing else, the keep will provide us food and shelter, and I'll have time to study and explore."

Nathaniel turned to Thomas. "What about you?"

Thomas shuffled closer and, after a moment's hesitation, formed a circle with his friends. The hint of a spark had returned to his eyes. "Will I need to study as much as Orah?"

Nathaniel's jaw relaxed, and he eased into a smile. "I didn't think that was possible."

Thomas grinned and spoke for them all. "Then the end of summer it is. You'll find Orah in Bot-a-ny. For myself, I plan to do most of my learning in the dining hall."

Thomas, as always, had found a way to make her smile, but this smile was short lived. Summer would fly by, and she and Nathaniel would have to negotiate the boundary between illusion and reality. For all her careful planning, she had no idea how it would end.

Chapter 28
Exploration

Orah slipped through a narrow passageway into a small room more cramped than her Temple City cell. She took a deep breath to calm her heartbeat. This place was far from Temple City — no teachings here. Like everything else in the keep, the builders had designed these chambers for utility more than luxury. The keepmasters had thrived in such quarters for fifty years. Surely she could survive a summer.

A friendly helper had assigned them each a warm and well-lit bedchamber. A straight-backed chair stood in its center, and to provide more space, the desk and cot folded into the wall. She asked the helper to lower the cot. Tiny gears hummed, so much quieter than those of the golden doors, and the cot stopped level with her waist. The meager mattress appeared as hard as the floor, but when she settled upon it, its strange material molded to her body.

She lay there, staring at the white ceiling and letting the tension drain from her muscles. For the past several weeks, she'd run a race filled with danger and doubt, and now that she'd reached her goal, she longed to stay on the soft surface.

One task left to do.

She rose and asked the helper to lower the desk as well, and then removed the long abandoned log from her pack. *Time to record*

191

the start of a new kind of quest – an adventure of the mind. She turned to the first blank page and began her entry.

> *The keep at last.*
>
> *Such a strange journey, so different from what I expected when I foolishly left Little Pond with my friends. Somehow, thank the light, we've reached our goal, but now what to make of the keep?*
>
> *Though I've yet to explore, I've seen a sampling of its wonders. Treasures lie here beyond counting, greater than I ever imagined, but not easily obtained. The keep offers more than any person could learn in a lifetime. In these scant few weeks of summer, my challenge will be to focus on one or two subjects. I pray to choose wisely.*
>
> *We've agreed to a simple plan: set our decision aside and ignore our impending fate, then pick an area of study and gather at dinner each evening to share our findings. Like Nathaniel, I'm eager to begin. Thomas professes disinterest, but I believe the keep will eventually pique his curiosity. It offers so much, the promise of a world reborn.*
>
> *My eyes grow heavy now. My hand lacks strength to write. Time to get some rest, for tomorrow my new adventure begins – a journey to discover my potential for greatness.*

***

Nathaniel yearned to set an example, to arrive at dinner with revelations so profound his friends would feel compelled to act, yet by the end of the first week, he had little to say. The keep offered an array of topics more daunting than he'd expected, and at his current rate of progress, he'd bring nothing to their meals but silence.

He decided to focus on history since all his knowledge of the past came from the vicars. They preached peace and perfection during the reign of the Temple of Light, but the brutal practice of teachings gave lie to what he'd learned. They claimed chaos and death had preceded its founding, but he'd seen enough of the keepmasters' world to know there had been more—bold undertakings and impressive accomplishments.

Orah admired accomplishments, the effort and cleverness that went into them. The more he found, the more likely she'd take up his cause.

The anteroom for history had the same appearance as the others, round with a recessed ceiling and lighting that bounced off the walls. Of the topics spiraling from its center, two sparked his curiosity: politics and religion.

He stepped up to the politics screen first. "Help."

A helper appeared, this time a young man with hair so short the white on the sides of his scalp showed. "How may I help you?"

"What is politics?"

The helper described politics as the ability to govern people, involving the creation of a system of rules to administer and control their affairs. Politics sounded like what the vicars spent most of their time doing.

"Then is it about how the Temple guides its children?"

A pause followed as some mechanism adjusted. The helper returned momentarily.

"Though the Temple of Light is the only system you've known, many others have come and gone throughout history. Please follow this corridor to learn more about them."

The very subject he'd been searching for. What made the Temple different from other systems? What weaknesses might cause its collapse?

But he had one last question before entering the corridor. "What is religion?"

The young man asked him to please stand by. Apparently, he wasn't the expert on religion.

The screen cleared and a woman in her middle years appeared. She had a strong chin and spoke with a high-pitched voice, making her words clipped and precise. "Religion is a set of beliefs concerning the nature and purpose of the universe, held in common by anywhere from a few individuals to entire populations. The larger congregations usually gather to practice some form of ritual observance.

"They also preach a preset moral code, which may be broad, declaring what's right and wrong in human affairs, or more detailed, dictating minutiae such as dress, diet and hairstyle. Often, compliance is left to the individual—a decision between each person and their god. In more extreme cases, the code becomes law and is enforced by authoritarian theocracies."

Nathaniel struggled to focus. The woman's statement would have earned her a significant teaching from the vicars. He chose to pursue the word she used last. "What is the-o-cra-cy?"

"Please stand by."

The helper on politics returned. His patience seemed endless. "A theocracy is government combined with religion. Using the force of moral certitude, theocracies tend to be more rigid and less tolerant. Generally, the civil and religious codes are one and enforced by a clerical class."

Finally, something tied to his world.

"Is the Temple of Light a theocracy?"

"Yes. One example. Please proceed to the politics section if you wish to learn more."

The time had come to accept the advice. He peered into the corridor next to the screen and proceeded down it as requested.

***

Orah was struggling. The library back home contained fewer than a hundred books, all of which she'd read years before. Now, as she wandered the keep, she found more areas of knowledge than books in Little Pond.

She searched for something familiar. The term "pharmaceutics" caught her eye, reminiscent of the village pharmacy. She located the viewing area and waited for the screen to light up. A man appeared who looked like an elder, with gray hair and a face creased with lines of wisdom, but in place of a black tunic, he wore a short white coat.

"Welcome to the subject of pharmaceutics. Here you'll find all you need for the assembling of medicines. Take a moment to look at the following list and select one by speaking its name. Some may be hard to pronounce, so you can also touch the word on the screen."

A list of words replaced his image, most with too many syllables and almost all unpronounceable. She tried to find one she recognized and gave up. She had more pressing questions.

"Help."

The elder reappeared.

"Where did these medicines come from? Are they a gift from the light?"

The man's image froze, waiting for her to finish before replying.

"Those of us who record our knowledge tend to forget how you were raised. I'd like to tell you these marvels were handed down as gifts from above, but nothing could be further from the truth. In my age, groups of dedicated researchers toiled for years to find cures for every ailment known. The Temple tried to take credit, but these medicines came as the result of hard work and individual brilliance."

He went on to explain how hundreds had devoted their lives to find a cure for a single disease. The vicars retained the knowledge to assemble the medicines, but the freedom of thought needed for research clashed with their beliefs, so the ability to discover new cures was lost.

Orah listened intently. What the helper said matched the vicar of Bradford's words, but she wanted to know more. "What would I have to learn to discover a new medicine?"

The screen went blank. The elder returned with a more formal demeanor.

"We're pleased you've chosen to pursue medical research. You've had a limited education as a child of light, but you will find all you need to learn here in the keep. Subjects you must master include...."

He rattled off a number of strange words — biology, chemistry, biochemistry, microbiology, genetics — until Orah stopped him abruptly. "I'm not following."

"If you'd prefer the course on paper, say print."

"Print."

A slot appeared next to the screen, and moments later a piece of paper slid out, on it the helper's list printed in the block lettering she'd always associated with the Temple. Another miracle demystified.

She spent the next several days trying to grasp these subjects, hoping to learn how to discover new medicines. The keepmasters understood the innermost workings of the body, but she found the underlying science too complex for a summer's study.

Undaunted, she searched for a simpler topic, one she might master in a matter of weeks, and stumbled upon mathematics. The word sounded familiar, like the arithmetic she'd studied in school.

A different helper congratulated her on accepting the challenge of mathematics, a daunting discipline mastered by only the brightest even in his own day. Given her limited education as a child of light, she should start with the basics, things called algebra and geometry, before undertaking the differential calculus. She approached the first topic with confidence—she'd always had a knack for numbers—but her experience here proved as inadequate as with medicine, and just as frustrating.

She studied hard, natural stubbornness stiffening her resolve. She'd show the helper—irrational though it may be—that given time, she could master anything. But progress came slowly. After a week, she'd had enough. She understood the need for medicine but had only a vague grasp of the goal of mathematics.

She dragged her fingers through her hair and summoned the helper. "What's the purpose of mathematics?"

"In addition to its abstract elegance," the helper said, "it expresses form and relationship throughout nature."

"Okay... if I master these subjects, you said I could proceed to the differential calculus. What's that for?"

"To measure rate of change as conditions vary."

"Give an example."

"Describing the laws of motion in physics."

"A more specific example, please."

"Predicting the path of celestial bodies."

She straightened in her chair, frustration turning to curiosity. "What do you mean by celestial bodies?"

"Objects in the heavens."

"Such as?"

"The moon, the planets, the stars."

She needed a moment to slow her breathing before asking the next question. "Why would you need to know such a thing?"

"To allow ships to rendezvous with objects at high speeds from great distances."

Ships going to the heavens? Her head spun. *What if Nathaniel is right? What if the keep is worth risking our lives?*

The question burst from her lips. "Are you saying you've traveled to the stars?"

The screen went blank. A new helper appeared, older than the former and, to her relief, less arrogant. He greeted her in the usual way. "Welcome to the subject of astronomy. How may I help you?"

She spoke the words as if crafting each for the first time. "Have you... traveled... to the stars?"

The image froze for a few seconds, an uncomfortable delay before he graciously responded, "Yes. We've traveled to the stars. Do you have another question?"

What more could she say? Her view of the world was changing too fast, a blur flashing across her mind and threatening to tear that world apart.

***

Orah fidgeted with her food, poking at one container after another but eating little. How could she tell her friends what she'd learned? She hardly believed it herself.

While she nibbled on a gob of reconstituted carrot, she grumbled between bites. "I feel so dumb in the keep."

She snapped a glance at Thomas, expecting him to pounce on her admission, but he merely grinned. "Just what I was afraid of. What chance do I have if you can't figure it out?"

She took advantage of the opening. "You never tell us anything. What are you doing? Do you ever leave the dining hall?"

"I'm using my time as well as you, only I'm exerting myself less."

"Really? What did you learn today?"

He leaned back and put his feet up on the table, carefully avoiding the containers of half-eaten food. "Today I learned the difference between light and darkness. It's more subtle than you'd imagine."

Orah glared at him, not sure whether to be interested or annoyed. "Please enlighten me."

"With the help of the keepmasters, I've discovered —" He paused for effect. " —something called custard. Custard comes in vanilla and chocolate, and is the perfect de-hy-drat-ed food. Vanilla is light and delicious, but I prefer the darker chocolate."

Orah slapped his feet off the table. "I'm so pleased you chose to waste your time. Do you know what you're missing?"

"No, and I haven't heard anything from you. Please enlighten me."

She flopped back onto her chair and blew away a curl. "I'm trying to learn but haven't found anything I can master quickly. If we ever came back, I'd choose one topic and stick with it for years. If the Temple fell tomorrow, we'd need at least a generation to relearn all this."

She took a bite of something claiming to be chicken, and then turned to Nathaniel. "What about you? Any more luck?"

"I've been studying history, especially the time the vicars call the darkness."

She set her food aside and sat upright. "What have you learned?"

Nathaniel hesitated, and a hint of doubt crept into his eyes. She'd known him since birth, knew him so well, but now a thin veil rose between them, as if he feared the consequences of what he was about to say.

After a moment, he dropped his guard. "The vicars were right. The so-called darkness was a time of chaos and war, but it was also a time of innovation and genius, just as the keepers claimed. The Temple of Light banished it all, both the good and the bad. Such events had occurred before. One period called the Dark Ages lasted over six hundred years, a time when scholars devoted their lives to recording forbidden knowledge for future generations while hidden away in places called monasteries.

"Once the Temple consolidated its power, the keepmasters came to believe a new Dark Age had begun. They saw it as their duty to save their knowledge from being lost, but unlike the scholars who preserved the past with parchment and quill pens, they recorded theirs using—"

The lights flickered.

Orah had barely enough time to catch the panic consuming Thomas before the room went dark. She pressed her eyelids shut, counted to three and opened them, but still saw nothing. As she strained to pierce the blackness, her sense of hearing became acute.

Something was missing—the hum that had accompanied them since passing through the golden doors. The heart of the keep had gone silent. In its place came a plaintive wail.

"It's the vicars," Thomas said. "They found us."

She jumped as a hand landed on her back, then relaxed when she recognized Nathaniel's touch. The two joined arms and shuffled forward, trying to find Thomas.

Before they reached him, a new voice sounded, the soothing words of a female helper. "We're sorry. A temporary disruption of power has occurred. Emergency lighting is being activated. Please stand by while repairs are being made."

The keep was healing itself. The dimmest of lights arose in the corners of the dining hall, but to eyes straining in darkness, they were enough.

Orah acknowledged Nathaniel with a nod, and spotted Thomas a few paces ahead, cowering on the floor.

He clutched her extended hand and scrambled to his feet, but quickly pulled away embarrassed.

She let him collect himself before asking, "Why did you think the vicars had come?"

As the color returned to his face, his answer echoed off the flat walls. "Because their weapon is darkness."

Nathaniel wrapped an arm around his shoulders and led him back to the table. "It wasn't the vicars, Thomas, but the age of the keep. Over time things will fail more frequently. Another reason why we can't stay."

Orah crept to the entrance of the dining hall and poked her head around, checking the corridor. Nothing. She held her breath and listened. Silence. She sniffed the air that usually shifted with a slightly cooling breeze. Stillness.

Convinced of their safety, she came back and urged Nathaniel to continue. "You were telling us about the past."

"The darkness," he said. "What we learned in school was true. People had always waged wars, but the age before the Temple's founding was especially bloody, pitting people against each other."

"But why?" Orah said.

Nathaniel shrugged. "Because they were different. We may not understand, since we've known nothing but the Temple of Light."

"Were they so different they needed to kill each other?"

Nathaniel shook his head. "Not that I can tell. All had some form of prayer, but their gods had different names. They prayed at different times, had holy days in different seasons. Most promised an afterlife if you adhered to their faith.

"In any case, they used thinking machines to organize those of like minds and turn them against everyone else. Then they fought with terrible weapons conceived from the same knowledge meant for good."

Thomas's eyes narrowed. His pupils drifted to the corners. "The people spoke different languages and worshipped different gods, and they used these languages and these gods to separate the people each from the other."

Orah waited until he finished, and then cautiously settled a hand on his shoulder, as if afraid it might burn. "Did they tell you that in the teaching?"

"Now we find it's true, just as the vicars claimed. The Temple of Light stopped it."

She turned to Nathaniel, desperate for a better answer. "Is that what the helpers said?"

The corners of his eyes sagged. "The wars forced elders to come together and make a pact to remove the differences, but no one would accept the other's faith. So they convened an historic conference to define a new religion, promising to preserve the best of each and set at its core a ban on violence. To speed acceptance, they made it easy to adopt, with few demands on people's lives. All the gods would be combined into a single concept called the light. Along with sins like murder or theft, they would deem anything that preceded it evil.

"Each leader brought large numbers of their followers. And why not? They'd kept the best, eliminated the worst and, most importantly, stopped the bloodshed."

Orah exhaled the next question. "So what happened?"

"Not everyone accepted the new way. The original leaders passed on and the next generation began to focus on ways to consolidate power. Over time, a different set of precepts emerged. Keep the population simple and small, control education, ban free thought, limit travel, discourage diversity, and most of all, erase the wonders of the prior age except those needed to keep them in power. In the end, they got what they wanted—a peaceful world with the vicars in charge."

As he spoke, Orah fiddled with the folds of her tunic until the edges crumpled into a bunch. She didn't look up until he finished. "How can so much harm have been done in the name of good?"

"I asked the helper."

"What did he say?"

"His answer was 'unknown.'"

As she stared open-mouthed, the keep sprung back to life. The soft lighting returned and the hum resumed—the only sound in the room.

***

Thomas sat and fumed long after the others had gone. He'd made a fool of himself when the lights went out, and had no power to stop it. He had no tolerance for the dark anymore. The vicars had marked him with this scar, and he'd never forgive them.

Now Nathaniel says the keepmasters were no better. To the darkness with the keepmasters and to the darkness with the Temple of Light!

Despite what he'd said, he knew his friends would never stay in the keep. They were different from him. He thought of dreams as a game— at least before the teaching had turned them to nightmares. But Orah and Nathaniel needed dreams like air, and they couldn't pursue their dreams in the keep.

For a time when he was younger, he'd imagined himself with Orah, but not for long. To bind himself to someone never content with the world? Not for him. Nathaniel and Orah were a matched pair, incapable of happiness without some improbable cause. Now the two fed off each other, each more desperate to prove their worth, their passion leading them closer to the brink.

If he had the power of the keep, if he could push a few buttons in the shape of stars until they lit up and destroyed the Temple in a hail of the old master's magic, he'd do so. But how could Nathaniel believe they'd defeat the vicars by themselves? Once the three of them left the protection of the keep, they'd be caught, and whatever scratches they might have inflicted on the Temple would only make their punishment worse.

Each day his friends edged closer to their doom. He feared a return to the teaching and would do what he could to save them from that fate, but he prayed in so doing, he wouldn't lose their friendship.

Chapter 29
Discovery

Weeks passed, but Orah refrained from telling her friends about star travel—she could hardly believe it herself. So she made astronomy her new home and devoted most of her waking hours to searching for proof in the stars.

The keepmasters confirmed the vicars' vision that the world revolved around the sun, but differed on all other celestial matters. They claimed the points of light visible in the night sky offered a mere sampling of the heavens. A few of the brightest were planets, other worlds that circled the sun, but most of the stars were suns themselves. And with instruments invented by the so-called age of darkness, they'd found millions of them. The sun, giver of life, was one among many, and not even the foremost of those.

She listened to lectures about the motion of heavenly bodies and discovered their movement followed not Temple dogma but the laws of mathematics. She even learned how to chart their course. The concepts, however, were too abstract—nothing that would convince her friends.

One evening while sulking in astronomy, her frustration boiled over into words barked at the blank screen. "If only I had a way to prove their claim."

The screen lit up, and the astronomy helper appeared. "I'm sorry. I don't understand. Do you have a question?"

"No. I was talking to myself."

The helper waited, uncertain how to respond. She folded her hands in her lap and studied her fingers. After a while, she stood and approached the screen. "You said you built instruments to explore the night sky. Do they still exist?"

The man appeared pleased with the question. "Ah. You'd like to use the observatory. Please step into the elevator and I'll meet you there."

She startled to a doorway appearing in the blank wall, exposing a hidden chamber. Unlike most rooms in the keep, this one was tiny, able to hold no more than four people. After a brief hesitation, she gave a shudder and entered.

A pale light shone rather than the usual soft glow, revealing stark metal walls broken only by a waist-high handrail. She barely had time to question its purpose when the door slid shut, locking her in with no latch or knob, or box with sixteen stars.

The room lurched and stopped. The lights flickered and dimmed. She'd become accustomed to problems, doors sticking, water spigots going dry, and other frailties of old age. Usually, the keep healed itself. But a day would come when the keepmasters' creation would fail. As she gaped at the featureless door, a ghost of herself gaped back, a grim memory from her teaching cell.

Before she could panic, a familiar voice sounded. "Please stand by. Repairs are being made."

Shortly, the lights brightened and the room began to accelerate—not nearly as fast as the flying wagon, but more disconcerting, it was moving upward. She clutched the handrail as her heart settled into her stomach.

When the room came to a halt, the wall at the opposite end slid open, and she gratefully exited into a domed chamber. At its center, a cylinder a dozen feet long slanted upward toward the heavens, with a seat anchoring its bottom.

Another of the ever-present screens sprang to life. The astronomy helper reappeared as promised. "Welcome to the observatory. Here you'll be able to view the sky, either with the naked eye or through the telescope. Which would you like to do first?"

She'd learned about telescopes and assumed the cylinder in the center was one of these, but she preferred to scan the heavens without it first.

A tremor crept into her voice. "My own eyes... if you please."

Gears ground and the roof of the dome retracted. Above her shimmered the same night sky she'd grown to love in Little Pond. She'd forgotten how beautiful it was.

The helper waved his arm in a broad arc, encompassing the round chamber. "You'll find markers on the wall that show direction. I can give you a tour of tonight's sky if you'd like."

"Yes, I would."

"At two hundred and thirty degrees to the southwest you will find the brightest of all lights, save the sun and the moon, a planet we call Venus."

She circled until she found the matching number, glanced up and beheld the evening star. Its light trembled and seemed to grow brighter as she stared.

"Venus is a world like our own, but revolves around the sun in a closer orbit. You can prove this by observing its phases. Part of the planet becomes obscured whenever it cycles behind the sun. You can see this phenomenon through the telescope."

The tube in the center whirred and swung around. She waited until it stopped before taking a seat. When she glanced through the eyepiece, her brows rose. An amber crescent shone, a third of a ball, with the remainder in shadow—the evening star as she'd never seen it before. *Another world like our own.*

The helper gave her time before continuing. "If you follow Venus for several days, you can track the phases as they change. Would you like to see more?"

"Yes, please." The tremor had gone, but her voice remained subdued.

"At eighty-three degrees east is Jupiter, a world farther away than Venus but much larger than our own. You can tell it's a planet because of the orbiting moons, with the four largest visible."

A third planet. Four moons. The open expanse made her giddy.

She located the appropriate number, cast in bronze on the chamber's wall, and glanced up. Though less bright than Venus, Jupiter outshone all the other stars.

"I don't see any moons."

"Let me position the telescope for you."

Orah clutched the sides of the chair as the cylinder adjusted and then peered into the eyepiece. Four bursts of white flashed close by Jupiter. She took a deep breath and then scanned the sky for another target. *So many stars and between them all, far more dramatic, the endless blackness.*

After weeks confined in the keep, she found the sight inspiring, and gave expression to her feelings. "What a view, and such a clear night except for that one cloud."

"I'm sorry. Remember, you must tell me direction and degrees."

Always respectful, she told him the location of the cloud, but her mouth dropped open at his response.

"That's likely not a cloud but a galaxy, a cluster of stars so far away they appear as a haze in the sky. I suggest you check through the telescope."

Once more, the cylinder whirred and stopped, but when she pressed her eye to the eyepiece, her vision blurred. She had to wipe the moisture away with the back of her sleeve before looking again.

Oh, Nathaniel, you should see this. She checked again to be sure she hadn't dreamed it. Through the lens, her mind filled with a million suns.

***

Nathaniel raced into the dining hall, eager to show Orah what he'd found — his childhood fantasy come true — but as he skidded to a stop before her, late and out of breath, she barely looked up.

"I found a map," he announced.

"What's so amazing about that? We have a map that shows all we need."

"Ours shows the world of today. The keepmasters' map displays *their* world on a screen."

She shoved the remains of her dinner aside. "Is this city on it?"

"Yes, and much more. Come with me."

She stood to follow, but Thomas didn't budge.

"You too, Thomas," Nathaniel said.

"I haven't finished eating yet."

205

"The food can wait."

Nathaniel grabbed his arm and tugged until Thomas shook him off. "Enough. I'm coming. This had better be worth it."

Nathaniel led them through a maze of corridors, never slowing to read screens. In a couple of minutes, they arrived at a viewing area like all the others. He urged them to sit while he stood next to the screen.

As soon as they settled, he issued his first command. "Show me Riverbend."

The screen flickered and a map appeared, more detailed than the third keeper's paper map and in color. The North River wound through the landscape in a ribbon of blue, and the forests gleamed a bright green. Shaded contours gave depth to the terrain.

Orah pointed to a thick black line. "Is that the road we took out of Riverbend?"

He nodded. "Watch. We can follow it." He barked out the word, "East."

The image scrolled, and the town vanished, but in the center of the screen the river curled northward.

Orah understood at once and took over. "North."

The picture changed. The river's bend now lay at the bottom left corner, and the broad roadway spread beside it.

"Can we keep going?"

Nathaniel barely contained his delight. "Go ahead and try."

She repeated the command and the screen scrolled again and again. Contours showed the trail rising. Soon, the four falls tumbled down and a new roadway jumped out of the mountain on one side, arched across the valley and entered the slope on the other.

Without hesitation, Orah changed direction. "East."

The image soared over the rugged terrain shifting again and again each time she spoke.

"Look how far the wagon flew. Don't make me wait, Nathaniel? How much farther?"

"A few more."

Orah barked out three more commands and gasped when the city appeared with its needle-topped buildings poking the sky.

She blew out a stream of air. "I wish we'd had this on our trek here."

Nathaniel nudged Thomas. "Your turn. Give it a try."

Thomas reluctantly rose to his feet, shuffled closer, and mumbled the words. "Show me Little Pond."

The screen stayed unchanged. Thomas frowned and fell back a step.

Nathaniel placed a hand on the small of Thomas's back and nudged him closer. "It doesn't understand Little Pond. I tried before. The village may be too small or the name may have changed over the centuries, but we can still get there." He faced the screen and spoke, "Show me Great Pond."

The larger town appeared by the pond of the same name.

"Go ahead. You know the way home from here."

Thomas eyed him skeptically. When he spoke, he sounded afraid he'd be denied again. "West... north... west." When Little Pond at last appeared, he brightened a moment before becoming wistful. "If only the screen came with a wagon to take us home."

"I'm sorry, Thomas. No wagon, but I have one more surprise."

He waited like a magician, letting the suspense build before performing a trick. Only after Orah slid to the edge of her seat did he speak the next command.

"West." Little Pond vanished from the screen. "West, west."

The granite mountains appeared—what the vicars insisted was the end of the world.

He gave his friends time to absorb the implication and then said, "West," again.

The mountains filled the right side only, but on the left, an expanse of blue appeared.

Orah came forward and brushed the blue on the screen with her fingertips. "Oh, Nathaniel, the ocean your knight discovered, beyond the edge of the world."

Nathaniel waved his hand and bowed. His show had ended.

But Orah wanted more. "Did you go farther? Did you try to find what's on the other side?"

He shrugged, surprised how caught up she was in the illusion. "I tried. Nothing but ocean. I'll show you." He took a breath and issued the command, "West." The screen turned all to blue. "West, west, west." Nothing changed. He waved at the empty sea. "The end of the map."

"Are you sure you went far enough? What if the ocean is so large we're still over water?"

"I tried a hundred times. The blue never changes."

"Ask if we can make it scroll faster."

He asked, and a helper told him to state the number of movements with the command. He ordered the map to shift five times, then ten. No change. In desperation, he hurled absurd commands at the screen. "West a hundred times. A thousand times. West to the far side of the ocean."

He turned to take his seat, tired of the show, but stopped when he saw Orah's eyes widen. Almost afraid to see what she was gaping at, he looked back.

The blue now filled only half the screen, with land on the left side, and on that land, a broad roadway led to a shining city.

The legend—every word of it—was true.

***

The next day, Thomas ventured from the dining hall without knowing why. Did boredom drive him, or had he finally succumbed to Orah's nagging? Whatever the reason, he found himself sitting alone in front of a screen.

When a helper appeared, he had no choice but to admit the reason he came. "Can you tell me about the darkness?"

The helper responded matter-of-factly, oblivious to the mood of his listener. "Do you mean darkness as in the absence of light or darkness as used by the Temple?"

"The darkness of the Temple."

The helper changed. The new one bore an unfortunate resemblance to the arch vicar, with thick eyebrows and a bushy beard, but when he spoke, he seemed friendly and enthusiastic. "Thank you for your interest in the Temple of Light. The vicars invented the term 'darkness' to mean the time before they came to power. Of course, the usage is simplistic. Any era has good and bad. The vicars justified damning ours by emphasizing the worst and hiding the best. I can show you examples of both and am pleased to discuss these further, but you may narrow the discussion by being more specific."

Thomas forced himself to recall his teaching. "Did they invent a liquid that melted flesh from bone?"

"The time before the Temple was a period of frequent wars, with atrocities committed by all sides." The helper warmed to his subject. "Combatants armed themselves with weapons that used the knowledge of the day, one of these was an incendiary gel composed of polystyrene, benzene, and gasoline, which—"

"Stop." One teaching confirmed. No need for details. "Did they drop an artificial sun from the sky?"

The helper resumed, unperturbed by the interruption. "The Temple coined the term 'artificial sun' to describe a super weapon dropped from the sky that could kill many people. The crass attempt at symbolism was obvious. Their sun, the giver of life, would compare positively with—"

"Was it ever used?" Thomas couldn't bring himself to look at the screen.

"I'm sorry. Please repeat your question."

Thomas squeezed his fist until the nails bit into his palm and spoke louder this time.

The helper hesitated as if reluctant to answer. Finally, he said a single word, "Yes."

"How many died?"

"Difficult to say. At least several hundreds of thousands, maybe millions if you count the long term effects of—"

"Show me."

The screen flickered and lit up, showing the same pictures he'd viewed during his teaching. His breath came in heavy bursts. Finally, he said, "Stop." The screen cleared, and the helper reappeared, waiting with an infuriating patience.

The word exploded from Thomas's lips. "Why?"

"I'm sorry. I don't understand."

"Why did they do it?"

The screen cycled through helpers as if unsure which expert to select. At last, the original helper returned, looked at Thomas dejectedly and said, "Unknown."

Thomas glared at the man, challenging him to come up with a better explanation. Everything the vicars claimed turned out to be true, and the keepmasters had no defense. He wanted to go hide in the dining hall and never hear of the Temple or the keepmasters again.

Then the helper began to speak on his own, his tone no longer pleasant but concerned. "I note your last several requests dealt with the horrors of our age—and we had many—but it would be unfair to limit yourself to such a negative view. I urge you to explore our achievements as well, the writings of our great thinkers, the scientific discoveries, the works of art." The helper opened his arms wide and waited.

Science was Orah domain, and Nathaniel studied history, but science gave Thomas a headache, and history revealed a time he'd just as soon forget. A part of him wanted to rush out into the ruined city and race through the buildings until one of them crashed down on him and ended his misery, but curiosity made him ask for more.

"What do you mean by art?"

The helper waved his arms as if to encompass the screen, the room and the universe. "The creative arts. We have so many forms—painting, theater, literature, sculpture, music."

The last caught Thomas's attention, and he repeated the word, "Music."

"I'm sorry. I don't...."

"Please show me music."

A new helper appeared, if anything more buoyant than his predecessor. "Welcome to the study of music. Music has evolved throughout history, an art form that constantly changes. Does any particular style interest you?"

Thomas had no idea. Most of what he knew consisted of the sound produced by two flutes and a drum, but a thought struck him—the vicars disapproved of music.

"Show me music from before the vicars came to power."

"We have many forms of—"

"Pick one."

At first, he believed the screen had gone blank, but then he realized he was watching a scene at night. Fire flashed. When the smoke cleared, a brightly-lit stage appeared with a dozen young men and women poised upon it, all dressed in black and made up in ghastly colors.

The drummer began, establishing the beat, and then the others joined in. The music blared louder than anything he recalled — until he remembered a similar sound from his teaching cell. The vicars had claimed the young worshipped death, but he perceived the noise differently now, a kind of music.

Had he finally caught the vicars in a lie?

He leaned in, needing to be sure. "Can you show me their faces?"

The screen zoomed in on the audience, not children worshipping death, but revelers at a kind of festival, their faces expressing pleasure, not despair.

Thomas settled back in his chair. The urge to flee had passed. He recalled the words of the vicar of Bradford: *The people of this era had enjoyed unlimited freedom of thought.* This music was chaotic, not to his taste, but these people enjoyed its sound.

The day had worn on, and his stomach began to growl. He decided to sample one more before joining his friends for dinner. "Can you show me something a little... quieter?"

The screen cleared for a moment before revealing a mass of players holding instruments the likes of which he'd never seen. Peering closer, he picked out a flute similar to his own, except larger, more polished and elaborately carved, and another wind instrument, even longer, with more holes and silver pieces to cover them. Most of the players clutched what he assumed to be wooden string instruments and held above them something like a thin saw.

The leader in front tapped twice with a stick. The musicians readied their instruments, with saws raised and pointing to the sky.

Then they began to play.

Thomas took a moment to connect the sounds — rich and sonorous and somehow woody — with the musicians sawing at their instruments. As he listened, he caught something else, not a single melody, but several going on at once. They didn't get in each other's way, but worked together, playing off one another to form a whole piece.

One of the higher-pitched instruments tossed out a melody. A lower one picked it up, changed it and tossed it back. Then all came together for a note or two, changing the — he had no word for it — and split apart again in a musical dance.

211

He found himself lost in a bouncing, floating joy, which made him recall trips to the granite mountains as a child, the thrill of winning a race at festival, the euphoria of finding the keep. It sounded like something he'd been dreaming about all his life—strange dreams that hinted of music from long ago—and now he'd discovered the joy again, better than he ever imagined.

When the music ended, the helper returned. "You've been listening to the first movement of the Brandenburg Concerto Number 2 in F major BWV 1047, by Johan Sebastian Bach, played by—"

"May I listen again?"

The screen went blank. The musicians reappeared and began to play once more, but this time Thomas focused on how the dance came into being, trying to understand the way the different melodies wove in and out. He reached into his pocket and pulled out the flute that had lain silent for too long, closed his eyes, and swayed with the sound until he felt it in his fingertips.

Then he joined in the dance.

Chapter 30
Enlightenment

The next morning, Nathaniel strode into a viewing area, desperate to learn more about the voyage across the sea.

He puffed out his chest and bellowed a command. "Help. I want to hear stories about heroes."

No helper appeared, but instead a catalog of titles showed. He leaned closer and scanned the list. One title caught his eye: *The Man Who Toppled the Temple of Light*. He repeated the phrase aloud, affirming what he'd read. The screen cleared, and a page of text displayed in place of the catalog.

Shortly, a helper with a rich baritone began reciting the words, which scrolled as he spoke. Before Nathaniel knew it, the story had captivated him. Abandoning his plan to learn more about the land across the ocean, he sat and listened. Hours passed as the speaker told of a courageous man who stood up for his beliefs in the waning days of the prior age. He traveled from town to town, declaring the truth about the past and urging the people to resist the encroaching power of the Temple. Many heeded his words, but none would act. In the end, the deacons drove him back to his village, where he was stoned to death by his neighbors at the urging of the vicars.

Nathaniel's hands clenched in sympathy with the persecuted hero, but the story hadn't finished. After the man's death, remorse drove the villagers to rebel against the Temple. The reaction spread like a wave, and soon an entire region had walled off the influence of the vicars. They reprinted banished books and resurrected forbidden ideas. Freedom of thought flowed once more. The story ended with the seeds of enlightenment planted and beginning to grow.

The tale left Nathaniel drained. He mourned the man and blamed the people for not supporting his cause sooner, but he exulted in the outcome. Though the man had perished, he'd made a difference.

Before he could dwell on it further, the screen cleared and a woman helper appeared, smiling graciously.

"Thank you for listening to the story of *The Man Who Toppled the Temple of Light*, author unknown. We hope you've enjoyed this book. If you're interested in similar stories, please ask and I'll be happy to make recommendations."

Nathaniel crumpled his brow. *Stories?* What had he been listening to? He recalled his original request and knew the helpers could be literal.

"Is this story true?" he said.

"No. *The Man Who Toppled the Temple of Light* is a work of fiction. I can show you a list of nonfiction books if you prefer."

"What is fiction?"

"Fiction is a class of literature that is the creation of the author, an act of imagination."

Orah's voice echoed in his mind: *What you see is an illusion.*

He forced his words to be crisp so the helper would understand. "Tell me more about this book."

She said the book had been written in the days before the keepmasters fled, and that the Temple censors had banned it. The work was one of the last rescued.

"What happened to the writer?"

"We can't be sure. Most likely, imprisoned or executed."

Maybe the story was no illusion after all. The author had invented the tale to show the truth and move others. He believed in his cause and had paid the price.

The day had flown by with no answers to his original question, but he'd learned a greater lesson—ideas combined with courage can change the world.

***

The next day, Nathaniel tried again. He raced through corridors, searching for information about those who'd crossed the ocean, switching from screen to screen, uncertain which question to ask. Each corridor led to another until he'd wandered as far as ever from the golden doors. Nothing remained but an unmarked anteroom with no screen and a solitary doorway.

He nearly turned back, sensing a blind alley, but curiosity drove him on. The passageway narrowed, barely wide enough for a single person, and its ceiling tapered downward until he had to duck his head to continue. The hall ended at an ornate archway opening into an elaborate viewing area. Unlike the others, this chamber was crowned with a marble dome, the keep's sole concession to grandeur.

Immediately, the air appeared to shimmer, and he struggled to distinguish between floor and walls. Elsewhere in the keep, the walls had been broken only by screens. Here, rows of boxes lined the surface, each a foot wide and a hand high, with their faces protruding. Each boasted an oval medallion at its center, inlaid with a glittering stone. These came in every shade and color—blue sapphires and red rubies, yellow and green opals, honey-colored amber and purple amethyst. The lighting in the room was directed not for the benefit of visitors but to highlight the stones. As Nathaniel drifted about, the refractions generated unsettling rivulets of light.

He groped along the edge of one of the boxes, his fingertips struggling for purchase, and pulled with no success. He tugged harder until the box groaned, shifting a hair's breadth. The movement had exposed a gap wide enough for his fingers to grasp. He positioned his hands, bent at the knees and grunted. The drawer slid an inch.

A pungent odor filled the air, distasteful but vaguely familiar.... Not a viewing area but a crypt. The boxes held human remains.

He slammed the drawer back into place and collapsed on a bench, resting his head in his hands. Dark visions filled his mind—the funeral for Orah's father, the tomb of the mother he never knew.

At his feet, another of the medallions lay on the ground as if waiting for a box of its own. In its center lay a chunk of obsidian, so much like the talisman he'd imagined hanging from the neck of his knight, at once clear and black throughout. It was the only one of its kind in the room.

As he stared, trying to penetrate to the heart of the stone, a flash from above caught his eye. The screen on the wall had lit up. A helper appeared, but different from the others, older and frailer, more like the prisoner Samuel than a keepmaster. The corners of his mouth glistened, and old age spots dotted his cheeks. Black eyes stared out from sunken sockets, giving him a mournful countenance.

For several seconds, the man stayed silent, as if he'd forgotten why he came, but then he started to speak. "I have neither time nor strength for formalities, so let me begin recording with three purposes in mind. The first is in my role as a descendant of the founders of the keep. Each of us pledged allegiance to our mission, our goal to impart knowledge, and I will do that. I'll recount the final days of the keepmasters. Second, I have a favor to request. With the third, I'll repay that favor as a man who is dying. I'll bequeath to you what wisdom I've gained, the lessons of a lifetime.

"The founders set guidelines for helpers to be cordial and impersonal but I am a person with a name. I'm called Kiran, which means ray of light. I don't know if my parents chose that name as a sign of hope or as a cruel jest, for I've never seen the light of day.

"After we completed recording the knowledge of our age, we did not vanish. The euphoria that accompanies all quests faded, but we went on with our lives. We married, had families and continued our research, but always, we feared being discovered. Over time, we developed our own religion, based on a dread of the Temple of Light.

"By my grandparent's childhood, leaving the keep had become unthinkable. I am the third generation to never venture outside. The fear gnawed at us and robbed us of reason to live.

216

Fewer couples married. Of those who did, many decided not to conceive children who'd spend their existence imprisoned here. And so we diminished. At times, it's been no life at all, but I lived nevertheless and will soon die, the last of the keepmasters.

"You, whom I never met, the seeker I awaited my whole life, can do me one final honor. You'll find before you a black stone, a color appropriate for the last of my kind. Behind you, in the corner of the topmost row, lies the box that awaits it. I chose this to mark my memorial. Please, take a moment to set the stone in its place, and to remember me and the rest of us who lived and died in the keep."

He broke into a coughing fit, reminiscent of the first keeper in his cell in Temple City. But to his last, Samuel had retained hope for the future. The man before Nathaniel had none.

"Now let me tell you what I've learned. In each of our lives, we have our mission, the life's work we choose that consumes so much of our energies, but we also have the little things we do with the hours and minutes of our days. As a descendant of the founders, I stayed true to their ideals throughout my life, but as a man who lives day to day, I failed. I recall my childhood aspirations—to play outside in the sun, to be free of fear, to welcome the seekers who would someday surely come—but these things exist in dreams. Each day, I had the ability to touch those around me, to repay my parents for their love, to embrace my wife.

"So what is the lesson of a lifetime, the truth I bequeath to you?"

He wiped his mouth with a soiled sleeve and stared out before continuing.

Nathaniel slid to the edge of his seat. The answer was simpler than he'd ever imagined.

"We should not be so seduced by our mission that we forget how to live."

The screen went blank. Nathaniel glanced at the floor and caught the glimmer of obsidian, the last keepmaster's despair trapped within it like the darkness. He cradled it in his hand and proceeded to the waiting container. Using his long arms, he reached up and snapped the stone into place. Then he stepped back and stared at it, trying to comprehend how it could glow so brightly and still be black as night.

***

Late August. As the deadline approached, the days weighed heavily upon Orah. She trudged about the keep as if still bearing her pack, and Nathaniel seemed no better. Only Thomas appeared unaffected.

That evening during dinner, as Thomas whistled a tune, Orah finally snapped. "Would you mind for once if Nathaniel and I had some quiet while we ate?"

"My whistling never bothered you before."

"I've never before been so close to being punished by *your* vicars."

Thomas remained unfazed, his childlike grin infuriating. "They're not *my* vicars."

"Then why do you defend them?"

"I don't defend them, though most of what they claimed has turned out to be true."

"Well I've found proof that their most basic precept is a lie." She'd blurted out the words without thought. For weeks she'd waited for the right moment, wanting so much to impress Nathaniel, and now her revelation had emerged in a squabble. She glanced at him out of the corner of her eye.

He stared back, brows arched in a question. "What did you find?"

She set her food aside and raised her chin. "The sun is not the source of all light, and the stars do not revolve around it. I'll never pray to the sun again."

All she'd discovered in astronomy poured out, how the stars moved in their own paths, how some were worlds like their own, but most were suns themselves—and the keepmasters had found millions of them.

Thomas gaped at her. "A million suns? Are you sure you didn't discover a vat of wassail?"

She turned from Thomas to Nathaniel. "I found a place where you can see for yourself. Come and I'll show you."

Nathaniel stood at once, but Thomas slumped back in his chair. "You don't need to show me. I believe you. But who cares if you found a thousand suns or a million? Our situation remains the same."

"You're being lazy, Thomas. Come with us."

When he refused to join them, insisting he had better things to do, Orah gave up, content to share her discovery with Nathaniel alone.

She led him along the familiar route and into the elevator, where she took satisfaction as he clutched the handrail when it began to rise. Once in the observatory, she ordered the helper to expose the dome to the sky.

She'd picked a perfect night, and Nathaniel reacted appropriately, spinning around and gawking at the view. When he'd seen his fill, she directed him to take a seat at the telescope and asked the helper to point the instrument at the cluster of stars.

"Now put your eye to the glass and behold."

He stared for a long time. Through the lens the cloud would become a brilliant whirl of lights, more than he could count in a lifetime, but when he finally looked up, the doubt in his face confounded her.

"Aren't you impressed, Nathaniel of Little Pond?"

He slipped out of the seat and drifted toward her, shaking his head. "I *am* impressed, but such wonders make me sad. So much damage has been done to our world. So much lost. We both know what our choice should be."

She turned away and bit her lip—not the conversation she'd hoped for.

He stroked her cheek with his fingertips, forcing her to face him. His doubt had changed to anguish. "But I no longer know if I'm willing to take the chance. What if the cost is too high?"

She'd always been able to read him, but her instincts failed her now, not because he'd become opaque—he was as transparent as ever—but because his thoughts seemed in conflict. "Are you saying you agree with Thomas that we should betray the keepmasters?"

"I'm not sure what I believe, but I understand better what's at stake."

"What's that?"

"The two of us. I'd trade all we've learned to go back to Little Pond and spend my life with you."

She rose on tiptoes and brushed her lips against his. He drew her closer until her head rested on his chest. *If only the helpers could freeze time and leave us in this moment.*

As she counted the too-quick beating of his heart, she struggled to find an answer. They could not stay in the keep; they must not betray the keepmasters. Then she remembered the other miracle she'd found.

She pulled away. "There's something more. They told me they'd traveled to the stars."

Nathaniel raised his chin and surveyed the heavens. "You believe them?"

She followed his gaze as if hoping to see a starship streak across the sky. "I... think so. I could try to explain, but it's too complicated."

"Did you ask them to show you?"

So simple, she'd never thought of it. She shook her head.

"Go ahead."

She turned to the screen. "Can you show us star travel?"

The screen cleared, and a roar filled the chamber. A long cylinder displayed, slowly lifting off the ground, a ball of orange flame and clouds of smoke trailing behind. Soon, a broad vista showed as if seen from a mountaintop.

As the land fell away, the answer she'd been seeking became a question, which Nathaniel gave voice to. "If they could go to the stars, isn't anything possible?"

She kept staring at the screen. Challenging the vicars might ruin them all, and Thomas would never go along. She needed more time to solve this riddle, a puzzle more complex than the rhyme.

"Summer's not over. We don't need to decide now."

But in that instant, she realized the harsh truth. Only by overthrowing the Temple of Light could she and Nathaniel have a life together. If the possibility existed on heaven or earth, she'd find a way.

Gradually, the roar diminished. The screen filled with the surface of their world, so far away now she recognized only the largest objects — lakes, oceans and mountains.

Then they beheld it all, framed in black, a great blue shining globe.

Chapter 31
A Plan for Revolution

Dear log,

The time has come to go silent. This day, I embark on the most harrowing venture of my life, one that might change the world or spell my doom. I've learned enough to believe this cause is just, but as always I worry.

Though I'm loath to admit it, I find myself thinking like Thomas. How I wish the realm of vicars and teachings would vanish from my mind. How I long to return to Little Pond, to join with Nathaniel and build a cottage of our own.

Which is the greater illusion – a life of contentment and peace, or the dream of a better world?

No matter. I have made my choice. The truth will drive me on.

Who knows where this journey will take me, what revelations I'll find or what trials I'll endure, but none of it will find place in this log, lest it falls into the wrong hands. This chronicle of my thoughts will travel with me, but I'll write no more, not until the journey's end, wherever it may lead.

I only pray this entry won't be my last.

***

Orah's mind was alive with plans. Was opposition to the Temple possible?

First challenge: if the vicars tracked their every move, the rebellion would surely fail. As her initial task, she needed to learn more about temple trees.

A well-meaning helper urged her to study the underlying disciplines, his purpose to provide an in-depth education, to produce an expert. She had a simpler goal: to disrupt temple communications.

She tried asking in a variety of ways. "How do temple trees work?" resulted in a lecture on something called microwaves. "What's their purpose?" produced nothing more than what she already knew. She found herself interrupting the helper with an increasingly abrupt "stop."

At last, she hit on the right question. "How can I make temple trees stop sending words through the air?"

The helper froze, apparently unprepared to explain how to make something fail. Seconds passed while the brains of the keep searched for an answer.

Finally, the helper awoke. "Temple trees get their power from a wire rising up from underground. You'll find a metal plate at the base of each tree for maintenance. Unscrew the cover and cut the wire to disable the tower."

A minor victory. The trees stood isolated and easy to access, protected only by the myth of temple magic. Disabling them increased their likelihood of success.

The helper, however, had more to say. "Be advised that what powers them is strong enough to kill you, so take the necessary precautions to protect yourself." He appeared pleased to have found an answer, and then added, "Do you have another question?"

For the rest of the afternoon, she thrashed about like a child trying to assemble a puzzle while the helpers teased by withholding pieces. Still she made progress, keeping careful notes and, when appropriate, printing pictures and diagrams.

The next day she focused on transportation. The Temple had banned all forms of fast travel, by animal or machine. What if the vicars had held something back for themselves? If the deacons could move faster than the seekers, she and her friends would soon be caught.

The topic led to more discoveries. People of the prior age traveled often and at high speed—mobility defined their age. Though few went to the stars, they took casual trips anywhere in the world. Did that include crossing the ocean? The helper told her yes.

"In great boats, big enough for ocean travel?"

"Yes," the helper said, "but only for pleasure, because ocean voyages took too long. Most people were unwilling to spend a week or more when they could cross in hours."

She'd witnessed the vastness of the ocean on the map and wasn't about to let such a bold statement pass. "What did they use to cross the ocean in hours?"

"They flew."

"Do you mean like the flying wagon that brought us here?"

"No. In flying machines."

"Do you mean like birds fly?"

When the helper responded yes, she hardly blinked, staying focused on one question—what machines did the vicars retain?

She learned most travelers used fast wagons. Some, like the giant snake that had brought them to the keep, moved hundreds of people at once, but only on a preset path. Other smaller ones went almost anywhere, and nearly everyone had one.

Flying machines, giant boats, fast wagons. Now time for the most important questions.

"Does the Temple possess flying machines?"

"No. The cost to maintain them would be prohibitive, and they'd be impossible to hide."

"Fast wagons?"

"We believe so, though they'd hardly be fast. No highways survived the Temple's purge. It's logical, however, to assume they'd keep some form of advanced travel for emergencies."

"Show me a fast wagon."

A broad roadway appeared, coated with the now familiar black rock. Hundreds of fast wagons rolled along it on four wheels, moving at incredible speeds. They raced across the screen, sleek and low, and wide enough to seat three people across. No threat here—no such roads existed.

Next she asked to view the wagons on dirt roads. Out of their element, they lumbered rather than glided, but still easily outpaced a grown man running. She recognized their flaw—too wide for trails through the trees. If the seekers stuck to the woods, the vicars would be unable to catch them.

She scoured her mind. What other obstacles might the Temple present? At once, she realized her oversight. She'd focused on the wonders of the past but had overlooked the horrors.

She crept closer to the screen and lowered her voice as if afraid the vicars might hear. "Did they keep weapons?"

The helper paused. When he finally spoke, he responded with the one word she'd come to dread: "Unknown."

An obvious next question occurred to her, but she hesitated to ask—at least until she thought of Thomas in the teaching cell. Anger overcame doubt. "Will you provide the seekers with weapons?"

This time, the screen blanked. When it brightened again, the woman who had first welcomed them to the keep reappeared. Apparently, this question required an answer from an elder. The keepmaster's lips stretched into a thin, unyielding line.

"The council knew the question of weapons would arise one day. We debated among ourselves and decided the abuse of knowledge had brought the world to its current state. It seemed foolhardy to encourage you down a similar path, so we determined to eliminate weapons from the keep. Of course, the foundation is here for you to re-invent them if you insist, but we refuse to help.

"The Temple of Light needed only ignorance to overturn our world. Let knowledge be your weapon to reverse the damage."

The image faded.

Let knowledge be your weapon....

The plan was coming together, but she still lacked a way to spread the truth. On a whim, she printed a picture of a ship that could cross the ocean—a curiosity to show Nathaniel. As the paper slid from the wall slot, an idea came to her.

"Is there a way to print my words?"

"Yes," the helper replied. "Say the command 'record' and as you speak, you'll see your words appear on the screen. Edit them as you wish. When done, say 'print.'"

"Can I print more than one copy?"

"As many as you wish. Say 'print' followed by the number of copies."

Dinnertime was drawing near. She'd be late if she tried now, but the solution seemed so close.

"Record."

The screen cleared.

"Nathaniel and Thomas are my dearest friends."

The words appeared as she spoke them.

"I would do anything to protect them from harm."

The new sentence followed the first.

"Change the word 'harm' to read 'the Temple of Light.'"

Instantly, the last phrase changed.

"Print."

Immediately, a page came out with her exact words in bold lettering.

"Print five times."

Five more copies slid through the slot in the wall. She checked each. Not a single mistake.

A new thought struck her. "How do you turn my voice into words on a page?"

"Your voice is recorded and stored. The sound is interpreted into text to be printed or displayed on the screen."

"May I listen to it?"

"Yes. Say play instead of print."

She took a deep breath and swallowed to moisten her throat. *Time to try.*

"Record." She paused to think through the words. "May the light protect my dear Nathaniel from this reckless venture." After a respectful interval, she said, "play."

Her voice sounded unfamiliar and timid, like a little girl scared of her shadow. Worst of all, the passion of it embarrassed her—the way she spoke Nathaniel's name.

"How do I make my words go away?"

"Say 'erase.'"

She did, and released a long stream of air when the helper confirmed they were gone.

Her stomach began to rumble, but she suppressed her hunger. Thoughts tumbled around in her mind and arranged themselves into a vision. She'd always been organized, but never before did she have to plan for a revolution. Unknowns abounded, yet for the first time, she believed their goal possible.

She gave the order again. "Record."

A shiver started at the small of her back and traveled up her spine. Steadying herself, she took a deep breath and spoke, her voice becoming firmer with each syllable.

The words burned into the screen.

They read, *The Truth about the Darkness.*

Chapter 32
The Potential for Greatness

The details of Orah's plan were snapping into place like the pieces of a puzzle, but one item remained unresolved: Thomas. Over the summer, she and Nathaniel had come to value what the keep offered. Thomas had not. With little sense of its wonders, he'd surely vote no. As the deadline loomed, she dreaded the choice: forsake the keepmasters or abandon Thomas.

She brought up the issue over dinner, hoping to provoke a reaction. "Summer's ending, Thomas, and soon you'll need to choose. I'd be happy to introduce you to the helpers if you'd like. In the two weeks remaining, you might still learn enough to make the appropriate choice."

"What makes you think your choice is appropriate?"

"I'm sorry. I didn't mean to judge. I was trying to remind you how little time is left. Visiting the helpers might give you a better perspective."

"What perspective is that? Nathaniel found maps that show an ocean we can never cross. You learned to predict the movement of the stars but can't change their course. Have either of you solved a problem or invented anything new, other than finding ways to blame the Temple for the world's ills?"

Orah grimaced. Too close to the truth. She'd learned much but mastered little, falling short of the keepmasters' expectations. Yet now, based on a belief in potential, she was about to cast her lot for a dangerous and improbable venture. She glanced at Nathaniel for support. He shook his head, intending to calm her down, but his unwillingness to confront Thomas fired her up instead. Better now than on decision day.

"At least we've tried, Thomas. What have you accomplished?"

Thomas displayed the grin that had infuriated her since childhood. "I mastered my own subject, different from yours, and I've gone beyond it."

"Are you going to amuse us again with stories about custard?"

"Don't belittle my accomplishments until you hear them. If you like, I can show you now." He shoved his meal aside and stepped to the door, waiting at the threshold for his friends.

Dumbfounded, Orah shrugged and followed with Nathaniel trailing behind.

Thomas led them through the keep, apparently more familiar with its layout than she realized. With no hesitation, he found the anteroom for art and strode down the corridor to music. In the viewing area, he asked them to sit while he stood beside the screen. Once they'd settled into their places, he bypassed the helper and announced some foreign sounding words followed by a number.

The helper vanished, replaced by a gathering of musicians clutching strange instruments. A man who seemed to be their leader called them to order with a small wand. The musicians arched their backs at the ready. Some of them positioned saw-like sticks over ancient strings banned long ago, while those with wind instruments raised them to their lips.

With a smile on his face, Thomas took out his flute and did the same.

They began to play, and Thomas played with them, note for note.

The music filled the air, gladdening her heart with its sound, but its interwoven melodies seemed complex, impossible to duplicate with the temple-sanctioned drum and two flutes, and far too challenging to master without weeks of practice.

Now Orah understood how Thomas had spent his days, and his time had been well spent. These musicians were likely the best of their age, and Thomas was their peer.

At the end, the music soared like ships taking off to the stars. The musicians went silent and set their instruments down, but Thomas continued to play, enhancing their tunes with his own creations.

This time, Thomas was right. Here was innovation reborn, the reason the keepmasters had locked themselves away for fifty years. But Thomas cared nothing for history or politics—only his music. He gazed out as he played, envisioning a place more sublime than any she'd ever known, and she could only applaud.

***

Nathaniel cradled the device in the palm of his hand. Orah had made remarkable progress, and now she'd handed him the final stroke—an opaque cube with rounded edges, slightly larger than his fist and fashioned of the same substance as the deacon's star. As he stared, trying to see through to its core, it took on the color of water. The cube bore no features save a red dot and a tiny lever on one end.

"Are you certain this will work?"

"Yes," Orah said. "The keepmasters have assured me. We only need to record the words, and this device will transmit our message at the appropriate time."

He pointed to the dot and lever. "What are these for?"

"The piece is too small to retain much strength from the sun, so it contains its own power source, but with limited duration. The helper said to slide this switch only when ready."

"How long?"

"He couldn't be exact. With no direct sunlight, a month at most. With some exposure, maybe more."

Nathaniel had spent the day with Orah composing messages. She'd fanned out the results on the table—four sheets of paper. All had the style of a Temple bulletin except for a title on the top and a signature at the bottom. The title described the content, beginning with, *The Truth about,* followed by the Temple claim under dispute—the darkness and teachings, medicines and temple trees. The signature read, *The Seekers of Truth.*

The truth simply stated would arouse the people, but this cube would provide the proof. All that remained was to record the message.

He handed Orah the script they'd crafted, but she declined. "I've heard my voice from the screens. No one would follow me."

"You underestimate yourself."

"Trust me, your voice is stronger. They're more likely to listen to you."

He began to argue but stopped as the realization came crashing down. The one who spoke from the cube would be interrupting the human embodiment of the light in this world. Recording this message was a death warrant.

He held out his hand for the script. "Show me what to do."

***

Thomas slipped into his sleeping chamber and ordered the helper to lower the slab. He recalled his first night, how he worried the bedding would be too hard, but as the strange material enveloped his body, he found the slab more comfortable than his bed back home.

He lay still, slowed his breathing and waited for the lights to dim, but after a restless minute, he asked the helper to leave them on. Aside from avoiding nightmares, he had a lot to think about.

Nathaniel and Orah had become secretive in the past few days, and now, instead of researching the keep independently, they worked together. Though the debate would wait until tomorrow, they'd made their decision, all except for his fate.

Despite the bright lights, exhaustion overcame him. His eyelids drooped, and his mind began to replay scenes from a younger day. A traveling peddler used to visit Little Pond each spring and bring some curiosity to attract a crowd. One year, he placed a wooden box on the ground and urged everyone to gather round. Thomas, as one of the youngest, took a seat in the front. With a flourish, the peddler sprung open the box, and out popped a squirrel on a leash.

With one hand, the peddler held the end of the leash, and with the other, he played a penny whistle. The squirrel began dancing to the music. At the climax of each refrain, the peddler yanked on the leash and the squirrel reared up on its hind legs, looking for an instant like a grotesque little man, tiny fingers grappling at the air and eyes bulging out.

People clapped and children laughed, but the spectacle horrified Thomas. That evening, he was too upset to eat. His father scolded him: *No squirrel deserves so much concern. Accept the order of things.* That night, he cried himself to sleep.

He shook off the memory, sat up and swung his legs to the floor. His friends were smarter than him and braver, but he knew something they'd overlooked—leaving the keep would seal their fate. Orah's careful planning might buy them a few weeks, but eventually they'd be caught and punished. Their only hope would be to barter the secret of the keep.

The keepmasters had caused their share of harm, and the vicars had done some good. With no clear idea of who stood on the side of right, better to avoid confronting authority. Better to yield to the order of things.

Yet he worried about his perspective. Was it his own, or had the teaching clouded it as Orah claimed? Had he now become the dancing squirrel, with the vicars tugging the leash?

***

Decision day. Thomas suggested they meet outdoors, in the place where they'd entered the Temple of Truth less than three months before. They settled on the landing with the gold plaque, on the topmost of the fourteen stairs.

A warm September breeze blew through the gap formed by the skeletons of once-great buildings. A few wispy clouds enhanced the blue sky, forming chevrons along the boulevard as if pointing the way home.

Thomas nestled between his friends and gazed at the bleak landscape. "So unlike Little Pond. By now, we'd have taken our final swim of the season. The pond would stay warm enough for another month, but a chill in the air would keep us out of the water till next summer."

Nathaniel picked up on the thought. "Soon our neighbors will take to the orchards for apple-picking. Remember how we picked—ten in the sack and one in our mouths, so crisp they cracked when you bit into them. By evening we all had stomach aches."

Orah had little tolerance for nostalgia. "Nothing can compete with childhood, but going back to being a child isn't one of our choices. The options before us are to stay in the keep, negotiate with the vicars, or fight for change. We can't stay here, and only fools would trust the vicars. That leaves one choice."

Thomas stroked the granite on which he sat. "You're so smart, Orah. Can't you think of another way? I'd trade anything to be sitting on a log on the banks of the pond instead of this hard stone."

She stared out as if searching for a different answer, then shrugged. "Sorry, Thomas. With what we know, the vicars will never let us roam freely, no matter what we offer. Look how they treated the first keeper, and he had just one scroll. Our only chance to go home is to confront them with the truth."

Thomas went limp. "I wish I'd never been taken for a teaching."

"But you were," Nathaniel said, "and through your pain, we learned what the vicars are."

Orah rested a hand on his arm. "I've only spent a short time in the teaching. I'll never understand what you went through, but we both witnessed the reason for teachings—to create fear. Don't let that fear keep you from doing what's right."

Thomas felt buffeted from either side, but his friends hadn't finished.

"Think about the music," Nathaniel said. "Would you lose it—not only what existed in the past, but all yet to be composed?"

Thomas stared at his boot tops and answered in a whisper. "I'd save the music if I could, but I wouldn't sacrifice my friends for it." He turned to Orah. "This isn't one of our games in the woods."

Orah reached behind her and traced the letters in the plaque on the landing. Her fingers lingered over the phrase, *potential for greatness*. "I understand, Thomas. Sometimes, I wish we'd never come here too. How much simpler to stay in the dark."

The breeze whistling through the empty buildings stilled as if stopping to listen. The three sat in silence for several minutes before Thomas tried one last time. "Can we really change anything? What if choosing this path makes no difference and costs us our lives?"

Orah twisted her mouth into a grimace as if she'd eaten something sour. "We're not back in school, and I have no right answers. With the keepmasters' help, the plan can work. How much of a difference will we make? I can't say for sure, and it's true, we may suffer for it."

"Well, I think we have little chance. The three of us are as unlikely to overthrow the Temple as—"

"If we have any chance," Nathaniel said, "we need to try, or the damage caused by the Temple may never be reversed."

Orah leaned closer, feeding off Nathaniel's energy. Her eyes narrowed and her voice deepened. "'Beware the stray thought.' Why do the vicars preach these words? Because what they call darkness is freedom. They feared its attraction and taught us as children to shun it."

Thomas studied them as they spoke, their faces beaming with zeal, their minds made up. He waited until Orah finished before posing his final question, the one he'd saved all day, the only one that mattered.

"Tell me this: if I say no, will you leave me here? I'm sure you've considered it, because you consider all possibilities. You both want this. Will you abandon me if I don't go along?"

Orah's frown etched wrinkles on her chin and around her eyes, making her look older than her years. "You're right, Thomas. I'd considered leaving you, but... I couldn't bring myself to do it. I believe in our cause but won't do this without you."

Thomas squinted up at the sky as she spoke. The warm breeze had broken up the chevrons of clouds, no longer arrows pointing home but random puffs like the fleeting hopes of man. When she finished, he tucked his legs under him and bounced up, stretched his arms over his head, and forced a yawn.

Then, he shuffled the toes of his boots to the edge of the plaque in the stone and invited his friends to join him. "Time for the Pact."

"You agree?" Orah said.

He eased into a grin. "You and Nathaniel... always such dreamers. Nothing ever mattered that much to me. I'm not the one to change the world, but now we're in a situation with no good end. You're my friends, and if you need to start this revolution, I'll go along. I just had to know if you'd leave me."

"If we all agree," Orah said, "then why the Pact?"

"To seal our friendship."

Orah and Nathaniel formed a circle with him around the golden words. Each covered their heart, reached into the center and clasped wrists as if they'd never let go.

PART FOUR
HEROES

"The hero is one who kindles a great light in the world, who sets up blazing torches in the dark streets of life for men to see by."

— Felix Adler

Chapter 33
Fearsome Odds

The temple tree loomed in the night, more than double the height of the surrounding evergreens, silhouetted against the stars. Beyond its unnatural height, its branches sprouted too evenly, and its boughs gleamed too green. Clearly made by man, yet for fear of the vicars, no child of light had questioned its purpose for a thousand years.

This made the sixth tree they'd encountered since emerging from the wilderness. At each, Orah had located the metal plate at its base but left it intact. Nathaniel and Thomas were itching to disable their first tree, but she held them off. From the helpers, she'd learned the gray friars monitored communications and would instantly detect a failure. If she disabled each tree in sequence, the deacons would eventually find them. Better a random approach.

Seekers no more, they were now the hunted, and to survive meant taking a devious approach. She'd devised the plan before leaving the keep: carry light-weight, dehydrated food to avoid relying on others—better to be self-sufficient; travel at night and rest in the forest by day—better to be unseen; plot an erratic course using the maps they'd found—better to be unpredictable.

Best of all, while researching the trees, she'd discovered a device that let her listen to Temple communications. Once within range of the first tower, the mechanism had crackled to life. Whatever words flew around, she could hear.

The conversations dismayed her. That which had awed her in Bradford impressed her no more. The chatter was cynical and bureaucratic, not the discourse of holy men. But once the seekers posted their first message, the words flying through the air would change, talking mostly about them. Until then, she'd eavesdrop on the vicars when she could — better to know your enemy.

The plan was straightforward. She'd printed three hundred copies of each message and divided the pages equally among them. The reason remained unspoken, but all understood why — so the mission could go on as long as any one of them survived.

She chose a region of several hundred villages, sufficient to make the pattern hard to predict but dense enough to form a front against the vicars. They'd meander rather than follow a straight line, never posting at two towns in a row. Few felt love for the Temple, and the messages would be burning tinder to dry wood. Sympathetic individuals would fan the brushfire, and once the flames of rebellion had engulfed the region, the seekers would muster the resources to protect the keep and teach others.

When they reached the temple tree, Orah removed her pack and entered the woods. Nathaniel and Thomas lingered behind, exhausted from the night's travel, and she let them assume another idle inspection, biding her time and building suspense.

"What're you dawdling for?" she said at last. "This is the one."

Nathaniel eyes shone in the dark. "Do you mean — ?"

"Come on, Nathaniel." Thomas raced toward her. "You wanted a revolution. Now's the time."

They located the plate at the base of the tree, fastened, like the others, by screws at the corners.

Orah asked Thomas for his pocketknife, but he refused. "You made the plans. I get to take off the plate."

She relented.

Thomas knelt and probed in the dark with his fingernails for the groove, then slotted his blade and twisted. The well-maintained screws gave with little effort. As he eased the last one out, she grasped the plate and yanked it free.

A black wire snaked up from the ground, exactly as the helper had described. While she admired her find, Thomas grabbed the wire and began sawing with his knife.

"Stop." She thrust a forearm into his chest, and he fell backward.

He rubbed the spot where she'd struck him and picked dried leaves off his tunic. "What did you do that for?"

"I just saved your life, Thomas. You forgot that cutting the wire can kill you."

While he scrambled back as if the wire might attack him, Orah rummaged through her pack and removed two items: the listening device, and the cutting tool provided by the helpers. The latter looked like scissors, but with a green coating on the handle. She turned on the device and listened to the familiar crackling noise, broken by remarks from faceless vicars. Then she picked up the tool.

Nathaniel grabbed her wrist. "I thought you said it can kill you."

"The helper promised the coating on this tool would protect me."

"Maybe I should do it instead."

She smiled at him. "The last time you tried to save me, you nearly became a vicar."

Before he could protest, she snipped the wire. At once, the crackling ceased.

***

No moon rose the next night, and thick clouds obliterated the stars. Orah stood watch at the edge of a nameless town, waiting for the last candle in a farmhouse window to be snuffed out. She'd insisted on going herself, but her friends had objected.

Instead, Thomas had picked three stones from the side of the road, all of similar shape, but one white like the Temple stone used to limit family size. He placed them in his pocket and rattled them around. "The one who gets the 'only child' stone goes first. Afterwards, we take turns."

One by one, they selected. In the dim light, she had trouble seeing who picked the white stone, but Nathaniel's swagger made it clear.

She grimaced as she handed him the four messages. "You be careful. Tread softly on those big feet and remember the one about the darkness goes on the deacon's post. Put the others where you see fit, but be quick."

Then she rose on her toes and gave him a kiss.

"What's that for?"

"For luck."

He nodded and headed to town, but she worried luck was a false companion. Even if it came in abundance, it would eventually run out.

***

The old farmer made a habit of going out for a morning stroll. He'd trek the fifteen minutes to the village center, where he'd circle the commons ten times before returning home for breakfast. By the time he finished, his right hip throbbed, but the exercise kept him spry.

On this day, a bulletin glared at him from the post by the common house. Notices never appeared before midday — the deacons who lived in town slept late, and no one was in a rush to read Temple news. He'd always stayed faithful to the light but refused to break stride for the vicar's nonsense.

At this hour, few people milled about. Like him, some enjoyed their sunrise stroll, and other unfortunates, like the baker, had work demanding an early start. Most ignored the bulletin, placing no import on its early arrival.

As he circled around, he counted those who bypassed the paper on the pole. He'd tallied up to six before the apprentice to the furniture maker stopped to read.

Oddly, the boy lingered, not only reading the document, but studying its every word. The farmer watched from a distance as the young man pulled others over. All clustered around and stared at the bulletin. Soon, a crowd had gathered. Despite the early hour, a lively exchange ensued.

On his ninth pass, the farmer stopped, curious to hear what they said. Their heated words became clear.

240

"This one's not from the Temple."

"It must be. Where else does such lettering come from?"

The old farmer nudged his way through the crowd. His eyesight had grown weak, and he needed to come near to read the words. The others jostled him so much he almost gave up, but then a path cleared. He turned to find a deacon hustling toward him, finishing dressing as he went. The image of the adoring family basking in the rays of the sun lay wrinkled on his half-buttoned tunic.

The deacon stared at the post while a second caught up. "What's wrong?"

The first deacon whispered to his friend, "Did you put this up?"

"Not me. Maybe one of the others?"

"I thought bulletins were your job."

"I said not me. What's the problem? Seems like a proper one."

The first deacon rubbed his jaw-line beard. "Dunno. Words ain't right."

"Should we take it down?"

Despite the morning chill, sweat beaded on the first deacon's brow. "Dunno. Never seen anything like it. We should check with the vicar."

The other agreed and the two ran off.

The old farmer chuckled to himself. He'd waited many years to see deacons so flustered. When he turned back to the post, the pathway remained open, so he stepped closer before the crowd filled in.

He nodded slowly at first, then faster. The paper had the look of a Temple bulletin, but with one difference. For the first time in his seventy-six years, he was reading an original thought.

***

The arch vicar scanned the faces around the table. Conferences with the grand vicar were routine, scheduled every Monday morning, and the broadcasts were uneventful to the point of boredom. Some of the vicars scribbled on notepads as the old man droned on. Others brought books to read.

Today was different, not a Monday, and the grand vicar had called this meeting in haste. Over the past few days, rumors had spread that the Temple was under attack.

The box on the table hummed while the grand vicar stated the facts. Blasphemous notices had appeared in twelve towns, possibly more, the messages printed to look like Temple bulletins. Somehow, the perpetrators had gained access to sacred technology. They'd even figured out how to disrupt communications. In response, he'd mobilized all assets, dispatching repair crews to the damaged towers and ordering the gray friars to localize the heretical activity. As yet, no pattern had emerged.

The arch vicar trembled at the threat to his Temple but also recognized an opportunity. He'd made the decision to release the young people, and their disappearance had left a black mark on his record. Now, the chance for redemption.

A hand shot up at the end of the table. The young monsignor always managed to have a question.

No time for politics. The arch vicar nodded and pressed the button.

"Holiness, how have the people reacted to these messages?"

A long pause. Had they disrupted the main communication line as well? When the voice returned, the grand vicar's answer chilled.

"The people have begun to pass this heresy on to their neighbors and question Temple authority. We must stop these enemies of the light. I've authorized the use of rapid transportation and other means at our disposal, clandestine or otherwise. All clergy have a responsibility to end this desecration before the darkness spreads."

Blood rushed to the arch vicar's cheeks. He'd believed in his plan for Nathaniel and his friends, but they'd turned out to be more resourceful than expected. The feisty old prisoner who had died that summer became placid after Nathaniel's departure, a sure sign he'd passed on the secret. The deacons had tracked them for weeks—everything going according to the plan... until suddenly they'd disappeared.

The arch vicar had guided his life with a dual purpose: to prevent the darkness from returning, and to rise up the hierarchy and one day become grand vicar. Now the two might converge. He'd atone for his mistake. The three had made clever use of stolen technology, but no one could master the secrets in so short a time. He'd spent years acquiring such knowledge.

Time to wield that knowledge against them.

***

The Vicar of Bradford bounded down the steps to meet his morning class, a favorite group of children between six and eight. Any of them might someday have replaced him as keeper, but that need had passed. The Seekers had come, and from the news burning up the network, they'd found the keep.

He ruffled a few heads before signaling them to follow. As he strode up the first step, one of them tugged at his robe.

"What is it, Richard?"

Richard regarded him with huge brown eyes from under a mop of untamed hair. He crooked his tiny finger and beckoned the vicar to bend low so he could whisper in his ear.

The child grasped his cheeks to make sure he stayed close and told him the story. That morning, when he went outside to fetch water for his mother, a pretty lady had appeared from behind a tree. She gave him a paper bag and made him swear to do two things: tell no one, and give the bag to the vicar of Bradford the instant he saw him. She promised he'd be rewarded with a sweet.

The vicar accepted the package from the child, unfolded the tightly-rolled top and checked inside. As he suspected, four scrolls nestled within, each with a surface like glass. A note lay next to them.

He waved the children to proceed to their class, all except the little messenger. When they were gone, he grasped the note from the bag and read the three handwritten words: *Just in case.*

He glanced to the horizon and then beamed at the expectant face of the boy, who with the blessing of the light might someday become anything he desired. But as vicar and keeper, he had one final task. He reached into his tunic pocket, pulled out a fistful of sweets, and dropped them into the cupped hands of the child.

Chapter 34
Eyes of Fire

Nathaniel roused before his friends in a clearing deep in the woods. *How odd to nod off beneath a dazzling sun and wake as the darkness falls.* He stretched his long arms overhead in a yawn. After days of dashing from place to place, at least he'd slept well.

He glanced about, trying to get his bearings. The day before, they'd traveled south and posted in a village at midnight, before racing off to the east. Last night, they'd switched to the west and avoided towns altogether. With so many twists and turns, hurries and delays, no wonder they'd dodged the deacons.

Orah had been brilliant.

He turned to watch her sleep. Her spirited heart beat calmly now, leaving her at rest. As a strand of hair fell softly across her cheek, a cruel vision crept into his mind—Orah wasting away in a teaching cell. Had she agreed to this venture for him?

The more they posted, the more likely they'd be caught. The chatter on the listening device now filled the air with their exploits. Every vicar and deacon in the world was searching for them. The race had begun—would the people rise up before the seekers of truth were silenced?

Nathaniel brushed the hair from her face.

244

She stirred and rolled toward him. Her eyelids fluttered and opened. She met his gaze, and her lips parted. "What are you staring at, Nathaniel?"

Once he'd have turned away embarrassed, but now he refused to flinch. "At you, my best friend. I'm staring at you."

***

The arch vicar stomped into the priory. The project was taking too long. He prowled the rows of brothers, pausing to glance over their shoulders as they stared at the screens. On each screen glowed a map of a region. On each map blinked a cluster of dots. A brother in the center found a match and punched a few keys. Another dot vanished.

The prior paced in the last row, hands folded in the small of his back. He stiffened when he noticed the arch vicar.

"Holiness, the brothers need sleep. They'll make mistakes if they're too tired, and we'll have to start over."

The arch vicar glared at the rows of gray friars. *Too coddled over the centuries.* Alone among the clerical class, they embellished their dress with preening accessories, the crimson sash and red skull cap. Now their skull caps lay next to their screens, and sweat glistened on their tonsures.

Wizards of temple magic. He'd learned more in the archives than any of them, and his youthful obsession was about to bear fruit. Not even the priors knew the systems as well as he. Not a one of them could devise this plan.

He counted on the young people's resourcefulness. Every communication device on the network displayed as a white dot on the dark screen. If they carried an unsanctioned device as he suspected, it would show as well. He ordered the brothers to check each dot against the records. When they'd exhausted the list, these so-called seekers of truth would stand out like a beacon in the night.

A brother on his right extinguished another dot, but too many still remained.

He whirled around to the prior. "No sleep for anyone. No sleep until only the unsanctioned device remains. Then you may sleep as much as you wish, and my work will begin."

245

***

Thomas forced his eyes to stay open, terrified the nightmares would return. His dreams of the darkness lingered but they'd evolved since leaving the keep. At first, his mind conjured up caves and fast wagons, flying at incredible speeds, but recently the images had changed. The wagons became hunters, and he was their prey.

He dug his nails into his palms to stay awake, but as the sun grew warmer and the air softened, he drifted off.

When the dream began, he struggled to name the fear, but a sense of expectancy raged. Then the wagons came at night with eyes of fire. He tried to flee, running away until a chasm loomed ahead. With nowhere to turn, he skidded to a stop. In no time, the largest of the beasts set upon him, and a door like the mouth of a snake opened and swallowed him whole.

Inside the belly of the beast, the darkness returned.

***

The middle of the night. Orah led them on a path with tree trunks encroaching on either side, too narrow for fast wagons. She'd become more cautious as the days progressed, always moving, never stopping on roads. They posted in fewer towns, more widely dispersed. They ran, they slept, they hid.

Why didn't the people rise up? What was taking them so long? She prayed they'd rise up soon, because she'd grown tired of risking the lives of her friends.

When the whining came, it sounded like an animal in pain. As it became louder, she sensed their approach, and then she smelled them, a pungent stench that burned her nostrils. In the distance, she saw lights through the trees. Ten, twelve, more each second, moving faster than the three of them could run.

Fast wagons. The vicars had come.

"Run deeper into the woods."

Nathaniel and Thomas hesitated only briefly. They'd learned to trust her and obeyed, but this time her judgment had failed.

She steadied her mind, trying to think as she ran. "Split up. Go in different directions."

When they were three steps ahead and fading into the dark, she slowed to remove her pack. Still moving at a jog, she groped for the device, and then stopped to make sure she'd grabbed the right one. Six weeks to the blessing—too far away—but she had no choice. She took a deep breath and flipped the lever. The red light glowed. She scanned the trees and picked one with a crook in its branches. Stretching on tiptoes, she nestled the device in its cradle and then sped off to her fate.

The whine became a roar. She glanced over her shoulder and spotted wagons unlike any she'd seen in the keep, smaller and narrower, with two wheels and a rider balancing on top. These could follow wherever they went.

The pursuers split up as well, swinging wide to form a circle around them. The glow of their lights pointed at her and her friends. They'd become the hub of a wheel whose spokes were beams of yellow made foul by smoke and dust—she could taste it on her tongue. The roar swelled so she had to resist covering her ears, and the lights inched forward, tightening the trap.

She whirled to the crack of a branch, and caught Nathaniel dashing toward her. By the light of the machines, she noted his clenched fists as he advanced on a rider.

She grabbed his arm, arching her back to add weight. He spun on her, easing off only when he recognized her. She shook her head until his arms went limp and fell to his sides.

The riders herded them to the road. Minutes later, a larger wagon rolled to a stop, its lights glaring in the darkness. Front doors swung wide. Several deacons emerged, each taller and broader than Nathaniel. One of them opened the rear door, and out stepped the arch vicar.

He came within two paces of Orah, a smaller man than she recalled, and thrust his face into hers. She held her ground, matching the clergyman's stare. No high bench between them now.

He signaled for one of the deacons to fetch her pack, and skimmed the papers inside. A sneer of delight came over his grim features.

"Orah of Little Pond, whose name means light. Will you still claim you've done nothing wrong? The darkness is a disease with no cure. You are sick with it and have tried to infect others."

Next he found the wire-cutter and a diagram of the temple trees. He fondled the tool, opened and closed it, and studied the diagram. Finally, he grasped the listening device and waved it before her eyes. "You tried too much, when you knew too little. Your arrogance gave you away."

He locked eyes, waiting for a reaction.

He'd get none. She'd frustrate this leader before whom others cowered, armed with the knowledge they'd found in the keep. No posturing by this frail old man could change that.

He pulled out her log. "What have we here? An unsanctioned book?"

Orah grabbed at it, but he snatched it away.

"It's nothing," she said. "Some scribbles with meaning only to me."

He fanned through the pages. "Then perhaps I might find it engaging."

He handed her log to a deacon and turned to Nathaniel.

"And so, Nathaniel, you lied to me, never intending to keep your vow."

Nathaniel tightened his jaw and stayed silent.

The arch vicar dug into Nathaniel's bag and withdrew the stack of messages. He leered at Orah and flipped the pages for show. Another ritual: read, humiliate, repeat.

He turned one last time.

Thomas collapsed to his knees. "Holiness, thank the light you've rescued me. They forced me to come with them, threatening to tell lies to the vicars if I didn't go. They didn't trust me anymore and were afraid to leave me behind. Me, their childhood friend."

A stab of despair struck Orah. She looked away, down to the ground, up to the trees, anywhere but to Thomas.

"Holiness, please, I know the darkness. I know it in my heart. Don't lock me away again. No second teaching. I know the darkness—"

The arch vicar waved him to silence and signaled for his pack. He found Thomas's knife. "From this object might grow a weapon if the darkness returns as you wish."

Thomas shook his head. His whole body shuddered.

Orah tried to forgive. This was no longer Thomas. Thomas had fled, replaced by fear.

The arch vicar found Thomas's flute. "Music corrupts the soul, and so the darkness has corrupted you."

He stepped inches from Thomas's face and held out the flute. His thick hands slid to the ends of the instrument and squeezed. The blood drained from his knuckles, and he snapped it in two with a crack.

Thomas fell face-down on the ground, his sobs the only sound.

The arch vicar signaled to the deacons. "Keep this one separate from the others. As for these two...." He turned to Orah and Nathaniel. "Bring them to Temple City, where they'll remain our guests for a very long time."

As the deacons led her and her friends off, Orah cast a glance to the east. Far off, deep in the woods, a pinprick of red glowed among the branches—a glimmer of hope in the darkness.

Then it vanished, snuffed out by the night.

Chapter 35
The Trial

Orah contemplated their cell, a space less confining than her prior stay, but with walls just as dreary. Deacons had placed them on a wooden bench at one end of a table—the only furniture in the room—and told them to wait for the vicars.

No. Not a cell, a holding area. A precursor to the rest of our lives. How many decades of dreary walls lay ahead?

She leaned close to Nathaniel while keeping her gaze on the door. "Have you seen a room like this?"

"Never." His voice sounded raw.

She tried to swallow, but her dry throat denied the effort. "I expected more pomp."

He turned toward her, but she kept still, viewing him only out of the corner of her eyes.

His lips parted easily with no tension in his jaw. "Pomp is for Temple ritual, theater for believers. It'd be wasted on us."

"What did they do with Thomas? Back to the teaching?"

"I don't think so."

She counted the seconds between his breaths. Normal, not rushed.

"I'm afraid he couldn't take it again," she said.

"He's not in the teaching."

"How do you know?"

"The teaching frightens only those who believe, not those who've learned the truth. The arch vicar found our messages, the tool to disable the trees, the communicator. He knows we've been to the—"

Her hand flashed. She pressed two fingers to his lips and shook her head. "They may have ways to listen. Secret places should remain that way."

Boot steps echoed in the corridor outside. She glared at the door, keeping it shut with her eyes.

When the guards had passed and the echoes faded, she released her breath and faced Nathaniel. "Will he tell?"

"He might. He told before."

Orah picked at the melting wax from a candle on the tabletop and molded it into a figurine. Before it hardened, she placed her thumb on its head and pressed downward until nothing remained but a splotch.

"He won't tell," she said. "I'm sure of it."

"Why?"

She glanced from the candle to the ceiling and sniffed the stale air. "Because I know him, my friend since birth."

***

The arch vicar waited for the deacons to bring in the boy. The others had earned the consequences. Not so the boy. His teaching almost a year before had revealed no strong beliefs other than loyalty to his friends. When he had come to the light at last, he was broken. The arch vicar loathed that part of his role, the need to imprint the precepts on the young, but for hundreds of years, such methods had kept the darkness away.

The darkness, always there, always waiting to pounce, to shred the existing order and cast the world once more into chaos. These young people understand nothing of the forces they might unleash.

The door opened and deacons dragged in the boy, supporting him under the arms so only the toes of his boots touched the floor.

The arch vicar signaled to the deacons to release their captive, and the boy collapsed in a heap.

The arch vicar stepped out from behind the desk and stroked the boy's head. "No one will hurt you, Thomas." With the tip of one finger, he lifted the boy's chin until their eyes met. "No more teaching cell, but the Temple needs your help."

The young man nodded, though his gaze darted everywhere as if unable to focus.

The arch vicar resumed his place behind the desk and waited for the boy to compose himself before using the voice of authority he'd learned in the seminary. "Thomas of Little Pond, where have you been?"

The boy began to sob.

The arch vicar lowered his voice. "Thomas, can you hear me?"

He nodded.

"Are you willing to defend the light?"

He nodded again.

"Say it."

"Yes, I'm... willing." The words trickled out, almost too soft to hear.

"Then tell me where you and your friends have been."

Thomas's eyes rolled up into their lids, his body trembled. Not a young man now, but a boy. Not a boy, but a child.

Finally, his eyes steadied, focusing on his boot tops, but his voice quivered when he spoke. "To the keep, Holiness."

The keep. The muscles of the arch vicar's jaw tensed and released. How often he'd dreamed about its wonders and the knowledge it might offer, but like the others of his race, he could not be trusted with that knowledge. If he discovered its location, he'd send those too ignorant to be tempted. Let them destroy it, and eliminate the temptation forever.

First, how far dare he go with the boy?

"Thank you, Thomas. I need one more thing from you." He waited for the boy's panic to subside. "Tell me how to get there."

Too much. The boy doubled over as if a deacon had kicked him in the stomach.

Once again, the arch vicar left the protection of the desk and went to the boy. His knees creaked as he knelt beside him. "I'm your friend, Thomas, and will do for you what I can, but you must tell me how to find the keep."

"I can't, Holiness," the boy protested between sobs. "They hid the way from me, blindfolding me at crossroads. No teachings, Holiness, I beg you." Then, looking around, trying to give anything to save himself,

252

he added, "There was a mountain, a waterfall, a cave. We walked for weeks, maybe to the north or west. No teachings, Holiness. That's all I know."

The arch vicar's brows drooped as he stared down at the frightened boy, the scars from his teaching still all too visible. Enough for now. He motioned for the deacons to take him away.

Had the boy told the truth? He'd betrayed his friends before, and they may not have trusted him. Only one way to be sure. His friends would confirm the story or reveal the lie—the reason he'd kept them apart.

***

The arch vicar strode into the meeting hall, paused at the head of the long table and sighed. A haze filled the air from the flickering fires of the braziers, casting shadows on the expectant faces of his colleagues. He'd struggled against the darkness for forty years, and would keep on until his dying breath, but he wearied of the younger vicars. In varying degrees, they believed in the light, but many cared more for power.

The questioning began before he'd settled into his chair. "Did they find the keep, Holiness?"

"Of course they found the keep. Where else would they obtain such technology?" He cast a quick glance around the table. Someone in this room had betrayed him to the council.

"Will they tell where it is?"

He opened a folder and reread the report but found nothing to change his mind. "Thomas Bradford gave the names of his friends in his teaching. They had reason to mistrust him. The boy is either unstable or extraordinarily clever. He may be the most likely to reveal the location if he knows it, but he seems terrified. The best way to gain the secret from him is with kindness."

The new monsignor's hand shot up, but he began speaking before being recognized. Civility was lost on these upstarts. "The keep is the heart of the darkness, Holiness. I'm familiar with these stubborn children from Little Pond. We should use force to learn the location."

The arch vicar's black eyes had served him well in exercising authority, and he leveled them now. "Would you violate the precepts to get it?"

253

The monsignor blinked and backed down, his answer left unsaid, but his intent lay bare for all to see. He'd violate the precepts if he sat in the arch vicar's chair.

"The Temple is best served by treating him well. I'll give him the opportunity to work in the kitchens. Of course, my men will supervise him at all times and keep him locked up at night."

Murmurs of approval and some nodding of heads. Finding the three had strengthened his hand, but a few took notes in the event of a failure.

"What of the others?" the monsignor said.

"The others are believers in the darkness. They're unlikely to tell."

"But, Holiness—"

"They're unlikely to tell, I said!" He raised his voice and added intensity to his glare. "Not with teachings, not with any method allowed under the precepts. No matter. We already possess what we need from the keep. As for the rest, our forebears rejected it long ago. The keep contains nothing more that we want. I'd destroy the place if I could, but what matters most is that no one ever finds it again."

Hands raised and mouths dropped open. Some even had the nerve to shout out of turn.

The arch vicar struck the table with the flat of his hand, and they fell silent. His eyes burned now, and his thick gray brows hovered over them like billowing smoke. "The keep doesn't matter. Only the knowledge of the keep matters. If we find it, we'll destroy it once and for all. If not, the secret will die with them. The two won't get the chance to stand before their people, and they'll never see the light of day again."

***

The chamber remained the same, but the circumstances differed. This time, the arch vicar sat alone behind the raised desk. Orah let her eyes roam up to the peak of the dome and down to the tapestry. The vaulted arches seemed less imposing, and she now saw the battle between darkness and light for what it was—a fantasy to inspire clergy, a nightmare to frighten those who'd be taught.

And Nathaniel stood at her side.

The arch vicar shuffled through a stack of papers on his desk. When he finally spoke, he used the thundering Temple voice. "Nathaniel Rush and Orah Weber, you stand accused of crimes against the light. The Temple relies on its rules, and you have violated many—blasphemy, praising the darkness and inciting others to follow. What do you say in your defense?"

Orah wanted to indict as well, to recite her own litany of lies and the harm the Temple had done, but this trial had only one outcome. Better to say nothing.

She glanced at Nathaniel, whose back had stiffened as he prepared to speak. She concentrated, trying to pass the thought through to his mind. *Be careful, Nathaniel. He's shrewd, dangerous. Don't let him anger you.*

But Nathaniel had changed, no longer the reckless boy of her youth. His passions stayed under control. "What we say doesn't matter. Your trial is all for show. Just... get on with it."

The arch vicar had wielded power for more than twice her life, but now reshuffled the papers for no reason.

Finally, he looked up and glowered. "Tell me where you've been."

"We left a trail of messages," Nathaniel said. "I'm sure you've tracked them all. Most towns we've now forgotten or never learned their names."

Good, Nathaniel. Say nothing he doesn't already know.

"Tell me anyway," the arch vicar said, "starting from Little Pond."

***

Orah quieted her mind. The tenor of the questioning troubled her—too easy. The old man asked, she parried, but a trap was coming.

She tried to disrupt the flow of the interrogation. "What did you do with our friend?"

"Thomas will be cared for based on his needs. Each child of light is treated according to Temple precepts."

Temple precepts. The Temple doesn't hurt its children. It harms the whole world.

The arch vicar leaned his elbows on the desk and rested his full weight upon them. "The Temple will treat him better than his friends did. He tells us you treated him badly."

Treated him badly? Thomas fought to be with us. Why would he say such a thing? Unless.... She glanced at Nathaniel. He bit down on his lip and stayed silent, but the comment required an answer.

Careful now. He's about to spring the trap.

"He's our friend. We'd never treat him badly, but after what you did to him in your teaching, we couldn't trust him."

The arch vicar tightened the net. "You never left him? He went everywhere with you?"

Think it through. Don't rush. "Yes, of course. We couldn't leave him alone. He'd have run off."

"Then he'd know the way."

Think, Orah. He's questioned Thomas separately.

The arch vicar settled back, his thick hands folded, a block of granite weighing down the desktop. He wouldn't be the next to speak.

"No. We made sure he'd never betray us again."

"How was that, Orah of Little Pond whose name means light?"

She felt like a child fighting the darkness with a stick. Her heart beat faster, but she took a cleansing breath and steadied herself. "At every major turn, at each crossroad, we used my scarf to blindfold him."

The arch vicar snapped a look at Nathaniel, and Orah followed his gaze. Her best friend nodded in agreement.

***

Nathaniel did his best to stay focused, but the questioning dragged on for hours. Orah had handled it masterfully. Their story stayed consistent with no mention of the keep.

At last, the arch vicar eased the folder closed. "Orah Weber and Nathaniel Rush, I take no pleasure in the judgment I must now hand down. You followed your beliefs, misguided though they may be, and will gain nothing from teachings, but you present a danger to the light. I rule you shall stay here as our guests for the rest of your lives."

The rest of your lives. Nathaniel had one last hope but the request stuck in his throat.

Orah turned toward him, her whole body turning, and uttered his request aloud. "Will we be together?"

"No. You'll be kept apart. I'd make it easier for you, but...." The arch vicar's thick brows drooped at the corners. "...you've done too much damage to the light. The answer is no."

***

Orah's spirit sagged. Bad enough to never see her mother or Little Pond again, but to live without Nathaniel....

The arch vicar rang the bell with the sun-shaped handle, and eight deacons entered, forming a box around the two.

Nathaniel forced his way through and approached the desk. "Will you let us share meals?"

The arch vicar shook his head and stood to leave.

A deacon grabbed Orah by the arms, but she twisted away. "One meal, Holiness. One meal a week."

The arch vicar looked at Orah, and then Nathaniel. Finally he settled his gaze on the floor between them. "No. This session is ended."

The deacons had secured her now and were dragging her toward the exit. As the shadow of separation hovered over her, she became lightheaded, overcome by despair. Was this how Thomas had felt at the end of his teaching? As she neared the doorway, she stretched out an arm to touch Nathaniel one last time.

"Wait." The arch vicar addressed the lead deacon. "Place the boy in the same cell as his last stay."

Orah held her breath.

"And the girl, lock her in the next cell, the one recently vacated by our late guest Samuel."

A gift. The peephole as dispensation. Blessed be the light.

Chapter 36
Temptation

Nathaniel slowed his heartbeat to allow himself to sleep. The weeks since leaving the wilderness had sapped his strength like a long illness. He and Orah both needed time to heal, to prove they were still alive. At first they talked incessantly, mulling over their fate until nothing was left to say. Their world had become simple—no goals, no plans, no future. Now they spoke whenever a thought occurred.

Orah had insisted on shifting their beds to the shared wall so they could sense each other even as they slept. He listened for her breathing, wondering if she was awake, but before he could gauge the rhythm, she spoke.

"Nathaniel?"

"Yes, Orah."

"I've been thinking about my father lately. I can picture his hands at the loom, delicate hands with slender fingers, not like a man's."

"Like yours." Nathaniel imagined she smiled.

"Like mine. I only need to glance down to recall them."

Nathaniel stared at dust patterns on the wall.

"Nathaniel?"

"Yes."

"I'm struggling to remember his face. I see him sometimes, telling me stories at bedtime, but I can't recall him at will. I wish I had a viewing area with a topic called memories. 'Help,' I'd say. 'Show me pictures of my father,' and he'd appear on the screen."

"Those pictures have lasted a thousand years."

"My father's been gone just ten, yet I'm worried I'll forget him entirely."

Nathaniel traced the cracks in the ceiling with his eyes. "In here, I may forget my father as well."

He tried to envision his father. Six months had passed since he'd last seen home. He shook his head to jog his memory, to summon his father's face, but only Orah's appeared.

"Move back," he said, "away from the peephole."

"Why?"

"I want to look at you."

He heard her shuffling away from the wall. "I'm ready."

He peered into the hole and caught her grooming herself, licking her hands to rub dust from her face, dragging fingers through tangled hair. She wore the same expression as when he kissed her at festival—eyes sparkling in the candlelight, a blush to her cheeks. What would he do if the vicars took her away?

He banished the thought from his mind. "Orah?"

"Yes."

"Would you do it again?"

"I think so." She laughed. It sounded like waterfalls. "Ask me in twenty years."

"What if I didn't race off to save you from the teaching? You'd be wiser in the light but would recover in time, as the elders say, and we'd both still be at home."

"Are you close to the hole, Nathaniel?"

"Uh-huh."

She slapped the flat of her hand against the wall hard enough for dust to fly. "Don't go having regrets. I loved that you came for me, and would never give up what we learned. Think of it, Nathaniel—a million suns."

Nathaniel pulled his knees to his chest and rested his chin on them. "I'm glad I went too."

259

No response from the next cell. No movement outside. Nothing but a candle flaring occasionally with a soft buzz. He checked on her once more. She was leaning on the edge of the table, staring at nothing.

He knew the thought would anger her but felt compelled to say it. "I should never have let you come with me that morning at the NOT tree. Then I'd be alone in this cell, and you'd be safe in Little Pond."

He peered through the hole. She was already striding toward him. For a moment, he felt grateful for the wall in between.

"Don't you ever think like that! How awful to have you missing, and I not knowing where you were. Better to be near, connected by this cursed peephole. Besides, how would you have found your way without me? You'd still be searching for mountains in Adamsville."

He nodded though she couldn't see. He was beginning to understand. "Remember what you said about having no illusions and needing to make choices. We've made lots of choices, but we believed in them all. Does that mean we should have no regrets?"

"I think so, like the old prisoner who lived in this cell. He made choices based on what he believed. Did he have regrets at the end?"

"No, but to the end, he had hope. Maybe when we're old we'll find a way to tell our story like he did." The corners of his mouth struggled upward, and he forced a glance to the unseen heavens. "Or our friend in Bradford might mount an expedition to rescue us." He shook his head. "There goes Nathaniel having illusions again."

"I don't know, but one thing's no illusion: being together."

He imagined what she'd do next if not for the wall. He leaned closer as if to savor the warmth of her touch.

"Orah?"

"Yes."

"If none of this had happened, or if by some miracle they let us go home to resume our lives, what would you wish for most?"

"Do you think it's a good idea to dwell on impossible dreams?"

He considered a moment. "Dreams may be all we have left."

"Then here is my list. I wish to win a race at festival as an adult, to have you win one too, so I can place a wreath on your head and embarrass you in front of the whole village, to weave enough cloth one year to let my mother get some rest, to go with you to explore the mountain pass and discover the ocean...."

Her voice trailed off, and he assumed his turn had come.

"My list is short. If none of this had happened—no teachings, no vicars, no seekers, no keep—I'd be content to spend the rest of my life with you."

When she failed to answer, he peeked through the hole in the wall.

She sat sideways on the chair, one arm draped over the back. The dim light of a candle flickered off her moist cheeks.

***

Three weeks had passed since the arch vicar had assigned Thomas to the kitchen. As another tedious day neared its end, he hobbled down the hall to the storeroom to fetch a sack of flour. He walked with an uneven gait, favoring his left side, and his head tilted left as well. His eyes flitted everywhere, aimless and unfocused.

Which allowed him to study his surroundings without detection—a perfect ruse. Only his friends would have seen through it.

Orah would be proud. He'd become a student of the dining routine, observing every detail, gathering information.

The kitchen provided meals for several hundred people and bustled with activity. Work began before sunrise when the baker arrived to fire up the ovens. Preparations for dinner started immediately after lunch, and setup for the next morning's breakfast followed the evening meal. Everyone raced about trying to finish as soon as possible and save a few minutes for their families. This made the hour after dinner the most frenzied time of day, ideal for avoiding notice.

He'd won the trust of Charles, the head cook, a round, hairless man with a thick neck and three chins, who liked to order people about using the familiar form of their name followed by the word *boy*—Willie-boy or Johnnie-boy. In turn, the others referred to the cook as Charlie-boy, but only behind his back.

Thomas played the simpleton so well the cook took to calling him poor-boy.

"Poor-boy, fetch me a sack of beets. Poor-boy, a crate of salted pork."

Thomas bowed, yes-Holinessed and shuffled off. He got away with asking foolish questions because everyone thought him feeble-minded, but he always managed to slip in one question for which he needed to know the answer.

"Holiness, why is the pork salted? Why are the beets stored in sacks and not crates? Why are the walnuts in cans? How does the food get to the vicars?"

He learned they served the clergymen first, and then the deacons. Next came the kitchen staff. Leftovers went to the guards below and, last of all, to the prisoners.

"How does the food get below?"

They sent the food from the kitchen using a moveable frame, hoisted up or down with a system of pulleys. The largest of these lay behind the brick ovens in a place left vacant except during mealtimes. It delivered food upward to Temple officials and down to prison guards. A second smaller one was set into the back wall of the storeroom. No one would tell him where that one went.

Everyone knew the arch vicar had sent him, and they watched him closely. When not working, they locked him away in a small room—but people relaxed around the simpleminded. Increasingly, gaps in his oversight showed.

After dinner, cooks, scullions and others of Charlie-boy's underlings hustled through the steaming air, rattling pans in soapy water, dragging crates of smoked meat and peeling potatoes for the next morning's meal. In the dimly lit alcove before the ovens, a washerwoman swished about on the stone floor with a mop.

The others considered the storeroom his domain, the one place he was allowed to enter unsupervised. With so many sacks and kegs, no one bothered to track how long he stayed inside.

He wound through the stacks of supplies and located the opening in the back wall, about half the height of a man but wider. On closer inspection, he spotted the entrance to a shaft downward. The frame lay in place, shelves empty, its work done for the day, but he dared not disrupt it for long. He fingered the thick rope—rough hemp and tightly woven. Good for a firm grip.

He inhaled through his nose and blew out a long stream of air. *Well, Thomas, you always thought your friends were braver than you. Time to be brave as well.*

262

He raised the shelf and slipped underneath. Once in the shaft, he clutched the rope between the insteps of his boots, pulled the shelf back into place, and lowered himself down.

The corridor at the bottom had barely enough light to see. The stale air coated his tongue with dust, and the walls were etched with decay. Heavy wooden doors lined the far side, each locked with a metal bolt.

His heart sank.

He spent his days in a bright room surrounded by people, while his friends stayed caged in these cells.

He took two steps to the nearest door, but stopped. A peek through a slat, a slip of a bolt and they'd be free, but what then? Too many unanswered questions remained, too many obstacles to freedom. Even Orah would struggle to stitch together such a plan.

He stared at the door and shook his head. No way to help them. If caught, he'd suffer a worse punishment than theirs, a useless sacrifice. He'd discovered a trifle so far, not a plan. He'd need many more trifles to make Orah proud.

He held his breath and listened. Were those the voices of his friends? Too muffled to be sure.

Afraid to stay any longer, he vaulted back into the shaft and shimmied up the rope.

***

A month had passed since Orah last saw Nathaniel with no wall in between. Now, as four deacons blocked her view and kept them apart, she peered past them to get a clearer look. He seemed thinner and more pale.

She suspected she looked no better.

The deacons led them through a maze of dimly lit corridors until she lost all sense of direction. Finally, they arrived at an arched doorway forming the end of a hall.

She suppressed a gasp. On the wall beside it sat a box with sixteen buttons in the shape of stars. The lead deacon knocked. After a moment, the door opened and the lone figure of the arch vicar filled its frame. He waved the deacons off and bid Orah and Nathaniel enter.

The arch vicar ushered them into a painfully familiar room. A soft glow rose around them, with no visible source. The furnishings differed from anything she'd seen in Temple City, with metal tables and straight-backed chairs. Every few paces, the plain white walls were broken by the rectangular windows she'd come to know as screens.

She did her best to disguise her reaction. "What place is this? Temple magic?"

"Well played, Orah," the arch vicar said, "but you fool no one. I know you've been to the keep."

She gritted her teeth as if pressing harder would prevent her from replying.

The old man responded with a look of his own, a glare of condemnation he'd used so often it had grown into his flesh and bones. "No need to answer, but tell me this: what made you so enamored of the keep? What about these people who valued progress over human souls impressed you so? What did you discover there that inspired you to throw your lives away?"

Orah glanced at Nathaniel; he licked his cracked lips and nodded. *Stay with what he knows.*

"You read our messages," she said. "They say what we found."

The arch vicar shuffled behind a desk. Arranged in a row upon its surface lay the four bulletins, and beside them, her log.

"Yes, of course, the truth about everything. I forgot. You are the seekers of truth."

He came back around and stood before her, so near her cheeks burned with the heat of his breath.

She rocked on her toes and raised her chin, refusing to be intimidated. "We sought the truth and wrote about what we found."

The arch vicar softened. This close, she perceived a sadness in his eyes.

"My child, when you've lived longer—that is, if we'd allowed you to grow old in the outside world—you'd understand there's no such thing as absolute truth. I'm sure you learned in the keep how much harm was done in the name of good."

"The same could be said of the Temple."

"I suppose. Which only proves that truth is elusive. We all act based on what we believe. I understand your little crusade, but I believe you are wrong. I can assure you of one thing: in the age of the keepmasters, you would not have been treated this well."

He returned to the desk and seated himself. Philosophical discussion had ended. Back to Temple business.

"Tell me how to get to the keep."

She bit her lower lip and stayed silent, but winced when the arch vicar picked up her log and flipped through its pages. "You write well, with such passion. So intent to right a wrong, to improve the lives of your people. But what of your fear—to be unworthy of another's love? Now you must make a choice. I can never allow you to leave, but if you assist me, I'll let you share the noontime meal every day."

She had prepared for choices, but not this. She brushed away a curl that had lengthened in the months of flight and discovery, upheaval and captivity, and breathed the words before Nathaniel could stop her.

"What do you need?"

"Only a hint, my child. I already know you headed east from Riverbend, looking for mountainous terrain and a path north along the river, but we've searched and found nothing. Help us take the next step." His voice became soothing. "Is that so much of a compromise compared to what I offer in return? Why miss the opportunity to be together?"

"River something?" Nathaniel said. "We've never heard of such a town,"

"Of course you have, as surely as you grew up in Little Pond. Beyond tracking you there, I have in my files the official testimony of the shoemaker's daughter... from her teaching."

Orah charged forward and planted her small fists on the desk with such force the arch vicar fell back. "She's underage, too young for a teaching."

"My child, the Temple is governed by precepts and rules. Precepts are handed down from the light and are immutable, but the council determines rules. An orphan may be taught early, if necessary. I had the authority to issue such a dispensation, and she has benefited as a result."

Orah swallowed hard and stepped back. Without taking her eyes off the arch vicar, she groped for Nathaniel's hand. Their fingertips touched, and their fingers wove together as one. His strength surged through her as she spoke.

"We have nothing more to say."

The arch vicar aged before them. His trappings of office lost their power. "Very well. I don't need to know the location of the keep, only that its secret will never be revealed. You'll be our guests for the rest of your lives, and the secret will die with you."

He moved a finger to press a button on the desk—a signal to the deacons—but his finger hovered, hesitating. He handed her back the log. "I'll summon you again in a month to check if you changed your mind. In the meantime, this belongs to you and has pages left to fill. If you run out of paper, tell the guards, and I'll provide as much as you need. You'll have plenty of time to chronicle your life, though I suspect you'll find little to say as the years of tedium drag on."

He took his seat behind the desk and scanned the messages as if rereading them.

When he resumed, his voice chilled like a winter wind. "I can do worse. I can put you in separate cells or send one of you to another Temple City so far away you'll never see each other again. Take a month to ponder this. The keep stayed hidden for centuries, and you only stumbled upon it with my help. Now you've spent weeks spreading these so-called truths, yet the children still live in the light. No one wants what the keep offers. Hiding its location will accomplish nothing but split you apart." He crumpled the messages and waved them in her face. "One month. Your final chance."

***

After they left, the arch vicar collapsed in his chair. He removed the black hat with the red stripes earned over so many years and wiped the moisture from his head. When he finished, the few strands of gray that remained lay plastered to his scalp.

What made them so willing to sacrifice so much? Had the founders of the keep left the world a better place? Was it so vital to contravene the order of things, to be able to fly or challenge the heavens? Did they need to develop such efficient ways to kill? He denied the darkness not because of what he'd been taught in the seminary, but because of the light he'd found in his own heart.

Yet these two also believed in something—the misguided ideals of the keep—with the same ferocity. He shook his head. They'd never tell. They'd tasted from the fruit of the tree of knowledge and would always want more. But despite their foray into the darkness, their friendship— their love—was of the light.

He'd used it against them.

What had the slightest hope of finding the keep made him do? Offer a choice that would torment them to the end of their days. Did their sin warrant such punishment, when he'd nearly succumbed himself?

He studied his oversized hands. They might have been the hands of a bricklayer, but he'd chosen to wield power instead. He'd been wielding power for too long.

No. He'd never follow through with his threat. He no longer cared what the younger vicars thought. Maybe he lacked the resolve to become grand vicar after all. If they refused to divulge the location of the keep in a month, he'd leave them be, to live out their lives locked away but with each other. Then he'd wash his hands of the whole affair. No need to do more.

The age of the keep had passed.

Chapter 37

Great Pond

The spinner was stacking yarn in the stockroom when the bell at the front door jingled — his wife and daughter returning from Adamsville. He dropped his work, brushed back his thinning hair and rushed out to greet them.

He hugged his wife, grasped the eight-year-old by the hands and inspected her from head to toe. "Two weeks gone, and as I suspected, you've grown an inch."

His wife laughed. "My mother gets to feed her only a few days each year and takes full advantage."

"How was your trip?"

"Long, as usual."

He noted their clothing, covered with the dust of the road — they'd need a thorough cleaning. "Any news from the towns to the east?"

The woman's face settled into a frown. "Odd things are about. Postings, like those of the Temple, but not from the vicars. For a while, I hear, they appeared daily, but then stopped."

"What did they say?"

"Complaints of the kind usually spoken in private. Accusations against the vicars, but with details to back them up. Here. I can show you."

His eyebrows shot up. "You brought some?"

She removed her pack and pulled out a wrinkled sheet of paper.

"Not the ones in Temple lettering. The deacons ripped those down, but people took to copying them by hand and passing them around. They say the spinner of Adamsville closes his shop at noon so he can spend the rest of the day writing. Look for yourself."

He took the page and started to read. As memories of his own teaching flared, his hands began to tremble.

His wife brushed his arm with her fingertips. "Rumors say it's the work of young people from Little Pond, two boys and a girl."

He glanced up. "The Weber girl?"

"And her two friends who went missing last spring."

He read another line but paused as a thought struck him. "Why did it stop?"

"What?"

"The postings."

"Caught, I suppose."

"The Weber girl?" His voice quivered as he pictured her in the hands of the deacons.

"Could be."

"I knew the father before he died. I still see the mother. With husband and daughter gone, she seems shattered."

He finished the page. At its bottom, it bore the words, *The Seekers of Truth*. Below the signature, someone had scrawled an additional phrase: *Please make copies and pass them on.*

"Do you have others?"

She reached into the pack and handed him three more.

"I'll need a pen as well."

"What for?" she said.

"I have copying to do."

Chapter 38
A Sliver of Moonlight

Orah startled awake to the sound of a bolt releasing. What now? The deacons usually left them alone this late in the evening.

She swung her feet to the floor and combed back her hair with her fingers, as if she cared what the guards thought.

But the intruder was no deacon.

"Well, Orah of Little Pond, you seem to be in a bit of trouble."

"Thomas!"

Her friend hushed her with a finger to her lips and squatted by her side. "Do exactly as I say. Count to sixty, saying one Little Pond, two Little Pond, as we used to when we played hide-and-seek. When you reach thirty, leave the cell. At forty, release Nathaniel. Be sure to close both bolts behind you. At sixty, be by the exit at the end of the hall. I'll unlock the door from the far side. Nod if you understand."

She nodded.

As quickly as Thomas had appeared, he vanished.

She rubbed her eyes. A dream? She longed to believe and began counting.

...twenty-nine Little Pond, thirty. She pushed and the door swung wide. Her heart pounded.

...thirty-nine, forty. Nathaniel stood within reach, gaping at her. His lips parted to form a question, but she froze him with a glance and led him away by the wrist.

...forty-eight Little Pond, forty-nine. She slid both bolts closed and dashed to the end of the hall.

...fifty-nine, sixty. The snap of a lock releasing, a creaking sound.

She gasped at the figure in the doorway. "Thomas. But how —"

He silenced her with a slash of his hand. "No more talking till we're out of the city. Now follow me."

He locked the door behind them and took off, leaving her and Nathaniel to hobble after. He flew down the hall and bounded up a stairway at its end, taking two steps at a time. When they finally reached the top, he yanked them into a doorway on the left, the entrance to the temple laundry, which had been abandoned for the night. In one corner lay a pile of soiled clothing. He handed each of them a set to put on over their own while he did the same. His guess at their fit seemed flawless, even finding a smock long enough to cover Nathaniel's arms.

Orah stretched a cook's cap over her head, stuffing her hair underneath.

"Now do as I do," Thomas whispered. "No questions."

He handed each a warm bundle tied in cloth, and limped off as if his feet hurt from standing all day. Orah drifted to one side and Nathaniel to the other, mimicking his gait. He whispered nonsense to them as they went, every so often breaking into laughter of the kind unlikely to come from someone trying to avoid attention. At one point, he dug an elbow into Orah's ribs to force a giggle and drive the terror from her eyes.

At the end of a passage, they came to an archway opening to the outside. A bored deacon slumped in a chair by the door. He roused as they approached, straightened his tunic and stood to block their way. "Leaving early tonight, are we?"

"Charlie-boy let me off," Thomas said in a hearty voice, only false-sounding to those who knew him well. "My birthday. Gave me a bunch of leftovers for the celebration." He gestured to the bags they carried, ripe with the aroma of freshly-roasted pork. "I brought plenty. Care for a bite?"

The guard's demeanor lightened when he inhaled the scent. He smacked his lips and rubbed his stomach.

Thomas dug into his bundle and pulled out a half-loaf dripping with meat. "Here you go."

The hungry guard accepted it with both hands. As he opened his mouth to take a bite, they waved and left the building.

Once in the street, Thomas insisted they plod along to maintain the pretense. One right turn, two lefts, and a secondary gate. Then Temple City lay behind.

Orah paused to breathe in the outdoors and beam at the full moon, but she had no time to savor the moment.

Thomas flashed his mischievous grin as he used to when playing a prank in school, but only for a second. Then he proclaimed in a whisper, "Now run for your life and don't stop till you're ready to drop."

***

Orah's lungs burned, but she refused to give in first. She reveled in the cold, the night sky, and the three of them together again. Her hope had returned, at least for a while.

Nathaniel jogged ahead, but slowed suddenly and threw up his hands, grimacing in pain.

She came to a stop by his side, with Thomas right behind. They'd been running for hours.

She lacked the breath to speak but motioned them deeper into the woods. Best not to take chances with their newfound freedom, and she needed to understand their circumstance.

Once out of sight of the trail, they peeled off their soiled kitchen clothing and buried them beneath a pile of leaves. Then the two former captives collapsed on a log, while Thomas passed out the water skins he'd brought.

"Thomas," she said between gulps of sweet water. "You are amazing. How did you do it?"

He told them about the two shafts leading downward and how he'd used his climbing skills to explore. One led to their cells and the other to the far side of the main prison door. Using a potato stolen from the kitchen, he'd stuffed a slice into the latch of his room, not too big to be seen, but enough to keep the lock from closing fully. That let him sneak out at will and practice until he could set them free, climb back up and unlock the exit, all within a count of sixty.

His eyes sparkled as he spoke, reflecting the slivers of moonlight that slipped through the branches of the bare November trees.

"You might have been caught. How did you know the way would be clear?"

"Every night, I waited until the guards and prisoners finished dinner, then I took a pouch of flour from the storeroom—too little to be missed—and climbed down the rope. I sprinkled a dusting on the floor and checked for footprints the next morning. I started early in the evening and late the next morning, narrowing the times until no footprints appeared.

"The rest was easy. I watched where the workers took the laundry carts. The hardest part was finding clothing to fit Nathaniel. I had no problem taking food—the kitchen folk always bring leftovers home. Then I waited for a moonlit night so we could run without breaking a leg."

Nathaniel slapped him on the back, and Orah viewed him anew. He seemed to grow taller before her eyes, as if the burden of the teaching had been lifted. "That's... brilliant, Thomas. So much planning, so many details."

She imagined he must have blushed, but his grin shone in the dark. "Maybe I spent too much time with you."

As she embraced him, a thought struck and she pulled back. "So how much time *do* we have?"

He narrowed his eyes and calculated in his head. "Six, maybe seven hours before they discover we're gone."

"Six hours. What are we waiting for?"

"I thought you needed to rest."

She glanced from Thomas to Nathaniel, ignored the ache in her chest, and sucked in a breath. "I'm ready. Let's go."

***

Thomas urged his friends to keep running until the sun rose above the treetops, but soon they began to stagger. Nathaniel stumbled twice, and Orah could hardly keep to a straight line. On his own, he might reach Little Pond in less than a day, but the newly released prisoners, weakened by weeks of confinement, wouldn't make it without rest.

He signaled for them to stop. "Enough, before the two of you pass out on the road."

Nathaniel doubled over, palms resting on his knees, while Orah braced her back with her hands, trying to expand her lungs. She shook her head long before she had breath enough to speak.

"We... keep going," she said between gasps.

"No," Thomas said. "We find a clearing in the woods and get some sleep."

She dropped to one knee, looking as though she might be sick. "I'm not going back. I'm never going back."

She tried to say more, but lacked air to speak—nothing remained but her will.

He eased her up by the elbow as he had the day they'd discovered the Temple of Truth. "No, Orah, this time it's my adventure, and I say we rest."

For once, she gave in. With his support, she lurched to her feet and collapsed in his arms.

***

Thomas sat on his haunches, watching his friends sleep and wondering. Why had he taken such a risk? For friendship, of course, but also for something more. To give them the chance to be together again, to grant them the happiness he hoped to find someday for himself.

He waited, tracking the shadow receding along the ground, hoping the sunlight would wake them. When neither stirred, he stepped closer and nudged them with the toe of his boot. "Time to go."

Orah sat up, stretched her arms over her head and turned to the warmth from above. "Praise the sun, giver of life. What a day."

"I thought you vowed never to say that again."

"I know, but the sunlight feels so good."

She staggered to her feet and attempted an awkward spin, but then stumbled and stopped. Her shoulders slumped as the reality of their situation struck. The exhilaration of the night's flight faded, and daylight exposed worry lines around her eyes.

"But where?" she said. "Where can we go that will be safe?"

274

Thomas shrugged. "I got us out of Temple City. I assumed you two would figure out the rest."

Nathaniel scrambled to his feet and tried to rub sleep away. "Where are we?"

Thomas waved his arms and circled about. "In the Ponds, I'd guess a day's walk from home."

Nathaniel gazed at the road ahead. "Little Pond. I'd love to go there, but won't the vicars be waiting with their fast wagons?"

Thomas frowned. "I did the best I could. Only two places offered hope — the keep and Little Pond. The keep was too far away, and a part of me longed to go home."

Orah pressed her palm to his cheek. "You did well, Thomas. The deacons have been searching Riverbend. We'd have run right into them if we got that far."

Thomas held his head still, savoring his reward, but not for long. The sun was racing across the sky. "They'll be after us by now. We need to get going, but where?"

Nathaniel strode forward, the resolve gathering in his eyes. "We'll go to the granite mountains and cross the pass I found to the ocean. No one will look for us there."

Orah glanced up as she combed mud and dried leaves from her hair. "Winter's coming. We'll need provisions and tools to survive, and fresh clothing. Mine are all wet, and I'm chilled to the bone."

Thomas watched the minds of his friends churn, planning as they'd done so often before. He was relieved to be free of the responsibility.

"We'll go to the NOT tree," Nathaniel said, "keeping to back trails. From there, we'll scout out Little Pond and check for deacons, then sneak in to gather supplies. We can rest in the shelter before heading to the mountains, regain our strength before scaling those peaks."

Thomas looked at him skeptically. "Then what?"

Nathaniel shrugged. "I don't know. Winter by the ocean, make a shelter or find a cave, catch fish to eat and wait till spring."

Thomas cocked his head to one side. "And when it's warmer...?"

Orah hooked arms with Nathaniel. She smiled and winked. "We'll build a boat and sail off to the new land."

275

"You've both gone daft in those cells. We'd have no chance."

"That's what you said about finding the keep."

Dreamers. I had to pick dreamers for friends. But he had no better option. He flashed his grin. "All right then. I never liked kitchen work anyway."

What did it matter? He'd made his choice on the steps of the Temple of Truth, on that near-perfect September day that seemed so long ago. Now the cost of that decision had come due. Better to die in the mountains or on the ocean than in the hands of the vicars. Better to die with his friends.

Chapter 39
Choices

Midnight had long since passed when Orah limped into the clearing outside Little Pond. The trek had taken longer than expected. They'd struggled in the dark to navigate the trail through the woods, and the flight from Temple City had left them bone-weary.

She stared at the remnants of their childhood sanctuary and sighed. Her damp clothing gave meager protection from the cold, but the NOT tree offered little more. The branches that wrapped it would provide scant shelter — their needles had turned brown and fallen, leaving the walls tattered and bare.

As she scanned the naked trees surrounding the clearing, so near to home she could almost smell the smoke from her mother's fireplace, a question crept into her mind. "Does anyone know what date it is?"

Nathaniel's eyelids sagged, nearly cloaking his eyes, and the rest of him sagged as well. "The leaves are down and the wind is brisk. That's all I know."

"The end of November," Thomas said.

"Festival already. Time's passed strangely this year."

Thomas shuddered. "This time last year, I was heading to my teaching."

An unexpected gust kicked up, making the branches on the shelter flutter in the breeze.

Orah wrapped her arms about herself and rubbed for warmth. "I'd love to go home to my mother, climb into bed and sleep for a week, and then gather for the lighting of the bonfire, but if I think that way, I'd be back in Temple City before the festival tree flares. Thomas would get his own cell, and Nathaniel and I would never see each other again."

She shivered, and Nathaniel draped an arm about her shoulders. She could feel his warmth, but his arm lacked strength.

He spoke in a murmur, with barely enough breath to slur his words. "Let's get some rest. We need to be up before dawn if we're to slip into the village unseen."

She nodded, turned and embraced him, clinging fast as if to allow no space for vicars or deacons or walls to come between them ever again.

After they separated, she noticed Thomas standing apart and went to him. "Whatever happens, Thomas, thank you for this chance at freedom, brief though it may be."

Then they entered the shelter and huddled together for warmth.

***

Orah awoke first, startled to consciousness by a yearning to be someplace familiar, safe and secure. The frozen ground had made her hips ache, and the wind whistling through the branches had troubled her sleep. She sat up, peered into the darkness and remembered — someplace familiar, but never again safe and secure.

She went outside so as not to disturb her friends, and settled on the flat rock. Her gaze wandered up to the treetops as they swayed in the moonlight and down to the dried leaves as they skittered across the ground.

She jerked around to the snap of twigs coming from the path to the clearing, and caught a solitary figure creeping through the trees. No need for panic. Deacons would come in greater numbers, not alone.

The hunched figure became more distinct, its movements deliberate and without stealth, but the face stayed shrouded in shadow until it breached the tree line.

Nathaniel's father.

"Orah, thank the light, I found you."

She rose to meet him, and they embraced.

Thomas stirred to their voices and stuck his head out from the shelter. When he recognized their visitor, he scrambled out to greet him as well.

Nathaniel's father glanced about fearfully. "Where's Nathaniel?"

She tilted her head toward the tattered frame. "Inside sleeping. Come, Thomas, let's leave father and son to talk alone."

The older man thanked her, bent stiffly and crawled inside.

***

Nathaniel awoke to no sound, but rather to a presence nearby, a specter kneeling over him praying. One eye opened, then the other. A vision of his father? He sat up and rubbed his eyes.

"What...?"

"I came to warn you, Nathaniel. Deacons roam the village. They intend to—"

"How did you find us?"

"Did you forget who built this shelter?"

"I didn't think you remembered."

"I'm still your father and always will be."

Nathaniel grabbed him in a strong embrace and held on for a dozen heartbeats.

After they parted, the two studied each other in the rays of moonlight filtering through the branches, trying to measure how each had changed, trying to understand the moment.

His father spoke first. "You've become a man, Nathaniel."

"I've been gone less than a year."

"I don't mean by time but by experience."

"The vicars haven't changed me. Their darkness doesn't frighten me anymore."

"Not in that way, Nathaniel. You bear a seriousness about you, like one who has faced death and made a choice."

Nathaniel looked away, embarrassed. As he turned back, a moonbeam fell across his father's face, revealing a right cheek discolored and an eye half-closed.

He reached out to stroke the wound. "What happened?"

His father winced and pulled away. "A misunderstanding with a deacon."

"I thought the Temple doesn't harm its children."

His father bowed his head and stared at the ground. "I've never seen them so ill-tempered, not even during my teaching. You must have done something terribly wrong."

"We're not the ones who've done wrong. It's the Temple of Light."

Nathaniel told him about the first keeper, discovered in the cells of Temple City, and the search for the keep. He described the wonders they found, a way to ask questions of the wisest people from a thousand years ago—from a time the Temple called the darkness—and a means to listen to their answers. He told of the medicines, the music, an instrument to view a million suns, ships that traveled to the stars and a thousand other wonders—all lost.

"I can prove their deceit in so many ways."

"I'd like to believe you," his father said, "as I believed you before, until the vicars came and claimed the darkness had seeped into your bones. They said you were no longer the son I'd raised."

Nathaniel had never been quick to anger, but now he became enraged. "They lied to you. They've always lied."

"As did you, Nathaniel. You told me you'd gone on a mission for the vicars. Only when they came looking did I learn you'd misled me. Whatever happened, I thought you'd be honest with me."

"You'd have been in danger if you knew the truth. I lied to protect you. Forgive me."

His father considered the response. "I forgive you. It's not the first time the Temple has forced someone to do what they knew to be wrong."

"But do you believe me now?"

His father glanced down as if counting the withered pine needles on the ground. He'd listened with a loving father's ears, but would he accept what he heard?

"If what you say is true, Nathaniel, it would turn our world upside down."

"It's true."

"That the Temple could do so much harm?"

"It's true. I swear.

"Even so, their precepts hold our world together. Is it wise to disrupt the current order?"

Nathaniel's eyes drooped at the corners. "Father, we found... dreams. Without the keep, we can be alive, do our work, live in peace and be... happy, I guess. But what are we without dreams?"

A look of anguish came over his father's face. "What's true no longer matters. It's too late. They're waiting for you."

Nathaniel's jaw tightened and his fists clenched, but before he could respond with defiance, his father silenced him with a wave. "I've been gone too long. The vicars and their men are everywhere. I was able to slip away only because of the darkness." He looked up, eyes pleading. "They're pulling people from their beds, assembling them by the commons and demanding they wear ceremonial robes. Leave, Nathaniel. Run as far as you can from Little Pond and never return."

The wind chose that moment to die down, and the rattling of the branches ceased.

***

Nathaniel watched until his father merged with the shadows and disappeared. Orah and Thomas waited nearby, but he could only look past them to the gap in the trees. All his life, his father had taught him to follow the strength of his convictions. Now, on the cusp of this most important decision, he'd urged him to run away.

But to where? The plan to cross the pass over the mountains had always been fraught with risk. Now, they'd need to do so without provisions, and the deacons might track them down, catch them on the way, and drag them back in shame to the village square.

Or they might flee to the east, sneak through the woods, steal food from remote farmhouses and survive like vagabonds, hoping some sympathetic soul might take them in and hide them in a woodshed or root cellar.

The muscles of his cheeks twitched and tensed; his jaw wavered and stiffened. He'd run once before to the granite mountains—a coward's journey. He refused to run again.

Orah stepped between him and the path to the woods. "What's wrong?"

He shook off the mood, seeing her as if for the first time. "Deacons, Orah. Deacons and vicars everywhere. They're organizing our neighbors for a stoning."

281

Thomas stifled a cry. "Then there's nowhere we can be safe."

Orah rested a hand on his arm. Her lips parted, but before she could comfort him, Nathaniel intervened. "You're right, Thomas. Safety is an illusion. We can never be safe while the Temple rules."

Orah stared deep into the woods as if hoping to find Nathaniel's father returning. "We can take back trails to the mountains."

Nathaniel shook his head.

"We can go east, find someplace to hide." She became more agitated. "People who've read our posts will support us."

"If our friends and neighbors won't support us, who will?'

"Then what can we do?"

"Do you remember the story I told you about the man who toppled the Temple of Light?"

She nodded. "You said it was a work of imagination, not real."

"But the idea is real. You and Thomas should flee to the east, head to Adamsville or Bradford, if you can get that far. Maybe you'll find support."

Orah's eyes had remained dry since her father's funeral, but found their tears in captivity. Now, once again, they began to flow. "Why do you talk like this? Why do you speak of me and Thomas without you?"

He wandered over to the shelter, grasped one of the poles and tested it—its base remained planted firmly in the ground. He hoped to sound resolute when he told her, but no amount of time could ease what he had to say.

He turned and faced her. "I plan to march into the village square. Little Pond is my home. I won't run again."

"You'll be killed."

"Better to die than to be hunted down, and I'll get the chance to stand before my people. Maybe they'll listen and believe. If not, they might regret my death and act later. You and Thomas can slip away while the vicars and their men are distracted."

Then he waited as his friends pondered his words. Thomas stared at him with sorrow, but Orah bristled with that fierce intensity that made her so beautiful.

"No, Nathaniel," she said at last. "At the trial in Temple City, I thought I'd lost you forever, and then I lived for the past weeks with that damned peephole between us. Each day, I feared they'd take you away. I'm not leaving you again."

She held her ground, eyes smoldering, daring him to disagree. He scoured his mind for a way to dissuade her, anything to keep her safe, but she believed as strongly as he did, and if their situations were reversed, he'd never leave her side.

"Very well," he said. "They're waiting for us. Let's not disappoint them."

Orah turned to Thomas. "Dear Thomas. We're sorry to abandon you at last. Run to the southeast, keeping to the woods. Once the vicars have vented their rage on us, they might be less intent on tracking you down. You may be fine. You've always had a talent for surviving by your wits."

Thomas surprised them by flashing his grin. "Are you kidding? I'm coming with you."

He held up a hand before Orah could argue. "My mind's made up. My feet hurt, and most everything else as well. Like you, I'm tired of running." He turned grim. "Besides, the prospect of stoning three of their children will make our neighbors think, and I can't wait to watch the vicars' faces when we march in together."

Nathaniel regarded his friend, no longer the boy of their childhood but a man like himself. He dipped his head, a sign of respect, and agreed.

Orah drew in a breath and began dusting off her clothing and combing her fingers through her hair.

"What are you doing?" Thomas said.

She smiled at him. "Getting ready. I want to look my best for the ceremony."

Chapter 40

The Edge of the Storm

Shadows in the night, marching with steadfast stride.

The people of Great Pond were on the move. All had read the messages copied and passed in haste from person to person. Deacons had come that evening as they had for the past few months, asking for the young people from Little Pond, but with an increased urgency. After midnight, a roar had approached from the east. Harsh lights had raced through the streets. People had been pulled from their beds and questioned. Houses had been searched.

Then the caravan of clergy left, heading west to Little Pond.

Now, the spinner and his wife led their neighbors in the dark, among them farmers, the blacksmith, elders and the young.

All walking west, shadows in the night.

Chapter 41
The Beginning

Orah paraded behind Nathaniel on the narrow path she'd traveled since childhood. Ahead, the harbinger of first light gave contrast to the commons, distinguishing its roof from the sky. Familiar shadows reminded her of festival—the mound of charred logs from the prior night's bonfire, the spruce waiting to be set aglow. Fond memories, gatherings with friends, and now their final approach to the square.

As daybreak loomed, the hint of dawn should have brightened the landscape, but the shadows deepened more than she remembered. When she drew closer, they transformed into the hunched forms of men and women. The whole village had arrayed itself in a half-circle guarding the commons. She felt as if she walked into a headwind, though the morning breeze had stilled.

Across from the commons, ominous mounds completed the circle. A noise sounded, like metal snapping into place. Then another and another. The mounds grew eyes that cast an eerie glow. Fast wagons, as she'd expected.

In the glare, she recognized the faces of elders and schoolmates, of friends and neighbors. Each wore a ceremonial robe and clutched a rock the size of an apple.

She strode to the center of the circle with Nathaniel and Thomas on either side.

Stragglers from more distant farms came stumbling in, and last of all, her mother and Nathaniel's father. They wore no robes, and their hands were empty.

Wagon doors opened and deacons emerged, followed by clergy — vicars and monsignors, bishops and arch bishops. The monsignor who had once ministered to the Ponds came to the front, cradling the sun icon in his arms. He used the temple voice to announce his superior. "People of Little Pond—the arch vicar of the Temple of Light."

The old man emerged from the wagon and stepped toward them.

A hush fell over the square.

The arch vicar raised his arms, fingers pointing to the glow from the rising sun, and spoke with an impressive force. "Children of light, your Temple is under attack. Three of your own have fallen under the sway of the darkness. I have petitioned his holiness, the grand vicar, to declare them apostates."

Grumbles from the crowd, calls of not possible.

The arch vicar waved them to silence. "You say they're blameless? You may be right. The Book of Light tells us, 'Beware the stray thought. Like water dripping on rock, it can erode the strongest mind and open a path for the darkness.' Now we understand the wisdom of the holy book. No one is immune. Sadly, these children have been infected by the darkness, and we must eradicate the disease before it spreads."

Orah marveled at his mastery—forgiving and damning them in the same breath. She glanced at her neighbors. Their eyes had glazed over as when the sun icon speaks.

The arch vicar's voice echoed in the chill air. "Would you allow the darkness to return?"

Mutters of no, no.

"Unlike the darkness these young people worship, the Temple has renounced violence. We stand defenseless and need your help."

A few nods, but otherwise silence. Fingers tensed around rocks.

"It is written, 'If there comes among you a prophet, or a dreamer of dreams, and gives you a sign or a wonder, saying, Let us return to the darkness, you shall not hearken to the words.'"

The nods ceased, but the children of light remained enthralled.

"'If your brother, or your son or daughter, or your wife, or your friend, who may be as your own soul, entice you saying, Let us abandon the light and serve the darkness, you shall not consent to him, but you shall surely kill him. Your hand shall be first upon him, and afterwards the hand of all the people.'"

His voice resounded like Thomas's music in the keep, rising and falling and moving the souls of its listeners. He shook his fist at invisible forces.

"'And you shall stone him with stones, that he die, because he has sought to thrust you away from the light.'"

He stepped aside, leaving a clear path between the villagers and the friends.

Time slowed for Orah, and her vision broadened. Thomas waited, frozen in place on her left, and to her right, Nathaniel stood tall, his head tilting ever-so-slightly in her direction. They might have enjoyed a lifetime together had they not been dreamers of dreams.

In a moment, the voice from the sun icon would speak, the judgment would be handed down, and rocks would fly.

She waited for her heart to pound, expecting her breath to quicken, but instead, she stayed calm as a spring day. Before the arch vicar could continue, her feet seemingly moved on their own as she separated from her friends and stepped toward the crowd.

"Look at us." Her words rang out, no longer the voice of a scared girl pretending to be brave. "We're your children. We swam in these waters with you and celebrated festival together here in this square. We're not infected with a disease or tainted by the darkness, but we've stumbled upon a truth, maybe through foolishness or luck, but a truth nevertheless. Things are not as the vicars claim. These wagons aren't magic. They were invented long ago by men and women who thought for themselves and dreamed dreams, people whose accomplishments and very existence the Temple hid from us and labeled as the darkness."

Confusion spread through the crowd. A few edged forward, rocks in hand, but most held back, shuffling their feet and eyeing their neighbors.

Deacons crept toward her, but the arch vicar dismissed them with a wave. "Leave her be. Let the people see how much the darkness has seized her soul."

She refused to back down. "In the privacy of your homes you complain about the teachings, but say they're necessary to keep the darkness away. Their real purpose is to make us afraid to think for ourselves. For light's sake, think for yourselves now. He's asking you to kill your own children, not for a crime but for daring to question the Temple."

She confronted the arch vicar, whose face had reddened in the rays of the half-risen sun, but the old clergyman was a believer, had fought what he knew as the darkness his whole life.

He met her glare and cut her off, his voice resounding through the square. "Look how she's revealed herself, this demon of darkness, twisting the truth to corrupt your minds. Is this what you want for yourselves and your children? She and her friends must be stopped or the darkness will spread."

Nervous feet shuffled forward, and more arms were raised.

The arch vicar's lips curled upward even as his brows sagged to meet them. He accepted the sun icon from the monsignor with both hands and lifted it above his head.

An evangelical fervor illuminated his face. "Oh Holiness, father of these children of light, the people await your judgment."

All movement ceased. Those assembled held their breaths, leaving no sound save the song of newly awakened birds, chirping to greet the dawn.

The sun icon crackled to life with the voice of the grand vicar, the human embodiment of the light in this world. "Oh, Sun, giver of life, we stand in judgment this day so the light may be returned to the village of Little...."

The grand vicar's words trailed off and a new voice spoke, not as strong or as well-trained, but to those who knew him well, the speaker was clear — Nathaniel.

"We are the seekers of truth, responsible for the postings. Now we speak to you directly through the sun icon. You may ask how we gained access to temple magic, but what you hear is neither magic nor of the Temple, but rather the genius of men and women from long ago, from a time the Temple calls the darkness. Here's the truth...."

The arch vicar's hands began to shake. Before another word could be transmitted, he cast the sun icon to the frozen ground, leaving a vacuum of sound, total silence in the village square.

But not for long.

Orah's mind became a spiral of swirling lights, bright thoughts, a glowing purpose—and at the hub of the spinning wheel, the power of an idea.

She recalled the speech she and Nathaniel had composed, and whispered to him. "Our words, your voice."

Nathaniel began reciting the next words so seamlessly they might have come from the shards on the ground. "Here's the truth about the darkness. We've stumbled across a place called the keep, where the best thinkers of that age spent their lives recording knowledge, committed to saving the past for this day. There we found wonders beyond imagination, ways to make our lives better without depending on the clergy. There we discovered our potential. The Temple would like to hide the keep from us, to prevent us from learning and growing. They claim we must fear the keep, but the darkness was not a time to be feared, but a time from which to learn...."

The arch vicar stood as if rooted to the ground, his jaw grinding. Finally, he signaled, and the deacons rushed forward.

Nathaniel raised his voice even as he struggled to evade their grasp, daring them to stop him. "The vicars offer us fear, a fear of thinking for ourselves. They've stolen a sacred right—the right of every person—" He twisted toward Orah. "—to have the potential for greatness. They offer us a world of limits. We can be much more. The future is in your hands."

He shook off the deacons and squared his shoulders to the crowd. Orah and Thomas joined him, and the three locked arms.

The arch vicar sneered at them and turned to the villagers. "You see the power of the darkness, which has gone beyond what I had imagined. Too late. Our leader has handed down his judgment. He has declared them apostates, and they must be removed from our world. Let them be struck down now."

As he spoke the final word, he slammed his fist into his hand. More arms were poised, more fingers tightened on stones, but before anyone could act, Nathaniel's father burst from the crowd.

"My son's voice. It's all true."

Deacons blocked his way, but he shoved them off with thick forearms and moved next to Nathaniel.

"I stand with my son."

The arch vicar grimaced, but motioned the deacons to step aside. "Now we know where the seeds of darkness were sown."

Then Orah's mother strode forward and came to her side. "And I stand with my daughter."

The three became five as the village watched. No more arms were raised, but none were lowered. The red morning sun had cleared the treetops.

Suddenly a buzz swept through the crowd. Fingers without stones pointed at a tramping noise, the din of marching feet.

Orah turned along with friends and parents, clergymen and deacons. Men and women began to arrive, first in ones and twos, then tens and twenties. When finally gathered, they numbered more than four hundred.

A middle-aged man with thinning hair came to the fore, the spinner Orah knew so well. His wife stood beside him, arm in arm. He needed a moment to catch his breath, but when he finally spoke, his voice sent tremors through the air.

"The people of Great Pond stand with the seekers of truth."

Nathaniel's father stared at them, assimilating the situation, then set his jaw and turned to the clergymen—facing them for the first time as an equal. "Take your wagons and leave the Ponds. If you return, it will be on our terms."

Flustered deacons formed a wedge around the vicars, a battle formation. Now at last, hands with stones found a target. Voices shouted. Arms were raised.

Outnumbered, the deacons backed down and retreated. Left with no choice, the arch vicar signaled the others to the wagons, but unafraid for himself, he lingered, a true believer.

"This is a sad day for the light." He pointed a bony finger at Orah. "You know not what forces you have unleashed. When the darkness descends upon our world, let it be remembered it started here in Little Pond."

The monsignor held open a door, and the arch vicar swept inside. The wagons sprung to life with a roar. People covered their ears as wheels spun, kicking up dust that rose twenty feet or more. When the dust settled, the vicars and their men had gone.

Arms relaxed, and rocks thudded to the ground. As quiet settled over the village, Orah found her neighbors gaping, waiting for someone to fill the void. Now her heart pounded and her breath quickened. No words came to mind.

Then she recalled the shoemaker's daughter and remembered her proud face reciting the pass phrase. She faced Nathaniel and grasped him by the hands.

"We have traveled far, but our journey has just begun. The true light drives us on."

He picked up on it instantly, her friend since birth. "May we find the end we seek and may the truth we discover hasten a new beginning."

She glanced back at the villagers, raised her chin and proclaimed: "Thus ends the age of darkness. Let the age of enlightenment begin."

Epilogue

Spring finally arrived. The seekers' bulletins had been read by thousands, and within weeks, thousands turned to tens of thousands. The rebellion had spread like wildfire, exactly as Orah had planned.

Thomas had muddled through the winter while elders from surrounding towns convened. As a seeker of the truth, he was obliged to attend these meetings, but at last the agony had ended.

Today, the people of the Ponds celebrated a new holiday, the festival of freedom, and tomorrow, the best of the region, led by Orah and Nathaniel, would embark on their initial expedition to the keep.

He didn't know if he wanted to go.

On this, the first mild day of the season, the trees prepared to spread their seeds to the world. He sat on a log and dangled his feet in the pond until he barely felt his toes, and then swung them out to warm. Sunlight filtered through the branches, causing ripples on the ground as they swayed with the breeze. Overhead, cream-colored pods from a honey locust floated down like snow.

December had been filled with bickering, demands from the people and righteous indignation from the Temple, until everyone agreed on conditions for the meeting. Adamsville was designated as the site. Nathaniel's father was chosen to represent the rebels, and the arch vicar would lead the clerics.

January consisted of posturing and pomp, with a plentiful smattering of sermons about the darkness. Eventually, necessity drove everyone together. The Temple had no means of support without the people. The people needed the medicine the Temple provided, and perhaps missed its spiritual ministrations as well. Most of all, after a thousand years, neither side had an appetite for violence.

In the midst of negotiations, the grand vicar passed to the light. The Temple council offered the position to the arch vicar. He declined at first, but when no one else wanted the job, they declared the old man the human embodiment of light on this Earth by default.

After long days fraught with ill will, the parties reached the terms of a truce. The practice of teachings would end. The people would accept ministrations from the vicars and continue to tithe. In exchange, the Temple would provide medicine and, most importantly, safe passage to the keep.

Orah worried that each day brought the keep closer to extinction. Practical as always, she proposed inviting the gray friars to accompany them, hoping they might use their skill to take over maintenance.

The council of priors had agreed at once. The brothers, it seemed, had more interest in tinkering with devices than arguing about the darkness.

This led Nathaniel to suggest a delegation of vicars come along. Their guidance might help avoid the mistakes of the past, and the gesture might ease the rift with the clergy. An outraged Orah accused him of dreaming again. Allowing the vicars near the keep seemed absurd to Thomas, but experience made him reluctant to doubt Nathaniel. Stranger things had happened.

His feet had warmed in the sun, and he swung them back to the pond. As the tingling spread to his ankles, he slowly shook his head. No, he'd pass on the trip. Once to the keep was enough, and he had better things to do.

That afternoon his newly formed group of musicians, a modest five with a drum and four flutes, would meet for their first session. He'd composed a tune for them but believed it needed a string instrument. While he'd heard many in the keep, he never bothered to study their construction, so now he sat on the log and tried out his newest creation.

He had chosen a backing of rosewood for the teardrop shape and, after some testing, had settled on spruce for the sounding board. He'd lovingly sanded the wood through the winter, until he could sense the grain with his fingertips. Then he'd tap the side with his thumb and gauge the vibrations, shake his head and sand some more.

Across the hole in the center, he'd strung catgut, which would produce different tones depending on how tightly he stretched them. To allow for adjustment, he'd wrapped them around pegs inserted into a short neck. For now, the instrument had five strings, but for next freedom festival, he might add a sixth. He twisted the knob to tighten the final string and plucked them in sequence. The first three sounded perfect, but the others needed tuning.

He remained undaunted. He'd call his new instrument a lute, after a similar one found in the keep. He might even name it a Bradford lute, since his had a unique tone, though not yet ideal.

But he knew he could make it better.

---THE END---

Acknowledgements

From start to finish, a novel is an enormous effort and would not be possible without a great team. It starts with my beta readers, including the members of my writing group, The Steeple Scholars from the Cape Cod Writers Center, and continues with Lane Diamond, Dave King, and John Anthony Allen. It finishes with the wonderful formatting and cover art of Mallory Rock. Through it all, the encouragement of others kept me going, my friends and family, including my dear wife, who has put up with my writing aspiration through the good and bad years.

I borrowed the quote engraved on the steps of the Temple of Truth from Robert Kennedy. The full text is: "The greatest truth must be recognition that in every man, in every child is the potential for greatness."

Finally, I want to acknowledge my readers, who are, after all, the reason I write, and especially for prodding me to make this book the first in a trilogy. So many of you wanted to know what happened to my characters after this book ends, that I was compelled to give them life once more. Orah and Nathaniel are grateful.

About the Author

The urge to write first struck when working on a newsletter at a youth encampment in the woods of northern Maine. It may have been the night when lightning flashed at sunset followed by northern lights rippling after dark. Or maybe it was the newsletter's editor, a girl with eyes the color of the ocean. But I was inspired to write about the blurry line between reality and the fantastic.

Using two fingers and lots of white-out, I religiously typed five pages a day throughout college and well into my twenties. Then life intervened. I paused to raise two sons and pursue a career, in the process becoming a well-known entrepreneur in the software industry, founding several successful companies. When I found time again to daydream, the urge to write returned.

My wife and I split our time between Cape Cod, Florida and anywhere else that catches our fancy. I no longer limit myself to five pages a day and am thankful every keystroke for the invention of the word processor.

You can find me at my website (www.davidlitwack.com), where I blog about writing and post updates on my current works. I'm also on Twitter (@DavidLitwack) and Facebook (https://www.facebook.com/david.litwack.author). If you'd like quarterly updates with news about my books, my works in progress, and my thoughts on the universe, please sign up for my newsletter http://bit.ly/1ronREk.

Whats Next?

THE STUFF OF STARS

(The Seekers – Book 2)
By David Litwack

Watch for the second novel in this dystopian sci-fi series, coming November 2015. For more information on this book, please visit the Evolved Publishing website.

~~~~~

But what are we without dreams?

Against all odds, Orah and Nathaniel have found the keep and revealed the truth about the darkness, initiating what they hoped would be a new age of enlightenment. But the people were more set in their ways than anticipated, and a faction of vicars whispered in their ears, urging a return to traditional ways.

Desperate to keep their movement alive, Orah and Nathaniel cross the ocean to seek the living descendants of the keepmasters' kin. Those they find on the distant shore are both more and less advanced than expected.

The seekers become caught between the two sides, and face the challenge of bringing them together to make a better world. The prize: a chance to bring home miracles and a more promising future for their people. But if they fail this time, they risk not a stoning but losing themselves in the twilight of a never-ending dream.

More from David Litwack

THE DAUGHTER OF THE SEA AND THE SKY

This literary, speculative novel is now available. For more information on this book, please visit the Evolved Publishing website.

~~~~

A world divided, a mysterious girl--a boat where none should be.

After centuries of religiously motivated war, the world has been split in two. Now the Blessed Lands are ruled by pure faith, while in the Republic, reason is the guiding light-two different realms, kept apart and at peace by a treaty and an ocean.

Children of the Republic, Helena and Jason were inseparable in their youth, until fate sent them down different paths. Grief and duty sidetracked Helena's plans, and Jason came to detest the hollowness of his ambitions.

These two damaged souls are reunited when a tiny boat from the Blessed Lands crashes onto the rocks near Helena's home after an impossible journey across the forbidden ocean. On board is a single passenger, a nine-year-old girl named Kailani, who calls herself *The Daughter of the Sea and the Sky*. A new and perilous purpose binds Jason and Helena together again, as they vow to protect the lost innocent from the wrath of the authorities, no matter the risk to their future and freedom.

But is the mysterious child simply a troubled little girl longing to return home? Or is she a powerful prophet sent to unravel the fabric of a godless Republic, as the outlaw leader of an illegal religious sect would have them believe? Whatever the answer, it will change them all forever... and perhaps their world as well.

~~~~

Praise for *The Daughter of the Sea and the Sky*:

"...a fully imagined, gripping read...." - *Kirkus Reviews*

"Author David Litwack gracefully weaves together his message with alternating threads of the fantastic and the realistic... The reader will find wisdom and grace in this beautifully written story..." - *San Francisco Review Book Review*

"... an enthralling look at an alternative world... thought-provoking, beautifully written and highly entertaining." - *Jack Magnus for Readers' Favorite*

"David Litwack's sweeping novel The Daughter of the Sea and the Sky is a powerful story that follows the journey of a mysterious but charming little girl whose mere presence seems to have changed the lives of those people around her... Superbly imagined with a tense plot which makes it difficult to put down..." - *the GreatReads!*

More from Evolved Publishing:

CHILDREN'S PICTURE BOOKS

THE BIRD BRAIN BOOKS by Emlyn Chand:
Courtney Saves Christmas
Davey the Detective
Honey the Hero
Izzy the Inventor
Larry the Lonely
Polly Wants to be a Pirate
Poppy the Proud
Ricky the Runt
Ruby to the Rescue
Sammy Steals the Show
Tommy Goes Trick-or-Treating
Vicky Finds a Valentine
Silent Words by Chantal Fournier
Thomas and the Tiger-Turtle by Jonathan Gould
EMLYN AND THE GREMLIN by Steff F. Kneff:
Emlyn and the Gremlin
Emlyn and the Gremlin and the Barbeque Disaster
Emlyn and the Gremlin and the Mean Old Cat
I'd Rather Be Riding My Bike by Eric Pinder
VALENTINA'S SPOOKY ADVENTURES
by Majanka Verstraete:
Valentina and the Haunted Mansion
Valentina and the Masked Mummy
Valentina and the Whackadoodle Witch

HISTORICAL FICTION

Galerie by Steven Greenberg
SHINING LIGHT'S SAGA by Ruby Standing Deer:
Circles (Book 1)

HISTORICAL FICTION (cont'd)

Spirals (Book 2)
Stones (Book 3)

LITERARY FICTION

Carry Me Away by Robb Grindstaff
Hannah's Voice by Robb Grindstaff
Turning Trixie by Robb Grindstaff
The Daughter of the Sea and the Sky by David Litwack
A Handful of Wishes by E.D. Martin
The Lone Wolf by E.D. Martin
Jellicle Girl by Stevie Mikayne
Weight of Earth by Stevie Mikayne
Desert Flower by Angela Scott
Desert Rice by Angela Scott
White Chalk by Pavarti K. Tyler

LOWER GRADE (Chapter Books)

TALES FROM UPON A. TIME by Falcon Storm:
Natalie the Not-So-Nasty
The Perils of Petunia
The Persnickety Princess
WEIRDVILLE by Majanka Verstraete:
Drowning in Fear
Fright Train
Grave Error
House of Horrors
The Clumsy Magician
The Doll Maker
BALDERDASH by J.W.Zulauf:
The Underground Princess (Book 1)
The Prince's Plight (Book 2)
The Shaman's Salvation (Book 3)

MEMOIR

And Then It Rained: Lessons for Life by Megan Morrison

MIDDLE GRADE

FRENDYL KRUNE by Kira A. McFadden:
Frendyl Krune and the Blood of the Sun (Book 1)
Frendyl Krune and the Snake Across the Sea (Book 2)
Frendyl Krune and the Stone Princess (Book 3)
NOAH ZARC by D. Robert Pease:
Mammoth Trouble (Book 1)
Cataclysm (Book 2)
Declaration (Book 3)
Omnibus (Special 3-in-1 Edition)

MYSTERY / CRIME / DETECTIVE

DUNCAN COCHRANE by David Hagerty:
They Tell Me You Are Wicked (Book 1)
Hot Sinatra by Axel Howerton

ROMANCE / EROTICA

COLLEGE ROMANCE by Amelia James:
Tell Me You Want Me (Book 1)
Secret Storm (Book 2)
Tell Me You Want Forever (Book 3)
Home Is Where the Heat Is by Amelia James
THE TWISTED MOSAIC by Amelia James:
Her Twisted Pleasures (Book 1)
Their Twisted Love (Book 2)
His Twisted Choice (Book 3)
The Twisted Mosaic – Specail Omnibus Edition
The Devil Made Me Do It by Amelia James
THE SUGAR HOUSE NOVELLAS by Pavarti K. Tyler:
Sugar & Salt (Book 1)
Protecting Portia (Book 2)

ROMANCE / EROTICA (cont'd)

Dual Domination (Book 3)
The Sugar House Novellas – Special Omnibus Edition (Book 4)

SCI-FI / FANTASY

Eulogy by D.T. Conklin
THE PANHELION CHRONICLES by Marlin Desault:
Shroud of Eden (Book 1)
THE SEEKERS by David Litwack:
The Children of Darkness (Book 1)
The Stuff of Stars (Book 2)
The Light of Reason (Book 3)
THE AMULI CHRONICLES: SOULBOUND by Kira A. McFadden:
The Soulbound Curse (Book 1)
The Soulless King (Book 2)
The Throne of Souls (Book 3)
Shadow Swarm by D. Robert Pease
Two Moons of Sera by Pavarti K. Tyler

SHORT STORY ANTHOLOGIES
FROM THE EDITORS AT EVOLVED PUBLISHING:

Evolution: Vol. 1 (A Short Story Collection)
Evolution: Vol. 2 (A Short Story Collection)
The Futility of Loving a Soldier by E.D. Martin

SUSPENSE / THRILLER

Shatter Point by Jeff Altabef
TONY HOOPER by Lane Diamond:
Forgive Me, Alex (Book 1)
The Devil's Bane (Book 2)
Shadow Side by Ellen Joyce
SUSPENSE / THRILLER (cont'd)
THE OZ FILES by Barry Metcalf:
Broometime Serenade (Book 1)

SUSPENSE/THRILLER (cont'd)

Intrigue at Sandy Point (Book 2)
Spirit of Warrnambool (Book 3)
THE ZOE DELANTE THRILLERS by C.L. Roberts-Huth:
Whispers of the Dead (Book 1)
Whispers of the Serpent (Book 2)
Whispers of the Sidhe (Book 3)

YOUNG ADULT

CHOSEN by Jeff Altabef and Erynn Altabef:
Wind Catcher (Book 1)
Brink of Dawn (Book 2)
THE KIN CHRONICLES by Michael Dadich:
The Silver Sphere (Book 1)
The Sinister Kin (Book 2)
THE DARLA DECKER DIARIES by Jessica McHugh:
Darla Decker Hates to Wait (Book 1)
Darla Decker Takes the Cake (Book 2)
Darla Decker Shakes the State (Book 3)
Darla Decker Plays it Straight (Book 4)
JOEY COLA by D. Robert Pease:
Dream Warriors (Book 1)
Cleopatra Rising (Book 2)
Third Reality (Book 3)
Anyone? by Angela Scott
THE ZOMBIE WEST TRILOGY by Angela Scott:
Wanted: Dead or Undead (Book 1)
Survivor Roundup (Book 2)
Dead Plains (Book 3)
The Zombie West Trilogy – Special Omnibus Edition

3

CPSIA information can be obtained
at www.ICGtesting.com
Printed in the USA
LVOW07s1744110517
534161LV00003B/147/P